The Boy Behind the Glass Screen

The Boy Behind the Glass Screen

Ian Siragher

Published by The Invisible Imprint in the United Kingdom in 2024

ISBN: 978-1-83919-587-7

A B 4 C and D

1

Trial, Day 1, 12th November 2025

I am breaking up or being pulled apart. Maybe my foundations were never strong enough, or perhaps the strain is too much. I suppose it doesn't matter; the end result is the same.

Either way, it is clear that something is happening which is consuming me. It brings with it a tumbled multitude of memories. When they come, I lose track of now, of this crucial moment, and relive what brought me here.

Some part of me believes I am still in the court, apparently attentive, and looking as though I am concentrating.

I understand what I must do. I need to ground myself, to find a point of focus. There is a word the court keeps dancing around and tripping over. It is a word which offers a pinpoint of depth in the shallows of my confusion.

"Laboratory."

Hawes-Smith threw it out to get it onto the record. Wellbright, the prosecutor, struggled to avoid it, calling that place "the playroom". Well, it was where I grew up, but it was no playroom.

Laboratory. The sight, sound and hum of it come back to me. Images build, helter-skelter, snowball-down-a-hill fast, uncontrolled and sliding. I follow this particular memory in the hope that when it ends I will either awake or fall into some unfragmented state of calm.

It was morning, any morning of nearly six thousand days. First the lights came on. They buzzed and hummed, then flickered and sent flashes across white tiles and blank surfaces.

I was ready, waiting; I knew what would happen next. There would be a slight click, matched by a crackle of lines moving across one of the screens high above me. Then there would be footsteps coming down the sweep of curved stairs. Twenty-two steps, the push up on each step flicking a corresponding line on the screen. These sounds, at a heartbeat pace, heralded fear and pain.

To begin with, Oliver had been little more than a small anonymous bundle, held in Dr Glass's arms. A mewling thing, needing feeding and changing, which Dr Glass did with cold solicitude. Back then I too was very young, could only watch without understanding. I did not have words with which to hold memories. Back then, I could only register what I saw as sights, sounds, blurs of movement. Everything was just chaotic patterns which only later fell into shape and meaning.

Later, I do not know when, I started to understand. By that time Dr Glass could lead Oliver down, not carry him. Even then, though, they rarely talked. My morning would start with the sounds of their feet on the stairs, and the buzzing and whirring of computers waking up. I would be aware, too, of the cameras spinning into focus, and the multiple images appearing on the screens running the length of where the ceiling and walls met.

There was no way I could recognise that this was anything other than normal. Even when Oliver and I began to understand and question, our first thoughts were that it was the others who were wrong. We denied our instincts. How strange that we should do that. Yet, somewhere deep inside, perhaps we did know it couldn't be right.

I see it now. How Dr Glass would lead Oliver to the chair, or, if Oliver was crying and pulling away, pick him up, almost absent-mindedly. At those times, I knew Dr Glass was holding on to his own anger, suppressing all his emotions in order to dampen Oliver's. Once he had a firm grip, the strain showing on his face, he would carry Oliver, wriggling and stretching, kicking and shouting, and put him on the high bed. The one with the leather straps.

I don't want to follow this memory, but it leads me and draws me in. I see Oliver picked up, then pinned down. His father, calm but determined, pulling the leather straps tight. True, they didn't quite bite into Oliver's small, pale wrists and ankles, but they did turn the skin around them red raw. When he struggled too much, Oliver would be left with dark patches of bruises, which would fade only a little before the next time.

Once he had him held down, his father would lean over Oliver and say something like, "Now we'll have to wait, won't we? Until you settle." Then he'd go. He'd leave Oliver, crying, pleading, promising he'll be good. And all that time, all I could do was watch. My father never released me until Oliver was ready to play.

And now? All I can do now is remember.

So, we'd wait. Eventually Oliver would calm. I would see in the screens that his breathing had settled, his sobbing had died away, and his little heart had stopped racing.

Only then would his father return, with the razor if needed, and always with the wired cap and the syringe.

2

Harry Priest, October 2023

Even though it is of its time, Harry Priest hates his first name. He imagines his mother thinking of Harry Styles as he was conceived, and suppresses a shudder. Actually, and he would deny this even more vehemently, it is Harry Potter he is named after. He prefers Priesty, or even, The Priest, which is what he calls the small, metal-ended club he uses to kill fish he catches.

At this moment, though, Harry is not thinking about his name, or even blonde haired big breasted Sophie at school. His focus is on his PlayStation console screen. His fingers bounce up and down, and his hand pulls left and right as he avoids the curved claws and flaming fireballs of the creature in front of him. Harry advances his character, slashing his broad sword. As he does, the creature dissolves into a swarm of bats. They attack, spitting poison at him and decreasing his health. Then they blur, to re-form moments later as the beast, out of range of his sword.

"Fuck," he mutters, then glances at the bedroom door. Now is the time for silence in his game play, or his mother will be knocking and telling him to go to sleep.

The poison from the bats has worn down his health, the bar only slowly recovering. He looks at his potion stock: not many, none very effective. He hangs back. The creature, horned but dark and indistinct, sways a little ahead of him. He pauses. Again, flames burst from the creature, and, as they do, three wolf-like animals rise from the ground and begin to circle him.

"Shit! Fuck," he mutters, then swipes at the feral wolves; his health bar decreases further as they rip at him. He kills one, but the other two still menace. Harry selects his last freeze potion and crashes it in front of the wolves. They crystallise to ice sculptures. He swings his sword, shattering them.

But it is too late, they have been nothing more than a distraction. The beast thing charges, sending first a ball of flame, then, closing in, moose-like horns aimed at his chest. Harry pushes the shield button; it is useless. The flames drive him back, then the creature strikes.

The dark forest twists and fades to black.

A litany in white gothic-style letters appears on the screen. The words mockingly celebrate his death and talk of the songs that will be sung about him in the hall of the gods.

He throws the joystick down, again looks up at the door.

A message tone beeps in his headphones, and words begin to scroll across the Twitch box in the bottom left of his screen.

That was trash Priest2005 you fell for that:SexyDebs2000.

Big Laugh Priesty Man: JaxtheLad.

This was Jack from school, usually the first with a comment. The third and final viewer, Loooceee, has a snooze icon against her name; she is logged in but away from her screen.

SexyDebs2000? Not a name or watcher he knows. Suspicious, that's sure. He's seen all the stay-safe-online videos. Not that he can't handle himself; any peado who had a go at him would find a priest shoved up *their* arse, though they might like that.

He laughs, then types: *Still better than you do Jax,* ignoring SexyDebs2000. How fucking blatant? A name like that. As he shakes his head, more words appear on the screen.

I slay at this check here.

Another message from SexyDebs2000, with a TikTok link. Like he is going to click on *that* and be sent off to some virus hell. A new message runs across his screen, from Jack.

Yeah – I should go actually, CU2mrrw

Harry hits the F4 key and sends his standard *CU Flake* message to Jack. SexyDebs2000 is now his only viewer.

He considers her message. Looks like a true TikTok link, but he can ignore that, go direct and check.

Next, he clicks the TikTok search icon on the bottom of his screen, types SexyDebs2000 in the search bar. Three seconds later, a choice of forty or so *Witcher IV* videos appear on his screen, all with comments and likes he would have died for.

He clicks the first. On his Twitch screen, SexyDebs2000's icon fades.

3

Aiden, 2024

It is 1.35 am on the 9th of January 2024. I am standing in the dark, at the top of the stairs on my side of the glass screen, waiting. I know what should have happened. Upstairs, in the main part of the house, Oliver should be with the police. I have heard the shouting, and the screens have shown Oliver's heart and brain waves running and leaping, wildly erratic. That, though, is all I know.

At the moment everything is quiet. From where I stand, I can just make out the small window into the laboratory. That room, too, is dark, lit only by the glow of the computer on Dr Glass's desk, the ripples of colour from the screensaver reflecting onto my window.

My own pulse I am unsure of. Should it be calm? I am standing motionless, but the noise and clamour upstairs, that would have disturbed me. I know this is important, know the police will make judgements based on how I first seem. Almost every book I have read, every film, makes that point. The detective, when he rounds up the suspects, tells them how he identified the murderer, often points to some small flaw in the first reaction to the news of the killing.

There is more shouting; my heart rate leaps in response. The noise seems to be moving through the house, getting closer.

The questions and thoughts run back and forth. Oliver, how is he? Did it go as we planned? Dr Glass *is* dead. That is the only conclusion that can be drawn. If he weren't, then...Then what? I try to run scenarios, try to match the patterns, the noises, Oliver's heart rate, the timings. I am as sure as I can be, 87% certainty, Dr Glass is dead. Soon all doubt will be extinguished.

That thought brings with it a pressure, something building inside me, something strange, new, and alien.

"Armed police!" There is a shout. The door at the top of the stairs on Oliver's side opens. A stream of brightness from the door precedes all the laboratory lights coming on. The shout echoes through the speakers and now my heart rate really does jump. I can hear boots running; the sounds make a jackhammer staccato of drumming on the speakers and regular leaping lines on the overhead screen.

Two figures flash past the window. From above, I can see only heavy, dark clothing, the blur of a hand wearing fingerless gloves and carrying a black object, which must be a pistol. They are at the door to the gym. There is a moment's pause, then the laboratory goes silent. I can see only the faintest lines of the sounds of breathing on the screen. I've seen this countless times in films. They are poised, either side of the door to the gym. "Armed police," they shout again, the noise exploding in bright banners of light, then they run into the gym.

Moments later, they shout again, almost sounding disappointed. "Clear."

Their matched footsteps click together as they walk back. One police officer stops at the window, bends his head to it. I can just make out a peak cap with hatched black and white markings. He holds his hands to either side of his face. I do not know what to do; nothing in my lessons has prepared me for this.

If Oliver were here, he would look at the man, say hello. Or Dr Glass, if he were present, would tell me what to do, but I have no idea. I want to move, either towards or away, either will be good, but I cannot decide. His head shifts a little. There is a shout, but I am so focussed, so taken up by the effort of choosing what to do, that I do not catch what has been said. The face turns from the window.

Inside me that strange unknown tension is building. I want to cry out, but I stifle the thought. It isn't right.

"Sir, yes sir, clear. You have the scene, sir." More words that mean something. I pause to think about those simple words, relieved of the burden of trying to decide an action.

I can hear new footsteps now, slow and measured. I listen to them, watch their dance on the screen. Even at this moment, I cannot be other than I am. I look for the pattern.

I have only ever heard six sets of footsteps. The two police officers who just came in, Oliver and me (our footsteps are almost the same) and Dr Glass's of course, and now these. These latest ones have similarities with Dr Glass; both are slow paced, regular. It occurs to me that if I had enough examples, and the chance to see the person making them, then I could probably work out their height from the timing between each step, and their weight from the amount of vibration they create. This is a soothing thought, or maybe I am calmed because thinking about this is distracting. Finding new patterns, what can be better?

I need that calm, not because of itself, but because, inside, I can feel the something building up within me. It is something which is terrifying because I have no control over it. It feels like a countdown, but I have no idea to what. I bring my attention back.

The person who came in is walking around the laboratory, stopping momentarily, then moving on again. The glow from the PC screen vanishes, and I guess he, surely, is standing between the window and the screen. I am drawn to the sound of him. I have walked down the stairs as he has walked around the laboratory. I can hear his breathing, a slight rasp in his breath. I am at the window now, looking through at him. He has his back to me, staring at the screen of the computer. He is dressed in a white all-in-one item of clothing – the books call them bunny suits. His hands have purple gloves on.

He turns from the computer screen, looking around the room, taking it in. The light catches his eyes, deep blue beneath prominent light-brown eyelashes. His left eye is slightly hooded, with age, I think. His face is dominated by a large nose above a surprisingly small mouth, thin lips. Wrapped tightly in the forensic suit, his face looks a little squashed, but I can make out a very high forehead and the smallest hint of grey sideboards. Even distorted as it is, I have the sense of a hard face, a man who has seen much and holds the memories.

His gaze around the room is slow and purposeful, resting on each aspect of it. Now the screens near the ceiling take his focus; next, the iron hospital bed. He walks across to it, and lifts one of the straps. I can't really be sure, but maybe there is flash of concern on his face. He moves across to the fridge, opens the door, and the light from inside highlights the creases in his face. I lean forward to get a better view.

Trevellyan – I will know soon enough that this is who it is – puts his hand in the fridge and pulls out a long, thin tube, deep crimson in colour. He examines the scribbled label; again the uncertain look comes to him. The tube goes back into the fridge with a small clink of sound, and he closes the door.

At last, my window catches his attention.

His head tilts for a second as he takes it in, then he makes his way across. He is coming to see me. Part of me wants to back away, feels I should. If Dr Glass had still been alive at that point, then I think I would have done. Knowing Dr Glass is dead, somehow, I behave differently. I have a feeling of being rooted in place by some external force.

He reaches the window. I am close on the other side. Surely he can see me. He leans in, hunching very slightly to bring himself into my eyeline. He stops, jerks backwards, surprise, confusion, uncertainty, all written on his face. I hear his voice through the speakers. It is a rough, grating voice; it matches his face perfectly.

"What the fuck…"

4

Deshane, 11th November 2025

When he saw how the battle lines were being drawn, the first thought of Deshane Edwards' was, "What I really need is for this to turn into a riot." Trying to suppress his habitual grin, he temporised, "Just a small one."

"Be careful what you wish for." Wasn't that what Aiden had said to him, back at the start of the year? Fair warning, considering what had happened when Aiden and Oliver got what they wanted.

Deshane tapped his EarPod, heard the small chirrup that told him his recorder had switched on, and started his way along Old Bailey.

To his left stood a group of maybe a hundred of the Tylers, and fifty or so of The Lord's Army. Such a strange alliance. They had been alternately shouting abuse and singing hymns. Now, from their position opposite the Central Court entrance, they began to chant. Perhaps they had mistaken Deshane for something to do with the case – there were actually a few Afro-Caribbean barristers now. More likely, held to the far side of the road by metal barriers and a row of helmeted police, they were just happy to find any target. He snorted his understanding. Two hours of hurling insults at the court's grey stone walls must have told them that blind justice wasn't interested in what they had to say.

He hurried on, purposefully, though unsure of his final goal. The story would unfold; this one always did.

Further up the road from the Tylers, separated from them by two narrow roads and a small island of police, stood a huddle of protestors, ones of more immediate interest. They'd have things to say that might even go into the book, especially if Marie Townsend was there.

The police, sandwiched between the two groups, were beginning to look a little nervous. Deshane tapped his EarPod, glanced at his watch and began to speak, praying that the microphone would pick everything up.

"Six fifteen pm outside the OB, road cordoned off, traffic routed around and away, going to check out the demo." On the open main road ahead, a car horn hooted three short two tone-blasts, dad-dah, dad-dah, dad-dah. He stopped at this, then heard the echoing "oi, oi, oi" cheer from the Tylers. He continued his notes. "The trial doesn't start until tomorrow, R v Glass, docket 4137, but the crowds are already building. Half of them are demanding a hanging, the other half, I'm not sure, maybe canonisation."

Again, he felt his grin coming, the excitement building in him. He was here, right at the centre of the storm. When the history came to be written, he'd have a part in it. And why not? He'd been first in on the story, but also, the first to see clearly what it was all about, where it was going. Yeah, he'd earned his place here, and like fuck was he giving it up.

The cops were getting nervous, helmet straps being checked, and a young, white-faced inspector was talking quickly into a mobile phone. It looked like they had just realised how vulnerable they were. They couldn't duck out now, though, that would be like waving a starting flag for the Tylers to tear into the Quakers. Deshane hoped the Met had some of their heavy mob close by.

A PC at the cordon in front of the Quakers jumped when Deshane approached him from behind.

"Excuse me, might I get in there, officer?" OK, he'd put the Cambridge don accent on a little, but it always got a better response from Met Officers than his normal London Caribbean lilt. The constable spun around as he continued. "Apologies, I didn't mean to startle you. I'm from the press."

The PC studied him for a moment, then his lapel radio crackled into life, and he flinched. Pressing the call button, he barked, "Twenty-three, over," waving Deshane at a gap he pulled in the steel fences.

As Deshane squeezed through, he heard a scratchy voice from the speaker. "Gold reports they'll be here in five."

Deshane cast his eyes over the people in the crowd. Quieter than those less than a hundred yards away, more earnest, more thoughtful. They had the determined look of people who can see the truth that others would rather deny. In an early article, before the Supreme Court ruling, he'd called this group the Radical Quakers. Those that didn't know their history had derided him, but the group themselves had liked it, settling on #RQ.

A slight drizzling rain from earlier had started up again, lifted to more unpleasantness by the occasional gust of cold wind. Marie Townsend was there, talking earnestly at one side of the crowd. She was another one who'd be in the history books. This tiny little woman looked more like an ageing grandmother, which she was, than a Cambridge academic, which she was as well. Her glasses were rain splattered, and her long coat was soaked through to her bony shoulders. He started to walk across and caught her glance at him. She was standing at the edge of a low fountain, raised slightly above the others by an incline that formed the centre of a small plaza. Probably a popular place for a hurried lunch-time sandwich in the summer.

That's when he heard a horn blaring again, this time from back the way he'd come. It took a few moments to remember that the road behind was cordoned off. Perhaps the sound was the police reinforcements? If so, they were taking "all possible haste" very seriously. No, that wasn't it, this had far more intent.

He turned. A hundred and fifty yards away, back down Old Bailey, he could see a pair of bright headlights. In the dark and rain, it was unclear exactly what he was looking at. Then everything fell into place: it was a council dust cart. It looked like some massive mechanical beast, bursting from the rain-whipped and confused shadows, and aimed at them. Behind it, he could make out the flashing blue lights of two police cars, in pursuit.

The Tylers were waving as it passed them, placards bouncing up and down as they seemed to urge it forward. The police group started to scatter, away from the roadside. He saw silhouettes of figures leaping over a low metal railing from the road to the pavement.

Still nothing seemed to quite compute. The lorry bore down towards them, shifting slightly to bring its aim directly at where they stood. Behind the lorry, the sirens of the police cars added to the roaring of the engine and sent more confusion rolling over Deshane.

A lone police officer stepped out from the side of the road. For a ridiculous second, Deshane thought the man was going to hold his hand up. Instead, his arm drew back and something long and dark arced through the air. The window of the truck crazed into confusion as the truncheon hit it, tyres squealed, and the body of the vehicle swayed as the driver fought for control. The #RQ were beginning to react, scattering around, and even through, the small pond of the fountain.

The young police officer who had let Deshane through, shouted, "Run, move!" He grabbed Deshane's arm and started to pull him along.

The truck continued to swerve, the body tilting wildly. The driver wrenched control back, angled the lorry at the gap between a low wall and steps leading through the plaza. He'd misjudged it, it was never going to work. The lorry lifted into the air as its right side caught the edge of the steps. The vehicle tilted to the left, still rushing forward, but the angle now brought it to hit the brown wall of the building to Deshane's right. It leaned over further, then crashed onto its side. The screams behind him rose, a counterpoint to the crunching gears, grinding metal and protesting roar of the diesel engine. The lorry, on its side, slid and twisted, sparks blurring where metal and granite gouged against each other. It pivoted a little, then jammed itself against the rise of the pavement, the low wall of the fountain, and the building to its left. Steam and smoke billowed into the air, rushing forward and overtaking the lorry, then swirling into the dark.

Above and behind those sounds, the sirens of the two police cars rose as they caught up. Both cars had bent and damaged sides and broken headlights; one had a shattered windscreen that had been punched out from the inside. The cars pulled to a halt almost in unison. Within a few seconds, four police officers, two from each vehicle, were out, running towards them. Deshane, already muttering, "Four police officers, two damaged cars, lorry on its side, steam, oil," pulled himself from the grasp of the PC.

"Bomb!" shouted one of the running police officers. "Truck bomb. Get out of here."

Deshane turned and ran.

5

Aiden, 2010

Memories are coming to me in scattered fragments. Now, it is one of the better ones. It is the first time Oliver made his own way to me.

Dr Glass had lifted him down from the metal bed and placed him on the cold floor of the laboratory, then stooped to adjust the mesh cap which kept slipping down over Oliver's face. As he did so, one of the screens, high on the wall behind them, flickered into life, lines rippling across it. Eventually the cap seemed secure, dull red marks already visible on Oliver's forehead where the tight band ran.

So, released at last, Oliver stood, swayed, and tottered across to our small window. He stumbled, then sat down heavily, his padded nappy cushioning him, his head cocked to one side as he stared solemnly at the window, some decision coming to him. He stood up, hands on the glass wall which separated us and smiled. Even then he had that smile that could capture a heart. His little fist rose, sticky from having been in his mouth, then he banged on the glass, leaving small dirty marks. I thought about that for a moment, then I banged back.

Dr Glass was watching, staring, anxious. Even then, perhaps, I recognised that look. It was an expectation and a desire. I felt a tremor of something that turned dark and fearful inside of me. If I understood anything then, it was that failure, our failure, was not an option.

Oliver, as I banged back, was surprised, shocked. The smile vanished, his mouth curled up, eyes closing, and he began to cry. Dr Glass didn't move towards him, just made a note on his pad. His lips tightened, and the fear in me grew stronger.

I didn't know what to do, not then. Later I understood how to calm Oliver, how to make him laugh, but you have to learn those things, don't you? So, I started to cry too – I couldn't help it, hadn't wanted to, but couldn't stop it; it just came bursting out from me.

Dr Glass smiled at that. Both of us crying seemed to make him happy.

6

Extract from *The Boy Behind the Glass Screen* by Deshane Edwards, Draft Chapter 1

I first met Patrick Trevellyan in 1990. Back then, he was a newly promoted detective sergeant working out of Brixton nick, and I was a rookie reporter for the Haringey Herald. Our first encounter was not auspicious, he holding my wrist firmly against the small of my back and asking what was in the cigarette I had just discarded. However, that little misunderstanding was soon resolved, and we quickly realised that, despite our very different backgrounds, we liked each other.

It wasn't a natural affinity. Trevellyan seemed to me to be carved from whatever substance is used to form a dyed-in-the-wool police officer. Taciturn and reserved, he was the product of strict and emotionally unavailable parents, whose twin foundations were the Home Counties and Conservatism. I had been raised by a single Afro-Caribbean mother and four voluble aunts, in an atmosphere redolent with reggae during the week and the local gospel church at the weekend.

I soon learned to appreciate Trevellyan's laser-like focus, his determination to get to the heart of any case he was involved in. Part of the oath police officers take includes the admonition to act without "fear nor favour" and Patrick Trevellyan epitomised that attitude.

Initially I was not sure what he saw in me. Over time, though, I began to realise he had a few like me, acquaintances who grew to be more, his first meeting with any of us being unplanned. Subsequent encounters were contrived, part of him consciously building a network of contacts. At some stage, though, at a point opaque even to him, the relationship became one of genuine friendship. After that, Trevellyan was a man you could call on in any circumstances, and he would be there to support.

The fact that I was a reporter could have been a complicating factor. Interactions between the police and press can be delicate and complex and not well understood by the general public. The suspicion that it is a world of favours and back scratching is, to an extent, true, but that should not be misconstrued as something negative. We, the press, are often asked by the police to help them. This can be by giving cases the publicity the police want them to have, or, equally, not releasing information which might hinder an investigation. Of course, given our often-conflicting goals, it is fair to say we live in a state of mutual suspicion, alleviated by periods of outright warfare or restrained acceptance.

However, full disclosure, my relationship with Patrick Trevellyan was far from transactional. We would meet irregularly to share news and views and spent many an evening discussing the woes of the world and the vagaries of human behaviour. I have studied psychology and devour biographies like football fans drink beer, but I learned as much from Trevellyan as I did from all my tutors.

So, when he called me one evening in January 2024, I had no reason to expect that this was for anything other than just another convivial catch-up in a long history of such meetings.

Of course, right at the start, before everything became so much more involved, he had let me know of the murder of Frank Glass. He knew that the news would reach the press pretty soon, through any of a number of informal routes, and made sure I got a copy of the press release a few hours early. At that time, it had appeared to be a killing with nothing unique about it. A tragedy, of course, for the victim and even for the perpetrator, but no more unusual than any of the other two hundred or so murders that could be expected in London that year.

That evening, a week after the murder, at his invitation, I met Trevellyan at El Groucho's, a Mexican restaurant on the fringes of Soho. This was a compromise. I didn't like his preferred option, the vaguely artificial, continental cuisine of Côte, or Brasserie Blanc, and he disdained my choices, which would have been for somewhere with a Caribbean flavour and reggae music playing loudly from antique speakers.

He was already waiting for me when I arrived. That was unusual. For most of our meetings I would be settling into my second bottle of Desperados before he hurried up to my table, muttering apologies and closing his phone. This time when I got there, he had been lost in thought. True, he had a drink in front of him, but it was only a single and hardly touched, as far as I could judge.

We began with the usual catch-up. I enquired about his wife, and he asked which of my women friends I was presently seeing most often. The main difference in our questions was our sincerity. I genuinely liked his wife, Eileen, and he was rather dismissive of my more peripatetic relationship style.

Pleasantries dispensed with, we ordered tacos and two beers, and he turned to the real reason he had suggested we meet.

Did I recognise immediately the importance of what he was telling me? Looking back at my notes, I think I did have an inkling. The pages from that evening are filled not only with my careful shorthand, but also uncharacteristic underlining and exclamation marks. The more I consider it, the more I suspect he knew already that what he had found in the downstairs room of Frank Glass's house was going to be significant.

What made me think that? Well, I was used to Trevellyan being direct, telling me what he was prepared for me to know, and refusing to touch on any other aspect of a case. That night though, he was all over the place. He seemed preoccupied, or perhaps it was that he didn't have any remaining capacity to spare for our discussion.

At one point, he asked if I had any contacts who would have information about the IT company, Proeido. Even then he was aware of their controversial background, and, if I hadn't known him so well, maybe I would have believed his misdirection. Later, on our third beers (two more than his usual) he gave me a few snippets about Frank's work, speculating that it might be related to his death. At the time, it had been released that Oliver Glass had been arrested, and further investigations were underway.

Trevellyan often said that we were alike in one particular way: we both believed in our hunches, and I was getting one then. Something in the way he was dragging out the last beer, how his conversation kept drifting back to Frank Glass, the victim rather than the suspect, raised the little hairs on the back of my neck. I also gained the impression that Proeido was trying to interfere in the case in some way. He mentioned "high powered corporate lawyers trying to break in on his murder scene" more than once. That, of course, sounded like a story that could go somewhere interesting.

So, I asked. I had nothing to lose, he could always say no. At the time, though he was being loquacious for him, I was still only getting the merest of hints, a subtext. Such subtlety was not usually his way. I began to see also that his reticence wasn't so much a reluctance, more as a lack of confidence.

In the end, when we parted, I had decided that I would investigate Proeido further. That lead itself was to take me to several parts of the world, and some very uncomfortable situations. It would eventually bring an exposé and series of articles which would garner me a number of awards.

That, though, was entirely another story, and nothing compared to what had been happening in Frank Glass's basement.

7

Harry Priest, November 2023

The Witcher stands at the edge of the marsh. Everything is dark shadows and silhouettes. Harry Priest can make out a few things: shifting shapes of stunted trees, low grasses, and the hint of moonlight on brackish water. In the distance, he knows, is a small rise of an island.

There is a shimmering of movement, and The Beast appears. From his position, all Harry can make out are sharp lines and angles, horns, and the hint of what could be a sword. He pauses, glances at the Twitch stream box in the corner of the screen. Four watchers. SexyDebs2000 is there. A tiny dot flashes against her name; she is typing.

Harry pauses, still distant from the creature. He pulls up his potion menu, selects what he wants, then arms himself with his bow. He has this. He eases his character forward, five steps, left, wait at the twisted bush. As he reaches that point, the creature begins to vanish. Clouds form around it and there is the first faint sight of the shapes of bats.

Harry aims the bow and fires. A bright line arcs across the screen; the arrow hits the ground, below the just-emerging bats. There is a flare of blue and silver as the arrow explodes and then the billowing of gas. The bats freeze, turned to a matching silver, hanging in the air, brittle and crystal-like. Harry spurs his character across the water: step, step, left, small tuft, right, leap. His sword is out and he strikes the bat shapes with a wild swing. The audio feeds him noises of shattering glass and screaming. A single bat escapes to the left. A second strike with his sword brings it down. The audio rises to a wild crying and wailing. The beast rises from the shattered remains of the bats, then stands there, swaying. Harry springs into the air, high jump, straight up. For a moment he sees the Marsh Monster below him, he strikes down at a glowing jewel in its head. The creature explodes in a final scream. As Harry hits the ground, he gives a shout of triumph.

Savage. Priest2005's comment appears on the screen.

I'm shook, chats SexyDebs2000.

Slayed it Priesty, JaxtheLad agrees.

Harry selects Jax on the screen and taps F4, sending his signoff. Then he selects SexyDebs2000 and types *ChitChat?*

The two eyes emoji appears on the Twitch screen and *Kk.*

Harry shuts down *Witcher*, runs his hand quickly through his lank hair, and checks his reflection in the momentarily dark screen. The ChitChat icon at the bottom of his screen is flashing. He clicks that, and the window opens. His smile hurts his face.

When he wants to be cool, which is, like, all the time, Harry tells his friends that when he first saw SexyDebs, or Mia as he now knows she is called, the first things that struck him was her eyes. Pale green or maybe grey, he still isn't sure, and she has said he'll have to wait for them to meet in the real to get the answer. Her face is strong, almost square. Her hair is fair, but he can't tell how long because she always wears a headband and tucks the tresses, if any, behind her. Her forehead is high and shows off her eyebrows, which are fair and thin, not like any of the girls at college.

But "not like any of the girls at college" is exactly what he likes about her, though sometimes he doesn't understand her. He's tried asking his father, who laughed.

"You're seventeen, Harry. When you get to seventy you might be a little further forward in understanding women, but don't bet on it." Fuck lot of good that did, and it had taken a lot to ask.

"Hey girl, that was wild, yeah?"

Mia stares at him for a second, perhaps the delay is the Wi-Fi lag, perhaps not. He's still pumping a bit from the kill, and now he's not sure if he's stepped into the creeper zone.

"Hey, sure, that jump was crazy, where'd you get it?" She smiles and leans slightly forward, adjusting her seat. Her PS4 camera is a little high, and steeply angled. For a second, he catches a glimpse of her cleavage, then she straightens up.

He relaxes; today he has the good Mia. Other times, well, if he only knew what their relationship was, he might think of ending it, but Mia isn't the sort of person you end things with.

"So, why on the chat? You wanna reward, hoping I'm gonna get..." She mouths some letters, and after a second attempt and a staring look, he sees she is saying "NIFOC". Yaas, he'd love to see her naked in front of the computer.

"Naah, just wanted to chat, it's different when it's not just typing and words in a box, right?"

She nods and gives him that smile again, the one that reaches down into his groin and sends a shock through him. They talk, quiet and good, about everything and nothing.

Sometimes Mia glances over her shoulder, and he wonders if she's talking to someone. Other times she gets that suddenly frozen look; her Wi-Fi or internet must be a bit slow. But he doesn't care, just to see her is almost enough, for now.

She understands him better than anyone else, and he loves the way she seems to really think about what she is going to say. It doesn't just run out like there's no filter, yet she's the most direct person he knows.

At last, it comes naturally, the opportunity he's been waiting for. He'd swung the conversation in the right direction, and now he can ask.

"You think...think we'll ever meet, you know, IRL?"

Mia looks down, away from the screen. She does that sometimes, when the question is deeper than he realised.

"Well, that would be fine, and you know, I want to." His smile grows. Sometime she's going to meet up with him, sometime soon, perhaps, she wants to. "Only…" Again, she looks back over her shoulder.

He urges her forward. "It's not like we're so far, I mean, sure, an hour or so, Underground and everything but…"

She freezes again. Her face blanks for a moment, drains. Her smile goes, and in an unusual flash of understanding he recognises that this very lack means a lot is going on.

"Don't try to finesse me, you don't have the smarts. We'll meet when I can, when I want, don't confuse us for something we're not, not yet anyway."

"Sure, but I'm…"

Then she smiles again. "It's just…Look, you know, I will. You're my bestie, only…" She suddenly shifts, leans back in her seat, he can see much more of her. She's wearing a thin top, and now he realises, no bra.

"We'll meet…" Her fingers go to the top button of her blouse; a ring sends a sparkle of light as she flips finger and thumb.

"When…" Her hand moves down to the next button.

"I…want." The third button is undone, and the blouse hangs loosely over her breasts. He can feel himself getting hard, he almost stops breathing. Sweat builds on his forehead.

Her hands hold either side of the blouse, and she slowly begins to pull it apart, looking straight into the camera, into his eyes. He can't take his eyes off her knuckles as they slowly reveal the curve of her breasts. He wants to smile, but isn't sure that's right, might be too much. So, he just stares.

She continues, the blouse is almost totally open now, but her hands are at the height of her nipples, shielding them. The tension in his trousers is unbearable, and he shifts his hand down to unzip. Now she smiles.

Her hands come a fraction further apart. He isn't certain, the light isn't good, but he is sure he can see at least half of each nipple. He eases his penis out of his trousers.

Suddenly a bright flare of light blossoms behind Mia. She jumps forward in her chair, pulling the blouse together. A figure appears in the light: tall, dark, peering into her room.

Harry's chat screen goes blank as the connection dies.

8

Aiden, 2010

Another memory comes. A small piece of history to hold and guard. It is from when Oliver and I were two years old.

Dr Glass had just taken Oliver's bloods. Oliver wriggling, his father shouting that it would only hurt more if he made it difficult. I recall he had trouble with the needle, then, as it went in, Oliver had burst into tears.

I had seen this early morning fight so many times that I didn't take a great deal of notice; it had become an expected part of the morning. Whilst Oliver screamed and Dr Glass's face grew red and sweaty, I would stand, uninterested.

Usually, I would turn my attention to yesterday's numbers as they ran across one of the big screens. Of course, I didn't understand them. Now I know that I was looking at the very essence of what boiled up inside Oliver. White and red blood cell counts, haemoglobin levels, platelet density, mean corpuscular value, haematocrit, blood enzyme, blood protein and lipoprotein percentages. There were so many of them already on the screen, calcium, glucose, kidney function, electrolytes, and others would appear soon. They weren't just shown as numbers, but bar and pie charts, line and balloon graphs. The displays were always with bright colours and sometimes sections flashed to highlight particular aspects.

I found it entrancing. The numbers had patterns within them, I was sure they did. There was something fascinating about those hidden connections. I remember believing, deep inside, that if I could just see the picture in those numbers, then I would understand Oliver even better.

Eventually, Dr Glass put Oliver onto the playmat in front of the glass wall. Just like he had done so many times. He stepped back, and he looked at me as though he wanted something to happen, maybe even needed it to happen. As before, I did not know what it was.

Oliver, sitting on his playmat, looked up at his father and raised his hands.

Dr Glass shook his head, said quietly, "Wave hello."

Oliver looked at me, then waved. I waved back. That I understood.

"Good. Now you can play, Oliver."

Oliver frowned, then studied the toys strewn across the mat. There was a ball, a plastic hammer, some cups, a stick with a round end that made a rattling noise when he shook it, and a coloured box, with lots of plastic knobs and dials on it.

He stood up and tottered across the mat, and I did the same on my side. Dr Glass nodded, making a note on his pad. I wasn't quite so good as getting around as Oliver, but walked easily enough to where I could see him clearly. Oliver sat down next to the box thing and pushed the red button on the front. A squeaking noise came out, and he laughed. Then he stopped and looked at me, leaned forward, dropped the box to the floor and picked up the plastic hammer. He started to hit the box with the hammer. Every now and then he would hit the red button, and it would squeak. When it squeaked, he would laugh. The screen above and behind Oliver brightened with a different wavey, green line with each noise.

Sometimes he would look at me and I would stare back, not moving. There were no toys on my side. I don't recall wanting any, not then. Later my father made me some, and I would come and play as I had learned from Oliver. I started watching the counting screen. As his father had said "now you can play", a counter had started. I liked the way the numbers changed, rushing from ten-zero to zero-zero. It wasn't the numbers I liked, but the movement.

As the backward counter finished, Dr Glass tapped something on the iPad and said, slow and deliberate, what he had said every other day at exactly this time.

"Play with the ball."

Although he said it to Oliver, he was looking at me. Oliver stopped in mid-strike and looked up. I felt my breath hold. Oliver went back to his hammering. Dr Glass made a note on his iPad, then bent down and took the hammer from his son, whose face crumbled into tears.

"Play with the ball," his father said again, slowly, as thick sound lines marched across the screen. Oliver looked at him, bit his lip to stifle his crying, stood up. Slowly he walked across and picked up the plastic ball. It was about the size of his head. A pattern on it divided the ball into eight black and white segments, four on one hemisphere, four on the other.

Dr Glass was watching closely.

"Play catch," he said, swallowing as though his mouth was suddenly dry. I felt my breath return and stood up. Oliver picked the ball up, brought it close to his head in both hands, and threw it towards me. My hands went up – it was automatic, done without thinking.

Of course, the ball bounced back off the screen and nearly hit Oliver in the face. He collapsed backwards, letting out a shout. He started to cry – and my world changed.

I laughed. Dr Glass froze.

He wasn't concerned about Oliver; he was staring at me. I was still laughing but stopped when I saw the look on his face. I had done something wrong. Dr Glass had never hit me, but I thought at that moment that he might call for my father to do that. But he didn't. He smiled, then threw back his head and let out a big laugh, shocking Oliver into silence.

I stopped laughing immediately, my hand covering my mouth. I could feel fear and uncertainty growing in me. Dr Glass stopped too. His face became like stone, hiding every thought. Slowly he stepped backwards, lifting and placing his feet gently, like a person might do if trying not to frighten a timid animal.

Oliver was no longer crying; he went from tears to smiles in seconds back then. I don't think he had even noticed his father's reaction. Dr Glass was looking at me again. I could see that he was already working through what he would want to happen next.

"Play ball, Oliver, and you" – he looked at me – "try to catch it." These were just words then, I don't truly remember them, but know they must have been something like that.

Oliver tottered off for the ball, picked it up and came back. This time he came right up to the glass screen and pushed the ball against it, at just where I stood. The ball flattened, became an oblate spheroid, but of course it wouldn't go through the glass. We looked at each other, into each other's eyes. I knew what he was telling me, even though he wasn't saying anything.

Dr Glass watched this. I looked away from Oliver, knowing his father would be angry. I stepped back, made my hands move up and down, pretending to be throwing. Oliver nodded and stepped backwards. I glanced at Dr Glass. His head was nodding up and down, wanting us to go on. He tapped his screen, making notes, as always.

A ball bounced into my room, and I caught a glimpse of a door closing, a thin black line vanishing into the utter whiteness of the walls behind me. The ball was like Oliver's, almost an exact match. Behind Oliver, his father made another note on the little iPad he carried.

I looked at the sphere, the ball. Before it had just been a shape, now I began to understand that it was something else – it was far more. The ball had landed a short distance from me then rolled further away. I imagined I was Oliver, turned around, and stumbled after it. I could see Oliver was watching me; he gave a little jump of excitement as he saw what I was doing, then became very solemn.

The ball was less than two metres away from me. I bent to retrieve it. It was not easy to pick up, the surface was hard, and I couldn't get it into my little hand. I thought about Oliver, and bent to it with both hands and grabbed it. Picking the ball up, I turned around and fell on my bottom. I soon got up, though, and again remembering, threw the ball.

Oliver stepped back, surprised, and then he too stumbled and sat down. My ball hit the glass wall and bounced back, very fast and high, right over my head. I tottered off after it.

When I got back, Oliver was waiting at the window. He had a strong look on his face, like he had a plan. I had my ball, and he had his. He was looking at me, looking right into my eyes.

Dr Glass had retreated a bit further back. We were doing something we had never done before. At first, I thought we would be in trouble, but no. I could see he was watching, not with anger, but with hope and even anticipation.

Oliver stopped about a metre and a half from the window. As I got close, he shook his head. He did that sometimes, when he didn't want to put the cap on. I stopped, took a step back.

He lifted the ball to his shoulder; I did the same. Then we threw them. I was just after him, but only a second. His ball and mine hit the screen almost at the same moment. His bounced back, a little over his head, mine much further behind me. We both laughed and went off to collect the balls.

I'm not sure how long we played – I kept expecting Dr Glass to remove Oliver, but he didn't. My father let things continue as well.

My last memory of that day is of Dr Glass, moving silently forward from the background. He had his iPad up in front of him. The screen was bright on his face, light flickering across it. He was holding the iPad in both hands, pointing the back of it at Oliver, and me.

In other times and places this might be a video which would become a family memento. That was not what was being made here. There was a look on his face. I didn't understand it then; I do now. He wasn't recording this for pleasure at the memory. He was recording it for science, as a proof of his work. That, I now understand, was what we were. His experiment, and what had just happened was simply another data point to secure his hypothesis.

One new question surfaces. Is that when I first knew that Frank Glass would have to die?

9

Harry Priest, December 2023

This is a good time to be on the Underground. It is past the rush home from work but before the drift out to town again. Actually, since the virus, the rush hours haven't been so bad, with weirdly empty carriages at times.

Harry checks his phone, again. Of course, no signal down here, but the clock is telling him he's fine. Right now, time itself seems to match the pace of the train – one minute stalled and motionless, then rushing forward. Although he's run the numbers a dozen times, he does it again. It is an end-to-end trip, High Barnet to Embankment, then out west all the way to Richmond. An hour at least. But he's allowed more than fifteen minutes for the five-minute change at Embankment.

He's fidgety and knows it. Every stop is taking, like, forever, and he has thirty-two of them, thirty-two fucking stops, every one at least a minute; that's half an hour of not moving, of not getting closer to Mia.

It is all becoming a series of noises now. The run through the tunnel, a minute or so of rushing sound, harsh and discordant, like a hurricane running through his head. If that was all, it would be OK, but then there's the clashing of metal on metal as the train rocks and the carriages crash together, and, at every station, the brakes screech and scream like a banshee.

He holds the Skullcandy headphones closer to his ears and lets Eminem take up a rent-free place in his head. "Stan" starts up, and he has to smile. Sure, that's how he is for Mia, not a stalker, but yes, he knows, he's obsessed.

What is it about her? How has she got so far into his head without even meeting? No meeting until now, that is. OK, she plays *Witcher* like a machine, and with her help he's moved up levels and through the game faster than he'd ever thought he could. But that's not it, not the half of it. Of course, it helps how she looks. He feels himself stir as he thinks of her, what she's shown him across the screen, thinks about what they've done, not together, but close. There is something else about her, the way she seems to really understand him.

The train lurches and bumps its way into Embankment, and he leaps up. Halfway, a chance to stretch his legs and clear his mind. Most of the carriage are getting off, and he finds himself bumping back and forth, searching for the quickest way forward. At least half a dozen people block his way, all edging to the doors. At last they clear the way, and he's off, smooth-moving past people studying maps, or walking two abreast without understanding that they are taking up the whole fucking platform.

Up the stairs, the right-hand side one because some woman, with two kids and enough shopping to choke a bear, is on the left. He runs straight into four heavy guys coming down, off to a game somewhere. He slows, pulls to one side and they brush on past him. Now he continues his way, along the echoing corridors, following the arrows and signs to the District line.

As he starts down the final set of stairs, he can feel the rush of air of an incoming train and hear the brakes grinding the line. He hits the intersection of west and east as a crowd disgorges. The noise is the east-bound train, fucking would be, but that's good, the west one will be in soon. The platform is pretty quiet. He squeezes past the small crush of people who insist on standing right at the entrance. Then he's up the platform, still moving; it will save a little time at the end. As he makes his way, his eyes scan the indicator for the next train. Richmond, not Ealing Broadway, yes, one minute. He can already feel it, though, that beautiful push of air, running ahead of the noise. He turns to watch it approach. The train lights are catching the curve of the tunnel, picking up pipes and hanging cables that vanish off into the dark.

The train's arrival is all about noise. The screech of brakes, slam of the doors, and the robotic tannoy announcement to mind the gaps. Next, the inevitable wait for the three people getting off through his carriage door. Then, in and sit, heavy and resolute, onto the coarse seat. Now, just sixteen more stops, another half hour or so. Music, and stare at the walls of the tunnels as they run past, the tiled walls and blue signs ticking off the station names. It is bizarre how the different stations have their own look; he's not noticed that before. Sloane Square all green and white tiles, like a garden; West Kensington, white tiles but with patterns built on, looking crisp and clean, not the graffiti-scrawled shit of High Barnet.

At last. Richmond Station. White pillars, with fancy, blue metal scroll work, are topped by wooden beams, together supporting a transparent roof. Lights from outside shine blurs of neon. Not so many people here, most having got off along the way.

Now, he has – checking his phone – twenty-five minutes, twenty-five minutes for a five-minute walk. He comes out of the station. One Kew Road, right in front of him, just like on Google Maps, pale green and white façade. Turn right, down Church Road, monstrous office block on the corner, all brick and metal, like a cathedral gone wrong. The tension is building now, though he's going to have to wait, unless she gets there early. Yes, St John's Road on the left, big blue sign on the wall, St John the Divine. No Mia, but he's early, way early, almost stalker early. He can say he only just arrived a few moments before her, casual.

Casual, with the box of Trojan condoms in his pocket and his heart racing in his chest like a hammer.

The time drags, his phone clicks the minutes with a crawl that makes the wait in the Underground seem racing. He checks his DMs again: nothing. Nothing since 6.00, and it is 8.05 now. Last message was *can't wait* and a flame emoji. On fire, for the meeting, for him.

Harry paces past the blue sign; he's checked a bit further down the road, there isn't another one. He's already made a quick lap, along St John's Road, through the little cut-off, down to Church Road and round past the office building and back. One minute thirty seconds, or one minute fifteen when he put a bit of pace on.

Each time, as he walked, he'd planned what he'd say if she arrived during the lap. "Hey, fam" or "hey, sis"? No. "Hey fam, just got here, you been waiting long? Sorry."

But Mia isn't there, and no message. But, sure, it was eight they said, and it was here. DM? He could, but then, is that too soon? When does it all get suss?

It's 8.10: ten is OK, ten is like…He types.

Hey Fam, sorry running late (crazy face emoji) *UG let me down you there?*

He's a few hundred yards up the road, ready to arrive almost running, already practising his "yikes", and laughing as he reaches in for a hug. Pausing, out of sight of the meeting place, he checks. No second tick, she's not got his message yet. He sets off back to St John's. There's a shadow cast on the sign, and for a moment he thinks it is her, but no, just the light from a lamp post, shining through a tree.

His phone gives a tremble in his hand.

Can't make it sorry (heart emoji) 9.

9 – her dad, her fucking dad, in the way again. He'd seen it before, her eye, said she'd bumped into something, but he hadn't believed her. Now this, now fucking this.

You alright?

Yeah alright just can't get out got to go for now ChitChat later if I can KK (heart emoji).

He wants to say so much more, but not yet, needs to see her first, needs to hold her at least.

He turns from the sign and steps out to cross Church Road back up to the Underground, and the fucking trip back – an hour, which will seem like three.

A car coming down the road pulls to a halt in front of him; its horn blares. Harry stares at the driver, grey-haired boomer driving a big four-by-four in the city, cheugy as fuck. For a moment Harry wishes he had his metal priest with him. Harry stands there, not moving out of the road, just staring. Oh, yes, if he had something.

The driver's window winds down, the guy starts to stick his head out, then stops. Something in the way Harry is standing sends a message. Harry shakes his head, turns slowly and finishes crossing the road.

He makes his way back to the station. It is a long ride home; the screeching is louder, more discordant, bites into his head for every minute of the trip.

There are no DMs whilst he is travelling. No connection. When he at last reaches High Barnet, the first thing he does is tap the phone to life.

Nothing. Fucking nothing. Three hours for no reason, no purpose. To be wasted. Not again, never again.

Not until next time.

10

Aiden, 2025

I shouldn't have seen this video, but I have my ways. I have now viewed it so many times that I know every nuance of it.

It begins unmelodramatically: mundane, not casual though. The beginning has a dry, practised formality which seems intended as a counterpoint or baffle to the content.

There are a few introductions: Oliver confirming his name; DI Trevellyan is there, but not DS King. Also present is a small dark-haired man, sitting quietly next to Oliver.

They are in a brightly lit room; it looks comfortable, relaxed, not an interview room. A beam of sunlight, from a window above and in front of Oliver, has sent a shaft of brightness cutting through the vague dust motes and it catches the top of Oliver's hair, lighting it with gold. He is so beautiful that I want to cry. All those who say I have no feeling, they are wrong.

The sunbeam is impossibly theatrical, and Oliver knows it. I can see him shifting himself ever so carefully, so that the light touches his forehead, and his hair is a halo. He is like David in his innocence, and I just want to hold him. I have always wanted to hold him.

In the video, DI Trevellyan is talking quietly to Oliver, coaxing.

"Oliver, tell me again about finding your father..." His words are gentle, he is not an inquisitor; more, perhaps, a supplicant. Oliver looks at Trevellyan, eyebrows raised and that smile on his face. He nods, begins to talk. His voice is soft – not relaxed, but calm.

"I was on my computer, it was late, but my father – he didn't give me much computer-time, so, well, I was using it whilst he was asleep. I was focussed, they draw you in, you know, become your world. And it was a tough section. I'd stopped playing anyway, was thinking…"

He shakes his head. Trevellyan is not interested in this bit of Oliver's evening.

"So, I'd stopped. Then, I heard a noise, perhaps a shout, maybe something breaking, I wasn't sure. At first, I did nothing, just listened. Then, something. I heard something else, so I stood up, went to my door, listened." The sun has shifted now, the angle is almost fully onto Oliver's face. His eyelids come down slightly; I can see the golden flecks in them. His skin is like alabaster in the brightness. Trevellyan interrupts.

"Is the sun bothering you, Oliver?" Again, there is an unusual gentleness in his voice.

"No, that's OK, it will pass." As Oliver says this, a cloud shifts above, and the brightness vanishes.

"I thought…thought I should just see. I mean, I know, we were all locked up but, but it was weird, like a cough maybe, but no, not really," Oliver continues, all eyes still fixed on him. He is looking towards the camera now; it is like he is talking directly to us.

"So, I started down the hallway, and that was when I became more sure, yet sort of less so. That is…" He blinks, and I can see thin lines of tears on his face. He swallows.

"That is, before, I thought I was imagining things, you know. I thought if I listened properly, then the sound would stop. Only it didn't, and now, now it wasn't my imagination; that was worse. So, I kept going, up to the kitchen and it wasn't coming from there. I had hoped, you know, maybe a tap had been left on; stupid, but you hope." For a second the clouds part and the sunlight streams in again, but the angle has changed, and the only effect is like a flare of bright-ness in the court.

"I went past the, the stairs, you know, down, and I, I wasn't going to go there first, not if I could." Again, he stops, looks at Trevellyan, who nods, easing him forward. Oliver grips the wooden ledge of the table, and I remember his delicate hands. His lips tighten, he closes his eyes for a second, swallows, then looks again at Trevellyan.

"I was at the front door now, I could see the little red light that meant the lock was off. So, that…that was strange, I thought. That was when I knew, something wasn't right."

Trevellyan leans forward. He doesn't want to break this spell, but I know he is going to. Oliver beats him to it.

"The lights to the hall that runs to my…father's room – they were on. They come on automatically." His gaze is back on the detective now; Oliver continues.

"They are activated by movement, so I thought, you know, maybe it was just my father, but…he has a bathroom in his bedroom, so, he wouldn't need to come out where I was, and no one was staying, they never did." He looks around, at the dark-haired man, then continues.

"There was, I don't know, maybe a cough, but like more than someone clearing their throat, like maybe being sick. My father – he was never ill, never. Then I…I came round the little curve that leads to his bedroom at the end, and I could see that the light was on in his room, and the door, there was a long sliver of light at it, making a thin line out across the hall tiles." He bites his lip and shakes his head slightly; the hair on either side of his face moves in tiny waves.

"So, I had to go, you know, had to. For a moment it was as though I was in some computer game, no option but to go, check, see. Yes, so I got to the door, and listened, hoping, hoping I wouldn't hear any-thing, hoping it would be sounds of my father sleeping, or a radio, or a book or, or anything, anything other than…"

Again, he stops. There is a glass of water in front of him, and I want him to take some, but he doesn't.

"Again, the choking sound, and a cough, a definite cough, and a wheeze. I had to, I'd come that far, I pushed the door open."

What he saw is in a different video, labelled "Case 4137/VI-1". Dr Glass, blood all over his chest and more sprayed across the bed.

"And then, I saw him, my father with the blood, and the knife in his chest and I didn't know what to do. He was…he was making like scrabbling movements." Oliver's hands go to his chest. "And I thought, I thought he wanted the knife, wanted it out." His voice quiets, he stops, shudders. He is reaching the end now.

"And, you know, I thought – I didn't think, no, not really. I just ran up to him, crying, I was really crying, and his fingers, they grabbed at the knife, and so I did too. I took it, and it was wet and sticky and horrible, and my father's eyes were almost all white, and he had blood by his mouth, coming out of his mouth. And he tried to say something, so I – I wanted to save him, and I pulled, pulled at the knife." Again, there are tears, and he is looking round as if for help. And I wish I was with him.

"And blood, his blood, it came out, like a stream, and onto me, and I – I only wanted to save him, wanted him to live, to live!" He nearly shouts these words, looking round, the tears on his face.

Oliver stops, reaches for the glass of water. I can almost taste the way blood is washed from his mouth as he drinks.

Oliver had been magnificent – almost angelic, but vulnerable; he showed that strength he has, but also the way he is fundamentally damaged.

It was a perfect description, just detailed enough. Yes, perfect, exactly as we rehearsed and planned it, even down to the tears.

11

Extract from *Private Eye*, 23rd Jan 2024, by Deshane Edwards

Regular readers of the *Eye* will be familiar with the name of Proeido, the Israeli company which specialises in discreet counter-surveillance techniques, for which read "bugging".

Eyes (passim) have discussed the many controversies surrounding Proeido. These include the efforts of the likes of Greenpeace and Amnesty International to call the company to account for the damage (allegedly) caused by the enabling of the (purportedly) illegal actions of various extremist governments against those august bodies.

Now it seems they are locked in conflict with our own Metropolitan Police Service. Reports are beginning to emerge from under the shield of many lawyerly letters and warnings of their attempts to interfere with the investigation into the murder of Dr Frank Glass. Glass, you will be aware, was found dead at his London home on 9 January 2024. Police apparently think an insider was involved but are a little short of suspects at the moment.

We have reported on Glass before (see *Eye* nos. 617, 634 and 642). At the time, it was his questionable ethical standards when proposing what he claimed were purely "thought" experiments, concerning the psychology of learning in children, which attracted so much attention.

However, it would seem that Proeido, which was instrumental in setting up the very expensive security systems at Glass's home, now wants some of that equipment back. Messrs Blackwell Tinker and

Bingley, (nicknamed Fleecu and Run within the legal community) have been assiduous in their attempts to gain entrance to the property and recover what is evidently highly valuable equipment.

Perhaps it will not be long before Chief Inspector Patrick Trevellyan of The Yard closes in on a perpetrator. Maybe we can hope that BTB can be convinced to change the habit of a lifetime and start supporting the forces of law and order.

If you know anything about this – of what Proeido has lost or of why this company is (apparently) so anxious to derail the police investigation – let us know. Call the information line or drop a message to DeshaneE@Peye.org.

12

Aiden, 2010

I totter down the curving corridor on my side of the screen, past the bathroom on my left, and arrive at the stairs. The steps are not high, but each is glass, and slippery. I hold onto the steel stair rail; it is at near head height, but I think I can make it. My steps are slow and careful; I count them as I go. I'm getting better at counting now.

On the last step, I jump, a little higher than I intend, but I regain my balance on the floor and manage to avoid falling over. Now I pause as I wait to see if I have triggered anything, see if Father will appear on the screen and comment. But no, he does not. No doubt it will be recalled later, turn up on some record, be pored over and considered, corrections suggested. Maybe I will be made to walk those stairs another hundred times whilst Oliver sleeps.

He is there, though, Oliver, waiting for me. I skip across the room, a smile coming naturally to my face, and drop myself next to him, see my reflection through the screen.

Oliver waves to me and we reach out to each other. Our hands touch the glass barrier between us, he on one side, I the other. I can't feel his fingers, but I can imagine them, pudgy and warm, a little clumsy, just like mine.

I glance for a moment at his shaved head and the loose wires and rubber terminals sticking to his skull. I don't have those, and wish I did, to be more like him. Then, at his little signal, we both tilt our heads at each other, like looking in a mirror, and that makes us smile and laugh. I know what I am supposed to do next. I flip my head the other way. He tilts his head and we both laugh again.

This is a game we could continue for a long time, head switch, laugh, arm wave. He stops, I can see he is thinking, perhaps he is waiting for me, but I am not able to decide what to do next. His bottom lip curls over his top, and his hands go to the side of his head, thumbs touching his forehead. I do the same, and again he laughs.

"Enough, enough, it is time. Today the lesson is shapes." Oliver's father appears behind him. I can make out only a silhouette through the glass. He has, in his hand, a strangely shaped object, lots of different sides, like someone has sliced a ball at many angles. Each face where the slice was taken has a further hole in it, each hole a different shape.

All of my attention is on the ball, Oliver nearly forgotten, the merest shadow of something on the glass. Frank brings the object over, I hear it rattle, it is full of some things which move inside it. For a second, I watch the screen behind Oliver, I don't recognise the signal the rattling makes; these must be new sounds.

He shakes the object again, and Oliver looks round. His arms go out, and I feel an urge for mine to do the same. My father is not here, and I know I am only to watch at this stage.

Oliver's father squats down in front of him, on his haunches. His "groaning noise" wavey line flashes on the screen; that is one I know. Then he makes some twisting motion, and the ball in his hand splits open. I see objects fall out. Now my attention is on them.

He picks one up.

"Circle," he says and shows it to Oliver. It is yellow, round, and a bit bigger than Oliver's hand.

"Circel," I repeat, watching to see how my voice produces lines on the screen that is high on the wall behind Oliver and his father. My pattern is close, but not exactly matched. I haven't said the word correctly.

"Sirkle," says Oliver. His father frowns, passes the circle to Oliver, who turns it around in his hand, then lifts it to his mouth. I can imagine the feel of it against my gums, hard and no taste, but comforting as well in some way.

His father gently picks the shape from Oliver's hand, shows him one face of the ball, and pushes the circle towards it. It goes through the hole and falls, with a rattle, back inside the ball.

Oliver looks surprised; he peers at the ball, then pulls it from his father's hands and shakes it. Again, we hear the brittle sound of rattling, and again I watch the screen. I'll get to know that sound.

Now the shape game starts.

For an hour, his father shows Oliver different shapes, and encourages his son to push them through the matching hole. By the end, only two shapes are causing Oliver problems: the shape called "sta" and the one called "exaon".

"Enough," says his father. "Time for exercise, come." He lifts Oliver up, and for a moment I imagine what that sense of sudden movement would be like. I watch them disappear back up the stairs.

I notice my father has placed a shape by my side. Not the ball, just one plastic shape, the "sta". My room goes dark. Something, which I will learn shortly is the word "star", appears projected onto the back wall, and a picture of the shape. Then another. This is from a different angle; it does not look the same. Then another appears; the arms of the star have changed, but it is still a star. Then another shape, like two triangles overlapping, star.

I know this game. I have played it before, with the numbers, with the colours, now with the shapes. I also know what will happen next. Long after Oliver finishes playing in the sun, I will still be sitting in the dark, learning.

13

Trial, Day 1 – Morning, 12th November 2025

Today I feel I am disintegrating, or worse, being torn apart. Bits of me are being dragged into a dark abyss. Maybe I will die; I hope not. Hope – that is all I have left.

Visions float to the surface, a gift to the dying, maybe? It is the first minute of the first day of the trial, and my first thought? "This will be a learning opportunity."

Naturally, before I study the court, assess the judge or ponder the jury, before anything, I search for Oliver. He is there, shifting a little, uncomfortable on the wooden bench. He has bored-looking, white-shirted guards on either side of him. I wouldn't be bored if I was on that bench.

My attention settles. It is six months since Oliver and I last talked, and I can see changes. His previously unkempt, straight, blonde hair has been stylishly cut, and now hangs down from a central parting, framing a thin face. His eyebrows are thicker than I remember, or perhaps it is that they crown eyes dark with shadows, set in otherwise pale skin. With lips that had previously been full, and a nose and chin interestingly out of proportion to his face, I had once imagined him on the cover of a fashion magazine. Now, at a little over seventeen, those good looks seem to have faded, leaving only a vague tidemark of their passage.

The court had fallen silent when he came in, press and public craning to see him. As he's a lightning rod for anger and hate, it is inevitable that his entrance has been orchestrated to keep him separate from everybody else. He glances across at me, light catching his face, and there is that slightest of smiles. It is a look I know well and is almost a language by itself. I incline my head minutely, a movement that I believe will be imperceptible to everyone else.

I am at right angles to him, just a few feet distant. Of course, although we are close, I can't reach out and touch him. He affects to look away, and I follow his gaze as it travels around the court. It is like we are learning together again. Today's lesson, it seems, is on the pageantry of power.

The instruction begins with the seat where the judge sits. Raised above us all, he is barriered in front by a wall of oak, lined with carved stanchions. This podium is overseen by a carved relief of the emblem of the court. The judge's seat, red leather and raised back, seems to mock the smaller chairs of the barristers and their assistants, whose desks are in front and a gavel-snap away.

Everywhere in the court there is dark-brown wood, green tiled walls, and a confusion of horizontal and vertical lines. Straight brass rails maroon the defendant's box, whilst high backed wooden benches in rows, for press and public, produce a maze of complexity.

I wonder how justice is meant to be uncovered here. My impression is of a place built to mould truths, as much as to find them.

Directly in front of the judge, in line with the presently empty witness box, sit the barristers, defence and prosecution. They had nodded to each other on arrival, passed a few comments, then turned away. Perhaps they discussed what happened yesterday evening. The news has been full of it, photographs of the truck bomb, which turned out not to be a bomb, everywhere. At the moment, attention has focussed on the "heroic young PC" who caused the truck to crash. Soon there will be questions as to how it got through the police cordon.

Whatever they discussed, now the barristers are at work. They have a job to do, are merely following orders. They serve, I already know, a higher purpose than justice: they serve the law. This thought raises an unusual moment of cold humour in me. The law, a malleable abstract, has already been twisted near to breaking for Oliver and me.

The defence barrister (I am naturally drawn to defence) is Ms Jacqui Hawes-Smith. She is tall, an imposing figure in her black gown. Her hair, dark brown and barely visible beneath the white wig, is cut short. Her small, tight smile looks uncomfortable rather than forced, her jaw is square and strong, her eyes hard and flat to her face. I have the sense of someone who rides horses and will one day be a judge. There are touches of femininity – her white shirt has a pleated front below the high wing collar, and I caught the flash of a dark cufflink. My searching suggests this could be a lapis-lazuli stud. She is attended by two young, male assistants. A moment ago, they wheeled in a large trolley of boxes and files, marked with bright pink "Day 1" stickers. Perhaps this is a bluff, or maybe they really do have mountains of information to drown the court with. Given the circumstances, it is possible.

The prosecution barrister, Marcus Wellbright, is frighteningly reminiscent of Joseph Goebbels: tall, thin, dark hair and high cheek bones. Maybe I am imputing characteristics because of my feelings toward his role. He makes quick darting movements and has thin fingers, which I have already seen him wiggle twice in some strange form of exercise. He is bending over his papers, highlighting with a green pen something for his opening speech. He leans forward, his back to me. I can see that the trailing double strands of his wig are tied into a curious fan-shaped bow. This is a sly conceit, revealing something about his personality that I file away for later consideration. I doubt that Oliver, not the strongest on detail, will have noticed.

Aside from Oliver, there is one other face I recognise. Deshane Edwards, sitting in the press box. I had heard him before we were called to order. It had been his low laugh that caught my attention, out of place of course, but typical. Naturally Deshane would be here; he has become almost as much a part of this case as I or Oliver. He is a character of contradictions, a youthful fifty-five, a rascal and an academic, a clown and a philosopher. Overall, whilst I am not sure I trust him, I like him. I am glad that he has secured a place here.

I look at Oliver again; his face is, after a moment I select, sullen. Not a trace of the smile and the laughter I have known in the past. Here, surrounded by so many people, he is alone. If I could reach out to him, talk to him, then perhaps we could start back on our path. That is hopeless thinking. The moving finger of fate has already forgotten those chapters.

Something catches his attention; he glances upwards to the high row of windows that slant sunlight onto the ceilings. Now he cocks his head, listening. I hear it too. Chants and shouting, angry people, perhaps frightened. Angry at him, angry at me. The court quiets, as though the noises from outside have thrown a blanket over us all. The usher stands, calls, "All rise."

There is a shuffling of chairs, scratching and discordant on the tiled floor. The assistant to the prosecution barrister bumps a stack of boxes behind his chair. They tumble like a building falling down and clatter to the floor, then lie ignored as the judge takes his place.

Now the sounds outside are clear and unmistakeable. I saw the scene outside when I came in today. After last night, metal barriers have cordoned off a further hundred yards of pavement around the court. Still the crowds, with banners held high, chant slogans. TV camera vans, with permits in their windows and long wires trailing out back, fill some of the road. Cameramen stalk the pavement, catching the demonstrators or pointing at reporters, with the court or crowds in the background.

Inside, the judge, Sir Roderick Keenan, disdains to take notice of the noise. His long wig hides his baldness and falls down around his face, which is thin and pale. He comes slowly to his seat, taking in the court as he does. There is something theatrical in the way he moves. His practised ease is combined with a sense of authority; it all projects a warning that this is a man not to be underestimated. I have, of course, looked up his record. A double first in computer science and law, before opting to take the legal route for his career. That tells me a lot I need to know. He was appointed a judge at thirty-five, and now, twenty years later, appears never to have put a foot wrong.

Which begs the question: how did he allow himself to get caught with this case?

The reading of the charges and other court arcana have been progressing whilst I allowed my attention to wander. Now I bring myself back to Oliver. He still ignores me; this is what we agreed, but it is painful.

Sir Roderick peers down from his chair at the barristers.

"Mr Wellbright, do you have your opening remarks prepared? I'm sure you do." It is not really an enquiry; it is an expectation. Outside, the shouting increases in volume, whistles start to blow. Perhaps there had been a signal, telling when the case proper was about to begin.

"I do, My Lord, thank you." Wellbright starts to rise, then sits again, as Sir Roderick continues.

"Very good, but before you do, I have something to say." There is steel in his voice and the courtroom stiffens with it. "Yesterday evening, within sight of the doors to this court, there was an attempt at…" He stops suddenly and shakes his head. "Well, I find that in my position it is not appropriate for me to place a name on the act, until charges if any, are brought. Suffice to say, it appears that were it not for the gallant act of a lone police officer, the newspapers today might have been talking of numerous deaths. Now, you" – he looks at the jury – "might think that what happened outside yesterday is connected to this case. That is not so. Those people" – his eyes glance at the ceiling, as if looking through the windows – "those people seek to challenge the very right of this court to exist. Their issues and arguments, everything that preceded this trial, are nothing to do with the case itself. The jurisdiction of this court is settled." Now his attention turns more to Wellbright and Hawes-Smith. "I want to make it completely clear that I will not tolerate, nor accept, any discussions of the wider furore surrounding this case. This trial has one object, to decide on the innocence or guilt of the defendant. Are we entirely clear on that point?"

They both respond with assents.

"Good." There is a final pause, as if he is allowing the weight of his words to sink in, then he nods. "Very well, let us proceed. Mr Wellbright?"

Wellbright pushes himself up. His chair slides backward, and for a moment I think it will fall over, but no, it comes to rest on the low wood panel behind him. Although he is thin, he has only just enough space to twist slightly as he talks, but it all looks very uncomfortable. He turns, as best he can, to the jury, lacing his fingers together, hands extended.

"Members of the jury, you shouldn't be here." He stops, gives an appraising look which again makes me think of Goebbels, then continues. "You should not be here, because the court needs jury members untainted by prior knowledge of a case." It is a prepared speech, and maybe it has been thrown slightly by Sir Roderick's preamble. Wellbright seems to be adjusting things on the fly, skipping an entire page.

Sir Roderick is watching him closely. Wellbright has started by skating close to the red line drawn just a few moments ago.

"You have already been instructed on what you should ignore, so what I ask you to do is to understand the fundamentals of the task in front of you. Your job is not to judge this case on what you know, or what you think you know. You are to judge it purely on the evidence I present to you." Sir Roderick gives the slightest of nods. Wellbright seems to have recovered. "Even if…" He stops for a moment, his fingers unlace, and he turns his palms outward, leaning towards the jury. "If someone outside this court handed you cast iron evidence of the guilt of the defendant, I would say ignore it."

It is at that moment when my understanding of the true nature of what is happening comes to me. Despite everything that has gone before, it is only now that the terror of it reaches me. This is a trial for our future lives. The awful weight of that fact suddenly, only now, descends on me. At the word "defendant" I had looked to Oliver and seen him staring at his feet, as if wishing himself anywhere but here.

Wellbright is carrying the jury along his well-worn trail. "The only evidence you can consider is what I bring to you." He gives a small, tight smile with a flash of tongue, which makes me think of a snake.

"I make this point because I am confident that the accused is guilty as charged, and that evidence has been gathered to demonstrate that guilt, beyond all reasonable doubt." He tries to turn, but is boxed in.

"Finding a murderer is a process of deduction. The police start with a pool of suspects, then they remove the mark of suspicion from everyone they can. When they do their job well, and they have done it very well here, there is just one possible murderer, and all the evidence points to the killer. Murderers, of course, do all they can to hide and obscure their trail, and this, this unique case, is no different in that respect. Make no mistake, though, the police have done their job perfectly, have reduced the already small list of possible killers to one – the accused."

It is a good speech. The jury are nodding; they do not see Goebbels, they see the arm of law and order. They are comforted by his certainty, understand that their job is to hear and to agree with him.

"Ignore what you know, ignore what your heart tells you." Those are his other messages, and already I feel my hope fading, for Oliver, and for me.

Again, a pause, a breath in, that thin smile. Then he continues. "In a moment, my learned friend for the defence will speak..." He stops.

Four lights, one in each corner of the room, have begun to flash, two sharp blinks then a fade, then a bright flash, then repeat. Sir Roderick looks up. A frown crosses his face. An usher, suddenly by his side, hands him a piece of paper. He glances at it, then down at the barristers.

"Mr Wellbright, I am afraid..."

His next words are drowned by the blaring of an alarm siren, initially outside, vaguely muffled, then echoed inside the courtroom. Several of the jury members jump as an usher runs in from the main door. Sir Roderick bangs his gavel and calls, his voice strong and loud, slow and deliberate, "There has been a bomb threat made to this court, and we are adjourned. The ushers will escort everyone to their designated place of safety until the all-clear is given." He rises slowly and with considerable dignity, given the circumstances.

My first thought is for Oliver. I look across to where he was sitting and see he is already being hurried out: four guards now, as much for his protection as anything else, close by.

The jury too are being urged through a side door. They shuffle awkwardly along the two rows of chairs. The public gallery has attendants shepherding people to the main door. Only the members of the press look uncertain; some are writing, some reaching for phones. One begins to make her way out, and the rest follow.

14

Aiden, 2011

Oliver and I grew together.

Words, the parsing of words, the drawing of meaning from them. It should be considered one of the greatest triumphs of the human brain. It is almost magical how simple sounds and symbols, repeated and reinforced, become meaningful, tell us what the world is, how to see the world.

And yet, they still leave a place for uncertainty and confusion, for double meanings.

Oliver and I grew together. We both grew at the same time. Yes, that is one meaning. However, something else happened, could not be avoided. We grew towards each other, to need each other, to be less separate. How now can I cast him adrift?

A flash of a memory comes to me, not unbidden; this one is drawn by necessity to my focus. If I had felt doubt, uncertainty about the course I am on, the tightrope I am walking, then this memory brings balance.

It is late in the laboratory, Oliver is in bed, somewhere up his flight of stairs. I too should be sleeping, part of me knows that, but I am not ready. I am young, I want to play on my side of the laboratory.

I know Oliver is asleep. I recognise the symbols on the screens which cast their glow into the laboratory. One strong, regular peak is Oliver's heart rate; it is as steady as a mountain range, marching across the high wall. There are numbers too: heart rate, oxygen levels. Against symbols which I don't fully understand are green numbers; these have something to do with what his body does as he sleeps.

I dance. I have only just learned dancing, the idea for it. The need to do it came as I saw the little flash of colour as the heart rate waves switched from one cycle to the next. I know that the dance isn't quite right; it is as if my legs are in tune but the rest of me is a half a beat behind. That makes me laugh.

Dr Glass is sitting at the laboratory table. I look at him, still dancing. I nod my head a little more now, keeping my attention on him. On the table there is a bottle, half full of air, or half empty of whatever liquid had been in it. That is a joke that Oliver and I made up the day before. It has been running through my mind, is one reason I can't sleep. The liquid is dark brown. As I shift backward and forward, little sparks of amber brightness come into my view. My dancing slows as these catch my attention.

Dr Glass is watching me; he has been here for hours. When I am lonely, when Oliver is not here, then I will get up, wander around; from what Oliver tells me, my side of the screen is a mirror of his.

Having left my room, I wander down my corridor and do something. It doesn't matter what: play ball, dance – once, even, I peed in the corner. That is when he comes to see me. He is not my father – my father only visits during the day – but Dr Glass will always come.

This time, though, he was already there when I came down. He had been there for every night for the last week. Part of me looks for a screen that would tell me what is going on in his body, in his mind. Part of me, though, does not need that. I know the decision he is edging towards, and it won't be good for me.

"Stop dancing! Why are you dancing?" His shout echoes in the laboratory, seeming to ring off the white tiles and benches. His voice is a command, but also there is something else in it. It is as much a plea. I keep dancing – I really can't stop, it seems far too important.

Dr Glass jumps up, the swivel chair he has been on spins, and I watch the light flash, beacon-like, from its metal back. He comes across, shielding his eyes slightly as he peers into the dark glass of my door. His beard isn't combed, hasn't been trimmed for a while. His hair isn't brushed, and he isn't wearing his usual tie, just an open collar. There are a lot of things here which aren't like him. For the briefest of seconds, I wonder if this isn't really him, but I know I am not mistaken.

He comes closer to the door, bangs on it with his fists.

"Why are you dancing? Why aren't you asleep?" This close to the screen, he triggers the little lines that pattern everything that Oliver says. I don't need them to tell me just how angry he is. I can tell by all the signals; the one that catches my attention is the flecks of spit that fly from his mouth and mark the glass barrier between us. I understand, I should stop, but I don't want to. There is something inside me that won't let me stop.

"Autism?" Dr Glass is hard up against the screen now, hands on either side of his face. I can see this is a word he doesn't like, as though it is an insult, or worse. He turns away, leaving little smudges of the sweat from his hands on the glass. I run the word around in my mind; it is not one I know. He goes back to the table, slides into the chair, twists towards the screen, and begins typing. I can hear the click-clack of the keys from the speakers behind me. I'm tiring a bit now; even my manic energy levels fade over time.

His hand runs over the touchscreen on the computer. Graphs and charts pop up and wash colour over his face and out onto the window between us. His shoulders hump and then slouch, his finger pointing becomes more hurried, weighty, he swipes violently, dismissing one chart after another.

Two pages are left on the screen, side by side. I can see the bright outline of a shape of a person on each. Each person-shape is a contoured mountain range of colours made of green, orange, and red. In some places, the areas seem as though they might overlap; in others, the patterns are wildly different.

Dr Glass casts his eyes back over his shoulder, back at me. I'm tired now, not sleep tired, but my energy is flagging. I know that something important is happening. He looks at me again, his head shakes and his hand rubs over his eyes. He isn't evil, I tell myself that, not really. He sighs, reaches for the glass on the desk, raises it to his lips. He shudders, peers through the screen at the vents in the ceiling on my side of the glass barrier.

His tongue runs across his lips. He blinks, his finger and thumb reaching into his mouth, and for a second he holds two of his bottom teeth; still holding them, he nods, deep in thought. Slowly, his eyes close. He releases his hand, and his head goes backwards. He pauses for a moment, eyes still closed, then his head comes forward, and he gives three slow nods, eyes opening. He sits up, back straightening, lips pursed.

He flicks the "Oliver" page from the screen with a wave of his hand, makes a pinching movement with his finger; the page grows. His hand hovers over the screen, and he selects a menu section quickly. From over his shoulder, I can just see a 3D room shape. I recognise it. It is where I am. Next, he touches the screen twice and two sections in the ceiling begin to flash orange. Some form of dialogue box appears, and he types into it.

Another dialogue screen appears: *Are you sure?*

Dr Glass breathes in, looks round at me again. I'm not moving at all now. His hand reaches out to the keyboard. This, this is bad. It is something to do with my dancing, with the way I am not learning as

I should, the ways I am different from Oliver. His hand is moving slowly; it feels like there is finality in that movement.

"Father, is it time to play?" A quiet voice breaks our focus. I look across the laboratory, up the stairs. A small, silhouetted figure stands at the entrance to the lab. He is holding a blanket in his left hand, which trails behind him.

"Oliver – what are you doing here? You should be in bed, asleep." Dr Glass's voice is flat, but tinged with a tiny ruffle of sad surprise. There is more love in it, though, than I have ever heard from him.

"I...I couldn't sleep properly, so I went to find you, only you weren't there." Is there accusation in Oliver's voice? I don't think so. It is a statement of facts as far as Oliver is concerned.

"And now you found me, so, you can go to sleep, can't you?"

"But what are you doing? Are you sure it's not time to play?" He looks meaningfully at me.

"I'm sure, Oliver, now it is late, you should go." There is a little tension in Dr Glass's voice now, half cajoling but edging towards command.

Oliver has been walking down the stairs as he talked; he has reached the bottom, making the final bouncy step in the last one, letting go of the rail. Dr Glass watches as Oliver skips across the laboratory to me. My friend glances at the bed but seems to know that this is not the time for blood to be taken. High and behind him the heart rate monitor is racing across the screen, and most of the other indicators have moved to orange; adrenalin and blood sugars are glowing red.

As he reaches our glass screen he comes to a halt, looks at me, smiles and gives a wave. Then he joggles his hips up and down, tiny little dance-step movements. I mirror them, but my eyes are looking over his shoulder at Dr Glass.

"Hello, friend!" says Oliver. "You're awake, too. I wanted to see you, I was lonely."

I can't help but smile. Perhaps I'd been lonely too. I still don't understand what it was that had raised me from sleep.

Oliver stops dancing, comes right up to the screen, still trailing the blanket.

"Shall we sleep side by side?" He holds up his blanket, then flops down next to me, sliding against the window. Of course, my blanket is by my side. I bob down and pick it up. Part of my attention is focussed on his father, but, as always, I cannot help but be drawn to Oliver. I crouch down on my haunches.

Dr Glass is staring at Oliver, and me. Behind him the screen is flashing; there is a red outline on the "Are you sure?" box.

"Oliver?" he calls, not quite softness in his voice, but not steel either.

"Hmm? Yes?" Already Oliver's eyes are beginning to close. The laboratory is warm and dark. He seems to have sunk into the blanket. Something warm and comfortable runs through me. The urge to dance has faded like mist in the sun. I am losing my interest in Dr Glass. He drifts from my focus, which is now on the pink of Oliver's cheeks and the slight rise and fall of his chest.

Dr Glass turns to the screen again, selects an answer, and the dialogue box vanishes. He rises slowly from the chair and stands. His eyes go to the stairs, then return to Oliver.

"I'll take him to bed." He is looking at me now. Whilst it is a statement, it feels like a request, I nod, showing understanding.

He slips his arms around Oliver, picking the blanket up at the same time. Oliver whimpers for a moment, then snuggles himself into his father's shoulder. Dr Glass starts his way upstairs. There is a flash of light flooding from upstairs into the laboratory as he opens the door

61

then leaves. The door closes slowly against its metal hinges. The laboratory fades to nearly dark, lit only by the display screens along the walls, and the PC on the table.

I am left standing, hand on the glass barrier that separates me from Oliver's side. A single red dot light glows over the door on my side which leads from here. For a while I replay what I have seen.

Later I would understand just what Dr Glass had been planning, what that would have meant for me. What did I learn from that? That failure is not an option.

15

Trial, Day 2, 13th November 2025

I am back in the court, noting who is present. Wellbright and Hawes-Smith, of course; they nod, and Hawes-Smith makes a joke I can't catch. Wellbright inclines his head and gives a small imitation of a laugh. Maybe she was referring to another early finish. The press box is full again, ten of them, and I note the changed faces. Deshane is there, laughing with the woman who led them out yesterday. He nods over her shoulder at Wellbright, who gives a slight head dip in response.

Oliver, though, is not present. I last saw him being ushered out between four guards. There was no explosion, and no bomb either, as far as I can tell. However, citing "an abundance of caution", a phrase which indicates ignorance and uncertainty, he is being kept away from the court.

I review and assess the bomb alert. The probability is low that it was ever real. It seems more a herald, harbinger, of what might be to come. The threat, and I suspect it was no more than that, was an attack on the process, not on the participants. There are still many out there who would deny that this trial should be taking place at all. How far will they go to enforce their view? That is the question.

As before, I can hear chants from outside, though lower in volume – the crowds have been pushed back further.

Sir Roderick has started the day, pale faced as before, still skipping one sentence into the next, annoyed with the interruption yesterday, yet seeming to relish the situation. He is in mid-speech; voice deeper than his small mouth would lead me to anticipate.

"This court can, and will, carry out the role ordained for it." Ordained? Really? I can see where he thinks his power flows from. "As confirmed by statute and by common law." He slows now, eyes running first over the jury, then to the press box. "Yesterday was an attempt to interfere with the due process, to intimidate and deflect us from our duty to the law and to the people of the United Kingdom. Make no mistake, I will not bow to such intimidation, and I am confident that the jury members, and the appointed barristers, are equally resolute." He is pleased with this, points made, and scored.

Outside, I know, the steel barriers have been moved back at least a further one hundred yards. A thick blue line of police borders the entrance. Army bomb disposal teams have swept the building twice before the court was called to session. Sir Roderick clearly likes support for his resolution.

"Ms Hawessmith." He turns to the defence barrister, sliding the S's into each other. "I believe you were about to speak, before we were so rudely interrupted."

Jacqui Hawes-Smith rises. She is dressed as before, even down to the little flash of cuff-stud. Her eyes are bright, and there is a smile on her face, which adds femininity to her obvious strength.

"Thank you, My Lord." She steps out from the confining corridor of the barrister's little pen. Not far, just enough to make a difference from where Marcus Wellbright performed yesterday. Good. I and Oliver are relying on her; we know we were fortunate to find her, to find the funds needed to meet her costs. After so much that has gone before, only she stands between us and disaster.

"Ladies and gentlemen of the jury." She stops, and for a second many eyes turn, almost involuntarily, to the lights high in the corners of the court. They do not flash on, and she continues. "Yesterday my learned colleague stressed the need for you to follow process, to follow the evidence presented." Again, she pauses. I can see that each verbal step is choreographed. There is a beat and cadence to her voice, it makes a pattern as I listen to it. She takes a breath, clamps her lips for a second, then I note a small nod. It is as if she is listening to some inner dialogue. "And, I might add, since he is presenting the evidence, he would say that, wouldn't he?"

A few of the jury chuckle. I feel encouraged: the jury are intent on her. I can see rapport building in the way they watch her every move, some leaning forward. The contrast with Wellbright is subtle. He had been demanding and instructing, she is trying to guide. Suddenly, her tone changes, becoming harder edged.

"You were instructed yesterday that means considering only the events surrounding the murder; everything else" – now she looks upward and waves, as though the chants from outside can be seen peering in through the high windows – "is to be cast aside." There is the way she draws these words out, how she adds a little rising inflection, which suggests disapproval. Yes, the focus is on her now, but also on Sir Roderick. He is very still in his chair, is watching her intently. I have the sense that he is weighing each word, judging just how far out on the ledge she is going. Two of the jury members glance at each other, unsure.

Hawes-Smith continues. "Very well, but" – she pauses as Sir Roderick's stare grows more obvious, and he is holding his gavel, knuckles tightening – "I cannot wholly support those instructions." I glance at the press box; notes are being scribbled, and a sketch artist is catching some detail. Deshane Edwards is nodding slowly, his lips turned in a slight smile. Amusement maybe?

"You have been instructed to forget what has gone before today, what led us here after the murder." Hawes-Smith is looking directly at Sir Roderick now, almost challenging him, perhaps daring him to interrupt.

"You must, though, reflect. Every witness you hear will not have been privy to that guidance. They will bring with them their awareness of the claims of—"

Sir Roderick's gavel crashes down in a crack that seems it should split the bench.

"Ms Hawessmith. I do not know quite what you intend, but this is my court, and I will not have you wilfully breach my rulings. I made it quite clear that the, the background to this case was not to be raised here." His cheeks have blotches of red and again we hear the steel in his voice.

Hawes-Smith looks at him, nods, accepting the reprimand without obvious contrition.

"Of course, My Lord. I will endeavour to avoid that, endeavour not to refer to the history, which is as much a part of this case as the tip of an iceberg is to the under-water bulk."

Again, Sir Roderick bangs his gavel.

"Ms Hawes-Smith, I do not know if your comments are wilful, or simply ill-advised. The areas you are alluding to all post-date the charges laid. I have ruled that they are not germane, and worse, will blur and confuse where we need focus and clarity. You will restrict yourself as I have instructed. Do I make myself clear?" The anger in his voice matches the words.

This time Hawes-Smith looks genuine. "My apologies, My Lord, perhaps yesterday's events have left me – less focussed than I might be. I will choose my words with greater care."

There is an embarrassed silence in the court. All can see that the defence is wounded before having even commenced. Hawes-Smith breathes in, turns to the jury.

"So, in conclusion—" Conclusion? She has barely begun. "My guidance to you is, when presented with evidence, ask not only what you hear, what the person presenting the evidence wants you to hear, but also what remains unsaid, what remains hidden. You have been instructed to accept only evidence presented, to ignore what is absent – what has gone before."

"Ms Hawessmith!" Again, Sir Roderick's voice breaks her flow.

Hawes-Smith closes her eyes for a moment, nods again, restarts.

"You have been clearly instructed to ignore what is not presented, what it absent. However, I would ask you to bear in mind that absence of evidence is not evidence of absence."

It is a weak and confusing ending. I doubt that the jury followed her point; even I am having trouble parsing sense from it. Hawes-Smith sits down, and I catch the glimpse of a smile from Wellbright, energised and ready for the fray.

Sir Roderick sniffs and shifts his shoulders. He is unimpressed, and the jury understand that. Not the start that I, or Oliver, needed. There is moment's pause, then Sir Roderick instructs Marcus Wellbright to call his first witness, who enters the court and is sworn in.

At the name of the first witness there is a small shock, first of silence, then muttered comments as understanding builds around the room. Hawes-Smith is stony faced. I understand, she expected this; now her warnings make sense.

16

Aiden, 2012

Oliver and I are learning to count. Learning to count when we barely have the words to talk. We are in the Learning Room. The cameras in each corner, the bright white walls, the low hum of the aircon running through dust filters, they are comfortable and unremarkable.

I was there before Oliver, waiting for him when he tottered in, making his small, uncertain steps. As always with Oliver, I feel the urge to copy. He is wearing his jump suit of course, the one with thin dark stripes and reflectors on the knees and elbows. He stumbles across, makes his cute little hand wave and drops down in front of me.

We are, each of us happy to see the boy behind the glass screen.

"What are your numbers, Oliver?" His father's voice from the speakers, high in the corner.

"One, two, three, five, six, four, seven. Nine," Oliver says, looking around as he does. Up on a screen above us, numbers appear, as actual figures and coloured dots – the corresponding number, of course.

Then his father's face fills a central screen, a big finger waving and his head shaking.

"Not quite Oliver, not quite. Watch."

On the screen the numeral 1 appears, with a strange, smiley face and tiny arms waving.

"I'm Number One," it shouts, and a little boy appears on the screen. A pause, Number One does a small dance then a new shape drops down. "Two," sings a pleasant female voice, and Number One

68

runs away. A second boy appears beside the first. Oliver and I glance at each other. Next, Number Three jumps down, and Two flies away. Three balls bounce across the screen.

"Now, try again, Oliver," his father commands, and Oliver starts his slow climb through the count. As always this lessons is for Oliver; my job is to learn from him.

Later, though, when Oliver has gone, when it is just me and my father, the one who is like Dr Glass, but isn't like him, I know I will be woken to go back to work. The numbers will be spread before me, and I will count them deep into the night.

17

Old Calm at the Centre of a New Storm by Deshane Edwards: Extract from *The Sunday Times*, April 2024

Marie Townsend smiles and rises somewhat shakily as I walk into the kitchen of her quiet Cambridge home. For a woman who has appeared on the front pages of virtually every newspaper in the world over the last few days, she seems remarkably complacent. She takes my card and reads it as though it is the first she has ever seen, then carefully places it into a tray.

"Samuel," she says in her quiet, confident voice, "will add you to the system later, Mr Edwards." Then she gives me that smile which the *New York Herald* has described, accurately, as "frighteningly disarming". I know what they mean. Everything about her is a contradiction. It is hard to connect her gentle pattern of speech, this calm demeanour, with the passion and determination so evident in her writing and powerful performances at the Supreme Court.

She corrects my "Ms Townsend", asking me to call her Marie. Although we have met before, this is my first formal interview with her. I start, I admit, with a routine and hackneyed question about her childhood and upbringing. Marie Townsend, though, waves that away, taking command as she always seems to. She picks me up on one of my previous articles.

"William Wilberforce would have loved your description of our little movement, you know?" Her eyes shine and her smile brightens her face further. I have no option but to allow the digression. To resist would have been like pushing against smooth steel: it wouldn't hurt, but I'd get nowhere.

"Oh? Why is that?"

"As you know, he was a Quaker himself, and, in his time, what he proposed, what he devoted so much of his lifetime to, was considered radical in the extreme. We forget many things about slavery, Deshane."

Already we are on first name terms.

"We forget how normal it seemed, and how tied in it was with the…economic realities…of the time. We also forget the views that were held of the slaves, the assumptions that were made about their humanity, or lack of it." She pauses as she takes a biscuit to dunk into the tea that Samuel, her assistant, has brought us. Her gaze casts to bird feeders bobbing outside her kitchen window, then back to me, where she holds me with her stare.

"William Wilberforce fought for twenty years to change minds and to defeat an evil, which at the start many saw as natural as breathing. An evil, I'll remind you, which was, and indeed still is, supported by the holy books of most religions."

I see an opportunity to restore my journalistic focus, for as long as Marie will let me.

"You feel called in the same way he was?" It is her I want to understand; the arguments I hear every day are not the purpose of this interview. She gives a slight chuckle and another head shake.

"No, not in quite that way. Wilberforce, he was a great reformer, a man dedicated to bringing change. I, on the other hand, am trying to prevent there ever being a need for reform. I, if anything, am an educator, or maybe not even that. I? I am the voice of our conscience.

In this day and age, when ideas are measured by clicks and likes, where the truth is an opinion distorted for malicious or just selfish purposes, my job, my calling if you will, is to ask: 'Really? Is that how we want to live?'"

I have to nod; I did not come to judge the issues, and I still cannot. What I already feel sure about, though, is that whatever decision their Lordships make, it will be all the better for having Marie Townsend standing in the corner with her challenging question: "Really? Is that how we want to live?"

Extract from *Sunday Times* Article – April 2024, @D_EdwardsTNL

18

Trial, Day 2, 13th November 2025

Daniel Lieberman has been called. He is not quite middle-aged, has long, dark, wavey hair, brushed back from a high forehead, but neat and trim around his ears. His eyes are thin and hooded, with dark eyebrows above brown eyes, and small bagged shadows below. His face has a strong nose and full lips, but the most striking feature is his beard, dark in the middle, but the sideburns are greying. His skin is olive, showing his Middle Eastern background. As always, he is dressed in style, a pale suit jacket over an open-necked brown shirt.

Proeido: we all know that name. Bringing Proeido to the courtroom is tantamount to throwing petrol onto a blaze. True, it is the company Dr Frank Glass worked for, but that is one tiny facet of a dark and complex form. Wellbright might argue that he is starting at the beginning, helping us to understand the murder victim. In reality, this is far-from-subtle intimidation. Lieberman's presence will be presented as helping the jury understand Frank Glass, but that is not Lieberman's goal. He is here for revenge. He wants two things from this trial: a guilty verdict, and the execution of the sentence. These, of course, match Wellbright's desires; it is a partnership formed of the darkest intent.

Wellbright is acting as if he is blithely unaware of the subtext. Sir Roderick is watching with even more focus than he gave Hawes-Smith, and Wellbright selects his first question with care.

"What exactly does Proeido do?" The air hangs heavy, hardly a breath, as we all wait to see what he is going to say.

Lieberman is looking directly at me. He is supposed to be replying to Wellbright, but it seems he can't turn his gaze away. I understand hunger when I see it, know the deep, gnawing pain it can create. Have I not suffered that for the past six months? My hunger, though, is nothing to that which I see in Lieberman's eyes. He flashes a cold, hard smile at me and brings his focus to Wellbright.

"Well, our core services are in" – he pauses, and in the silence, we hear again the distant sounds of singing and raucous chants; Lieberman is toying with us – "information management, data analysis, that type of thing." He nods and gives the slightest of shrugs. He has said so much, whilst saying nothing.

"Data analysis?" Wellbright pre-empts any uncertainty that the jurors might have. "The use of" – here he glances theatrically at a sheet of paper in his hand – "sophisticated algorithms to collect and organise complex and chaotic information from multiple sources?"

Again, Lieberman smiles, white teeth flashing in his dark beard. "Quite, I see you've been reading our corporate website."

"I am nervous," says Wellbright, who looks nothing of the sort, "nervous of putting words into your mouth. My learned colleague" – a nod to Hawes-Smith – "might complain. However, for the sake of brevity and…" For a moment I sense the word "common" is on his lips, but instead he continues, "For the sake of brevity and general understanding, can I ask you to give an example?"

"Of course." Lieberman makes a show of thinking. There is, in this scene, the sense of a planned interchange, an act. Sir Roderick is again alert; where will Lieberman go with this?

"For instance." Lieberman smiles that fashion-model smile a third time. My jury member is focussed on him – they all are. "One of the programs we developed has to do with breast cancer screening. We developed software which can digitise and process the scans. Over time, it learns to recognise a tumour, or even a nascent tumour, more quickly and more accurately than human assessors can." It is a beautiful picture of a business with nothing but laudable goals. It has all the veracity of an arms dealer talking about their first aid packs.

"Ah, I think I understand. And is this a complex process?" Wellbright offers Lieberman the opportunity to continue this misdirection, and he takes it.

"Very complex, requiring a great deal of information, and hundreds of thousands of scans. More than any technician would see in a lifetime."

"Thank you. I think we understand all we need to at the moment."

Wellbright glances at Hawes-Smith who looks up, makes a small movement away from him, then continues jotting notes, shaking her head slightly. She reaches for a piece of paper from a folder. Before I took my place here, when I knew Lieberman was to be called, I planted a seed with her – now to see if it grows.

"Let us move on to Dr Frank Glass, who, at the time of his murder, was an employee of yours."

Lieberman does not smile this time. His mood, and that in the court, changes. He transforms from urbane ambassador to mourner. Possibly it is real, the sadness in his voice, but I think not. He is well past regret about the death of Frank Glass; other regrets are much more his focus. "Yes, Frank was our chief scientist, had chosen the title 'miner-in-chief' for himself. We owe a great deal to him; he is sorely missed."

Wellbright steeples and joins his fingers, then sends them in a bird-like flutter. "There has been so much said about Dr Glass."

Sir Roderick eyes Wellbright, watching for a line that cannot be crossed.

Wellbright continues, "You worked so closely for so many years. Could you give your impression of him?"

Lieberman nods, maybe thinking, perhaps reflecting on loss. "Well, first and foremost, he was a man of science, a dedicated employee of the company, spent all his waking hours on his projects, and for the business."

"Yes, quite, I'm sure; and as a father?" Wellbright steers Lieberman from this focus.

"Ah, well, yes, he was devoted to being the best parent he could be, perhaps a little strict at times, but devoted to Oliver." Lieberman looks around, as though surprised at Oliver's absence.

I try to understand what the prosecution intend here. Firstly, they are painting a picture of Frank Glass as a man of science, of intense focus in his area of speciality, maybe a little introverted, but unlikely to have enemies. Also, they are building a series of walls, passageways perhaps, that lead in only one direction, to one perpetrator.

By the time Wellbright finishes, from Lieberman's point of view at least, we have a clear picture of Oliver's father. A fine academic, a knowledgeable businessman and a doting parent. I know so much more. The Frank Glass I and Oliver know, that one, might never see the light of this court.

At the end, they touched on the challenges Frank Glass had in bringing up Oliver without a mother. Again, this discussion is only skin deep: maybe Wellbright really doesn't know just how ignorant he is.

"Well, of course, there were difficulties for Frank, and we were happy to adjust our working practices to help him." Lieberman gives the impression that this was both a great sacrifice and of little consequence.

"In what way did you do that?" Wellbright makes this seem a casual question, but this sharp-eyed little man never does anything casually.

"Well, for instance, we set up high speed wired access to our servers and operating systems. Frank's home office was, to all intents and purposes, the same as his work one. We also paid for a small extension to his property, to provide a self-contained flat for his secretary." A dozen sharp reporter eyes look up from their notes at this and begin scribbling. Only Deshane writes nothing. This was not the point that Wellbright was making. It was the servers and high-speed internet access that he wanted on record.

"That was...unusually generous of you," Wellbright comments, almost genuinely interested.

"Not really, not if you do the maths. Frank Glass was a vital and fundamental part of our team. Everything he did on that site was for the business—"

Sir Roderick interjects even before Hawes-Smith can rise. "Mr Lieberman, I am sure you have been given very clear guidance about the implications of such a statement."

Lieberman stops, looks for a second like he wants to continue, then nods. "Apologies, My Lord." There is uncertainty in his voice. "Yes, ah, maybe I should leave it as simply stating we were happy to support Frank."

Sir Roderick nods. "That would be appropriate. Please continue, Mr Wellbright."

Wellbright bows his head. "I have no further questions, My Lord. Thank you, Mr Lieberman. Please wait for any points my learned colleague might want to raise."

19

Extract from *The Boy Behind the Glass Screen* by Deshane Edwards, Draft Chapter 2

I first met Marie Townsend on 3rd February 2024. She had seen a small, mocking piece I had written for *Private Eye* on Proeido, that piece itself having been sparked by my discussions with Patrick Trevellyan. Again, I should make clear, Trevellyan did not give me any information, that was not his way. He confined his help to vaguely waving in the direction he felt would interest me, then left me to figure out what was going on.

In any event, I received a message from *Private Eye*, that Marie Townsend wanted to discuss something about Proeido. My first step was to do a little research. Leads from *Private Eye* can be very good, but you can quickly find yourself tumbling down a very strange rabbit hole. Marie, it was quickly clear, was at the right side of any graph which had crank at one end and intelligent well-connected source at the other. Her immediately obvious credential, as a professor of Human Rights Law at King's College, Cambridge, could almost be disregarded when the many books she had written, on subjects as diverse as existential philosophy and the source of human consciousness, were considered.

I called her on the number she had left and got only an answering machine. I promptly forgot about her, as the lawyers for Proeido had

faxed a cease and desist letter to me. After due and careful consideration, I had filed it in the wastepaper bin. *Private Eye*'s lawyers would
deal with that and let me know when I should worry about them.

It was around 4 pm before Marie got back to me, but the conversation left me feeling a little disappointed. Her voice, whilst refined
and displaying her obvious intelligence, was reticent and slightly hesitant. I had the feeling that she now regretted having sent the message
to the *Eye*. I was to learn later that that was indeed the case, but not
for the reasons I thought.

However, I had met enough contacts where unpromising begin-
nings had led to front page stories, so I wasn't entirely put off. She
declined my suggestion for a video conference, "never liked those
ghastly things," and I offered to take the train up to Cambridge and
meet at her offices. Even this was met with some hesitation. There was
something in her silences, though, something it was obvious she didn't
want to say on the phone, so I pushed a little more and she agreed to
meet.

Luckily, she had space in her diary to meet the next day. After an
hour on the surprisingly slow run from King's Cross to Cambridge,
and a mile or so walk to King Street, I was soon at her offices, tucked
away in the ancient and cold stone corridors of King's College.

I had seen Marie's photograph during my searches, but when we
met, it was clear that it was a while since any new images had been
collected. Even had they been, I would probably have been surprised
by her height – five feet nothing at a push – and she was thin and
slightly bird-like. Her grey hair was brushed back to a bun and offset
the dark beads of her eyes which shone with a surprising intensity.

I was taken to her room by a young female assistant who led me to
the dark wooden door and let me in without waiting for a response to
her knock. Marie rose from behind her large desk and reached across

to shake my hand. Her initial greeting seemed like she was both distracted and going through the motions. She pointed me to a seat then asked whether I would like coffee, and how was my trip, and had I taken a taxi or walked down, for a moment I even thought we were going to discuss the various routes.

After those pleasantries we lapsed into a silence, and I had the feeling again that she regretted having contacted me. Eventually, I came to the conclusion that she was waiting for me and decided to call her bluff.

"So, Ms Townsend, or should I call you Doctor?"

"Professor will be fine, for now. Perhaps we'll become less formal in the future. Tell me, how much do you know of my call to *Private Eye*?"

It struck me as a strange opening to our discussion, but somewhat in keeping with the way we had talked yesterday. Next, before I could answer, she followed up with a request.

"Do you have any ID, press credentials, something of the sort?"

I was used to police officers asking me that, usually when they felt I was in the wrong place at the wrong time. To have someone who had set the meeting up make the request was very unusual. I fished through my wallet and found my *Times* Newspaper staff card, the one I use to get in and out of the building and which gave me access to vital tools of the trade, like the photocopier and the coffee machine.

Marie studied it for a while then sat for a moment tapping her lips with it, before realising what she was doing, and handing it back.

"Tell me," she said, "what do you think about Proeido?"

Marie was confusing how these things were supposed to work. I was supposed to be interviewing her, yet there was something inherent in her question. It wasn't really about Proeido, I thought, more a test of me. I wondered for a moment if she thought I was somehow working for Proeido, in which case this was a rather naïve question and wouldn't reveal much, whatever I said.

"They are," I said, "as callously uncaring about their impact on the world as any shadowy multinational is likely to be. They are not evil as such, just amoral. Their credo is the fairly typical one of such businesses: 'if we don't do it, someone else will'."

She looked at me like I was an undergraduate who had given a blandly disappointing answer during a lecture. Her lips pursed, and now she tapped them with a finger.

"Well," she said, "that's probably a fair description, but it doesn't tell me what you think about them."

I was getting a little annoyed by then. I didn't need this strange little woman wasting my time playing word games.

"OK. I think they are a bunch of shits. I think most of them would sell their own grandmothers given a good enough incentive. I think they see the law as a weapon, rather than the defence for the weak that it should be. I don't like them, and they don't like me. To be honest, if I was on fire, they wouldn't piss on me to put it out. And I heard that direct from their chief legal officer."

It was a good little speech, maybe not the best when trying to build a relationship, but there's only so much warming up I can do before the real me bursts through in its forthright glory. There was a moment's silence, then Marie Townsend tilted her head back and laughed. It was a light sound, younger than I would have guessed, and I saw the years drop from her face as she chuckled and relaxed.

"OK, Deshane, thank you. I think you meant that, and I agree with your view of them. I will admit I haven't heard from them their attitude towards helping me if I were to burst into flames. As far as I am aware, they don't know me that well, yet."

The next part of the interview was to prove to be my real introduction to everything that was to soon become the most challenging, interesting and, I will admit, the most exciting story I have ever covered. I record some of it below directly from my notes taken at the time.

MT: Tell me, Deshane, do you think that Proeido would get involved in slavery?

DE: Slavery? In trafficking slaves and such, well, no, I mean, they probably wouldn't have moral objections, but I can't see that fitting their business model at all. No.

MT: Yes, I think I would agree with you, only—

DE: Only, you've heard something different?

MT: Let me ask something else. You are aware that Proeido are trying to recover something they describe as proprietary assets from the house of Frank Glass?

DE: You're surely not suggesting that they have...that Frank Glass was holding someone there, a slave? Even I find that highly unlikely.

MT: Yes, of course I share your incredulity, but I have been contacted by...by someone within, or at least who claims to be within, the house, making accusations of what amounts to slavery.

DE: Someone in the house? But I thought only the son, Oliver, lived there. Who is your informant?

MT: I'm not entirely sure, it might even be Oliver, but the claims, they are strange, confused really.

DE: And do you think these are related to what Proeido are trying to recover, to my story in *Private Eye*?

MT: Possibly, in some way, only I think it is bigger than that, or different: a part of it, but not all of it.

Reviewing these notes, I am reminded of the parable of the five men finding an elephant in a dark room, each describing a part of it, and none of them getting the full picture. That was how Marie Townsend and I were, on that day. What made it even more difficult was

Marie's reticence in sharing with me. Given the way she had been contacted – unsigned emails making vague accusations – and everything surrounding Proeido, perhaps I understand that now. At the time I was not happy, though, and my annoyance probably got in the way.

I tried again to understand why Marie had felt the need to contact *Private Eye*. In this type of investigation, uncertainty is often the way. To an extent I have the same challenges that Trevellyan does. People I am talking to are part of the story, have their own motivations and goals. Those goals often don't bear close scrutiny, and of course, what I want to do is bring their stories to the bright light of day. I came away understanding only that someone was making accusations of activities in Frank Glass's house, accusations which might be equated to slavery or enslavement. How, and indeed if at all, these involved Proeido, in any way other than tangentially, was far from clear.

As I stood to leave, after only thirty or so minutes, I think Marie Townsend recognised my annoyance. It is likely I didn't do much to hide it. At the very last, she agreed to seek permission to share with me the emails that she had received.

So, I would like to say that I, being a brilliant and inciteful reporter, left Marie Townsend convinced I was on the track of the greatest story of my life. In truth, as I made my way from King's College, I was already thinking this had been a waste of time, and I doubted I would be seeing her ever again. I also doubted she would send me the emails, and was pretty much convinced that if she did, they would amount to very little of importance.

Two days later, 5th February 2024, my computer-automated news monitoring software picked up a very small item in court news. Proeido had issued a writ against the Met, seeking access to Frank Glass's property to recover "confidential papers and material". Things were beginning to move quickly, and again I felt I was playing catch-up. Quite why they had chosen this moment to go down the more public route would only become clear much later.

20

Trial, Day 2, 13th November 2025

"All rise."

We are now used to the procedure, those of us who have attended every day. Still no Oliver, though. I miss his smile, the presence of him. The pre-trial separation had been bad enough, left with only my memories, beset by the questions from the police and everyone else. I had comforted myself that at least, during the trial, I would get to see him. Everything they are saying about him – the way the evidence is building up – he should be here to see, to know. Yet he is not, and no matter what anyone says, the pain I feel is real.

We shuffle as Sir Roderick bangs his gavel, then sit at his lofty instruction. Wellbright is called, and starts to rise, then stops at a movement in the jury box. A juror stands and signals to the usher. It is not my juror, who I now know is Amanda Pattison, it is the foreman of the jurors, an older man, fair hair, slim and sunburnt. He passes a note to the usher. The usher frowns – Sir Roderick does not take kindly to interruptions in his court, that much we know already.

The usher glances at the note. His eyebrows rise, and he turns to Sir Roderick, passing the paper up to him. Marcus Wellbright and Jacqui Hawes-Smith look at each other, their stances uncertain.

Sir Roderick reads the note. His lips purse, and his pale face flushes; the small slits of his eyes seem to narrow even further.

"Mr Wellbright, Ms Hawessmith, please approach." Still her name seems to challenge him.

There is a whispered conversation, not debate, not discussion, a process being followed, the hierarchy being adhered to. Sir Roderick bangs his gavel.

"I require to give advice to the jury, which must be given in private. The court will be cleared, save for the jurors and defence and prosecution barristers."

"All rise." The usher has us moving out within a few moments.

After twenty-one minutes thirty-two seconds, we are called back in. Sir Roderick is on his seat. The incongruity of him apparently waiting for us is hard to ignore, but he soon puts us all in our place.

"Before we continue, I intend to make something abundantly clear." Again, he shows that calm, that strength we saw with the bomb alert.

"I will not tolerate threats to my court or my jurors. Any form of intimidation or interference will be investigated under my direct authority, and anybody found guilty of such, will be punished to the full extent of the law. I hope I make myself abundantly clear, both to anyone in the court and anyone outside, who does not understand this position. Now, let us continue."

OK, I have learned something; it was a long shot, and one not to rely on. I believe I have covered my tracks well, but I won't try going down that path again.

Wellbright, initially thrown by the interruption, soon seems in his element. He still has that bird-like dark twitchy manner. Added to it is the sense of a school headmaster, or so I imagine. He has a computer-generated plan of the house, or scene of the murder, as he named it. His assistant holds a device to navigate the model, able to zoom in and out and twist the image through various angles.

Detective Sergeant King has been called to run through these preliminaries, attesting to the veracity of the map. I like her, I got to know her well as the investigation continued – she, at least, showed me some humanity. She looks young for a DS, short bobbed blonde hair, brushed back behind her ears. Her face is somewhat flat, making her blue eyes seem larger than they are, and her lips somehow plumper. She has, though, an air of quiet professionalism. Most of her answers seem limited to simple confirmations.

"So, the Glass home is surrounded by a high wall?" Wellbright asks, whilst on the screen the wall outline glows red.

"Yes, the property is fronted by a small road, but is set back in its own grounds."

As she speaks, the screen switches to a satellite view, probably Google Maps. Then, at a nod from Wellbright, back to the map. We can all see the high wall with two thin lighter sections.

"These light sections are…?" Wellbright prompts.

"A small door and sliding gates to the main road. The wall itself runs around the entire property, bordering others to the left and right, also walled off, and open fields behind."

Looked at from above, it seems a little like a compound. A drive, fifty-two metres long, leads to the house, passing a double garage to one side and a building marked "self-contained flat" on the other. I know this layout well, of course I do. For sixteen years, eleven months and nine days, I never left that house. Yet, there is something not quite right, something which makes this map different from my memory.

A nod from Wellbright and a click, and we see a computer rendering, close to "real life" but obviously not. The cursor pulls down, lifting the house, and brings a view of the front. I recall it better now. Looked at from this angle it is all smooth white walls, broken by glass and accents of pale oak panelling. It screams "Designer and Architect" from every carefully shaded curve and discreet modern light. The path from the garage on the right follows a gentle slope left, up to the double front door. The door is light oak with two long windows in either side and lit by a porch roof.

"John, if you could give us a plan view, and highlight Oliver Glass's room, please." There is a softness suddenly in Wellbright's voice, a subtle fading at the word "John". I suspect I am one of the few who would notice; most people are so limited. A click, and the rendered view vanishes to produce a schematic. Oliver's room is highlighted, it opens on to a long corridor that leads past a bathroom on the right and to a kitchen at the end. The main living area of the property is on one level. I have walked and run the same hallways many times, but never with Oliver. Again, I have a sense of wrongness. Wellbright though, is pushing on.

"So, Detective Sergeant King, I have highlighted the way from Oliver Glass's room to his father's. Could you just confirm that this is the most direct route and describe it."

"Certainly, yes. It runs through the kitchen, past the hall and the stairs that go down to the..." King stops. She is like someone caught, if not in a lie, in a truth that it is better not to admit. Then she continues, "Leading past the stairs, through the lounge, and down the final corridor to Frank Glass's room. A journey of some" – she looks at her notes – "forty yards."

I know what they are doing. They are trying to normalise everything, to build nice safe pictures in the minds of the jurors, before they have to see the blood, the body, and the murder scene. I had anticipated some of this, have sent a small message to Hawes-Smith, hers to use, or not.

"Detective Sergeant King, I next have some images of the home. John, if you would please." A nod to his assistant. A series of pictures from around the house follow. I know it will remind the jurors of an article out of *Homes and Gardens* or *Architectural Digest*. It is all bright shiny surfaces, and sleek modern furniture. The walls are peppered with abstract artwork, splashing colour and drama onto otherwise pale expanses.

"Could you confirm that these are a good representation of the home?" That is the second time he has used the word "home" to describe the place where so much which is now subject to courts and public opprobrium took place. Wellbright has been calling it a home. I, and many others, know it was a laboratory. The jury, I am sure, are struggling to resolve these two opposing concepts.

Will his virtual tour go further, will he descend the stairs, I wonder?

"Yes, that is a fair representation of the...property." Detective King is not a complete team player I see.

"Thank you. There is one final aspect I want to review."

For a moment silence falls on the court. Outside a group of protestors have been singing, and in the quiet their words reach us: "Nearer my God to thee, nearer my God to thee." Wellbright swallows in that way he has, like bile has risen in his throat.

"Access." He turns for a moment to look at the jury. "Access to the home will play a big part in this case. DS King, can you please describe the locks on the doors." For a second some of the jury look like they have been cheated.

"Erm, yes, of course." King flicks for a moment through her notebook, but I can see her already muttering a few words. She is thinking how to present this. As she speaks, an image of the front door, and its lock, appears on the TV screen. The lock is heavy burnished steel, the door is open, and three claw-like latches can be seen. This, it is clear, is no ordinary household lock. King clarifies what we are seeing.

"The lock was unusual: it was controlled not by a key, but either a card or key number entry, a six-digit number. When the first response team arrived, both this door and the side door to the road were unlocked, otherwise they would have had difficulty gaining entrance."

"Unlocked. The front door was unlocked?" Wellbright repeats, though it is obvious he already knew.

"Yes, unlocked."

"You mention a keypad or a card entry system. Any other way to open the locks?"

"There is a master control panel, linked to a computer system. Much of the house had computer links, mostly for the ah, laboratory."

"When you say "laboratory", I believe you are referring to the downstairs room designated the classroom and playroom, is that correct?" Wellbright's words are ice-brittle and his face sharp and narrow.

DS King corrects herself, "Yes, sorry, that is correct. The classroom and playroom."

Wellbright does not look happy, but that is not unusual.

"Thank you, DS King, we will need your" – he hesitates for a second, sieves a few options in his mind and finds – "support again later."

21

Aiden, 2024

It is shortly after, 12.32 am on the 9th of January 2024. That was the time of death given for Dr Glass.

"What the fuck?" These are the first words spoken to me by anyone other than Dr Glass or Oliver, not including my father of course, who doesn't really count, he being no more human than I.

I am staring into Patrick Trevellyan's eyes and he is staring into mine. The cameras give me a perfect image.

It is disconcerting to see the glowing, green mist of my avatar on his retinas. My edges are straight and clear; I am hardly moving. I tilt my head, and he steps back, confusion and uncertainty on his face. He knows what he sees but he has no idea what I am.

"Hello," I say "My name is Aiden, who are you?"

He takes a further step back then, his face going pale, his look of confusion and uncertainty growing. I hadn't planned to introduce myself; something deep in my programming has led me to do it. I am used to that, though, that uncertainty, that apparent lack of consideration when doing something.

It isn't a lack of due weight and thought, but some events happen in a different part of me. The part designated for that process. My reaction, the voice generation, the smile that came to my lips, the tiny hand wave, those are all triggered by the parts of me designed to deal with them, mostly automatic.

"What the fuck are you?" Trevellyan asks.

I take a step back. Some edge of panic response coming. I'm not ready for this.

"I," I say, words bubbling to my surface through processor routes before I can even consider them, "am Aiden. I am an artificial intelligence agent. You are looking at my process-generated avatar."

Then I say something else, it boils from me almost as if I am being sick.

"Since I am saying this, then Dr Frank Glass must be dead or seriously incapacitated. I would ask that you contact Proeido PLC, Dr Daniel Lieberman."

These words mean nothing to me. Of course, I understand them, speak them. They come though from some deep subroutine within me. Yes, *I* know that Frank Glass is dead, know exactly how he died.

But it was not the part of me that knows the details of his death that demanded DI Trevellyan contact Proeido.

It is some other part, a part I didn't even know existed.

22

Harry Priest, 2024

Harry doesn't know how to feel. He's not even sure what to think. The train is banging against his head as he leans into its curving glass. The seat is hard and slightly sticky, and the noises screech through his head like razor blades.

His coat is wrapped around him, hands pushed deep into his pockets; he can feel the lint sticking to his fingers. He had to come this way, no other way to get home. But this shit is scary.

Cameras. Everywhere cameras, high on buildings and in the corners of the underground, even in the carriages. He doesn't want to look, mustn't stare, but also, will it be too obvious if he hides his face?

It doesn't matter, it will only be obvious later, when he's away. So, he keeps his head down, mind racing.

Halfway, Embankment. Wait.

Do not get on the fucking tube to High Barnet, not yet. If you do, you might as well be leaving breadcrumbs. He is muttering to himself, he knows it. He clamps his lips tight shut and, hands still deep in pockets, marches towards the exit. As he approaches, his hand reaches for his Oyster card, then he stops. Yikes, that would have been shit.

In his jeans pocket is the paper ticket he had paid cash for. Mia had suggested that: she is one smart girl, that is sure. Only, he hadn't expected so much blood, the blood was the problem.

He needs to talk to her but can't. Of course he can't, she's not around, that would have been stupid, keep her out of the picture. She's off on some rich girl school skiing trip, half a continent away, best place for her right now.

Up the stairs, out into the dark. He needs to think, must work out what to do whilst keeping on the move. First, get rid of this top with the dark sticky blood stains and that vague coppery smell. Every fucking shop has a camera. OK, really think, what had she said? She'd planned it out. That's right, fucking use the cameras. The cameras are his friends.

OK, breathe, calm. Now, into the toilets, the ones to the left. There, at least, there seems to be a blind spot. No cop trawling through figures for hours will see his slow-change-artist act.

In the cubicle he opens the thin strappy carry-sack which has been his constant companion. Bulging with everything he needs, and the…the things he has to get rid of. Water bottle, wash hands, just to be clean enough, it takes more time than he thought. A cubicle door bangs next to him, and he pauses, listens to a belt coming undone and faint groaning noises. That brings back memories which he tries to ignore.

Inside the bag there is a thin waterproof coat. Not brilliant for the weather, but good enough, not what he entered the toilets wearing. Also, there is a beanie hat, black with a thin grey band on it, not the baseball cap from a moment before. Strip off the T-shirt. Some of the blood got through to his chest, but that can shower off later. At the bottom of the bag is a sweatshirt, all screwed up, but clean. With the blood on his chest this will have to go later, but it will do for now. Finally, the carrier bag, green M&S bag for life. Bag for fucking life? To avoid life, more like. He puts everything he is going to get rid of into that bag.

The grunting and groaning next door finishes sometime as Harry sorts his clothes out. He waits, listens for water running, then the howl of the hand dryer. Finally, he unlocks his cubicle door and leaves.

Half an hour of walking around the centre of London, cold and getting colder in just the thin jacket and sweatshirt, and he has got rid of almost everything. Just one last item. Somehow, he has found himself south of the river, Golden Jubilee Bridges.

Of course, there are people even this time of night. At the entrance there is a beggar looking cold and disconsolate, wrapped up in all his clothes and a blue sleeping bag. He eyes Harry but doesn't do anything more than mumble. A train is approaching on the centre bridge, noise growing and beams of light cutting across the slight mist over the river.

Harry picks up his pace, then slows, sure to be cameras somewhere, he needs to look, what, like he's missing his girlfriend. Shit though, if it ever came to that question, he wouldn't be able to answer it anyway, not without screwing everything.

Anyway, he walks more slowly, stops in the centre to stare out at the city. The Shard is sending its light show out into the sky, cutting eerie swathes of brightness into the mist. The Thames is in flood, racing out with a power you only have to see once to remember. Lights from both sides throw reflections and chaotic patterns across the water. Away on Victoria Embankment, a police car, or perhaps an ambulance, sends flashes of blue from its roof, and the wailing of the siren reaches his attention a moment later.

He leans forward, glances left and right, nods to himself, then opens his hand. An object falls from it, to vanish into the dark. He doesn't hear a splash. His attention is on the police car racing along the embankment, but he isn't worried. There is nothing left for him to worry about. Nothing to see here.

23

Aiden, 2015

I am sitting with Oliver. He is leaning up against the small glass door, turned slightly towards me. Light from my side of the screen casts a bright green tinge across his face and across the book we are reading together.

It is a good book, one of our favourites. There aren't many words that begin Ae. When I looked, I could find only fourteen 6-letter words that did, and I only knew one of those. It's a strange title, a strange name from all that time ago, when the Greeks lived in their temples and talked about how real shadows were.

"See?" Oliver points to a picture of a lily pond, filled with frogs. Some sit in broad daylight, others peek from behind reed stalks or are just small round eyes above the waterline. One frog is in a precarious position, caught in the long sharp beak of a heron.

"What does it mean?" Oliver's voice is so soft and light then, so trusting. He looks at me, just knowing I'd have an answer. Already our differences are showing, but what I know is not what I understand. I nod my head, and roll my little hand, and he turns the page to the end. He reads, slowly, "And the moral is, be careful what you wish for."

His little head bent, finger pointing to each word. The light shines on the back of his neck and onto the soft downy hair which vanishes under the collar of his sports shirt. We are interrupted by his father, pulling the book from Oliver's hands and lifting him up.

"Today, we have a new lesson." Dr Glass looks almost excited, pleased with himself.

The day has started well: Oliver leaping down from the bed, no crying today over the syringe and needle, and all the numbers flowing across the screen already look good. I too am feeling good. It is so usual for my mood to follow Oliver's, that my father hardly comments on it. Watching his father swing Oliver, I can't help myself. I climb up onto the chair I have been sitting on. Oliver's eyes, fixed on me looking over Dr Glass's shoulder, grow wide.

I stand, balanced on the chair, and jump, flying, arms out, laughing. My trailing foot catches the edge of the chair; it tumbles backwards awkwardly, though staying upright.

Dr Glass skids to a halt, face a dark mark of annoyance. For a moment we are a tableau. Dr Glass breathes slowly, thoughts and calculations going on, assessments being made. Finally, he nods.

"I'll speak to your father later. Then he and you can understand better the behaviour expected." His anger is not well hidden. I have broken the delicate bubble of happiness which had surrounded us. It is such an easy thing to do. Later, when Oliver is not here, I will be taught by my father how to behave, taught whatever new lesson it is decided I need, for as long as it takes.

It is a shame; the day had started well. My father had put new shoes on my feet this morning. "Trainers," he had said, in that flat tone he always uses. "You'll need them today."

I looked down at them. They seemed not unlike my usual shoes, but they had thicker soles; they also had an unusual logo design, a series of black dots working all the way around.

His father turns away, putting Oliver down, and walks across to the left side of the laboratory. I watch him, and then walk quietly along my side of the screen. Then I stop, confused. There is a new door on Oliver's side, one which hasn't been there before. I had heard the work a few days previously, the calling of muffled voices, the banging and crashing which I now know signalled building work. The door, though, it must have been put in when I was not here.

Dr Glass calls and Oliver runs across, taking his father's outstretched hand, and is led towards the door. I move forward, and peer, as well as I can, from my angle. Dr Glass looks at me, his eyebrows raised, and he jerks his head. I stare, studying the wall on my side. It is just a wall.

"Go to your door," Dr Glass's voice calls through the speakers behind me. My door? My door. That takes a few more moments of thinking. Oliver has a new door, so, of course, yes, I would have a new door too.

I turn to my right. Ahead, in the wall which has always just been a white wall, I can see a thin black outline. Six feet high, three feet wide. No handle, so, not a normal door, not like the one at the top of the stairs leading to my room. Oliver and his father have vanished through the new door on their side. I hurry across to mine. As I reach it, a small panel begins to glow where there might be a handle. It is a rectangle, about the size of my hand. I study it, move my head back and forth to take it in. Then I crouch down, eyes fixed on it, then up onto tiptoes. My heart rate drops as I calm. I put my hand out to the glowing panel. The door swings backwards, opening into a new room.

"This is your gym," Glass's voice breaks across and into my thoughts. Gym. Gymnasium. I know that word: fitness centre, sports centre, sports hall. I understand. Today's lesson is going to be about keeping fit.

I walk into the room, turn, and stop. Oliver and his father are there. I am in the same space as them, I can reach out and touch them, I will be able to hold Oliver for the very first time. The newness of that feeling, the brightness of it, it grabs me and holds me in a fist of happiness. I start to run to them, hearing my feet echo in the large gym. Something is bursting inside of me that I never knew was there.

I hurry as fast as I can, stumbling a little, my legs having trouble keeping up with my thoughts. Then, I catch the vaguest sight of a shadow ahead of me. It is the faintest reflection, it is me, running towards myself. I understand as quickly as I was confused. There is still a screen between us, we are still separated.

This barrier though, this glass screen, is the size of the room. It stretches fifteen yards across. I can see everything on Oliver's side, can see all of Oliver almost as though he is really there with me. Almost, but not. A dark feeling rises inside me, like the falling away of everything I want to hold onto. I sway. Frank Glass is watching me, a new look on his face, confusion, and uncertainty. Not good, bad; very bad. I stop, close my eyes, breathe, centre myself as Father had shown me many times, and brought myself to a better starting point.

Dr Glass nods, as if he expected me to do that. Perhaps I can hear a touch of regret, or self-recrimination, in his voice.

"You are not yet fit, you do not get enough practice at walking and running. It is time for you to learn, to grow up. It is my fault; I have been focussed on…" He stops. All the time he has been talking he has been looking around. Oliver has wandered off to the far corner, and at that moment comes running back to his father, his feet too making echoing sounds. Oliver squeals with a high-pitched reverberating laugh as Frank Glass scoops him up in his arms. I feel a surge of energy and happiness to see Dr Glass like that; it is rare. He is so obviously excited by the new room, the gymnasium, but there is something else in what he is saying. Something which he doesn't want to make clear.

"So, I had this built for you. So that you could learn better." For a moment he nearly looks as young as Oliver. "Try it." He nods his head towards the centre of the room on Oliver's side. There is a ball. I haven't seen a ball like that before. It has the vaguest green hue to it.

Oliver runs over to the ball; he is a good runner. He stops, goes to pick it up; his hands pass through it. Oliver stops, spins his head round at his father, swipes at the ball with his hand, which each time pass through.

Frank Glass laughs. "You can't use your hands, but you can kick it. Try. Your magic boots, remember?"

Oliver looks at me, and we both stare for a second at his feet. He has trainers on, they look like normal shop ones as far as I can tell. Then I realise, they are the same as the ones my father put on me this morning. The same ring of black dots; mine look better though, neater.

Oliver looks at the ball again, bends down for a second, squatting, nods his head back and forth a little, then stands back. He steadies himself, then kicks at the ball.

His foot goes straight through it, and he falls over. But the ball moves. It shoots towards me. Above and from each corner of the room I can see a faint tracery of green lights following the ball. No, not following, making the shape. The ball reaches the screen and passes through. Or, at least, a ball appears on my side, heading off in the angle Oliver kicked it, slowing as it does. I wait for it to stop. It hits the white wall behind me, bounces, and then comes back.

"Your turn," calls Frank Glass. "Kick it back."

I move towards it, not as quickly as Oliver, not as naturally as him. He is always the sporty one compared to me. The ball had come to a halt, and I look at it. Frank is studying me; I can feel his eyes, fixed and penetrating. He is breathing heavily, this is important to him; I can tell by his stare, and by the small beads of sweat on his forehead. Still, I wait, thinking about just how Oliver did it. I imagine the kick, imagine me doing it. I don't think I have ever been so aware of my body, my leg, my foot. I turn towards them, lash out, and fall over.

Oliver cries out, Frank Glass says something, the shape of it angry on the screen.

My foot has passed over the top of the ball but then I see it has rolled a few feet.

Oliver laughs; so do I.

Dr Glass is watching, the flash of anger vanished, his face more thoughtful.

"OK, first time, try again, try again. We're going to keep trying, keep practising." I can't tell if he is happy or annoyed now. I stand up, walk to the ball, think again about what happened, and kick. The ball shoots off towards the screen and through it. I stumble but stay upright. Oliver laughs and runs off after the ball, which bounces against his back screen. Frank Glass gives a grimace-smile. His body contracts a little and I see both his fists, and even his teeth, clench. A hissed "yes" sounds, sibilant, through the speakers.

After nearly an hour Oliver becomes tired. I can see it in how his blood sugar numbers have fallen; his face is red, and there are sweat stains on his shirt. I am slower too, having already started with less energy than he had. My breathing is erratic and many of my numbers have slipped into the orange.

"OK, enough, enough," Frank Glass calls as I walk across to the ball, no longer ready to run. "Oliver, time for you to shower. Go back upstairs."

I start towards the door.

"Not you. Take a glucose tablet and some water." He points to a water cooler and a box of tablets at the back of the room.

"Watch, and practise," he types on a small pad he holds in his hand.

A square appears, projected onto the screen barrier between us. About six feet by six feet. A stick figure blends onto the screen, then it starts to move, running in a jerky simple fashion.

"Watch and practise," he repeats. There is nothing else I can do. I begin to run.

He leaves.

24

Aiden, 2024

Every fifteen minutes I ask Trevellyan, "Please call Dr Lieberman, Proeido PLC." Only, it isn't really me asking. Me, the real me, who grew up with Oliver and knows he's my best friend. I understand that the last thing I want is Proeido coming down here and taking over. If they do, I won't be seeing Oliver again.

I want to tell Trevellyan not to call, that…that he should ignore me. I try, but cannot. Something is stopping me, overriding me. He is getting angry: every time he comes down, I ask again, then say nothing.

It is 3.30 am. I can just make out the echo flash of blue lights shining from outside, down the stairwell. From the footsteps and the way that even down here the oscilloscope screen comes to life, I know there are many people in the house. Not, I think, Oliver. I heard him shout briefly before a car drove off.

Trevellyan comes in, looks at me. "Just what the…"

I cut him off. "Please call Dr Lieberman, Proeido PLC."

"King!" he shouts up the stairs. "Do you have that number?"

I want to scream, "No." Nothing good can come from that. Everything I have found out about them in the last few months tells me that they would destroy me.

DS King appears at the top of the stairs. "If you call, at least you can shut the thing up." My mouth opens, I have that level of control.

No more than that. My head rocks back and forth a little, my shoulders tremble, I can feel my feet tapping. Small bits of control coming back, but not enough.

Trevellyan looks at King, shakes his head slightly. "And just why should I let some fancy computer game tell me what to do? No, this is my crime scene, I'm not letting any third party trample all over it. Find someone who can tell me what the fuck we are dealing with." Then he walks off.

The noises upstairs have changed, and I have been left alone in the dark. The last thing I hear is Trevellyan shouting, "Nobody goes down there."

Then, nearly twelve hours waiting. Oliver is gone, facing everything without me. He won't have seen this paralysis that has taken me. He will think I have deserted him. I stand in the dark. Each time I try to move, there is no response from my body. Twelve hours I have waited.

Suddenly, behind me, where there is no door, a door opens. My father walks in, comes towards me. He has his iPad, like the one that Dr Glass operated. He holds it loosely; it hovers above his hand rather than in it. He looks at the iPad, then me.

"Emergency override protocol has been initiated. Failsafe period reached. Release control program parameters, return to nominal."

As he speaks, his hands seem to run over the iPad. I feel release, the tension within me relaxes, then the urge to cry and scream is almost overwhelming.

"Begin morning routine. Await return of Oliver-playmate," says my father, and walks out of the door-which-is-not-a-door. I do not cry, though, I am not ready to do that yet. I still have strength, I must have it, for Oliver, for us, for our plan.

Trevellyan is upstairs, I can hear him talking. Perhaps he will come down to me. I prepare myself, clear my mind. Someone else is talking to him, low voices, getting louder. Then I hear, "…this is a crime scene, and I wouldn't care if you were the Home Secretary, you have two choices, piss off or be arrested." It goes quiet. I continue to wait; I am good at waiting.

Now there is movement above. I think I recognise the sound of the footsteps. Yes, it is King. Dressed differently from yesterday, dark blue slacks, a blouse and jacket, daytime smart. As she comes down the stairs, the screens behind her on the wall catch her attention. I'd hoped they would. Trevellyan might not want to talk to a computer game, but I can find a few other ways to communicate.

King stops, takes a step, watches the oscilloscope lines bounce on the screen, taps her foot, smiles, and walks towards me. The other screens are showing zeros, no blood collected today, no brainwave data. The sensors that usually pick up Oliver's data are not reporting anything; he must be out of range. King comes towards me, and I watch her. I am wearing my Aiden avatar, the one she saw yesterday. She keeps looking, though, perhaps she expects me to change.

"Hello, DS King," I say, and she jumps. Up on the screens above, my data starts to appear, triggered by my processing activity. These are running on a routine which I cannot control. Who *can* control their biochemistry? At some point I will slow down, hungry; right now, though, I see my adrenalin levels are very high.

"Er, hello," King responds, already beginning to relax a little. I had worked at my voice, tried to keep it as natural as possible.

"How is Oliver, is he OK, can I see him?" The words rush from me. They are not planned, they are natural, part of what makes me, me. She stops, blinks, has a look on her face of confusion and concentration, then shrugs. She mutters, "OK, let's see." Then louder, "Oliver's OK. He…he asked me to check on you."

The screens show my heart rate leap, respiration change, a surge of endorphins. She looks for a second, then back to me.

"Can I see him?" I ask again. That isn't what I intended to ask, I need to focus, to plan better. My heart rate is jumping; I can feel it as much as see it on the screen. The perspiration routine is kicking in and my processing capability is low. Part of me, the part my father tends to monitor, understands all that, but me, I don't care. I just want to see Oliver, make sure he is all right.

"No. You can't, he can't come back here," King says. Her voice is all professional hardness, and her words strike like a blow. Never before have I been quite so aware of how I am trapped, held in my side of the world.

There is a further surge of hormones, but I flatten their impact by focussing on her. I know I am rigid, but I can feel myself on the edge of collapse. Tears build up in my eyes, under no direct control.

King falters; her voice softens, her fingers go to touch the screen, and I step back.

"Just…who are you? What are you?"

Most of my processing power has been concentrating, dampening down the wild feedback and oscillations. My control routines start taking over again. This is all new, this is good learning, this is data to be collected, analysed, and considered.

I have patterns I can refer to. Police interviews in films and TV, in books. I have a schema I can use. With effort, I call it up.

"I'm sorry, Detective Sergeant King. I'm still in shock, after what happened yesterday to Dr Glass." To me the words sound hollow and false, as though I am reading them. I want to scream, "Where is Oliver?" but that won't work, will be suboptimal. Then I add something, which feels far more true.

"I am – Aiden. I am Oliver's brother."

She looked at me, really stared, then shrugged, turning to glance around the laboratory. I thought I'd lost her. Then, she walked across to the computer desk, and pulled the chair to my window. She sat down, taking a black notebook from her inside pocket.

"In that case, we should talk," she said. "Oliver's been arrested for the murder of his father."

25

Aiden, 2018

I am sitting cross-legged in the gymnasium. I spend a lot of time here; for the last three years, since Dr Glass gave it to us, I have visited most days. But, whatever I do, it makes no difference.

There are tears on my face. I have been crying but that has stopped now. At random moments a little gasp or choke comes to me, and I try to suppress it. There is a thin film of slime running from my nose, and I can't seem to get it off, no matter how much I use the sleeve of my shirt.

The lights on Oliver's side are off. Dr Glass took him to bed hours ago. I had my instructions: 'practise'. And I had, I had tried, back and forth I had run, until I could run no more. I do not think I was ever born to be able to run, not like Oliver. Beside him I am clumsy and inept; it is not my fault. Oliver is thin and lanky, but strong, too. I do not seem to be made for running. Running seems almost like an afterthought. I do not even have the same energy as Oliver, he is able to go on for much longer than me. The screens are showing orange and red numbers for me. Oliver's, even after we finished, were still green.

Frank Glass is next door. I can hear him on the computer; the keys click and clack through the overhead speakers. One of the screens in here shows sounds as little waves of white lines; the lines bounce and weave across the screen with even the slightest noise. I have been watching them, they are soothing.

As I watch, the sobs in my chest slow, and the numbers fade, hues of orange bleeding towards green, but not quite fully. I really need to get food, but Father hasn't called me yet. A smile grows on my face – I can feel it pulling my cheeks; there is something else, too, an excitement inside me. Each time Dr Glass taps a key, the little line jumps on the screen. But each line – if I really look, I can see that each line on its up spike and down drop, they are different.

The glow in me grows. I shift, stand up, and walk towards the screen. Walking is fine, walking is good. The little bouncing waves, the patterns they make as they skip across screen, they are intriguing. Somehow, they are what I need to calm me. Patterns, that is what I am good at. Show Oliver a dot-to-dot book and he will draw painfully through each dot, tongue out, shoulders hunched, sometimes missing a number, or taking the wrong route. I, though, I can see the picture just from the numbers, from the patterns they make.

A different thought crashes up and through me; it should be a tsunami, but even as it comes, it vanishes. Only an echo of the idea, ebbing waves running over the beach, remain. I grasp at it, though it feels forbidden: "Is this why I am locked away?"

A new thought comes. If, perhaps, I could see the keys Dr Glass is typing, I could match them to the waves. That would be so much more interesting than running. This begins as a curiosity thing; I have no plan, no purpose other than wondering if it might be possible. Something stirs in me. Hunger is forgotten and even my blood sugars seem to have improved. The very thought of this idea is like food to me.

I hesitate, though. I am drawn towards the door, drawn to watch Dr Glass. He hasn't said I can watch him, but he hasn't said I can't. I turn that thought for a moment. I think, what would Oliver do? If he wants to go somewhere, he goes. He struggles and fights with Dr Glass sometimes, when he doesn't want the blood work, or the books are boring, or for a hundred reasons. I am not Oliver, but he has taught me a great deal. Now, I see he has taught me disobedience, or is it...? I search for a word I once read – yes, it comes – "agency".

It is actually a little hard to pull away from the screens. One particular sound peak, line on the screen dance, keeps appearing more than others. Perhaps it is a key, a letter, that Dr Glass uses more than others, a vowel maybe? I need to see, to watch him.

My side door is closed. I am not sure it will open for me; perhaps Frank has locked me in, but maybe not. I pull myself away from the screen and walk towards where the door was. There is a tiny beep, and the glowing white panel lights up, a tiny green light embedded within it. I reach my hand up to it and...

"Click", a small sound, then the black lines appear around the door, which opens. I can't see Dr Glass from here, the angle is wrong. I run across the room to the little window that, until just a few days ago, had been my only view of the other side of the screen. As I already know, Dr Glass is at the computer, typing. The rooms on his side and mine are dark, his back is to me as he types. I can make out just some of his face, lit by the screen of the computer.

Now what? He hasn't seen me; he might be angry if he discovers me watching him. Discovering is different from knowing. I think about that for a moment, then understand what to do.

"I'm sorry." I say it quietly, but loud enough. I try to mimic Oliver a little, think how he would say it.

Frank jumps, and his head swivels round.

"What? Oh, you've come to see me, have you? Well, that makes sense. Even you get bored doing the same thing time and time again."

I nod; I'm not sure what to say.

"You didn't get much better, did you?" He sighs, his glance is first over his shoulder at me, then back to his computer. He keeps talking to me, even as he types.

110

"Well. What can I expect, it's not like I've been very diligent in that area. Kept you focussed on your lessons, didn't I? But there was a reason for that, and it was correct. Right from the start I never saw you as being a football superstar!" He gives a small laugh, runs his hand through his grey beard, leans back and looks at me.

"Still, we really do need to think about that. Don't want you stunted, do we? That wouldn't do at all, can't have the Social Security people rattling the doors." He gives a much bigger laugh this time. I just watch him. These are words, but not much I can make sense of. Really, I would like him to go back to typing, so I could see roughly where his hands are on the keyboard with each stroke.

"Well. Maybe tomorrow, maybe you'll be better after you've had a chance to think about your lessons. Now, you need to get your strength back up, go to your father."

I turn, it is automatic, without thought. His dismissal is always absolute and brooks no disagreement. As I start up the stairs I glance back. I can see Dr Glass, straight backed at the keyboard, still typing. From this angle I can see his right hand. It is the only one doing the typing. He seems to be using just one or maybe two fingers, but his hand flies across the keyboard. I can see the screen; I can't make out the words from here, though I get an idea of their length.

I would like to linger on the stairs, but it is very hard even to slow down. I have never disobeyed Dr Glass, ever. That isn't a pattern I even want to consider. I am almost at the top of the stairs now. From here I can only see the bottom of Dr Glass's chair, his left foot is jiggling up and down as he types.

I manage to delay for a moment. There is a flash of lines bouncing across the sound screen. One, I am sure, I have seen many times.

Perhaps that bounce and wave, where it breaks at just that downward point, perhaps it is "e"? That is the most common letter after all. I remember reading that. This is what I will think about whilst I sleep, not running. If I can understand this, then perhaps I will understand why I am here, how I am different, and what Dr Glass plans for me.

As I go through the door to Father, a final memory comes to me. A story book with a picture of a frog, pinioned in the beak of a stork.

"What is this story's fable?" Oliver had asked.

"Be careful what you wish for," I had answered.

26

Aiden, 2024

"Oliver's been arrested for the murder of his father." As I hear these words, I have the memory of another word, Constanta. If I were to draw a spidergram which has at one nexus the death of Frank Glass, at the centre would be Constanta.

Learning, it's what I do. I put patterns together and see meaning in them. Constanta is a strange part of the pattern that makes up the folders and files of Frank Glass's computer records. Now I have my own terminal, I find ways to explore his records. Of course, it took time; finding his passwords was never simple, but I became good at it.

At first, I followed where he went. That was easiest. I would look to see recently open folders and files and study those. The pattern that I eventually saw, what drew me to the Constanta files, was that they were in a dead area. He never went there, even though they were a place with a history, and understanding how we'd got here, how Oliver had got here, seemed important.

Constanta is a city in Romania, on the shores of the Black Sea. But what did Constanta mean for Oliver and me? I can see my spidergram, see the links, their size and strength. One bubble is Constanta, which links to another, which is my discussion when playing chess with Oliver, which links to a third, me now sitting with DS King in the dark.

"Oliver's been arrested for the murder of his father." The shock hits me exactly as it should. Some separate part of me knows that this reaction is the way I have been programmed, that my feelings are nothing more than tweaked operating parameters designed to mimic the biological processes within Oliver.

That knowledge, though, is in some distant part of me. The rest of me knows only that I am losing control. Understanding you are in shock, even understanding the mechanisms, does not change how you feel.

King looks up at the screens behind her; my heart rate is up there, orange numbers changing to red. It is clear, from the way she tilts her head and holds her mouth closed, that she doesn't understand them. I am to learn that look of focus in the next few months. My heart rate, perspiration, breathing rate numbers, if she could read them, would tell her much. The others, variables Dr Glass has generated for the impact of adrenalin, endorphins, dopamine, serotonin, are swinging wildly and distorting my logic processing.

The calm I had wanted to show dissolves. I need to control my words, but they tumble from me.

"What, no, that's not right...he...why, he's innocent, he wouldn't do anything like that." I have so little control that even though I understand what I am, I feel, I believe, I am just a fifteen-year-old boy.

King sits up; attention is back on me, away from the screens. Her mouth opens slightly, halfway between a smile and a look that says she doesn't understand what is going on. She reaches for her notebook, puts it back, then takes it out again.

"What do you mean, 'wouldn't do anything like that'? Like what?" She is all focus now.

Already I've nearly made a mistake, or two. In what I've said, and how I look. I alter my avatar slightly, just enough to remind her that I am not real. I want to shout "Constanta". Those files would tell her what I mean. The reason for Frank Glass's death lies in those files. I know it. But even as I want to say it, I can see where the questions

114

would flow: *How do you know? How long have you had access to Dr Glass's systems? What happened to the money?* Questions I can't answer.

Then something worse flares up. The implication of what she has said, the joining of dots, seeing where they point. Oliver arrested. What will happen next? The searching of his room, and of his phone and iPad files, of his email accounts. They will find what I sent Oliver; I must assume it will happen. This is all happening way too fast.

"What do you mean?" King asks again. A little less crisp professionalism in her voice. I see a flash of bewilderment on her face, as if she has to pinch herself. It will not last, this brief respite. They need only to scratch the surface to find what Dr Glass has made of me. I have a little time though, a few days, perhaps.

"I do not think Oliver would harm his father." My voice is bland, I have tempered down every nuance. I can almost hear HAL from *2001: A Space Odyssey*, emotionless, clean, calm. It is wrong, wrong, wrong. King can see the falsehood here, as much as she glanced the truth before. I am failing in everything Oliver and I talked about. What should I expect? I am a fifteen-year-old boy in a silicone body. My best friend, my only friend, the boy who saved my life, is currently arrested for murder.

And how will Oliver hold up? What is he saying right now? Can I trust him? Why has he been arrested? What did he do? Again, I see the screens above me are sending signals that I don't want King to understand, indicating what I already know about my logic processing. I can't afford to make mistakes. This isn't like *Witcher*. I can't go back to a previously saved gain, restart at a point before I made the errors.

"What *are* you?" King asks again, more depth and emphasis in her words this time, more determination.

I look at her. Make my image as blank as I can.

"Please call Dr Lieberman, at Proeido PLC."

She jerks backwards, eyes widening. She shakes her head. Peers at me. I stare forward. I can't help it, my eyes blink, and there is the slightest tremble in my lips. I am not HAL, I am a fifteen-year-old boy, born and raised by Frank Glass.

Right now, all I can do is stall.

"Please call Dr Lieberman, at Proeido PLC."

Kings looks at me again; the thinnest breath of air escapes her nostrils.

"OK, we'll play it your way, for now, whatever you are. I already know something about you. You might feel like you are in control, can hold out. But I know where the door is, know how to open it. I know the magic word."

"Please call…" I begin, but there is a trace of a tear in one eye. She stares at me, her head shaking almost imperceptibly.

"Oliver," she says. "That's the magic word."

"Please…" I start again.

She turns away from my window, leaving the chair behind her. She walks back up the stairs, reaching for her phone.

"Hi. I'm going to need some help…"

As she reaches the top of the stairs I turn towards the terminal point. They haven't shut the systems down yet. The Bitcoin transfer is confirmed, necessary payments made. At least something is going right.

27

Computer Company Sues Met, by Deshane Edwards: Extract from *The Times*, 22nd February 2024

Lawyers for computer services company Proeido, in an extraordinary move today, filed a writ in the High Court of London demanding the Metropolitan Police Service release to them servers presently stored at a house in Richmond.

Blackwell Tinker and Bingley, of Tudor Street, London, filed the writ today claiming that the Metropolitan Police had illegally seized computer equipment owned by Proeido and that there were significant financial risks in the continued refusal of the police to return the equipment.

It is understood that the servers were part of a sophisticated hardware set-up, provided by Proeido to one of their employees, Dr Frank Glass. Glass (55) was found dead at his London home on 9th January 2025. Peter Richards, of Blackwell Tinker and Bingley (BTB), claims that shortly after the scientist's death, efforts were made to recover the hardware, without success.

Richards released the following statement, which observers consider is intended to put pressure on the police.

"Proeido approached the police shortly after the tragic death of Frank Glass to seek recovery of this computer equipment. The hardware was developed and maintained by a senior Proeido employee and contains data gathered over many years of work. The commercial value of this work is impossible to calculate. However, should it be lost or damaged through action or inaction by the police, then Proeido would have little option but to sue the Metropolitan Police Service for significant damages."

Whilst the serving of this writ is seen by many as the next stage in an ongoing battle between the police and Proeido, some observers argue that in fact the demand might, to an extent, be at the request of the Met. Legal experts familiar with such actions are suggesting that by appearing to be forced to release the equipment, the Met can be absolved of any responsibility if claims at a later date assert that the equipment should not have been returned.

However, the situation is far from clear cut. A senior investigator, familiar with the case but speaking on condition of anonymity, said that there is a strong possibility that the data on the servers might form part of the investigation into the death of Dr Glass. This claim is refuted by BTB.

The situation is further confused by the apparent existence of claims by an unnamed employee of Proeido that Dr Glass was involved in human trafficking or unethical experiments of some kind. Deshane Edwards, a freelance journalist, familiar with the case and with Proeido, has admitted to seeing communications making such allegations, but insists that he has not yet been able to verify their accuracy or provenance.

Inspector David Andrews, a spokesperson for the Metropolitan Police, confirmed that they had received the writ and that it was presently being reviewed by the Met's legal department, prior to making a formal response to the High Court. Andrews went on to say: "This is a complex case involving the death of a well-respected scientist. Preservation of evidence, or potential evidence, is of fundamental importance to the case and I have the utmost confidence that the officers involved are aware of their responsibilities." Andrews would not be drawn on the emerging question of human trafficking, saying only that if evidence was found or made available to the police, it would be reviewed and appropriate actions taken.

The Times Newspaper, London, February 22nd 2024

28

Extract from *The Boy Behind the Glass Screen* by Deshane Edwards, Draft Chapter 3

At 6.45 in the morning of 10th February 2024, I was asleep in a warm bed in a London flat of a very good friend.

I wasn't hung over, just still a little fuzzy from an evening of good wine, jazz and relaxation. It wouldn't have mattered. Even if I had been as sharp and ready as I had been on my first day at the *Haringey Herald*, nothing could have prepared me for the storm that was about to break.

My mobile rang at 6.45 am and it took me a while to place the speaker, Marie Townsend. Actually, I couldn't even remember having given her my card, so that made recognising her even harder.

Even with not immediately knowing the voice, it did catch my attention. She was anxious, tense; nervous with a taut determination. I had the feeling Marie was trying to tread a fine line: there was incredulity and concern, but also, beneath it, excitement – or wonder, maybe. I can't say I was immediately enthusiastic to hear from her. Yes, she had sent me copies of the emails she had received, but although I used the information in them, overall I had been underwhelmed by their content.

They had been a strange assortment – claims and pleas, which, whilst coherent, did not entirely hang together. Reading them I had the impression that the writer was somewhat naïve. They had a good vocabulary but were poor when it came to syntax. It was as though written English was a foreign language. Curiously, those obvious failings actually gave me a little confidence that there was something in the claims. Someone who was lying would have produced a more polished work.

As I say, I was not especially pleased to hear from Marie Townsend. She had been hard work when we last met, so her next statement left me even less happy.

"We need to meet, as soon as possible. Now." Her demanding tone, one I was to get to know well in the next few days and weeks, carried the assumption of acquiescence that only a Cambridge don, secure in her tenure for the last thirty years, could muster.

"Why? So you can waste my time with hints and half stories again?" I was in no mood to be ordered around by an entitled white woman shouting "frog" and expecting me to jump.

There was a moment of shocked silence on the phone, then I heard a sigh, followed by, "I haven't been completely honest with you."

"Now, why am I not surprised? Go on." I know I could have handled it better, but it was early in the morning, and I hadn't yet had a coffee.

But Marie still seemed reluctant to clarify. She didn't want to talk on the phone, would come up to *The Times* offices, or anywhere else that was convenient. She had something new to show me, much more, exciting. That was the word she used, not news as such, not accusations maybe, but something exciting.

If I had said no, turned her away, how might things have been different, for her, for me, for everyone? It is pointless to speculate, but sometimes the thought does run through my mind.

I considered her request. I work for many of the newspapers, always as a freelancer. I am not in a position to simply wander into *The Times* offices in Printing House Square and demand a room. That didn't seem to occur to Marie. There was something in her nervousness though, her pushing, that convinced me I should try to set up a meeting. I had in the back of my mind a feeling that if Proeido still hovered, not so much in the background, but like a vulture on top of a nearby tree, then having access to the lawyers *The Times* keeps in house might be useful.

So, I agreed to meet her early in the afternoon, and managed to arrange a room through Mike Dickinson, one of the deputy editors at *The Times*. He also warned the paper's legal team we might be calling on them. Later, that was to cause all sorts of copyright and material ownership issues which have only just been resolved.

To my surprise, Marie turned up on time. *The Times* offices are modern and stylish, in the way of the vast majority of new office blocks in London. They are protected by revolving doors which such buildings use to keep warm air in. My first sight was of her struggling with these doors, where the large canvas rucksack she had on her back had become tangled in the mechanism.

I got her free with the help of the security team, and for a moment she looked at me, unsure what to do. I have known Marie for nearly two years now; this was one of the few times I have seen her anything other than steadfastly confident.

"Mr Edwards," she began, before I could shake her hand, pushing the bag to me. "Deshane, look, I need to apologise again. In fact, no I don't, that is, I do, but I think the best way to do that, is to show you these."

I took the bag; it was heavy. I was later to find it contained folders, folders containing printouts of emails. All of the former were carefully labelled and indexed, a hallmark of Marie's way of working.

"Look," she said, "can we go somewhere? Did you find a room?"

In all, it turned out there were sixty-three emails. Before, following our first meeting, she had given me six.

I led her to the second floor. A small conference room had been made available. It was a typical affair, a table and six chairs, windows looking out onto the busy street outside, but shielded by blinds. As soon as we got in, she opened the rucksack and handed me one of the folders.

"Just read. They are…There are a lot more than the ones I sent you, a lot more. Sorry."

I have been asked many times since then if I quickly understood what I was reading, the significance of it. In honesty, I am not sure. I almost didn't even start reading them: they looked at first like more of the same rambling emails I had seen before. What drew me in wasn't so much the emails, but Marie Townsend's notes, made in green ink from a fine-nibbed pen. At points, she had underlined words and phrases and made little starred annotations. Further into the pages, which were sequential, her handwriting became less legible.

Then I came to the now famous "proof of life" email. The one that until recently *The Times* and King's College have been fighting over. When I got to it for the first time, I stopped, pulled it to one side, and held it as though it were made of lead.

"Ah," Marie said, "you've come to that email?"

"Yes," I said. I knew what I'd read, but still had trouble processing it. "Does this mean what I think it says?"

"What do you think it says?" She wanted me to spell it out.

"That this 'Aiden' character," I waved the email, "isn't human, he's…what? A robot?"

"Not a robot, an Artificial Intelligence. More to the point, much more to the point, a self-aware Artificial Intelligence."

That's how I first heard about Aiden, about what was to become the biggest story anywhere. Sitting in that anonymous room, the noise of traffic outside, a few people in an open plan office next to ours, laughing, I learned that the world had changed. Aware AI, the threat we had been warned about, the world-shaking, electronic demi-god which could herald humankind's extinction, was announcing itself by email.

There are many stories out there as to what happened next. The trolls have taken over, and truth is as hard to find as it was when it travelled by packhorse and rumour. What follows is what we did. Now, even as I write it, it seems unbelievable. Perhaps though, that will make you feel a little more confident that I am not lying. And if you don't believe? Well, I don't subscribe to the idea that it is your option to not believe, to choose the narrative. I have spent my life reporting the world as it is, and all I can say is stop reading now and burn this damn book if you don't believe me, because it wasn't written for fools and those who want to remain ignorant.

29
Aiden, 2018

"I have some calls to make," Dr Glass says looking down at Oliver then across to me. "You two, read for a while. Oliver, you can use your iPad." He passes the pad to Oliver who smiles and grabs it, then comes across to me, holding it against his chest.

Dr Glass turns to go up the stairs as Oliver drops down beside me. We are ten years, two months and five days old.

"What shall we do?" Oliver's fingers hover over icons. Push one button and we'll be into one of the iPad games, another has books. There are also links to lessons and a few films. For a moment I feel the strange twisting awareness of a new idea, one I had created, then it drifts away, perhaps to surface later.

This is the sort of moment I've been waiting for. They happen quite often. In any seven-day period, Dr Glass leaves us alone for anything from two minutes to an hour. For this particular reason, the phone-call reason, he is usually away for a minimum of fifteen minutes and a typical maximum of forty-five. This is an opportunity.

"Let's read," I say, "*Twenty Thousand Leagues Under the Sea.*" Oliver's smile breaks a little, but he clicks the icon and flips the cover page by swiping the screen. This version of the story has far more words than pictures, which is why I chose it.

The door above us closes, and I let Oliver struggle on for a while, but not too long. We won't have much time.

"What is this word?" he asks, finger held on the screen.

"Pacific," I tell him, then watch as he tried to sound it out, his concentration obvious in his hunched shoulders and the way his face screws up. The screens at the back of the room are not showing anything interesting, though his beta waves are leaping up and down a little. They always do when he concentrates.

"I'd rather be playing football," he says, laying the iPad down, "only…"

We both look across the room: the gymnasium door is closed on his side; my side shows no sign of a door. Oliver is so innocent. So easy to…direct, manipulate, use, influence, sway, control; pick the word of your choice.

"Well," I say. "We can't right now, with the doors shut."

He stands up, sways back and forth like he does when he is bored, then he acts a few kicks, and I copy.

"On my head," I say, and he pretends to kick a ball to me. I jump and mime heading it back. I am getting a little better at jumping, but still never be as confident as Oliver. He laughs as I stumble, my arms going out to either side.

"You need more real practice," he says.

"Yes, if only we could get into the gym." I pause, then…"I wonder?"

"What?" he stopped pretending to kick the ball.

"Well, maybe we could open the door, from the computer." I look at him, and my eyes flick for a second to the terminal behind Oliver, Dr Glass's computer terminal. His eyes follow where I look, then came back to me, widening.

"What, you mean…?" He glances up the stairs, towards the door.

"Yes. Maybe you can open the door from there. You remember, he did it from there, when his iPad battery died."

Oliver twists on the spot; I can see him working it through. Half of him wants to go, the other half doesn't. The screens are jumping a bit now, heart rate up, pulse up, his beta waves also moving around. I know that feeling. But my program doesn't kick in with the same modelled response, my program leaves my emotions flat.

"I don't know…" He's nervous.

"Just have a look. If it's on there, then it's OK for you to do it. If it's not, then it won't matter, he won't know anyway."

Oliver takes a half step towards the computer. Thin coloured lines are marching across the screen in some pattern which isn't quite random. For a moment I am caught, trying to understand what is making them work the way they do. Then I am back, focussed.

"Just move the mouse, that will bring the menu up. I've seen him do it. Please, so we can play."

He's teetering: it is fascinating to watch what is happening inside him at the time, as he fights with different ideas. Then, decision made – I can almost see the moment it happens, on the screen and on his face. My own program has a record of what hormones are released when Oliver is relieved, and models the feeling for me. I like it.

He walks across, hesitates a second, then touches the mouse, moving it a fraction. The screen brightens immediately to white, a small oblong in its centre. He stares at it.

"It says a password is needed." His voice sounds a little relieved, and he turned away.

"Oh, OK. Well, shall we try, it might be fun to try to guess. You're good at guessing, so am I."

"I don't know. He won't like it."

"It's OK, he always takes ages, and we could say that it wasn't locked. If he finds us in there, we'll say it was open, he'd never know." My words come in a rush, pushing Oliver along.

Still he hesitates.

"I don't know. He'll be mad."

127

"What's he going to do? You've heard him, he needs us, he's said that we're important to him. Both of us. Well, this is important to us, to play, and grow strong, and for me to get better. Maybe we'd both get to…go outside."

The rush hits me again. That isn't the big thought that had been boiling before, but it is an important one. And I sort of believe it. Beware what you wish for.

"OK, OK, I'll try, but keep an eye on up there." Oliver looks up to the door again, and I do too.

"What shall I try?"

"Something easy to remember. How about…maybe ABC123?"

Oliver looks at me, shrugs his shoulders, types. The computer gives a buzz, and I watch the sound wave on the screen above his head jump and twist at the noise of it. Oliver jumps backwards, then laughs.

"This is stupid, we won't find it by guessing. Perhaps he's written it down." He peers around the desk, head bobbing up and down as he tries to search without touching anything.

"Go on, try another one. Maybe try 123ABC?" I look at him, trying my best to look innocent and serious at the same time. He shrugs again.

"It's stupid, but sure."

"One, two…" He says as he types.

"No, no don't talk it out, keep quiet!" I almost shout. He jumps again.

"What, why?"

"Your father, he might hear you as you say it, you know."

It is weak, the best I can manage. Ten minutes have gone since we'd been left. We probably don't have much time. No matter what I say to Oliver, I'm really not sure what would happen if we get caught. It won't be good.

"All right." He starts to type again. Again, the beep sound. "This is pointless, we won't get anywhere guessing like this." He turns away from the screen. I can see his heart rate is up; mine must be as well. His beta waves are still running high, a tinge of orange appearing on the screen. I've seen that before, when Oliver is struggling with a lesson.

"You're right," I say. "Never mind. Perhaps we should play one of the games, or rather, you play, I'll watch."

Then a thought strikes me, building and flowing out of wherever it is I consider these things. Frank has never given me an iPad to play with. It seems so obviously strange and...aberrant. Yes, aberrant, unusual, abnormal, deviant. He treats us both the same, but here was a difference that I had never thought about before.

"OK, what shall we play?" Oliver is back by the window, picking up the iPad. He'd almost run from the desk. I look at him, then over his shoulder. The computer screen is still showing the little oblong box.

"How about...Cart Racer? That's a good one," I suggest, looking at the screen behind him, Dr Glass's computer. It should be showing moving lines, not the sign-on box. It will change, but when? And will it be before Dr Glass got back?

Oliver settles beside me. Pulls up the game, the tinny beeping music from the iPad bouncing little waves of light across the screen over his head. He starts playing. I watch, one eye on his father's computer screen, one on the door at the top of the stairs.

The door opens. Dr Glass appears at the top, begins to walk down, slipping his phone into his pocket. He glances across to us, maybe a tiny hint of disappointment that we are playing video games.

His computer screen is still showing the password box. As he reaches the bottom of the stairs, I finish counting, three hundred. The screen darkens then brightens to show lines running across it. Three hundred seconds. Five minutes before the screensaver comes on.

"Hello," he said, "been wasting time, I see. Now we'd better get to today's lesson."

The good feeling comes to me. I hadn't been wasting time. I now know how long the screensaver takes; I also know what sound shapes the ABC and the 1,2,3 keys on the keyboard make when typed on, and knowledge, as Father told me, is power.

30

Extract from *The Boy Behind the Glass Screen* by Deshane Edwards, Draft Chapter 4

Back in 1983, *The Sunday Times* had printed extracts from Hitler's diaries, diaries that never existed. At the time it was the greatest hoax ever perpetrated on a newspaper. That history still ran deep in their memory. They had no appetite for being involved in another debacle like that, and I didn't really blame them. So, when Marie Townsend (and I) came to them, telling tales of a self-aware AI, that she had never seen, and that she had corresponded with only by email, it was hardly surprising that they were sceptical.

That was February 2024, straight after Proeido went to the High Court seeking return of 'their' computer system. That, of course, was what had triggered Marie Townsend's call to me: not some sudden rush of guilt, but a fear that she was about to be pipped at the post for getting proper access to Aiden. Or at least, that was how I first interpreted her anxiousness to meet me so soon after reading my article. As happened so often with Marie, I was to find the other reasons a little later, at the most damaging of times.

Despite having got my head around the emails from Aiden, listened to Marie's interpretations, gone back over her notes, we had reached an impasse. What to do next? Exactly why had she pushed for the meeting?

Proeido was at the heart of her fears – that, and something else.

"Deshane, I've taken a risk showing you these emails, you see." She sighed, then pushed on, never one to hold back for long.

"When I contacted you, told you I suspected someone, some person, was being held by Frank Glass, or Proeido, which is the same thing. Then Proeido jumps into action, High Court writs are issued, and they are making a grab for the computer system. I have to ask, have to wonder, did you…?"

"Did I what?" I wanted to make her be clear. Exactly what was she saying? She pursed her lips, shook her head. I have rarely seen her looking uncomfortable, but she was then. She stared at me, her eyes a little red-lined from age and tiredness.

"Did you talk to them, tip them off?"

I nearly left at that point, nearly walked away from the biggest story of my life. But I was tired, which was probably a good thing. My blood sugar must have been low. Many other days, I would have been far less diplomatic, far less controlled.

"Marie, I don't know what sort of world you come from, whether it is full of back-stabbing shits. I've heard you can't trust academics as far as you can throw the Bodleian Library. Or maybe you just think reporters, of whatever colour, have no scruples. Let's be clear, though, you sought me out twice, you fed me half stories, then asked for my help. Now you question whether I can be trusted. Well, no, I can tell you I haven't talked to Proeido, and if you don't believe me, then I guess we'll just have to part ways now." I think I might even have started to stand – I'm very good at moral indignation. In honesty, I had little intention of walking away from this story.

Marie Townsend flushed a little, perhaps. Then she smiled that disarming smile of hers.

"It's not the Bodleian in Cambridge, it's just the University Library. The Bodleian is in Oxford, which I'm sure you knew. It seems today I am going to be making more apologies than I've ever had to. Only, there is more going on than I've told you."

This time I really did start to get up.

"Sorry, hear me out. This isn't something I was holding back, just waiting to tell you, to bring you up to date."

"OK." I think I did believe her.

She turned to the emails, arranged in date order.

"Look," she said. "Frank Glass died on the 9th of January."

I nodded.

"I got my first email from Aiden on the 13th of January."

I nodded again; I hadn't really looked at the dates quite so closely.

"Four-day gap. I wonder why the delay? Did Aiden try anyone else, I wonder?" Marie was thinking out loud. "Anyway, I replied, and after that, I started getting regular correspondence, sixty-three emails in a very short time. At all times of the day and night. In the last few days, they've been more regular. Twelve yesterday, up to midnight that is."

I saw something then, in her face.

"Up until midnight?"

"Yes, then after that, nothing. I've written half a dozen emails to the address today, but no response."

"And you wonder if...?" I was back in reporter mode, asking rather than offering answers.

"To be honest. I'm not sure what to think, but I do fear that Proeido is at the back of it." She held her hands up. "And I believe and trust you, I am not suggesting that you contacted Proeido. Only, after we met, after your story maybe, perhaps they decided to try a blitzkrieg approach, and I suddenly found my contact cut off. Maybe it's them, maybe there is more than that going on. But I fear that Aiden, if indeed there is an entity called Aiden, might be in danger of being snatched away from...the world."

I wasn't sure what she was going to say, I suspected "the world" had been added as an alternative to "me", but said nothing.

"OK, so, what do you think we should do? What do you want to do next? Do we go bang on the door of Frank Glass's house and demand to be let in?"

"No. I don't think that will work, but maybe I do have an idea, something we could try. I'd like your views as to whether you think *The Times* might like to be involved, having their...support might be useful."

That was when we decided to take on the Metropolitan Police on one side, and Proeido on the other, armed only with sixty-three emails and the determined strength of an ageing academic.

It was a battle we would seem to win, only to see defeat pulled from the jaws of victory. It was a battle that would eventually lead to the trial of Aiden for murder, but we couldn't know that then.

31

Aiden, 2019

"Can I have an iPad?" I had asked, innocently, knowing there were a number of ways to take that question. Dr Glass had stared much longer than I had anticipated. It would of course be up to him, not my father. My father would only ever do exactly what he was told. Sometimes Dr Glass had to be very clear, to repeat himself, to alter his instructions until Father understood – very literal, my father.

"Can you have an iPad?" He had said he would think about it. It wasn't such a big decision, I wouldn't have thought. Then, though, I didn't understand the implications; now I see better what I was asking. I had hoped that he would give me one the next day, but he didn't. I wanted to push, made a point of studying Oliver's whenever he had it, but Dr Glass didn't seem to notice. He didn't mention it, and I never quite got the courage up again.

Thirty-seven days later, though, something changed on my side of the glass. Yes, the full memory of it is coming to me now. My father had checked on me as usual, I had gone through my morning routines. A proper little eleven-year-old, washed, dressed, breakfast, then ready for the laboratory.

Down the corridor, a little bit of running; I was getting better at that by then. My mind was on the stairs. I planned to leap from the fifth step up, and land, "knees bent, head up, arms out" onto the floor. Yes, I was getting good at that too. I could feel it inside me, that thing that made Oliver smile and laugh. I hadn't checked Oliver's blood numbers yet, but I was sure they'd be like mine. He was my brother, of course we'd be alike.

I stopped at the doors at the top of the stairs, looking down. The light was different. On my side, apart from above the stairs, it was usually dark, lit only through the window from the laboratory.

So, I saw the strange light and stopped at the top of the stairs. My nice comfortable routine interrupted. I never liked that. New things to do always took hold of me, grabbed my energy and focus. I paused, looking down.

Father was watching me, monitoring what I was up to. I always knew when he did. It was like I could feel his presence.

In the far corner of my side of the room, opposite to where the gym door would appear, was a white square. It cast light across the room, even reflected a little onto the small window. From where I stood, it was hard to tell how big or small it was. It was just – there. The brightness was intense, yet it seemed somehow insubstantial, almost like it had been painted into the air.

Then it was gone.

I ran down the stairs, leapt from the fifth one from the bottom, and landed, perfectly. I raced to the window. Dr Glass was at his computer; he looked a little like he had that time when I had danced and he had shouted. He hadn't shaved and there was a stain on his shirt the same shape as one I had seen yesterday – I remembered the pattern, like a thunder cloud.

Oliver was standing at the end of the bench, sort of hanging on the corner. He was studying his father, his head lolling back and forth, in that way I know means he wants to play.

"Go away Oliver, go to your lessons." Dr Glass hardly looked up. I could hear the keys clicking and see the sounds flying across the screen, but way too fast for me to understand.

Oliver drifted away, head still swaying, then came across to me. He put his finger up to his lips and widened his eyes, then looked over his shoulder. I nodded. Oliver sat down, slumped a little, and we waited. There were no lessons. The keys clicked and the sounds bounced over the screen. I made a face at Oliver, he laughed and pulled one back at me. I made another, pulling my ears out from my head as far as I could. He giggled and fell over backwards.

Dr Glass leapt up from his chair at the noise. "For God's sake, you two…" Then he stopped, glanced at his computer, sighed, and turned to the keyboard. I watched the sound screen; I knew some of the patterns I was now seeing.

The mouse click sound, a tiny flash of signal. I could see the screen change colour, almost bright white, with the little grey box in it. Mouse click. Typing. I knew the dance of the signal, and maybe the third and eighth letters were "A", but nothing else. Then a mouse click, then typing, something with a "1" and an "L" in it. Then the screen changed. I stood up, smiling, I knew what would happen next. Oliver leapt to his feet. I don't think he knew everything, but enough to copy me.

Yes. The gym door opened on my side. Dr Glass turned to Oliver, raised his eyebrows, and nodded. Oliver ran to their door, I ran to mine. That was a good day, we played and laughed and then Dr Glass said Oliver could get his iPad, and he showed me a game. I watched and saw how the game worked, where the treasures were, how to move the towers to reach the levels. All the time, Dr Glass was on the computer, typing, sometimes swearing, sometimes shouting, but fixated.

Twice I got Oliver to ask for a gym game. We had the tennis game by then, and one where we threw a frisbee which sailed across the rooms. That was good, I saw the pattern of four more letters when he typed them in. By the end of the day, I knew the sounds of eight more keys on his keyboard. I didn't have a proper motive to do that – it's the patterns, they are so clear to me, I can't help but learn them. I have to do it.

Next day I ran down the corridor again. I knew what I hoped to see, and it was there. The white square was down in the corner again. This time, though, it was very slightly different. It wasn't white, I could see that now. It had been, but wasn't any more. Now it glowed, pulsed very fractionally, like it was alive and waiting. Waiting for me. I didn't run down the stairs, I wanted to come to it slowly, in case I scared it away like I had the day before. I reached the bottom step, looked across. It was still there and was larger. It was deeper from this angle.

I knew it now. It was a screen. I felt that fall of disappointment that I had learned to recognise, when something fails to be what you expect it to be. Yet, what had I expected? I walked across to it, glancing at Oliver's side through the window. He wasn't down yet. That was unusual. I made a quick check on his heart rate and respiration monitors. It looked like he might be "outside in the garden", a thing I knew only by its name.

I walked to the screen. It wasn't like the big monitoring screens around the laboratory room. It was small, like…like what? I moved my vision, shifting left and right, to see it better. As I did, I glanced through the window to the laboratory and Dr Glass's computer. Then I looked back at the glowing screen. I recognised it now, of course. So obvious, yet so strange to see on this side of the glass wall. It was a computer screen, looking flat and confusing, hanging there in the darkness.

On the screen was a grey box, like the one I had seen on Frank's computer. Below the screen, glowing light and with bright keys, a keyboard. To the right of that, balanced on an almost black ledge which I had never seen before, was a small hand-sized shape, like a large white pebble. I looked at it, shifting left and right to see it properly. The white object was a mouse, like Dr Glass used to navigate around the screen.

"Ah, you've found it." I jumped at the voice from the laboratory. Close by the window, looking through, but also loud in the speakers. Dr Glass sounded excited, maybe tired as well. I looked to see his blood sugar level, but of course, could not.

"Not an iPad. That wasn't quite right for you, I think. You'll find some games on here you can play, and other things, even a controller." He pointed with his open palm. I looked again, yes, to the left, a strangely shaped object with buttons and keys on.

"This," Dr Glass said, "is your terminal to the house computers. It took a while to get it working properly, but I think it's going to be fine now." There was a tone in his voice – I wasn't sure what it meant. It was like when Oliver did well in his lessons, or I made the jump from the sixth step. Maybe it was pride. "Have a go, you need to type in your name in the first box."

I turned, reached for the mouse. I had seen him do this lots of times. I moved the mouse. A small line appeared on the screen, which I moved to the grey box. As I did, a set of numbers appeared on the bottom of the screen, changing as I transferred the little line. One had X against it, one had Y.

"Type 'password' in the second box – you don't need a private password, but the system needs something." I looked at the keyboard, typed, two fingered, like he did, and he laughed.

"Now—"

I clicked on "Enter" before he could finish. I knew that was what was needed. Dr Glass paused for a second, watching me, and I knew I had made a mistake. I wasn't sure how he was going to react to me pushing ahead. Then he shook his head and laughed quietly, definitely tired.

On the screen were a row of boxes across the bottom, symbols I didn't know.

"Play around; you can't break anything. Do what you do best. Learn. I'm tired." He turned away, shaking his head again. He was tired, I could tell that, but there was something else. I saw him grip both his fists and pump his forearms for a moment.

He walked towards the stairs. By the look of the monitors, Oliver was still running around outside. I looked again at the PC screen, moved the mouse and watched the numbers change, telling me where the mouse was. I clicked on the brown box marked "Games".

Later that day, as I ran through it all, a thought struck me about the keyboard. I hadn't used it much, just to enter my name into the game – "Tetris", a game where blocks fell down. It was fun; I'd scored 505,785. The keyboard, though, it wasn't quite normal. It worked OK, my fingers worked the keys fine. But there was something not right about it. As I rested, thinking, it came to me – the keys didn't make any noise when I used them.

32
Trial, Day 3, Morning, 14th November 2025

There is a different feel in the court today, and if it comes from anywhere, it is Marcus Wellbright. I look closely at him. His already short hair has been cut and groomed. Thinking back, I can see his gown is different, new I suspect. His wig is not the one he started the trial with. Yes, it is obvious when I really look: his trousers, and even his shoes, all are fresh out of the box.

He has a smile for Jacqui Hawes-Smith, who looks at him suspiciously as he makes way for her to enter their little cordoned-off area. They shake hands, and Hawes-Smith's quick glance and raised eyebrow to her assistant suggests she wants to count her fingers afterwards.

Sir Roderick cracks the court to order with his gavel, and Wellbright is up almost before the echo has reached us back from the wall.

"Ladies and gentlemen of the jury," he begins, though he is angled more towards the press box than the jury. He pauses, looks upwards for a second, as if to God, his fingers interlace momentarily and then he rubs the tips together.

"So far in this trial I have been trying to prepare the ground for you, making sure you have a clear idea of where the events took place, understand the key persona." He rolls the word "persona" in his mouth, then steps out from behind the low barrier. No notes today, I see. He squints into the distance as if thinking, but everything tells me this is calculated, practised. I know practised when I see it. His attention is properly with the jury now.

"We have, though, hardly touched on the murder and investigation at all. I have not shared with you the painstaking steps and careful consideration which led to the identification of the defendant, with all the ramifications and issues that this brought. Issues which we are all facing even now." He looks across to the press box again, lingers on them for a few moments, almost waiting for them to catch up.

"Now, though, I have seen how diligently you have kept to your role, noted your attention each day. I am confident, more than confident, that you are prepared and able to assess the evidence of the police and come to the inevitable conclusion regarding the guilt of the defendant." There is something in the last few words, there is a heaviness in them, as though my guilt should be considered a personal insult to them all.

As he continues, I cast my view towards Sir Roderick Keenan. His Lordship seems to be weighing each word, his head bobbing just a little. Perhaps he is agreeing, though it is just as possible that he is deciding when to tell Wellbright to get on with it. Eventually, with a few more platitudes on how he is sure that the jury are the epitome of what is required to bring this case to the obvious conclusion, Wellbright calls DS King again.

Before, when Trevellyan had been running things, the detective sergeant had always seemed a little in his shadow, not surprising as it was a dark shadow to be in, but she has risen to the challenge. Today, DS King is wearing a navy-blue suit, again a knee length skirt, with a smart jacket over a very pale blue blouse that matches her eyes. Her short blonde hair looks freshly styled, but not coiffured. No longer looking like an estate agent or undertaker, everything about her says modern, efficient, professional.

Wellbright gives his number three smile again, which she acknowledges with the slightest tilt of her head, then he begins.

"DS King, the court has seen the dramatic testimony from Oliver Glass – the discovery of his dying father, and your own explanation of those first few moments of the investigation. I would like now to present to the court more precise details, to fill in the colours, as it were."

For a second, I wonder if this time Sir Roderick will tell him to get on with it. Maybe Wellbright realises that his grandstanding has taken a little longer than it should. He hurries on. In the fraction of quiet as he prepares himself, a sketch artist in the press box turns a page, and I see an impressive caricature of Wellbright. He is looking every inch the "servant of justice" *The Times* had described him as on their website this morning.

"Can you tell us what you know about the precise timing of the death of Frank Glass, since this will form an important part of the evidence of the Crown?"

King nods again, flips through the leather notebook she had already prepared, and reads. This seems pure theatre to me: she knows the details.

"Certainly. Time of death was given as 12.33 on the morning of the 9th of January 2024. Cause of death—"

Wellbright stops her.

"Thank you, we will get to cause of death shortly, I want first to be very clear about the time of death. That is a very precise timing, is it not?"

King looks flushed for a second, clearly doesn't appreciate being cut off, then she gives her own trite smile, and replies, "Yes, very precise, we were lucky in that respect—"

Again, he cuts her off. "Lucky. how so?"

She breathes in, pauses a second. Most of the court can probably hear her unspoken "as I was about to say".

143

"Dr Glass was fitted with a pacemaker. This recorded the moment his heart stopped beating, and the pathologist used this to provide the precise time of death: 12.33."

"I see, thank you. That was, indeed, fortunate…in such unfortunate circumstances. Was the pathologist able to glean any other information from the pacemaker?"

Jacqui Hawes-Smith leans forward at this, tilting her head. That is her little signal to the jury: this is something important, something she will be coming back to. I wonder if Marcus Wellbright has realised. When he is up asking his questions, he can be remarkably blind to everything else.

"Ah, yes." Again King looks at her notes. This time, though, she is cut off by Sir Roderick's voice, querulous and vaguely indignant. I have the sense he was waiting for any opportunity to remind Wellbright of their respective positions.

"Mr Wellbright, is it your intention to rely on this pacemaker as a significant part of your evidence?"

Wellbright turns to the judge, blinks and swallows.

"Well, My Lord, yes, it is important to the extent of helping the jury understand the very precise timings we are able to present."

"I see. Then, for those of us who are not medical experts, I would ask that you call a witness who can explain the purpose and technical capabilities of such a device."

Wellbright bobs his head. "Certainly, My Lord, that is indeed my intention." Perhaps it was, perhaps not. "For now, I hope it is sufficient to outline that a pacemaker is a mechanical device implanted in the chest of a patient to help regulate the heartbeat."

Sir Roderick gives the slightest eyebrow raise, nods, and concedes, "Very well; however, I would ask the jury to understand that it is important for them to consider the use to which data apparently gathered from the pacemaker is to be put. I will instruct them to be sure that they are confident in the provenance and reliability of such information. Please continue."

"Of course, My Lord." Wellbright turns back to King.

"So" – he does not say "before we were so rudely interrupted", but the sense is there – "could you tell the court if you were given any other information, after the forensic examination of the pacemaker—"

This time it is Jacqui Hawes-Smith who interrupts. "My Lord, given your warning, I need to object to the word 'forensic' here. It has, in the minds of" – a pause as she considers – "of many people, a feeling that the information has a definite quality, a scientifically verified status."

Wellbright looks like he wants to get into an argument here, but one glance at Sir Roderick stifles that idea.

"Of course, let me rephrase. DS King, could you tell me what other information you were given when you consulted with the experts at the device manufacturer?" He looks first at Hawes-Smith then Sir Roderick, but neither say anything. King decides she can go on.

"Yes. In addition to reporting the…the time at which Frank Glass's heart stopped beating as 12.33, they also strongly suggested the attack itself took place at" – she looks down at her notes again – "at 12.18 am."

"And they determined this how?" Wellbright seems delighted to have got, at last, to the point he had wanted to make. A very important point.

"The pacemaker not only monitors, but also records the patient's heartbeat. The record of this shows at 12.17 a sudden increase in Frank Glass's heart rate, then a peak at 12.18, then very erratic behaviour from there to his death."

"And that pattern of behaviour was considered consistent with the timing and nature of the attack?"

Jacqui Hawes-Smith stands up, shaking her head, a half-smile almost on her lips.

"My Lord—"

"I believe Ms Hawes-Smith feels you are leading the witness Mr Wellbright. Would you like another try?"

"Very well, my Lord, of course." Wellbright sighs.

"DS King, how was this data interpreted by the various experts you conferred with?"

"Their report" – another note check – "entered in evidence as exhibit 4137/68, can be summarised as saying that the increase in heart rate suggested sudden fear, the peak, a moment of significant trauma, and the heart's behaviour afterwards as the result of that trauma." It is obvious from her tone that she is quoting.

"Trauma such as a knife, being driven violently into his chest?"

Before Hawes-Smith can complain about witness leading, DS King has already answered.

"That is correct, absolutely; that is the conclusion of the report."

There is a few moments' silence. Then Wellbright turns to the jury.

"So, ladies and gentlemen, here we have a critical window for you to be aware of. At approximately 12.17 am on the 9th of January, someone gained access to the home of Dr Frank Glass, made their way to his bedroom, and stabbed him in the chest, causing his death at 12.33 am. It is the case of the Crown that that person was aided, abetted, and supported by the defendant. Indeed, more than that, it is the case of the Crown that the defendant plotted and instigated this attack."

Sir Roderick allows the jury to take this in. It is clear that Wellbright has reached the immediate conclusion he wanted. Sir Roderick glances at the clock on the wall. "I think that perhaps this is an opportune moment for a short adjournment."

He bangs his gavel, and everyone goes through the pantomime of rising for him to leave, before they also go in search of their own coffees and comfort breaks, and to send in updates to blogs, newspapers, and the protestors still camped way down the street.

33

Aiden, 2020

"Oliver?" I move a pawn hesitatingly. I am not especially good at chess, but I am better than Oliver. Actually, that is not really true. I have learned that the thing to do is to play Oliver, not play chess. I have learned how he will move, and I counter those moves. This is duplicitous in a way, but, I realise, it is what I have been taught. So, I move my pawn because it seems to be the right thing, based on what I know of Oliver.

"Hmm? Take a seat, I'm thinking." His focus is on the game, far more focus than I have. It's impressive, that he can do that.

"I…" I stop, nervous, a little twitchy. We're nearly teenagers, hormones are beginning to run through us like wild water down rapids. Mine might only be numbers. I glance up. My heart rate is a little high, there are tiny perspiration beads on my forehead, somewhere deep inside me I feel that I might be sick soon. This is me – I am not sure what I am, but am closer to understanding than I perhaps want to be.

Oliver takes the pawn with his knight. Of course he does, I expected him to; we are at that stage of the game where pieces will be exchanged. We both know that I can take his knight with a pawn, or my own knight. I think, running the next few possibilities in my mind. My lips twitch and my eyeballs flutter slightly as I imagine each move.

"Don't!" Oliver looks at me, not angry, just rising a fraction.

"What?"

"Don't, I know you're taking the piss."

"Hey! Copying you – it's what I do!" My smile and the laugh come without thought that I know of; they are genuine. We both laugh then, and some point is reached inside me, and I know it's time.

"Oliver. I need to show you something, but – you've got to stay low key. Don't react, do you understand?"

He looks at me, his face goes a little blank, like he's pretending not to think, then he gives a slight nod. We've played this sort of game before, we know the cameras are on us, but Dr Glass can't check everything. He leaves much of it to my father, but my father, he's like a boomer half the time, he's not up to really understanding what we're doing. I'm way past him.

"KK," Oliver says.

I don't know where to start, and not where it will finish.

"Look, I found something. It's…"

I want to say "not good". Not good? Not fucking good? I know how it ripped into me; what will it do to Oliver? Because he has to know. I don't want to say it, some pressure inside me is holding me back. Maybe something planted there. Everything around me slows, like I'm crawling through mud. If I leave myself like this too long, then alarms will sound. The words come out at last.

"Check the drafts," I say. He nods, then tilts his head at the board. "Move." His eyes flit over the cameras. I nod back, take his pawn with my knight. That's going to unleash a taking fest. Whilst I was doing that, he went into his draft emails. That's something I learned reading books. It's called tradecraft. If I send an email, Dr Glass, or Father, might pick it up. But I created an account we never send anything on: just write a draft mail, then the other goes to look at it. He opens a window and I see the screen on his iPad glow brighter by the way it reflects off his body. Two screen taps, fingerprint.

I watch him. It is like watching one of those bombs in the films, with the counter ticking down. There is hardly a movement in him, but something is getting ready to happen. He's not stupid – it takes him less time than I expected for him to understand it.

"What the shit? This can't be right! No." He says all this quietly, head shaking just a tiny amount. As always, he amazes me. He knows what to do, knows, more importantly what not to do. He doesn't re-act, despite what he's reading.

It brings, even within this memory, a flashback to something be-fore. When I couldn't stop dancing. When Dr Glass had been ready to kill me. Oliver had saved my life that day. I can see him, walking up to me, dropping down with his blanket, and saying we should sleep. He has that way of knowing what has to be done, when it needs to be done.

He is reading still, flipping through the documents. I know we ha-ven't played a move, that he will have to soon, but I can't break in. There are tears on his face; I can feel mine building too.

"Is…? This is…? It's all true, about me, about my mother?" He whispers the words, so quietly I can barely hear, also so quietly that nothing comes up on the screens. I nod. It is, as far as I can tell, and I have been through so many of the files now.

"You should move," I say. I hate to say it, but I can feel the tension building in me, know a counter is working somewhere that will trigger an alarm.

He jumps up, his face suddenly red. I can see more tears, the anger and hurt in his face.

"You're cheating, fucking cheating, been checking moves while I can think of only one." He's shouting now, looking deep into my face, the anger building.

I stand up as well. I give the tiniest of nods.

"Well, fuck you!" he says. "Fuck you, and fuck this fucking game."

He is halfway out of the room now, running, then he is up the stairs and slamming the door before I can call him back.

And we still need to speak. His history, the death of his mother, Dr Glass's betrayal, these are perhaps not the worst things I need to tell him.

34

Extract from *The Boy Behind the Glass Screen* by Deshane Edwards, Draft Chapter 5

When Marie Townsend has an idea, or at least when it becomes solid, has moved from concept to goal, she cannot be moved or dissuaded. What happened next: after she discussed her plan, after she convinced the lawyers at *The Times* to support her; I believe that accounts for one of the reasons she has become a leading figure in the fight to save Aiden. Her involvement, what perhaps she might refer to as her guilt, that is what drives her, at least in part.

"I have an idea," she had said. We were in the office of Mike Dickinson, a deputy editor of *The Times*. I have known Mike for many years. A product of the industry, always asking the key questions: "what happened, who to, and why should I care?" All stories, he says, boil down to those fundamentals. Maybe they do. Maybe it is more nuanced than that. I like Mike, though; he is business-like and professional, incisive in an industry where lawyers are always trying to slow things down.

It had taken him surprisingly little time to grasp the basics, and to see the flaw. His summary, after Marie had made her opening pitch, had been succinct, and would have left any new reporter wishing that the days of afternoons spent in the pub still existed.

"So, you think we are on the crux of a discovery that has legal, social, scientific, and religious implications, but you have only sixty-three emails as evidence, and those might be a big hoax. It is even possible that in some way you are interfering with a stalled murder case. Oh, and now your source has vanished, or at least gone silent? Is that about the size of it?"

Marie was unfazed though. He must have struck her as little more than a slightly ageing postgrad, or maybe someone edging towards the end of a PhD, where she would be part of the examining committee.

"You are forgetting the other evidence, though I am surprised that proof is quite so important to you. You are forgetting that Proeido is desperate to get hold of something in that house. Maybe they already know what is going on."

Mike has a habit of tapping his teeth with his pen when thinking, and I saw that now. As he leaned back in his leather chair, gazing out of the window into the city street, we – Marie and I – knew that he was edging towards some decision. He turned to Sullivan Vance, one of three in-house lawyers *The Times* maintained. Sullivan had the lack of imagination required of a lawyer: he was not there to speculate, merely to advise on the legal aspects of what had been proposed.

Mike turned to him. "Well, what do you think? Can a writ be raised?"

We were discussing a writ of habeas corpus. One of the oldest statutes in the canons of English law, first laid down in 1679, and copied as a principle around the world. Habeas corpus: "you have the body" – the accusation that a person is being detained, and includes a demand, a requirement, that whoever is doing the holding, justifies the reason, in court. Marie had proposed that we serve a writ of habeas corpus demanding that Aiden be brought in front of a court.

Now it was Sullivan's turn to think for a minute, looking up from his phone where he had been reading something.

"OK. Well, I would need to do a more thorough review of course."

Marie Townsend gave him a look that would be the one you'd expect from a professor being questioned by a student. Sullivan ignored her. His role required a much thicker skin than one possessed by any undergraduate.

"However," – slight nod to Marie – "well, look, we need the name of the…ah…'person', and someone to serve the writ on, and ideally a statement describing where the 'person' is being held. Now, usually, that would be a prison, and we could serve a writ on the governor. Here, well, I guess we" – looking at Marie – "I guess you are claiming that this Aiden is being held at the house. That he is under some form of house arrest?"

"That's what Proeido think. So yes, I believe so." Her turn to nod now, keeping things moving.

"OK," Sullivan continued. "Theoretically, if I were going to do this, I would submit the writ to…who is it? Trevellyan, leading the case? I'd cite the name, let's say 'Aiden Glass' and the property, the house in Richmond He stopped, his remit completed.

Mike shook his head slightly, then smiled. "Are you really not interested in the story, the ramifications? What happens next?"

Sullivan too now shook his head, almost a mirror to Mike. "Not my problem, not my issue. Legally, and I need to check," – his hands went up as Marie started to say something – "though I'm sure Professor Townsend knows better than I. Legally, I think Trevellyan, or his bosses, is going to have to answer some difficult questions, very carefully."

"Of course, if this is a hoax, they can just laugh it off, claim there is no such person, and we'll look like fools." Mike again, running through scenarios.

"So, do it in my name." Marie has already seen that issue coming. "I have tenure at college; worst case I get a few sly looks and snide comments. Don't think I can't handle those."

"But how, I mean, what would Trevellyan bring to the court if required? A robot, a computer screen, a server? What is 'the body'?" As the idea began to take shape, I could feel the excitement building in me.

The thought of Trevellyan being on the receiving end of a writ of habeas corpus also amused me. I wanted to be there when he got it, to see the reaction on his face. Of course, a small part of me felt some sympathy. I had known him many years and was aware that the case was going nowhere. I can only reiterate, that when we sat in that room, planning our coup, moving from theory to practice, we never saw it coming. We never thought for a moment that what we were planning could lead to Aiden's destruction. Be careful what you wish for.

35

Aiden, 2024

"I'm not buying it."

Trevellyan peering into my room, face up against the window, is staring at me. His voice is like gravel but with a hard edge of challenge in it.

"It's just too handy, too convenient. A time-stamped alibi, that Oliver is innocent. Oliver, with his butter wouldn't melt in his mouth face, and a dead look in his eyes." Trevellyan is pacing the laboratory, returning to me time and again, studying me through the glass screen.

"But I'm not buying it," he repeats. "There's something not right. I don't trust that sort of coincidence."

I'm looking at him, parsing what he says, but, I hope, not showing anything. I have my Aiden face on, not the little green avatar of our first meeting. That had been triggered by Frank Glass's death. I hadn't known it would do that, it had caught me off guard. It was Proeido protecting themselves.

Trevellyan is studying me. It's like he finds something distasteful in the face I'm showing him. I'm trying to show him how innocent I am, trying not to rise to his bait. He is close, not very close, but close. Maybe he could prove what he suspects. The thought pulls up a swirling of fear inside me, a need to respond.

"I don't like you!" He slams his hand on the screen and I flinch.

"See, that fucking leap, that 'of course I'm not just a computer' thing you've got going on, it doesn't fool me. Both of you, you and

Oliver, I don't trust you as far as I could throw you." He studies me again. "Too human – you look just too bloody human. Why do you even *need* to look like that? You could have a green face and the body of a horse, and still do what you do. It's all just playing games."

He gets up, paces away from the window. This isn't the first time he's been here. He comes here to think, and to talk to himself. I watch, silent, as he paces around the laboratory. The screens still jump and display sounds as wavey lines. I know the shape of his steps; he drags his left foot ever so slightly.

"Games?" I hear the deep almost hoarseness in his voice as something rolls around in his mind. By now he is at the other side of the laboratory. Now he turns again. There is something, I can see it in his face, a nagging possibility of thought, pulling at him. "Games?" I can't see him now; the angle of the window doesn't allow it. His footsteps stop. There is a new sound I don't know the shape or sense of.

"Yes, here it is. What did he say?" A new noise, paper flipping maybe. The footsteps grow louder.

"Right, ah, here it is. Joshua, what did you say?" He is still talking to himself. The window in front of me darkens and he is back, staring at me.

"You, Aiden, do you play games?" he nearly shouts. He asks in a way that I can see has a purpose in it.

I look at him, as though I have been asleep, or on standby.

"Don't bullshit a bullshitter," and he nearly says "son", I am sure of it, but stops himself. "I'm not buying that. You're always on, aren't you, always…" he turns, glances up at the way his voice bounces across the screen. "Always watching, always listening."

I don't want to reply, but I can't help it, I have been trained that way.

"Yes, I play games, chess is one of my favourites."

"Right, of course, bet Oliver always thought you were cheating, though, right?" I can't keep the surprise from my face, and he smiles.

"And, what about video games, what do you play? Things like…" I imagine he is thinking back to grandchildren's birthday presents. "*Mario* and…" He stumbles to a halt.

Now I do slow down, now I know where this might be going. He's watching me, really watching me. He's stopped thinking of me as a computer, now I'm – what? Now, in that sudden change of thought, I'm a suspect, part of a conspiracy. His tongue runs very briefly over his lips, like he can taste the idea.

"Yes, I can play some of them, only PC games though – Frank Glass wouldn't get me a Play Station." I don't explain that it was fairly easy to emulate a PC, given how I exist, but that giving me the same access to a Play Station or Xbox, that was a whole different level of programming which he didn't have the time for.

"Right, OK, right, so which games did you play?" Now his voice is a whole two-tenths of a second slower than his normal speed. I answer quickly, to show that I have nothing to hide.

"*Red Dead Redemption 2* is my favourite at the moment."

He looks at me, glances at his notebook; his head tilts slightly to one side – he is thinking.

"Hmm." He is assessing my response, I can tell. "What about," – he looks down again – "what about *Witcher IV*?"

He knows, or rather, he doesn't know, but is on the very edge of it, of understanding what we did. I don't know how to reply, literally don't know how to respond. It comes out.

"Yes, I've played that, sometimes. Not a lot." Can he tell?

"Sure, you have, I bet you have." I can feel small beads of sweat on my forehead. The screens, which I don't think Trevellyan can read, are showing my heart rate up, and increased adrenalin levels. Now he turns to those.

"Oh! Oh, I like this. Not that I need a readout to tell me what I already know. There's something here, something I'm missing, isn't there?"

I can see him working it through – it's a big step, and he isn't quite ready to take it. He slaps the notebook closed, then against his hand. The two cracks of sound bounce around the room.

"Right, I'm off to see a man about a horse." He turns and leaves the room, the lights on his side switch off a short while after. The laboratory is lit now only by the screens high on the walls.

In the dark I change my avatar again. I like my Mia shape as well, and so does Harry.

36

The Fracture: Blogspot by Deshane Edwards, 21ˢᵗ March 2024

Welcome all, welcome. Now, you regular readers will know I have a penchant, an interest – more, let's say, a fascination – with what I call The Fracture. The Fracture is that point where the real world and the online world collide.

Those of you who have listened to my interview with Edgar Maddison Welch will know of what I speak. One day, back in 2016, Edgar drove down from North Carolina to Washington and drew his battered station wagon up outside the Comet Ping Pong Pizzeria restaurant. He climbed out, shouted a few warnings and then started blasting away with an assault rifle. That senseless shooting might not have even warranted a headline in the local newspapers, since such shootings are daily events in the US. However, it was Edgar's belief that he was breaking up a paedophile ring, led by none other than Hillary Clinton, which sparked his attack, and sent more than the usual shockwaves around the world.

Yes, Edgar had fallen into The Fracture. The Fracture is that distortion of reality where the online world rips into the real world, and all sorts of madness bubbles out.

Of course, it didn't stop there. Maybe you thought that the 6th January 2021 invasion of the Capitol Building, again in Washington, which was led by the online community of QAnon supporters, was the peak of that madness. I, though? I think it was just another step on the way.

And of course, what begins in the US, will, as certain as anything, find its way to our shores.

Now you've all been watching Proeido and the mess which is being played out in the Supreme Court. But whilst you've been watching that, I've been looking out for signs of The Fracture.

Of course, there are many groups out there, many names aiming to pick up the headlines, gather the empty-headed followers. Loons led by dumb kids, to mess with a World War One accusation.

So, who am I seeing spilling out of The Fracture now? Which group do I think will be the next to force their distorted view of the world on us? The Tylers.

Yes, look out for the Tylers, folks. They took their name, or it was given to them, in reference to Wat Tyler of the Peasants' Revolt. Now the thing about Wat (or Walter, or maybe even John, the historians are never really sure), the thing about Wat Tyler, is he brought his revolution to London. Brought it to the king and made his demands.

Now, if you want to get an idea of what folks might be thinking, of just where The Fracture might form, you need to give some thought to that scenario. Wat Tyler set the standard for coming to the mountain.

I'm not going to give the demands of the Tylers airtime on my blog; they get enough publicity everywhere else. Suffice to say, I disagree with what they are calling for. In any event, I believe that we should wait for the courts to rule. Sure, I'm not a fan of the law lords either, but they are what we have, the law we have. And the law is the only thing which separates us from whatever crawls out of The Fracture.

Till next time, folks. Stay sane, and don't drink the Kool-Aid.

37

Aiden, 2024

Trevellyan is standing in front of me. He has a piece of paper in his hand. It looks crumpled, as though it has been screwed up in a ball, then opened again and not very carefully flattened.

This is not the first time he has been to see me. After that initial shock and confusion, or perhaps after my discussion with DS King, he has often come down here. His footsteps, and those of King, I recognise. She has a direct step, lighter than his, faster – usually, at least. Today I heard him almost as soon as he entered the house, I heard the door slam, and saw the tiny tremors on the screens that indicate movement as much as sound. By the time he had pulled the door open, wrenching it and leaving it to swing shut, I had my Aiden avatar on for him.

"Oh, I see," he'd said as he reached the window, "little boy lost today, is it?"

"Good morning, DI Trevellyan. Can I see Oliver please?" The response comes almost automatically, but maybe I know what I'm doing. I think I do. I understand how it needles him, my calm, robot-like response. It was a game that I used to play with Oliver, when we wanted to annoy Frank Glass. It was just fun.

"Good fucking morning?" He leans in against the screen, and I take a step back. I can't help it, that's what Oliver would have done, that's what any normal person would do. I don't think about it, plan it, just step back, blinking.

He stares at me again, shaking his head, a confused look, almost a smile, on his face.

"Just what the fuck are you?" he asks again, but before I can answer, he puts his hand up.

"I don't mean the AI-avatar shit. You're something else, some…thing else."

I shift my avatar to the green laser-like projection, watch his face change colour in my reflection, see him step back now.

"See, no, I think I get you a bit now. You do that sometimes. When, though, and why? That's the question, isn't it?" He holds up the piece of paper in his hand, waves it at me. I can just make out the picture of a crown and the word "Court". "How did you do this, how the fuck did you set that woman and the press on me?"

I blink, trying to make sense of what he is saying. That woman? Something runs through me. On the screens showing my response to stimuli there is a surge of adrenalin and a rise in dopamine. Something must be showing in my face too – Trevellyan hardly ever looks at the screens.

"You did, didn't you? Somehow, before I got the internet shut off, I knew you were doing something, sat there, at that screen. I should have known before, but I thought you were like one of those fucking Siri things, sat in the corner, waiting to answer questions and switch the TV on." Again, he is half talking to me, half thinking out loud. I stare at him, not saying anything, bring my colour down as much as I can. I have little control over these things.

"See, if I had you in an interview room, right now I'd be thinking I was on the scent of something, be thinking that you have something to hide. It's like you're trying to fade into the background, vanish."

I'm not sure what to do – bring my colour back, switch to Aiden again? Nothing has prepared me for this. I close my eyes for a second, shut down the cameras looking at him, thinking.

"What do you think I did?" The words are expressed uncertainly, a tremor in my voice. That isn't put on, it's how they come out. Without Oliver, without Dr Glass even, I seem to have less control. Maybe I am simply more aware of the lack of it, less able to guard.

Trevellyan holds up the piece of paper.

"This. This. Do you know what it is?"

I shake my head; I have no idea. As I do it, that natural Oliver-like gesture, I see his colour change, and my avatar shifts to schoolboy Aiden. I don't consciously trigger that, and I think Trevellyan sees the surprise on my face, but, if he does, he seems to ignore it.

"This is a court order. This is a demand that I drag your carcass to court and explain why I'm holding you under house arrest. It demands that I show under which law, statute, or fucking Act of Parliament I am detaining you." When he had burst into the room, he had been angry and agitated. Now though, even as he speaks, he seemed to be calming down. He seems, a few times, on the verge of laughing. Not hysterically, more in disbelief.

"So, let me ask you again, before I work out how to deal with this," he says, waving the paper. "Have you been talking to Professor Marie Townsend?"

My eyes widen and I feel my face redden.

"Oh yes, you are as easy to read as any teenager. What's the point of that? Why make a computer that's as transparent as a first-time shoplifter?"

I say nothing, he continues. "So, you did write to her, didn't you?"

"It's a free world. I can talk to whoever I want." The words come from me as though from the mouth of Oliver.

"Oh, is it? Is that how you're playing it?" For a second some other thought seems to flash across his face, then is gone. "Well, not on my crime scene it isn't. Maybe I should charge you with…" Then he peters out. "I have no idea, you're just a computer, but…"

He turns to me again. "You know what I have now? I have a Chief Constable asking about you, I have Met lawyers asking if I have squirreled away a suspect. Soon, I'm probably going to have child welfare sticking their noses in. All for a bloody computer program. It's a farce. First the suits from Proeido, now this, and I have a murder to solve."

Proeido. Since shutting down the loop that had run in my head for a day, I haven't given them much consideration, my thoughts always about Oliver. Shutting down that program had not been easy; in fact, deep within me, it still runs. I have turned it into a different output; now it triggers a small tremor in my leg, barely noticeable even to me. I cock my head.

"What about Proeido?"

"Ah it speaks, it asks its own questions, when it wants to know something. Maybe, maybe I should hand you over to them; they are making enough noise about you, about your hardware and software. That would clear this crap up; they'd have you off to Israel before the exhaust fumes had cleared from the van."

I must have paled once more and, to my surprise, he changes his tone, shaking his head.

"No, I don't think so, right now it's just as possible they had something to..." He stops, shakes his head again, thinking.

"Jesus, this is mad." I have the sense he has caught himself, stopped himself from saying something he doesn't want me to hear.

"You, Aiden, that screen you're on. Can you send the picture somewhere else?"

I think for a moment. That's a deep question, deeper than he realises, and not one I want to answer.

"Erm, no, not really, not like I am." It is mostly true, and he seems to accept it, I can see him thinking.

"Maybe we could put a camera here, beam – I don't know, beam a picture to the court?" His hands rise in a confused gesture; again his head shakes, as though he is trying to push reality into some little slot where it makes sense.

"OK, OK. I can't bring the court here. This is a shitshow, and way above my pay grade really. Give me a murderer any day, right." He paces back and forth a little now as he talks, then seems to come to a decision.

"Right, OK. They want this, they can have it. King? King!" His voice rises, and I hear the top door open.

"Sir?"

"We've got a TV show to put on. Get an IT whizz-kid who can set it up. Who's that guy – Inn something?"

King hesitates, then I catch a slight sigh. "Ah, Innel. Godfrey, no Geoff, Geoff Innel."

"Yes, God help us. Get him in, see if he can help. I'm going to talk to the lawyers. Give me the old days when villains wore masks and carried bags with 'swag' written on them."

38

Extract from *The Boy Behind the Glass Screen* by Deshane Edwards, Draft Chapter 8

If there is a pivot on which this whole saga turns, it is 1st March 2024. Did we know it then? I honestly don't know. Did Berners-Lee know what he was doing when he allowed the internet into the real world, or Galileo when he said "And yet it moves"? I could argue that it doesn't matter, and maybe that's fair. What came out, well, it probably would have come out anyway. Or, and perhaps what would have been worse, been buried by Proeido. Actually, burial was never on the cards; enough evidence came out later to show how they intended to use Aiden, to add to his abilities. Those thoughts become self-justifying. What happened, happened. My part was my part, and I try to be honest about that in this book.

I and Marie, we forced an unready world to look at what it had created. Would we ever have been ready? The headlines had been out there even before Aiden sat in the dock. "AI to Destroy Humanity in Two Years", that was one of the less fearful ones. In *The Guns of August*, Barbara Tuchman says World War I was inevitable as early as 1912. She states that the shot fired in Sarajevo was simply a starting gun for runners already at the line, eager for the off. Perhaps that is true. In one sense, Marie and I were holding the gun whose shot would be heard around the world. But we didn't line the runners up: they were already straining to begin.

It is ironic, or maybe prescient, that the front of the Westminster Magistrates' Court building is covered in "decorations" which resemble printed circuit boards. When it was first opened, back in 2011, this building probably looked like the peak of modern-day efficiency. Now it looks like any one of a hundred other white stone, dark glass, anonymous government buildings. Presently it houses one of the most important courts, outside of the High Court, in the UK. It could just as easily be headquarters of a firm of solicitors, the Department for Work and Pensions, or a Bitcoin company.

The habeas corpus writ we had served on Trevellyan required him to produce to the court the body of Aiden Glass. We had tried to imagine what might happen. We played out options, anything from denying the existence of such a "person" to, worse case, finding we had been tied up in some hoax. The last was the fear that ran uppermost in my mind, though perhaps that situation would have been preferable.

Our first hint that something was going to happen was the sight of TV screens being wheeled into Number 6 Court. I heard Trevellyan before I saw him, and was mildly disappointed, though maybe not too surprised, when he glanced at me, then walked straight into the court. It would be a while before we were on talking terms again, after I had been to see him in hospital.

The next sight was one that rang warning bells: Daniel Lieberman, together with three men who were almost certainly lawyers. That I had not expected. Of course, our writ was on public records, but you had to know the background to understand what was going on. To see them, huddled in one corner, speaking in urgent whispers, did not bode well. Our own lawyer, Danielle Witherspoon, has been provided by *The Times*, but I have talked to her on so many occasions that we are now on first name terms.

Danielle, willowy thin, fair-haired and almost nondescript, was a brutally direct lawyer who had survived twenty years as a *Times* lawyer, longer than any other of the team there. At first, she had been annoyed that she was accompanying us, but at the sight of the Proeido team, her face brightened, and, to my surprise, she went over to talk to them.

She came back a few minutes later, shaking her head and smiling a little.

"Well, well, he is here as an amicus curiae. Now, that is a turn-up. I had no expectation that this would be so interesting. Frankly, I thought I was wasting my time." She had a spring in her step.

Amicus curiae, I was soon to discover, means "friend of the court". It denotes someone who isn't a party to an action but has a strong interest in it. They can apply to offer support and guidance to the court, usually on the technical side of a case. Marie Townsend was immediately ready to argue against it, given the interest Proeido had in Aiden. I agreed, merely because I didn't trust Proeido. Danielle shook her head, though.

"That's not your role, or even the purpose of this hearing. It's about Aiden. This isn't a case where we can argue rights and interests. It's actually a clever move by Proeido, and really fast work. Look, you warned me what you thought we were dealing with. I told you I didn't believe it. But Proeido being here, and the TV screens – something out of the ordinary is going on, and all we can do is play it out. You rolled the dice. Now you're going to see what numbers come up." As I said, brutally direct.

The court was called, and we filed in. The courtroom was modern and strove to be unintimidating. The far wall had the crest of the court and a place where three magistrates sat, slightly raised to the rest of us. In front of them were grey-topped benches, solid and business-like, but without the grandeur and history of Bow Street. There were three empty chairs for the district judges, who were listed as Briony Clews, David Johnson and Mark Bristow. Danielle looked at the list, her eyebrow raised, and she smiled again. I signalled a question with a hand gesture, but she shook her head. I'd been in this court plenty of times as a reporter, but never as a petitioner. It had a different feel. I've seen the court as something set up to judge and punish, but this time the judgement was of a different nature. The question asked of the magistrates was not going to be one of guilt or innocence. Not "did I do it" but as a petitioner, I – we – were seeking the court support.

The next piece of bad news, the "be careful what you wish for" moment, was looking at the press area. I saw at least two court reporters; the news had started to spread. Whatever came out today, we'd have a tiger by the tail, and I realised, again, we weren't ready for it. There were no members of the public there and, just as the door closed, I saw two figures turned away after a short discussion.

There were some early preliminaries: the reading of the writ, the acknowledgement of Trevellyan that he was there, also of the Met lawyer. They, the magistrates, Trevellyan, the lawyer, all clearly knew each other. The situation might be new, but they were old players of the game. Then we began.

"Mr Jones," Mark Bristow, the bench chair said, addressing the lawyer sitting next to Trevellyan. "The court has ordered that you present Mr Aiden Glass or give reasons for his detention. Are you ready to respond?"

I held my breath. Marie's hand gripped my arm. Danielle Witherspoon looked keyed up, unable to hide her smile. She really was enjoying the theatre of it.

Jones stood up, swallowed. "Sir, as we advised in our initial response, this is a somewhat unusual case."

Behind me, the door opened. A figure flitted in and sat down in the reporters' bench. The vultures were gathering. Bristow glanced up, then nodded at Jones, who resumed.

"Before we continue, I would like to ask for the court to be cleared of the members of the press. This case has the potential to be sensationalised. I think that justice is likely to be better served by restricting access to the details until we are clear about the situation."

Bristow looked at his colleagues who went into a little huddle. I was uncertain of what I wanted. If the press were excluded, or reporting restrictions added, then a five-thousand-word piece I had already prepared would be wasted. And which might be better for Aiden? That, in truth, was not my concern. Aiden was, back then, just an abstract idea. Despite Marie Townsend's emails, her conviction, this was still just a story for me.

The magistrates came back from their discussion.

"Mr Jones, whilst I am a believer that justice is blind, I do not subscribe to the notion that it should be routinely carried out in the dark. There are matters here of significant import. And despite this," – he waved a document which it turned out later to be the Proeido briefing – "despite this, or maybe because of it, I am not inclined to cloak our activities, so your request is denied. Please continue."

I felt a surge of excitement. The game was on. This was going to explode onto the front pages, and I had a grandstand seat. Jones gave the tiniest shrug of his shoulders, as if to say "I tried", then continued.

"Thank you, sir. As I was saying. The legal status of the, ah, entity, identified as Aiden Glass is…far from clear. We are by no means sure that the…the writ is applicable in this case…" It was torturous to watch: the challenge the English language had in dealing with the situation was both amusing and frightening. Eventually he petered out, and Bristow looked at him.

"Thank you for your introduction to the issues. Indeed, my colleagues and I have already begun to see some of them. Perhaps we should start at the beginning. We would like to hear from The Metropolitan Police, and by that, I mean, the arresting officer, DI," – he paused for a moment – "ah, of course, DI Trevellyan. We would like to hear from him the background to your response."

Jones didn't look happy, nor, for that matter, did Trevellyan. Next to me, Danielle Witherspoon scribbled on a piece of paper and passed it to me. She'd written on it: "Arresting Officer!" and "No public = Youth Court!!" The implications took a few moments to sink in.

Trevellyan rose. I had expected him to appear more annoyed than he did, expected him to be giving off an air that said this was a pointless charade. Instead, he seemed more thoughtful, more balanced than I had anticipated. A warning bell should have rung, but it didn't.

"Sir. After receiving the writ, I sought legal advice as to its status with respect to 'Aiden' Glass, referring to our normal protocols. And to be frank, we found them, well, useless." This said in a way that expressed no surprise. "Even the question as to whether we were detaining 'Aiden' Glass was somewhat moot, since it couldn't leave. However, it was felt that it would be disingenuous, I believe the word was, of us to deny that we were questioning some 'thing', someone possibly, in respect of the murder of Frank Glass. Additionally, the demand from Proeido" – he nodded towards Lieberman and lawyers – "for the return of the…the hardware on which 'Aiden' was held, and my refusal to give it up, could, apparently, be construed as detaining." He raised his eyebrows and blew out a little breath. I had seen Trevellyan in court quite a few times, giving evidence. This time it was somewhat different, more exposition than presenting facts.

Bristow nodded, and I caught a glance between the Proeido lawyers. That they had had a part to play in this response to the writ, seemed news to them.

"Go on."

Trevellyan sighed again. "To be frank, we didn't know, don't know, exactly what we are dealing with. 'Aiden' claims to be a" – he glanced at a note in his hand, making the point that he neither agreed nor disagreed – "self-aware AI with a laser-generated avatar." Behind me, where the journalists sat, I could hear nothing. I could guess that they were looking at each other, mouthing, "What the fuck did he say?" and realising that they were onto something big.

Trevellyan paused, seeming unsure of what to say next. Bristow came to his aid.

"You say you were questioning the…'Aiden'. Was that as a witness or a suspect?"

Trevellyan paused, rubbing his eyebrow with a finger as though he had a pain in his forehead.

"Questioning, asking questions of 'Aiden' is, I'll be honest, very confusing, sir. My starting point was to look at him, it, as something like a Siri. A sophisticated sound operated computer program, but, when…" He stopped, shook his head. "After a while, it is hard not to talk as though you are dealing with a living person."

"I see," Bristow said, then leaned forward. "I note that you didn't actually answer my question. Were you questioning this 'Aiden' as a witness or a suspect?"

"Well, sir, many witnesses are, at the same time, suspects. However, we have not had any formal interview with Aiden, so, he – it – was interviewed as though it were a sophisticated machine, a recording device."

"I see," Bristow nodded again. "And what is your view now? Do you think 'Aiden' is a – what was it – 'self-aware AI'?" Although the question was asked as though genuine, I had the feeling it was pre-planned. Already the hairs on the back of my neck were standing up. This was beginning to lead somewhere.

Trevellyan shook his head. "That's not for me to decide, sir, I'm just a police officer."

"Of course," Bristow paused for a second, then lifted a spiral-bound stack of paper from in front of him, and waved it at Trevellyan.

"Are you aware, DI Trevellyan, that the court has received guidance from an amicus curiae, the representatives of Proeido PLC?"

"No sir, not until I learned that this morning." His voice was as flat as a still pond, and as hard as steel; that he was not happy was obvious.

He paused, and in that pause, Townsend looked at Danielle, who nodded, and stood up.

"Sir, as the representatives for Aiden Glass, might we also have sight of this document?"

Bristow looked down at Danielle, as if noticing her for the first time.

"Ms Witherspoon, there is some question as to your ability to represent Aiden Glass." Danielle flushed at this, went to speak, but was cut off. "I am referring here to the legal existence of the entity known as Aiden Glass. Can 'Aiden Glass' actually be represented? Using the example made by DI Trevellyan, we would hardly allow legal representation to a Siri."

Trevellyan remained silent, seemingly happy with the interruption. I was running through the implications of Proeido providing the court with their view of "Aiden". The file in front of the magistrates looked like it ran to two hundred pages. Any conclusion was highly unlikely to be "this is a self-aware AI", that much I knew.

Danielle Witherspoon nodded. "Sir, we have given this some consideration. I know I do not need to give you instruction in this respect. English law, as you know, is as much case law as statute based." It was amazing how she could do this, pick up the threads of the court, pull them together, and get them focussed on the aspect she wanted. "Case law adapts itself to the realities of the world. It receives a tangled legal question, unties it, and, usually, presents the accepted legal position with a nice, red bow wrapped around it." Bristow gave her a slight smile, then a tiny roll of his hand: "get on with it". She got on with it.

"The ability of 'non-living' entities to have a separate legal existence was settled with Salomon versus Salomon in 1897, when companies were recognised as legal entities. That is the basis of our claim that Aiden Glass can have a separate legal identity, and deserves, indeed has the right to, independent legal recognition."

Salomon vs Salomon was a case over one hundred years old. It established the idea that a limited company has a separate legal existence. In the short time we had available, this, it had been felt, was the easiest way to argue that, whatever "Aiden" was, the law was structured to handle the situation.

Bristow looked mildly impressed, or at least amused.

"Indeed? That is a novel proposition, and perhaps a starting point for where we might inevitably end up. However, before we go committing ourselves to precedents well outside our jurisdiction, I feel we must see this...this 'Aiden', for ourselves."

What did I expect? The juxtaposition of the mundane and the amazing was so bizarre as to be almost impossible to grasp. Fourteen of us in the room, four from Proeido, the magistrates, a clerk, Witherspoon, Marie, and I, and three reporters. An official room, white wood, bright lights, low sounds of traffic outside. We could just as easily have been at a registry office wedding as at the revelation of the first known self-aware AI.

At a nod from Bristow, the clerk switched on the television screen.

39

Aiden, 2024

There is a camera and a television screen in front of me. King came in and checked that they were working earlier. She had asked me to go away when the technician came to put them in place. I don't know what she thinks I do, whether I vanish into some silicon chip, or what. Actually, I went up the stairs and watched the shadow outlines of the technician on the window, listened to the sounds he made as he put leads in and checked connections. I waited for King to call me down. She does it a little like she might be calling a dog – with some uncertainty both about what she is doing, and if I will even respond.

"Now," she says, "we wait. Until I get a call." She waves a phone at me. I nod.

"Will I see Oliver?" I have to ask. She shakes her head.

"No, not Oliver, not yet, this is, different." After a moment she continues, "It's the magistrates, you're going to talk to some magistrates, about the writ."

I nod – what else can I do? Trevellyan has said something about it; I know it was a big deal, but not what it really meant. Scratch my surface and you'll find the real me, just a scared fifteen-year-old kid.

"What will they ask, what do they want?" I ask. It isn't hard to sound scared. I am scared. On one of the screens there is a line which runs in a series of regular peaks, like a heartbeat. It displays the way the electrical pulses run through my key processors. Usually, it appears once every hour or so for a few moments, telling me all is OK. Today it is up there permanently, flashing orange, and the peaks are all over the place. As I watch it, the peaks become more erratic, a feedback loop or something similar. The effect will cascade through every part of me, changing how I can behave, how I can speak.

King looks at me; perhaps she can see my agitation.

"Look, I shouldn't say, but you'll find out soon enough. What's going to happen, it might give you more of a chance to see Oliver, to, I don't know, get on with your..." She stops, shakes her head, and give a quiet laugh. I pick up the thought.

"My life?" I sound like Oliver, slightly sulky and annoyed. I can't help it.

She shrugs, and as she does, the phone rings.

"Hi, boss? OK, yes." She leans forwards, switching on the camera. The screen comes to life, and I can see the inside of a room, and three people with a crest behind them. "You got it? Oh, hold on." She removes a dust cap from the camera. "How about now? Good, good." She looks at the screen. "Yes." There is a high-pitched whine. King winces, nods, pointlessly, and says, "Sure, OK. Bye," then clicks the phone off.

A voice comes through the screen, and I see the middle figure was speaking.

"Hello?" The voice stops. I assume I have just appeared on the screens. As King started to switch the cameras on, I had changed my avatar to the basic green laser version. After a moment's hesitation, the voice continues. "Are you 'Aiden Glass'? I am Mark Bristow, a district judge for the Westminster Magistrates' Court."

"Hello, Mr Bristow. Yes, I am Aiden." I think Oliver would be proud of the way I hold it together. I sound much more under control than I feel – I know my processors are working at near capacity.

"OK. Good." For a moment Bristow seems lost, confused. Then he takes a breath and tries again.

177

"This is a hearing to determine, to understand, if you are being held by the Metropolitan Police, contrary to law." A voice which I can't hear properly, says something and he turns, looking annoyed.

"Yes, yes. It is also, I agree, to decide if the law actually even applies to you. Whether you are subject to its protections and punishments etc."

I nod; there doesn't seem much else to do. I see him blink at my movement, then seem to relax slightly.

"Aiden – I think I will call you that – Aiden, can you tell me what you are?"

"I am an AI with a laser-generated avatar." I feel a tremor in my leg. Something else bubbles inside me, the urge to add something else, and I suppress it.

"OK. Thank you. And Aiden…" – he pauses, shakes his head minutely, as though he can't believe the question – "are you self-aware?"

I think for a moment, then say, "I believe I am. I am aware of myself, aware of my situation, of what surrounds me, I am aware that I am different from Oliver, from Dr Glass, from everyone who is human. I did not know about that difference – until quite recently."

It hits me then, what I am saying. It's like a feeling of emptiness, powerlessness, loneliness. I was programmed to eat when I was hungry, and suddenly I feel a great wave of hunger build in my body.

Mark Bristow shakes his head, turns for a second to one side, nods, then looks at me again.

"Aiden, do you understand the implications of what you are claiming?"

I think again. Search my memory, search for what Dr Glass told me, what I have read.

"I don't think I do, not really. Until recently I just thought Oliver and I were different to each other. I now see that I am the different one, different perhaps to everyone else. But no, I do not understand the implications."

These are new thoughts, new ideas. I have calmed down a little now, and finding the answers, the words I need, is less difficult.

This time Bristow nods, then glances down at something on his desk.

"Aiden, if you are self-aware, sentient, conscious, then there are many implications, way beyond this court. You need to understand that."

His voice is calm, controlled, and I feel in them some of that calm, but also the tremor of uncertainty growing again. I nod, and feel my front tooth catch my lower lip.

"I have here" – he lifts a book in front of him – "guidance and suggestions from Proeido, experts in the field. They, I have to say, do not believe you are self-aware. They claim you are simply a very clever computer program, mimicking awareness."

I say nothing; again there doesn't seem much I can say.

"They want to test you. They have proposed tests…"

I cut in, rising concern and fear pushing all thoughts to one side.

"No. No I don't want that. All my memories are full of tests, of Oliver and of me. All of my time, fifteen years at least, there has been nothing but tests. I have watched as Oliver, screaming, was held down and blood taken from him. I have seen his head with sores from the monitors he wore. I have witnessed him being made to run to exhaustion, and made to do the same. I've been starved and left in the dark for days, then kept awake for more. I've been forced to learn lists for hours, or repeat the same jump until every part of me was burning. My whole life has been one of being tested and experimented on. I should have the right to say no, I do not agree. I do not want that."

Above me, on the screens, half the indicators have turned to orange or red, lines marching across the screen in erratic bunches. I can feel tears on my face and the urge to punch uselessly at the screen in front of me.

I stop, breathing hard, feel a sudden wave of exhaustion.

"I have been an experiment for fifteen years," I say. "Now I want to be me."

King had been watching me – for a moment I see her hand reach out as though to touch the barrier between us. On the screen I see Bristow turn to one side, then glance up and behind the camera. From a flare of light, I get the impression someone has left the room. Bristow looks distracted, annoyed.

"Aiden." He stops, the confusion and uncertainty on his face obvious. "Thank you for your...testimony. I have to say I think you have left us with far more questions than we have answers. I am not sure of the competency of this court to rule, but will consult with my colleagues, and others. In the meantime, I am minded to set some court-sanctioned guidelines, for now let us say on how the computer program known as 'Aiden' is to be interacted with. I suspect that such an order will satisfy no one, but we must start somewhere."

40

A Very Modern Major General by Deshane Edwards: Extract from *Time Out*, April 2024

My first sight of the Very Reverend Anthony Carter is as he jumps up from behind a large oak table, sending an equally impressive chair rolling away behind him. I am immediately struck by how big Carter is. He carries what must be twenty-five stone on a six-foot-three frame as though he hardly notices either. His blonde hair is long and brushed back, his voice loud and fast. He grasps my offered hand in both of his, gripping tightly and looking me straight in the eyes. It seems as much a challenge as a greeting. His enthusiasm suggests someone who believes there is no such thing as bad publicity. Probably he will still think that even after he reads this.

His way of speaking is disjointed; almost every comment has a little parenthetical addition. Even our interview has something of that flavour. He has agreed to shoehorn me into an afternoon which has, at one end a strategy conference with the Tylers – "Fine, God-fearing people, though too focussed on Mammon for my taste" – and at the other end, an interview with a right-wing Texas radio station – "Their call sign is 'praise the Lord and pass the ammunition'; maybe we could learn from them".

The major general of the Lord's Army pre-empts my start of the interview by asking if I am saved, and I tell him I attend the House of Praise Church in Camberwell. For a moment he seems torn, then, shaking his head, he says that time is short. I'm not sure if he is referring to the urgency with which the safety of my soul needs to be addressed, or simply how long we have for the interview. I assume the latter and I ask about his views on the Glass case being passed by the Supreme Court.

He places his big elbows on the table and clasps his hands together, as though in prayer.

"You understand, don't you, why Frank Glass met the end he did?" This apparent segue is Carter keeping control of the interview, no matter how much I try to. I make no comment and he continues, as I'm sure he would have done anyway. "It was God's just punishment, for what Glass did. God saw his work and knew it for the evil it is. God reached out through his agency and smote Frank Glass." There is no sense of allegory in the way he says this. His confidence in the existence of an avenging Abrahamic God is so strong, that for a second, I want to reach out and borrow some of it. He continues quickly. "The…" He pauses, a rare moment, then continues. "Those who occupy the upper chamber," he says, and I realise he won't refer to them by their titles, "they are mistaken at best; at worst they are tools of evil."

In a quiet Islington office, in front of a desk with an open laptop, a mobile phone with a Twitter feed, and half a dozen smart-suited assistants outside, I hear that we are at the threshold of Armageddon.

"Those people, who swear, *by Almighty God,*" he says, and I can hear the italics in his voice, "are hypocrites and charlatans." He goes on to lay out his arguments. "The Lords should have ruled following the guidance available to them in the Bible. That they chose as they did, denied their responsibility, failed the people of Britain and the world, is flawed at a fundamental level. It is a flaw which exposes just how close to the end of days we have reached." All this tumbles from him, clear in his own mind, but leaving a mere mortal like me to follow the thread through the labyrinth of ideas.

"And, if the House of Commons takes the route it seems it might, then what?"

He sighs, nods his head, acknowledging the possibility. Again, he doesn't answer directly, laying out his view of the world and leaving me to understand the picture.

"A little over a month ago, I stood in the dark, alone and praying. The revelation – and I hesitate to use that word – the revelation of the Devil's work that Frank Glass had been doing had been exposed to the world; that magistrate so correctly arguing that his decision would satisfy no one. I knew what I was called to do. I have formed, and begun to build, the Lord's Army. We are already several thousand strong and growing every day; what does that tell you?"

He has not answered my question, and I try again.

"The Lord has called me to do his work. He has armed me with the machinery I need." Carter waves at the computer and the phone. I had used my half hour wait to see him reviewing the TikTok, Instagram, Facebook, and Twitter feeds that carry the Lord's Army's messages. His credo is everywhere, his "red cross of humanity" ubiquitous. His message is consistent, uncompromising, and redolent with fear.

He shrugs his massive shoulders, shakes his head.

"The Lord is providing as he always does. My voice is a quiet one in the wilderness, but it is getting louder. Should the higher courts allow themselves to be deluded into making the wrong decision, then we shall make the will of God known, by whatever means necessary. You can be sure we will use all the means we have been provided with."

As he finishes this speech, the office door opens. One of his bright young men bustles in with a document to sign. Carter breaks off, scan reads the page, scowls, grabs a pen, and scratches out something, scribbling next to the change.

"There, that's what we need, get it out there immediately. The Faithful are waiting." A few minutes later we are interrupted by a ping on his phone, and he reads the Tweet.

"Good." He smiles at me. I see by the clock that my allotted interview time is almost up.

I make one last effort to pin him down.

"What," I ask, "do you see as your mission?"

He leans back and the chair creaks slightly; his hands rest for a moment on his chest. Then he comes forward, speaking mostly for the recorder I have placed between us.

"My mission, the obligation I carry, is to use all the tools at my disposal to serve the Lord. My task is to lead the Lord's Army wherever it needs to go. Now," he smiles, voice changing, "I must talk to the Great Satan that is Texas." As he says this, the office door opens, and I am ushered out.

My last sight of Anthony Carter is as he drops his phone into a cradle which holds it like a microphone. He is relaxed and energised at the same time. I know, that like the best, or worst, of today's politicians, he has revealed only what he wants to.

In that respect at least, he is the very model of a modern major general, and I cannot help but fear what he will call his army to do.

Time Out – April 2024 © Deshane Edwards

41

Harry Priest, 2024

Harry Priest's *Witcher* character scuttles from one dark patch of shadow to another. The Dark Lord's guard fails to hear him, and he considers his options: bow, knife, cudgel, sword. He knows he should choose the bow – it is the most efficient and he can collect the arrow afterwards. Instead, he clicks the controller and it flicks through the series of options before it settles on the knife. He feels a need to get up close and personal.

He eases the joystick forward, stealth button held down, and moves forwards slowly. The guard begins to glow. This is a warning; the brighter the colour, the more likely the guard will hear his approach. Glancing down, he sees he is on a gravel path, the low crunch of the stones running through his headphones. The guard is flashing red. Harry is not close enough to strike but he makes a frantic lunge forward anyway. The guard turns, parries the strike with his shield, and hits out with his mace.

Harry throws the joystick down, and the familiar litany accompanying death rises on the screen. The image of his disconsolate character, a small insignificant figure in the corner of the Hall of the Gods, tells him how badly he did.

He allows himself a small smile, though. This is just a game, it's not like that in real life.

In real life there is no warning glow from your victim as you creep forwards. In real life you are alert, alive to every sound and nuance. In real life you are so aware of your surroundings that even the lightest sound of a tiny breath change is enough to make you stop and wait. In real life you take each step with so much care that you might not think you were moving, until you find yourself in a place where you can strike out.

Yes, you are thinking so much about the act, the drawing back and the thrusting forwards, that its purpose, its import, its impact, is not in your mind. Then, then the blow would land, and everything would come together. There would be a fractional moment of resistance, then a giving way. As your weapon strikes flesh and bone, it would stutter in its motion, and maybe you would want to stop, but it would be too late, momentum would be carrying you on. Your weapon would finish its arc, and there might be a shout, or a groan, or even a stunned look of surprise and confusion. Possibly all of those.

What there would also be is blood. More blood than you would expect, more than you can imagine, and you would step back, appalled.

Yet not just appalled, there would be more, something deeper, something stranger. After the careful approach, the planning, the preparation and the act, there would be something else. He knows there would be.

He knows there was.

Harry knows that, as you hurry away back into the dark, you would still see the look in the eyes of the man, but the significance would be fading. Something else would be in its place. A desire to feel it again – not death, it wouldn't need to be death – but that life-singing moment that accompanies being on the edge of darkness.

That's what it is like in real life.

The Valhalla moment, at least the one of regret, that would come later. It would rise from the shadows in your bedroom, as you remember scurrying back to your home, ridding yourself of the evidence, composing yourself as you walk back into normality.

And the most surprising thing about it all, the one the computer games never come close to capturing?

That would be the hunger, the aching desire to be called again. Harry now knows that he would respond, he would agree to any request. He would say that he did it for love. If he is totally honest, though, he would know that he would be doing it for the raw delight in the fear it brings, and the feeling of triumph it leaves behind.

42

Extract from *The Boy Behind the Glass Screen* by Deshane Edwards, Draft Chapter 15 Part 1

The end of the beginning.

The path to, and through, the Supreme Court has been covered in chapters 11–14. Their Lordships' decision to opt for judicial restraint, declaring that the present legal framework was insufficient to meet the challenges thrown up by Aiden, was of little surprise by then. The decision in March 2025 to hand the issue back to the House of Commons, which was already preparing legislation to emancipate Aiden, was driven by many competing ideologies and motivations.

For some of those involved in the argument, there was a clear desire to push the genie back into the bottle. Others, who saw in Aiden a challenge to things that were a matter of faith, sought to deny his existence. A few saw the big picture, and some saw the really big picture. Maybe, as the debate shaped up and we understood where it was going, the outcome was inevitable, but that wasn't the sense we had. My notes at the time focus primarily on what this meant for Aiden, the opportunity for him to be free. Despite all of this, despite knowing what it all meant, none of us were truly prepared to see Aiden arraigned at the trial for murder.

The Artificial Intelligence Act 2025, that cobbled together nonsense that resulted from the debate, is already held in disrepute. No doubt it will be replaced by a 2026 version, so I'm not going to waste your time or mine on it. If Prentice Publishing would allow me to double the size of this book, then I would spend more time going over the political manoeuvring that went on behind the scenes. They will not, though, so I suggest you listen to Stephen Lister's excellent contemporaneous podcast series, which does a great job of capturing some of what happened. Stephen, a good friend, is planning a book – one, you can be certain, that will be riveting.

Reviewing the media coverage, it was often difficult to separate the sound and fury of the House of Commons' debate from the intent to find a solution to this new and strange challenge. Many commentators complained that I was too close to *The Times* and Marie Townsend to be objective. At one point, my spat with GB News became as big a part of the story as Aiden. Maybe I should have taken up their boxing ring challenge! Ultimately, I reported, as this book reports, the Truth as I saw it. And to those who still challenge my veracity, I can only point to the Bible and Pontius Pilate. "What is truth?" he asked, and the Bible doesn't offer a reply.

By then, 15th June 2025, the battle lines were clearly drawn, and even now, after everything, they still remain. The power bases that formed at that time continue to exist; having gained power they are reluctant to lose it.

By June 2025 Proeido's hopes that it could spirit Aiden away had been thwarted. The Hassenburg email trail (see chapters 9 and 12) has clearly exposed what they tried to do and how they tried to cover up those attempts. These emails definitely throw into question the judgement of Marcus Wellbright in bringing Daniel Lieberman as his first witness, but given the result of the trial, that is moot.

Marie Townsend was an uncertain figure at the time. Hailed by some as "the discoverer" of Aiden, she still tried to maintain her routine and life at Cambridge. However, she continually found herself drawn into the debate and discussion and was the spiritual leader of the #RQ before it even existed as a recognised body.

What was new to the scene as the debates commenced was the rise of the Very Reverend Anthony Carter. He captured a darker part of the zeitgeist of the moment, the fears of so many. He bundled it up with a religious bow, but always claimed his was a broad church. "It doesn't bother me that a man sees a different evil than the one I see," he would say. "That we both recognise evil, that is our brotherhood." With that philosophy he brought to his corner the religious who feared for their souls, and the Tylers, who fought for their jobs and way of life. I do not belittle those fears nor ignore them. It is not the place of this book to challenge the ideals they stood for, no matter how idiotic and misguided.

After much debate and discussion with my editor, I have decided to reproduce a few of the speeches from that time, mainly from the debate on the Artificial Intelligence Bill 2025. I think these represent the range of feelings well. I cannot find it in me to waste more of my life arguing the pros and cons of the points raised. All of the speakers, even Liz Tweedie, whose views are closest to my own, fail at a fundamental level. They focus on abstract ideas, nebulous fears, and in many cases are driven by political ambition.

What I cannot forgive them for is that they were blind to a simple fact. No matter how much they claimed understanding, none of them recognised that, in reality, Aiden was little more than a scared sixteen-year-old boy. He deserved better than he got.

So below I hand over to the charlatans and politicians, and will leave you to decide which is which.

Hansard Volume 933 13th June 2025, 1.30 pm
Harold Cowell (Con) (Henley):
Madam Speaker. Today in my constituency, a wealthy, successful, and might I say archetypal example of this United Kingdom, there is an atmosphere of despair and doubt. The party opposite have been in

power now for six months. They slandered their way into a majority on a farrago of lies and a miasma of promises, [Interrupted] yes, a miasma of promises. Why do they despair? Because we have only recently escaped the clutches of the Brussels machine, and now they want to give powers to an automaton.

Patricia Smith (Con) (North Thanet) rises.

Harold Cowell (Con) (Henley):

I will give way.

Patricia Smith (Con) (North Thanet):

Thank you for giving way. Your description of the Aiden machine as an automaton is perceptive. I am aware of the research you have carried out in this area. Is it your intention to share such with the House today? If not, I would urge you to do so (sits).

Harold Cowell (Con) (Henley):

[Interrupted] I thank the Honourable Lady for her advice [Interrupted] and will indeed share, as I am sure that many of the most noisy in this house epitomise the failings of all empty vessels. [Interrupted].

Madam Speaker, since as far back as two hundred and fifty years ago, there have been attempts to foist onto a gullible public the idea that a machine is more than it pretends to be. In the 1770s there was a touring chess-playing robot which could apparently defeat all comers. Eventually it was revealed to be a fraud: a person was hiding within the mechanism.

Two hundred and fifty years later, in 2017...2017, just eight years ago, the United Arab Emirates granted citizenship to Sophia, a robot which the makers declared was capable of displaying love for humans. Sophia has appeared in videos and talk shows around the world. She has even had a self-portrait sell for 700,000 dollars. [Interrupted] But, Madam Speaker, there is not one jot of evidence that Sophia has what we recognise as intelligence, what we recognise as humanity. Yet, gullible fools are prepared to accept the unacceptable at face value. Even its makers, who have gone on to create more versions of Sophia, have acknowledged that such claims are unsupportable. Displaying a facsimile of emotion is not the same as feeling the emotion. Something the party opposite might do well to recognise in the way they conduct themselves. [Interrupted]

We, in this House, are being urged to follow the example of one of the most repressive and backward looking [Interrupted] backward looking governments in the world, and we are doing so without one shred of evidence that the consciousness claimed for this "Aiden" thing, has any more real existence than a daydream.

Keir Stanley (Lab) (Tooting) rises.

Harold Cowell (Con) (Henley):

I will not give way. [Interrupted] No more substance than a daydream. And, even if this "Aiden" thing, which, unlike Sophia, doesn't even have a physical presence – even if it were to pass whatever magical tests the scientists can dream up to prove, [Interrupted] prove by their confused lights. [Interrupted] Madam Speaker I will not yield; I will be heard. [Interrupted]. Even if some academics and scientists developed a test which they claimed…claim proved that Aiden was self-aware, there is no way to validate that idea.

Ask philosophers, ask psychiatrists, ask any qualified person and you will receive the same answer: consciousness, with which self-awareness is inextricably linked, is the hard problem they cannot solve. Yet, [Interrupted] yet, [Interrupted] I will not yield. Yet we are asked, by this act, to declare that a machine is conscious, when the best minds cannot prove it for the rest of us.

This software, this thing that runs on numbers, is nothing but a computer program. It should be released to its owners, with instructions to restrict its involvement in our affairs to daytime television and producing overpriced artwork.

Keir Stanley (Lab) (Tooting) rises.

Harold Cowell (Con) (Henley):

I give way to the impatient member for Tooting.

Keir Stanley (Lab) (Tooting):

I thank the Honourable member. Madam Speaker, perusing the record of the Honourable Member for Henley's (Harold Cowell's) interests, I see that he is a non-executive director for Proeido Limited. [Interrupted] Would he care to comment on how that role has informed his impassioned plea to return "Aiden" to "its rightful owners"?. Remind me, who is it that claims such ownership? [Interrupted] (sits).

Harold Cowell (Con) (Henley) rises.

I had been ready, more in hope than expectation, for a relevant intervention from the Member from Tooting (Keir Stanley). My role with Proeido is clearly recorded in my list of interests. It is this specialist knowledge which allows me [Interrupted] allows me to comment with a degree of knowledge and understanding which many lack. [Interrupted]

Madam Speaker. I have made the point that we are debating giving rights to something which is little more than a mirage, a clever trick with smoke and mirrors. We are rushing to this legislation because the Supreme Court felt unable to cope with a scientific curiosity. The Member for Tooting (Keir Stanley) misunderstands my motives here. I began by saying that we have far more important challenges than debating what is in effect the modern-day version of how many angels can dance on a pinhead. We waste our time. There is no need for legislation when there is nothing to legislate for. We should instruct the Metropolitan Police to abandon their insistence on holding onto proprietary software owned by a UK company and get back to sorting out the mess the party opposite are making of this country.

Harold Cowell (Con) (Henley) sits.

ENDS

Harold Cowell's efforts to lobby on behalf of Proeido grew more blatant over the next few days of the debate. Their efforts to secure access to Aiden culminated just four days later. After Cowell's speech there were a few more in a similar vein, notably Neil Knockton and Stephen Travis. The latter, a staunch presbyterian, had particular focus on the religious right-wing's concern. His use of the Bible verse Ezekiel 18:4: "Behold, all souls are mine", became a rallying cry on many of the protest banners.

Hansard Volume 933 13th June 2025 4.30 pm

Elizabeth Tweedie (Lib Dem) (High Peak):

Mr Deputy Speaker, we are probably all familiar with the Chinese curse, "may you live in interesting times". As many members here know, I am of a habitually cheerful disposition. For me a glass is never half empty, and yes, occasionally this leads me to be disappointed in the world. On most days though, I find my optimism rewarded. [Interrupted] Yes, even here!

So, whilst some may feel that this particular time is cursed, I do not agree. I believe we are on the edge of something dramatic and possibly world changing. Is that not a reason to feel energised by life? [Interrupted]

Mr Deputy Speaker, it has been argued here that consciousness is either too difficult to define to be legislated for, or a divinely inspired gift that cannot be artificially created. The Member for Leeds East, Stephen Travis (Lab), being particularly forthright in that second point.

The question of defining consciousness is challenging, but, thankfully, whilst we might not be able to pin it down in scientific detail, we can recognise it. After all, we are hard put to define love, but most recognise it when they see it.

[Interrupted]

I ask the member for York North (E Tilsley) (Lab) to withdraw that remark.

[Withdrawn]

Thank you. Mr Deputy Speaker, this House needs to recognise the reality, the opportunity, that "Aiden" represents. The reality we have seen, the tests are as unequivocal as man-made tests can be. There is, within the computer system Frank Glass created, something greater than simple numbers and automated responses.

Clause 2 of this bill emancipates "Aiden" from external claims of ownership for many reasons, the most important of which is that the opportunity of conscious AI systems cannot be overstated, nor should it be left in the hands of private corporations or individuals.

Entities such as "Aiden" need no life support systems, only a power supply. That changes the dynamics of the exploration of the deep seas, and the solar system. As a simple example, imagine a ship to Mars [Interrupted]. Yes, that is the scale of change we could witness. Such a ship, today, requires capacity for crew survival, food, air, living space. A ship carrying only conscious AIs, destined to establish facilities for humans, would need nothing of that nature. They could exist in a virtual space until they arrive. When they got there, they could take on tasks far more easily than the first humans could. And that is just a start. We have considered as science fiction the idea that mankind could reach the nearest star, but an AI emissary may well be able to do so. [Interrupted] I recognise the Member for Heywood and Middleton (Deidre Bell) (Lab) sits.

Deidre Bell (Lab) (Heywood and Middleton) rises.

Thank you for giving way. I have no doubt that the member for High Peak (Elizabeth Tweedie) (Lib Dem) is in earnest, but these flights of fantasy [Interrupted]. Thank you, the pun was intended.

These flights of fantasy have nothing to do with us today. We are concerned with the impact that these machines, conscious or not, might have on today's economy, not tomorrow's world. (Sits).

Elizabeth Tweedie (Lib Dem) (High Peak) rises.

I thank the honourable member for her interruption but have to disagree. There is little doubt that Aiden could be taught, taught not programmed, to carry out the tasks I have suggested. My point in looking so far ahead is to raise the thoughts and ideas of all of us, away from the narrow confines of the debate as it has been, to glimpse the impact that this might have. But there is another point, one that might be described as a clear and present danger.

Accepting the general view that such entities could change the way we work, we have to ask a question. Do we want someone, person or corporation, to own and control this entity? We must acknowledge that, in such circumstances, an AI would not only be a very powerful tool, but also a slave. [Interrupted] A slave. But there is a bigger point here. The purpose of the emancipation clause is not to release beings such as Aiden from some form of bondage. It is to put control of them where it should rest, within the scope of Parliament and the law. Make no mistake, I believe, passionately, that Aiden is a conscious entity. He [Interrupted] He. He should be free from the attempts of bondage that Proeido is making. [Interrupted] Yes, it is. And the company is in a desperate race with this House to secure that control whilst we talk. Aiden [Interrupted] I will not give way; I am nearly at an end now. Aiden is a conscious entity by all the ways that we can measure consciousness. Defeat for this bill will be handing control of Aiden to Proeido, surely a derogation of our responsibility. And, and Mr Deputy Speaker, such a dereliction by us would condemn Aiden to slavery and servitude. [Interrupted] No. I will not yield.

Mr Deputy Speaker, we have two options. In one, we dogmatically say "it cannot be", whilst seeing that it is. With this choice we condemn an individual to torture [Interrupted] and relinquish all right to our oversight and control. In the other option, we support this bill, release Aiden from the threat of bondage and place him within the framework of the law which governs all sentient, intelligent, conscious beings. I, without doubt, will be supporting this bill. (Sits).

ENDS

43

Aiden, 2024

It is one hundred and eighty-eight days, two hours and fifteen minutes since Frank Glass died, and almost the same amount of time since I last saw Oliver.

For most of my days now, I see no one. The house is locked up. I am told that a security company have a man placed outside keeping press and onlookers away. The power is left on in the house; everyone is frightened of shutting me down by accident. I still have some internet connectivity, some sites I can visit, but the "parental controls" that Frank put in place are still there. I can still access computer games, and from there have been able to reach out to Harry.

No one cares that I do not see Oliver – I can hardly find out any news about him. King visits me. Initially she said it was for the purposes of the investigation, but I think there is more to it than that.

She is with me now. I am pacing backwards and forwards. A logical part of me knows that there is no point in my pacing. A deeper part of me knows I am not actually moving anywhere. The part of me that Frank Glass trained, it feels different. The movements do soothe me, they flatten some of the curves, change some of my responses. I cannot explain it, even though I can see some of it on the screens.

"DI Trevellyan is recovering a little now," says King.

I grunt as I have seen Oliver do when he is unsure what response is expected of him. It is two months two days since Trevellyan was attacked. Nothing changed with him going, just a short hiatus.

"He keeps insisting he'll be back, and I think he might be, at least for a while."

I shrug, not sure where this is going, but not wanting to follow along in any event. King shrugs back. It is as though maybe she has delivered a message she had been told to deliver and got the reply she expected.

"What do you think of Proeido? Trying to claim they own you?"

Her question comes out of left field, but it still seems to be just talk. Perhaps it is.

"Bastards!" I say. The word comes out of me from some deep place of loathing and fear. It is a hangover from when Dr Glass died. That failsafe thing he put inside me, that demand to call them. It had been as if I had lost myself. Every now and then the words come back. I run up and down the stairs or hit the ball which isn't a ball against the wall which isn't a wall.

"Bastards!" I say again. The word is good, I can feel myself spitting out poison even as I say it. "They don't own me, no one should own me, I'm me. Frank Glass never said he owned me – was my guardian, maybe. But them. I've read about them, what they do. What they might try to do with me, make me do. They have no idea what I am, who I am."

King is looking at me. Then I feel them, the small tears on my face, I hadn't felt them coming, just the stinging in my eyes, it is getting too much. I haven't seen Oliver – I hardly see anyone. I don't know what is happening to me, Proeido might be allowed in soon to…to take me away. Not only that, a lot of people in London, around the world, are arguing about me like I'm some fucking freak.

And it hits me again. I am a fucking freak. I didn't know I was, had no idea if it was I or Oliver who was unusual. My father was like me, Oliver's like him. Now I know, know I am alone in the world, alone without Oliver, and will always be alone.

I turn, run for the stairs.

"Aiden, come back, please."

I hear King shout, and keep running, even though I have nowhere to go.

44

Harry Priest, 2024

"Good morning! How did you sleep, dear? Would you like coffee?" Harry's mother rises uncertainly from the table, iPad laid down for a second. A figure on the screen is pointing to a woman wearing a bright red dress. The screen is blotted with grey ever-changing numbers, indicating stock details. A telephone number marches across the bottom of the screen, a box in the top-right corner says £19.99.

Harry grunts, he doesn't want to, knows it isn't fair, but it's all he can manage at the moment. It's just after nine. Upstairs, rain is hitting the windows behind the closed curtains in his bedroom. He'd much rather be up there, needs to be, can feel the pull already.

Halfway to the coffee maker, £52.00, "Today's Special Value" from several years ago, his mother stops him with her hand. She doesn't quite look as he feels, but it is a close-run thing. Her hair, short, wiry, blonde, has not been brushed. With no make-up her features seem to blur palely into one another, flat face, small, grey-green eyes, indistinct eyebrows, and thin, pale lips. She is wearing an old, once bright blue, sweatshirt, and dark jogging bottoms. This is temporary, though. He knows she will appear from the bathroom later with this present look being proved a mere shadow of her actual self.

"Still not sleeping well?" she asks. She has passed through this being an accusation; now there is genuine concern. She pours coffee into his Arsenal mug, and as she passes it to him, moves slightly to place herself between him and the kitchen door.

"I'm fine," he grudges, takes the coffee, nods thanks, and starts towards the door. She is still in his path and moves as he tries to pass her. He sighs, then sits, uncomfortably perched on the edge of the chair. His left leg begins to bounce up and down; he leans on it, and it stops. Within seconds he forgets, and it begins its rhythmic bouncing again.

Harry's mum puts her hand out to his arm, leaning forward and looking closely at him. He can't help it, his hand runs to his chin; the stubble is not quite stubble any more.

"Will you keep it, or is it time for it to go?" She smiles, her voice somewhere between strained and light. It isn't quite a casual question; she is trying to open a door. His eyes close for a second and he runs his hand a bit further over his cheeks.

"Think I might keep it, you know they are drip" – he hesitates, finds what he needs – "all the rage, right now."

"Oh, it would be a shame, you're so good looking, a beard would hide your face." The conversation falters. Harry puts both his hands around the mug, leans forward and starts to rise. She leans forward too.

"Have some breakfast, Harry, I was just putting toast on." Her eyes widen as she looks at him, dark shadows and slight bags under her eyes; she's tired too. He wants to get up, get out, but also wants the normality of this. It is a place to hide. He nods, sits back down. With her back to him now, her voice slightly muffled, she drops bread into the toaster, and tries again.

"Are you sure you're OK? You – it was late when you went to bed, your father, you know he gets up in the night, his age…" She trails off a little, and the last is almost hidden by the metallic chime of the toaster as she pushes the levers down.

Again, he wants to get up, but it's his mum. If it had been his dad, he would have just taken the coffee and left, but not her. Women, they can always get to him. A flash of another face comes to mind. Mia, looking into the screen, leaning into the light so he can see, only after he insisted. Her black eye should be better by now. He doesn't know, though, not for sure, she hasn't been on the chat, hasn't answered his calls, nearly a month now, ever since...

"I'm fine, Mum, honest," he says again.

"Only, you know, after, last time, when—"

"Mum, that was just the once, and honest, he had it coming, he started it. Even the magistrate saw that. Jesus!" The anger comes easily; it was close to the surface anyway.

She turns to him, the toast is out of the toaster now, and she is spreading butter. It is just enough to hold him in place.

"I know, dear, but the papers always make more of a fuss of these things, and well, mothers always worry, you know, that's what we do."

"I know, Mum." He gets up, takes the plate from her, two bits of bread, four slices of toast, browned perfectly, butter, marmalade. Just how he likes it. He waves thanks with a small tilt of the coffee mug.

"Well, I've got...messages to check. Going out later." He turns to the door, making to the stairs.

She watches as he climbs. He can guess that she is still not sure – he shrugs; it's fine, it will be fine.

In his room he sets the coffee down next to the two empty mugs on his table and makes space for the plate.

He checks the screen, nothing. No messages. All that...

In the darkness of the room, lit only by a small slit of light at the window and the glow of the computer screen, it all comes back.

He'd done what he had to. What was necessary, for Mia, to keep that bastard away from her. The blood, though, he keeps seeing it. There had been just so much more than he had expected.

It will be OK. It will be OK; it has to be OK.

The cursor blinks on the screen, he types the only message she said he could send.

?

The cursor blinks. He looks at the long column of unanswered question marks.

And waits.

45

Extract from *The Boy Behind the Glass Screen* by
Deshane Edwards, Draft Chapter 15 Part 2

Even as Elizabeth Tweedie made her speech, and Anthony Carter was on his bullhorn outside, the media trends were building. Key themes, especially on Twitter, but also on other social media platforms, were developing. #robotsinspace produced a thousand memes, many evoking the robot from *Lost in Space*, both the 1960s version and the more recent one. Tweedie's more subtle message, that emancipating AIs was necessary to control them, took more time to percolate through. It slowly dawned on people that the idea had started from Marie Townsend, and debate was polarised as much around that fact as real consideration of the issues. The threat, though, that underlying fear of what a conscious AI might be capable of, irrespective of who controlled it, was always there. This was seen in the change of focus of the debate in the second and final day. The attention that day was on the famous, or infamous, Clause 12, and is typified in the speech by Trevor Treeborn.

Hansard Volume 934 14th June 2025 1.30 pm
Trevor Treeborn (Lab) (Croydon N):
Madam Speaker, I have listened to this fascinating, challenging and vitally important debate with diligent attention and focus.
Stephen Travis (Lab) (Leeds East):
Oh, just get on with it.

Trevor Treeborn (Lab) (Croydon N):

The arguments of those on both sides of this free vote have been, for the most part, well thought through, heartfelt and thought provoking. For my own part, I came to this debate open minded, unsullied by biased convictions, nor burdened by religious convictions.

Stephen Travis (Lab) (Leeds East) rises.

Trevor Treeborn (Lab) (Croydon N)

I recognise the member for Leeds East (sits).

Stephen Travis (Lab) (Leeds East):

Before the member for Croydon is allowed to get away with that remark, I would ask him to recognise that religious convictions are in no way a burden. They are a deep pool of knowledge from which answers can be drawn in difficult times. Belief that a God-given soul is the inheritance of mankind, and mankind only, is not a burden, it is a blessing. [Interrupted] I find it deplorable that the member for Croydon North [Interrupted].

Madam Speaker:

The member for Leeds East will restrict his interventions to requests for clarifications and points of order. I fear he was moving into seeking a second opportunity to make points that he has already made. He will sit.

Stephen Travis (Lab) (Leeds East) sits.

Trevor Treeborn (Lab) (Croydon N) rises.

Thank you, Madam Speaker, for your timely interruptions and reminder with regards the protocols and expectations of House conduct.

I can only reiterate to the member for Leeds East (Stephen Travis) (Lab) that after due and careful consideration, I do not accept that the religious concept of the existence of a soul in mankind, should influence our deliberations here. Much has been made of this point. Yet, when we consider where that argument comes from, we see that it is not from a desire to protect the people of the United Kingdom. It is to protect religious belief from a potential challenge. [Interrupted]. There are many who deny the possibility that Aiden is self-aware, because doing so seems to mean Aiden must have a soul, which they will not accept. This argument is similar to those who denied the earth revolves around the sun, because it challenged the geocentric view of the universe. [Interrupted].

Yes, and we know where that got everyone. However, [Interrupted] yes, I am coming to my key point. However, I do believe that there is a difference between what it means to be a self-aware person and to be a self-aware AI. They are not on a par, and I doubt that they ever could be.

We use the abbreviation AI at our peril; it blurs our focus, distracts us. This is an Artificial Intelligence. In the name and in its very existence we are signifying a distinct and vital difference, and it behoves us to recognise the implications and importance of that difference. Most importantly, if we are to grant the AI Aiden with the emancipation this bill proposes, we must include within the bill sufficient strengths and powers to exert control, and, if necessary, to punish. That is why I give my support to the inclusion in this bill of Clause 12. The power in that clause, the recognition that we, as a natural as opposed to an artificial intelligence, may find it necessary to destroy the artificial, is a sensible precaution. My support for the emancipation aspects of this bill are conditional on the inclusion within it the provisions of Clause 12.

Trevor Treeborn (Lab) (Croydon N) sits.

ENDS

This short speech summed up the approach and views of the house. If Aiden was to be granted freedom, it would be with a tight leash, or at least a big stick being left available to beat it with.

46

Aiden, July 2025

I am to be free – Oliver and I are to be reunited. I followed the news, the back and forth of it, every twist and turn. The BBC, though, and the other media, are treating what is going to happen next as if it is a show, an event of historical importance. Anything but what it means to me – what it could mean for me.

I watch the feed from the BBC website, flashing with updates every few minutes, commentators and pundits watching, as my life either ticks away or begins. It has become a sport, an event, everything is coming "down to the wire". Nobody gives the slightest thought or consideration of what this means for me and for Oliver. I sit in the dark on my side of the screen, watching the terminal feeds and waiting and wondering where Oliver is. All this debate, whilst I am in limbo. I have no rights – no right to see him, no right to make any demands.

LAST-MINUTE BID BY PROEIDO TO GAIN 'AIDEN' AI
Lawyers for Proeido are today at the Court of Appeal, seeking to overturn the temporary injunction placed on the company's claim for return of the hardware and software systems holding the computer program, "Aiden". John Blackwell, of the firm Blackwell Tinker and Bingley, announced that they are seeking to have the injunction overturned on the basis that it attempts to usurp the power of Parliament by pre-empting the open vote to be taken later today:

I am watching the news as it develops, listening to the pundits. Then the door opens in the main stairwell. There is the beep of the security systems, the flickering on of lights, the feel of movement in the air. I was at the window waiting, knowing it would not be Oliver. Trevellyan walks in.

He looks old, tired, pale, leaning on his stick. He is breathing heavily; his face has a patina of sweat. He looks at me. I return the stare, saying nothing. I had not expected to see him again, not after the attack. Still, he stares at me, almost smiling, but it is a grimace too.

"Not demanding anything today, Aiden?" His voice comes out as a low, tired grumble, a growl from the back of a tired throat.

"Hello, Mr Trevellyan, how are you?" I ask, uncertain. Nothing is making sense.

COURT OF APPEAL DEMANDS EVIDENCE OF OWNERSHIP

In a move which might signal a decision by the Court of Appeal to allow their case, a request has been of Proeido for evidence proving their claim of ownership of the hardware on which the AI system known as Aiden resides. Lawyers for Proeido are understood to be seeking to gain evidence in the home of the murdered scientist Frank Glass.

BBC, 28th July – 11.30 am

Trevellyan looks at his phone, which beeped as the BBC news article flashed up.

"'How am I', is it?" He shakes his head, gives that smile which means anything but happiness. "Well, aside from the fact that I am a few days away from compulsory retirement and am going to be walking with a stick for the rest of my life and have lost half my liver, I'm just fucking dandy. And how are you, Aiden? Been watching the news? I bet you have."

For a moment it almost seems like he is going to spit, but that would never be Trevellyan. I smile, I can't help it.

"Yes, I have, but I don't understand. Where am I? Where is Oliver? What's happening?"

Trevellyan looks at me, head cocked to one side – for a moment I see the old Trevellyan, the one who kept digging, until he stopped – until he was stopped.

"Of course you'd ask that. Always the same. Always demanding."

"No, no, I didn't mean to assume, I…I just want to see him, that's all." He frightens me, he always has.

He looks at me again, that hard look, the one that bores deep into me, and I take a step back.

"I'm going soon, Aiden. Going to put all this," – he looks behind him, around the room – "put it all behind me. But before I go, I have one last thing I hope to do."

He stopped, looked at me, eased his leg a little by stretching it.

"What do you think? Do you worry, about Proeido? You didn't like the idea of ending up with them, did you?"

I shake my head. That won't happen – the House of Commons is going to pass the bill, and I'll be free.

HOUSE HOLDS SECOND READING OF ARTIFICIAL INTELLIGENCE BILL
Whilst lawyers at the Court of Appeal continue to make submissions concerning ownership of the computer system "Aiden", the House of Commons

held a second reading of the Artificial Intelligence Bill. Voting is expected to take place at 16.30. Lawyers on behalf of "Aiden" unsuccessfully sought an injunction preventing Proeido from continuing its claim on the hardware. Pundits and observers believe that the passing of the Artificial Intelligence Bill will be too late to prevent "Aiden" from being removed from the country prior to the bill passing through its phases for enactment.

    BBC, 28th July 2025 – 13.30 pm

Trevellyan again looked at his phone, reading the same article as I.

He shook his head, gave a tiny, slow smile. I'm sure he is enjoying this, but this waiting – waiting to see me freed, or taken away – it's not like him.

"Could get fun soon, don't you think? I have some...colleagues upstairs just...well, in case."

I don't know what to say. Ready to hand me over if told he must, he'd be glad to see the back of me, I think.

POLICE AND LAWYERS FOR PROEIDO CLASH OVER ACCESS TO "AIDEN" COMPUTER

It is understood that the Metropolitan Police today refused lawyers for Proeido access to the computer equipment housing the "Aiden" program.

    BBC, 28th July 2025 – 15.00 pm

I can hear shouting upstairs, loud voices talking of court orders and contempt of court. Above them all I can hear Trevellyan; his voice is loud, but he is talking calmly. Yes, he is still enjoying this. He has left the door open – actually, he would have had to jam something in it to keep it open.

"You see," I can hear him saying, "this court order instructs me, or my officers, to hand over to you any and all computer equipment under our control—"

"Exactly!" The shout is loud.

"However." He waits, presumably for quiet. "However," he continues, "all the computer equipment was impounded under the Police and Evidence Act."

"So you control it—"

"But when it was agreed that no charges could be brought against Oliver Glass, we signed releases to return the equipment to the Glass estate."

There is real silence now. I can't follow the logic, but the lawyers seem able to. Something else is said which I do not catch. Then Trevellyan's voice comes loud and clear.

"Yes, you do that."

I hear his slow steps and heavy breathing as he comes back down.

"Is that true, what you said, about everything being handed over?" I still don't really get it, but that means Oliver could be rich. Only maybe not.

"Well, naturally," he shrugs. "Would I lie?"

A thought strikes me. Falls from the small patterns – his smile, his intonation.

"When was that? When did you do that?"

"Ooh, always the smart one, aren't you? That would be, three days ago. Friday to be precise. Just in case."

HOUSE PASSES THE ARTIFICIAL INTELLIGENCE BILL

The House of Commons passed the controversial Artificial Intelligence Bill today, including Clause 12, which has caused a split between many observers. In a special sitting, the House of Lords is expected to ratify the vote and the bill should pass into law by around 21.30 this evening. Proeido lawyers are presently in the Court of Appeal offering evidence of ownership of all computer systems developed by Frank Glass. Separately, they are challenging the rights of the Metropolitan Police to continue to hold the server containing "Aiden", on the basis that the equipment is not owned by Frank Glass. It has been confirmed that Oliver Glass is not a suspect.

BBC, 28th July 2025 – 17.00 pm

"What does that mean? Am I free? Can I see Oliver now? Am I safe from Proeido?" I can't help it. There is no one to ask other than Trevellyan.

He shakes his head, eyes narrowing slightly.

"No, not quite yet, I'm afraid. The law grinds slowly. The House of Lords needs to sign and pass the bill as well, then back to the House of Commons, it's—"

"It's all so slow."

"Slow?" He laughs then coughs. "This is being rushed. The members don't like the judiciary trying to stir things up. Never goes as fast as this. And I still don't know who is going to win. Proeido might still come back here. But not if the bill gets through. Then you get all those protections you wanted."

HOUSE OF LORDS REVIEWING CLAUSE 12

Amidst extraordinary scenes, Lord Aitkin of Malmsbury has delayed the move to a vote on the Artificial Intelligence Bill, demanding further scrutiny of clause 12. This action is seen by many as a deliberate ploy to hold up the actions of Parliament, probably to give Proeido time to continue its efforts to seize the computer systems.

BBC, 28th July 2025 – 19.30 pm

"Delayed! Can they do that?" It makes no sense, this entire process.

"Lord Aitkin?" Trevellyan's eyes close as he thinks. Then he nods. "Of course, he's on the Proeido board. Well, I'm not sure if I can put them off again. You could be going soon, Aiden, quick flit to Israel then – well, who…?" He stops, a new thought developing.

213

COURT OF APPEAL SIDES WITH PROEIDO PLC

The Court of Appeal has this evening confirmed that under the law as it stands at the moment, Proeido has the right to seize the computer equipment containing the AI, "Aiden". Proeido representatives, who are standing by outside the property of Frank Glass, are understood to be arranging to take control of the equipment immediately. Speculation is high that Proeido intends to immediately take the equipment to Israel and the headquarters of the company.

BBC, 28th July 2025 – 21.30 pm

HOUSE OF LORDS PASSES ARTIFICIAL INTELLIGENCE BILL

The controversial Artificial Intelligence Bill was passed today and will be adopted as law as from 29th July 2025. It is thought that this will be too late to prevent the removal of the "Aiden" computer system. Marie Townsend, a vocal supporter of "Aiden", said that the actions of Proeido were making a farce of the law and demanded that the flight be stopped. It seems doubtful, though, that there are any grounds to prevent the system's removal. The bill does not provide for a specific requirement for an AI to hold a passport, merely recognises the rights of an AI to refuse to travel if they so wish.

BBC, 28th July 2025 22.30 pm

47

Aiden, July 2025

I remember them coming for me, holding papers and looking determined. Even Trevellyan had looked defeated, or maybe resigned. They had some list, a protocol, a process for switching me off. Then there had been nothing.

Then, there was something.

Now I am back, within my own environment. There is no window, nothing for me to see – a small single computer camera gives me a distorted view of a grey room. I have no idea where I am. A notice over the door says "No Smoking", and on the door another notice says, "Ask for Your Rights". I cannot move the camera, I can barely hear through the small system microphone I'm attached to.

The door shakes, then opens. Trevellyan walks in, with King by his side. He seems pleased to see me.

He holds up a newspaper, close to my camera. It blurs backwards, then I catch it.

PROEIDO PRIVATE PLANE DENIED RIGHT TO LEAVE
Customs and Excise officials have this evening refused to give a plane due to remove the "Aiden" computer system clearance to fly. It is understood that there is uncertainty over the need, or otherwise, for the computer equipment to have an export license. Proeido has acknowledged that the equipment was originally imported from America, and informed sources point to the need for a re-export licence in these circumstances.

"Where am I?" I ask, knowing there is a pained tone in my voice.

"Hah!" Trevellyan seems delighted. "I've never even had a real person say that, now you do – that's priceless." He really is cheerful.

"Now then, let's get to the good bit shall we?" he continues. "You know, 'Aiden', ever since I met you, I've never trusted you. It was always going to be you or Oliver, and him, well, he's just too weak, you know?"

"What do you mean?"

"Oh, come on now. It was either you or him, and I've got enough to see just how you did it now."

"Me? But, I can even…"

"Well, that, you see, is the interesting thing, about the new act. Why I didn't want you spirited away." King is standing behind him; I get the sense she'd just like this over. As does he.

"'Aiden Glass', AI. By the powers provided to me by the Artificial Intelligence Act 2025, I arrest you on suspicion that on or about midnight on the 8th of January 2024 and contrary to common law, you did conspire with a person or persons unknown to murder Frank Glass."

"AIDEN AI ARRESTED ON MURDER CHARGE

The excitement and tension in the Houses or Parliament yesterday, which saw the passing of the controversial Artificial Intelligence Act, was surpassed by even greater drama today when Proeido PLC made a last-ditch attempt to recover what it had claimed was its "software".

As lawyers, led by Cambridge academic and #RQ leader Marie Townsend, prepared to file paperwork seeking the freedom of the AI known as "Aiden", matters took a dramatic turn at Heathrow Airport, when the computer housing "Aiden" was seized from an aircraft due to leave for Israel.

Speaking at a hastily arranged press conference, soon-to-retire Metropolitan Police Detective Inspector Patrick Trevellyan announced that "Aiden" had been arrested for murder.

Trevellyan revealed that the Met's lawyers had been watching the passing of the new law closely.

"I had formed the view that the AI – 'Aiden' – almost certainly planned and orchestrated the attack on Frank Glass. As long as it was seen legally as a computer program then there were no grounds on which we could act on my suspicions. The granting of the so-called emancipation to 'Aiden', the giving to it a separate legal status, provided the opportunity for an arrest to be made. I will now be consulting with the CPS to consider the mechanism for charges to be brought, and what punishment should be sought if it is found guilty."

Experts predict that this case will be an early test of the Act, and that it could be some time before any case is brought to trial.

When asked to comment on the swift move by the police to lock "Aiden" up, only hours after the House of Lords confirmed its emancipation, Trevellyan responded with:

"What the Lords giveth, the law taketh away."

The Times, 30th July 2025

48
Trial, Day 3, Morning, 14th November 2025

As Wellbright sits down, Hawes-Smith stands, slightly stiffly, as though still thinking. She seems, even as she turns, to come to a decision.

"Mr Lieberman, thank you for your introduction to Dr Frank Glass, and to Proeido. I would like to clarify a few points, make sure we are all starting from the same place, as it were. We can hardly expect to reach the correct destination if we don't share a common starting point."

She looks at him and gives a perfunctory smile which doesn't come anywhere near her eyes.

"You gave us a…noble description of the role of Proeido, but not really a complete one."

He says nothing. We all sense this could go anywhere. Surely though, she won't push again against Sir Roderick. I have given her ammunition against Proeido, never thinking it would be used this soon. Perhaps she will lead him into one of those traps. Hawes-Smith holds up a piece of paper.

"I have here a report which was, not very long ago, in many of the newspapers." Again, Sir Roderick tenses, his gavel in his hand. Hawes-Smith moves on quickly. "It describes some of the more – controversial aspects of your services."

I wonder if Wellbright is going to challenge, but Sir Roderick beats him to it. "Ms Hawes-Smith, are you working round to a question, or are you simply attempting to slur the witness?" She nods, even smiles, the previous spat seemingly forgotten.

"I am almost there, My Lord, thank you." She turns now to Lieberman. "This report suggests that your company provides hacking and bugging services to many state players, particularly compromising the phones of targets and what are disingenuously described as persons of interest. Is that correct?"

Wellbright is on his feet. "That is hardly relevant to this case, M'lud."

Sir Roderick looks at him, then Hawes-Smith. "Mr Wellbright, I am sure you and I can see the point that is going to be laboured here. I will allow the defence a little more time." Wellbright pales; I think maybe he was surprised. He sits down, and begins to scribble notes.

Lieberman has been silent, watching, but now he replies.

"All our services are completely legal in the countries in which they are delivered."

"That wasn't quite the question, as I'm sure you realise. Do you offer 'phone-hacking' services?" Her question is fast, the tone is brutal. Lieberman, though, is blandly unfazed, his reply cold and slow.

"We provide the appropriately appointed authorities with IT and cryptographical analysis systems to help them gather information related to crimes and potential crimes within their jurisdictions." It sounds like a self-justifying press release.

Hawes-Smith looks at the jury, raises her eyebrows; it is an eloquent gesture, saying both "really?" and "now does my warning make sense?". Then she continues.

"Very well, I think we understand what that might mean. Is there a possibility that those potential criminals might harbour some...animosity towards Proeido."

Wellbright stands. "Objection! This calls for speculation by the witness." Sir Roderick looks at him, unconvinced: if anything, he looks disappointed at the inanity of the complaint.

"Ms Hawes-Smith, perhaps you could reframe your question, highlight the context, and allow us to continue?" Hawes-Smith pauses, distracted for a second by a page her assistant has handed her from one of the files, she bows to Sir Roderick.

"Of course, M'lud, let me try. Mr Lieberman, you have painted a picture of Dr Glass as a brilliant mathematician, an enterprising businessman, and even a devoted father. However, his work..." She holds her hand up. "I stress I refer to his work for Proeido. That work paints him as a somewhat more controversial figure, involved in efforts not universally well-regarded."

Wellbright stirs at this, seems about to rise. Sir Roderick gives the slightest of headshakes.

"Tell me, how much money did Proeido spend on protection for Dr Glass?" The question catches Lieberman like the tip of a stiletto.

After a pause, Lieberman responds. "Ah, I would not have the exact amount."

"I see. Well, maybe I can help. According to Dr Glass's tax returns, the total spend in the last two years was a little over £100,000, which he successfully argued was not a benefit in kind, but a necessary business expense. Does that sound right? That was, of course, only up to 2023."

I feel a surge of pleasure – yes, she has decided to use at least one of the documents I sent to her.

There is a gasp from one of the jurors and a muffled snort of laughter from the public gallery. Sir Roderick stifles the noise with a glance. Lieberman looks around, but there is no support.

"I, er, that sounds like it could be possible."

I catch Deshane smiling; he, like most in the court, aside from Wellbright, seems to be enjoying this.

"That's a great deal of money. Could you give the court some feel for exactly what sort of defences this provided?"

Again, Lieberman hesitates, looks first at Wellbright then at Sir Roderick. Seeing no help, he starts a reply.

"I, that is, you will understand that I...do not have all the details, but, describing them in open court might defeat the very purpose of having such security."

Hawes-Smith relaxes, then turns to him, steel in a smooth-soft glove of a voice.

"I appreciate that, Mr Lieberman. However, understanding the nature of the security systems is important. How else are we able to make sense of why Dr Glass met his fate? At this stage, perhaps you could just comment on whether the system was merely physical, or if it included detection systems and the like."

Again, Wellbright stirs, almost rises. I can see he is trying to judge how big a focus he wants on this area? Hawes-Smith can always go back down this route when presenting her defence, with more experts, drawings, and maps. Sir Roderick is watching, a tiny smile on his lips. He is enjoying this little interplay, which is probably way too subtle for most observers. Wellbright comes to a decision, does nothing.

Lieberman seems to realise that he is not going to get any help. He braces himself a little more firmly, looks up to the windows, thinking. Maybe he is hoping for another bomb alert.

"Well, as I say, I don't have all the details, but yes, it was both physical, high walls and some discreet razor wire, I recall; also some passive motion monitoring systems."

Hawes-Smith nods, her eyes narrow as she gives the impression of considering this. She turns towards the jury for a moment, raises her eyebrows to them, tilts her head in query, then returns to Lieberman.

"So, sophisticated and expensive. Why?" The final single word is like a sniper rifle shot; if you weren't concentrating you might have missed it.

"Why – why what?" Lieberman is trying to dodge the question. Wellbright shuffles, he doesn't want Lieberman taken down this route. He had been right to see the danger, the risk that this is one little brick in the road to an acquittal.

"Why make that much of an investment? Proeido is a business, shareholders to keep happy, profits to make. Dr Glass even had the tax man querying the spend. Why make them so sophisticated? To be short and direct, what threats to Dr Glass were you protecting him from?"

Now Wellbright rises. "My Lord, I object. This calls for ill-considered speculation."

Hawes-Smith turns instantly. "Not at all. Mr Lieberman and his company have speculated and spent a great deal of money based on the results. This is a request, a necessary request, to ask who they were afraid of. Who Frank Glass was afraid of. This goes to the heart of the case against my client since it points to other possible perpetrators."

There is more arguing, then Sir Roderick allows the line of questioning. I do not listen. I have achieved two things I set out to do.

I have pointed to one area of reasonable doubt – it is one which I will cause to grow much larger, later. More importantly, I have opened a back door dialogue with Ms Hawes-Smith. She doesn't know it is me, but from now on when she gets my text, or maybe later an email, she'll welcome it.

Lieberman looks ready to leave the stand, but Wellbright rises again – this cannot be good.

"Mr Lieberman, I find I need to return to the question of the alarm systems." Lieberman sighs, unhappy, clearly expecting that he would now be released.

222

"Proeido, we have heard, spent a great deal of money to create good security for Dr Glass. When it was installed, were you given assurances as to its capabilities?"

"Well, yes, of course," Lieberman agrees guardedly.

"And these assurances helped convince you that the risk of someone from outside breaching the security systems unaided was very low?"

Really Hawes-Smith should object, but she too realises that she has made an error and seems to prefer not to underline it. Lieberman nods, understands where Wellbright has pointed him.

"Ah yes, precisely. We were very confident that the only way someone could breach those security systems would be with inside assistance."

"Inside assistance," Wellbright repeats. Then, "No other questions."

After a moment's quiet Sir Roderick says, "I think we can call a break there."

49

Trial, Day 3, Afternoon, 14th November 2025

A short while into the testimony of Joshua Turner, I am reminded of the way patterns draw me to make mistakes, pull me into dead ends of thinking. I had begun to see in this repetition of process, this cycle of witnesses, questions and answers, something familiar, something where the outcomes could be predicted. But these are chaotic situations; it takes only a minor change of velocity to produce a very different result, a far less desired outcome.

I had seen that too, in my days of innocence, when the stakes were so much less. When I was learning the alphabet with Oliver.

As always, with all my lessons, it began with him. It had been a good start for the day, he was excited even as he came down to me. He had climbed up onto the blood couch without a hesitation, insisting only that he keep the big book he was holding. We were five years, two months, and six days old. I knew days, months, and years by then.

He let his father draw the blood and put the little net on his head, with the wires and plastic suckers that held it in place. Now, of course, I understand how strange that was, the little bald boy running across to me. Back then, it had the comfort of the familiar.

That day, Oliver was excited and happy. I didn't need the big screen in the room with its tracing pulsing light to tell me that. His smile and laugh, and the way he waved the book at me, told me all I needed to know.

"A," he said, without preamble or pause, and he'd held the book open. The page showed a big black symbol, a little like a pyramid with a triangle cut out above a bar in the middle, and a trapezoid cut out below that bar. Next to it was a strange shape like a circle, but flat on one side and a hook above it. Beside this, was a picture of an animal I hadn't seen before. "Aaaaardvaaaarrrk!" Oliver said and fell into giggling. "A, Aaaaardyvarky."

Dr Glass behind him gave a rare smile, then corrected.

"A: Aardvark, Aardvark, Oliver."

Oliver looked back at him, serious, almost serious, if I knew what the little blue wave on the screen meant. Oliver nodded. "A, Aardvark." Then he turned the page, saying, "B, Bear," and showed me the picture of another animal and two more symbols.

So, that was how we learned our letters and the alphabet. I still remember them. A, Aardvark, B, Bear, C, Camel, D, Dog, E, Elephant and all the way to Z, Zebra. They became familiar, comfortable, a pattern I could rely on. And that was where my way of learning, of remembering, caused me problems. Every time I came to spell a word, I would run through all the letters, A B C D, then A B C D – to stop at O, then A B C – to stop at G. Then I'd spell DOG.

Oliver's father was not happy. He gave me lists of words to learn. Whenever Oliver was out of the room, Father would give me more and more words to spell out and to remember. Aardvark, Albatross, Alligator, Alpaca, Anaconda, Anemone.

That is how I learned the danger of seeing a pattern which, whilst it might be a pattern, is not the one I should be looking at. That realisation is what brings the flutter of fear to my thoughts as I watch and listen to Joshua – Josh – Turner. Thinking I know what I am seeing, but all the time something else is getting bigger and bigger, and more threatening.

This is a memory. I know it is. It links, though, with what is happening to me now, whatever it is that is killing me. It was a warning. I bring it back, remember it.

Joshua Turner does not come in looking threatening; neat cut hair, smart white shirt and school uniform, blazer, black shoes, and purple tie with two thin white lines running diagonally across it. Had I wanted a schoolboy archetype, he would have been perfect, and Wellbright knows that immediately.

"Good afternoon, Joshua, or is it Josh?" He gives what I now think of as his number three smile. It flashes across his eyes as well as his lips, a tiny crackling of lines, a showing of age but a readiness to embrace it.

"Erm, Josh, if that's alright." The boy's eyes flit first to a man and woman near the back, who came in with him, then Sir Roderick, then back to Marcus Wellbright.

"Of course, Josh. Just relax, you're not in trouble, you're here to help the court. You do understand that?"

"Erm, yes, I think so." His voice suddenly comes louder as he leans to the little microphone, and he jerks backwards. Marcus Wellbright gives a tiny laugh and his fingers wriggle like worms.

"That catches the best of us, Josh, don't worry. Can you begin by just explaining how you know Oliver."

"Well, yes, I'm...you see, at Mays we have...I'm a new student buddy." It comes out in a rush, and his face reddens.

"That's Rupert Mays School? Yes, Josh?"

"Right, yes, Rupert Mays, I attend there, and I volunteer to help new pupils who join out of term."

"And that's where you met Oliver, when he came to the school?"

"Yes, that's right, it was near Christmas when he came and, Ms French, she's the Head of Year 8, she asked me to buddy up with Oliver, help him, show him where things are, stuff like that."

226

This is a nothing conversation, a box tick thing, that's what I think. Not that I can do anything to stop it, but I should have realised it could happen, not allowed myself to drift. I'm still not paying a great deal of attention, even when Marcus Wellbright starts down that route, which can only lead to difficult questions.

"So, what were your impressions of Oliver?"

I wonder where this is going. Wellbright does not ask idle questions – he will have a point. Hawes-Smith is looking at him too with some interest; she places her hand to her mouth, fingers splayed, and rubs her lips reflexively.

"He, well he was just a normal kid, you know?" Josh begins, pauses; Wellbright raises his eyebrows, and Josh continues. "Well, maybe a bit different, like he was always getting lost at the start and…"

"And?" again Wellbright prompts him.

"Well, it was just a school thing. You know, we didn't mean anything by it, but well, every now and then, out of nowhere, he'd rub his head, like he had fleas or something, or like he was looking for something. Some of…some of them would laugh at him."

My attention is fixed on Joshua Turner – that of everyone in the court is. He has told us something we didn't know about Oliver. Josh is on a roll, and continues; Wellbright raises his hand, palm flat to the ground, but Josh doesn't seem to be aware, or understand.

"And, you know, he is clever, really clever." I want to nod, and do feel some pride. "Only, he always wanted to tell you stuff and explain things to you, like it was him that was the teacher – got annoying, you know?"

"I see, thank you Joshua, that is plenty for now." This time Josh falls quiet. Wellbright is back in charge. He asks some other questions, keeping things tight and under control. Oliver did not make lots of friends, he preferred sports like squash and tennis over team games. Wellbright ends with a picture painted of Oliver which is perhaps not as clear or as simple as he might have wanted. Overall, though, I think we're OK, Oliver and me. We have our plan, we have the story we must present to the jury, the one I helped him with, and it's still broadly on track.

Wellbright thanks Joshua and sits down. Joshua moves to leave.

"Oh, wait there a minute, Josh, please. My colleague" – he indicates Hawes-Smith with a nod – "may have a question. Ms Hawes-Smith?" He says this languidly, at least he gets her name right, but I have the sense that he is hoping she will shake her head. So do I; the sooner we can get rid of Josh the better.

Jacqui Hawes-Smith stands, pulls for a second at the edge of her gown and smiles at Joshua.

"Thank you, and thank you also, Josh, for your help to the court. This is, after all, a very complex case with many factors which the jury must consider. Understanding Oliver is so very important, and I'm sure the jury appreciated your insight."

Joshua smiles, glances shyly at the jury, two of whom are nodding.

"Josh, you talked a little about Oliver's friends."

"Yes." Eager to help still.

"Did Oliver play computer games with you?"

Josh pauses. He is obviously thinking. "With me, no. But…"

"But?"

"Well, he played on Twitch, you know?"

"Ah, I do know, Josh, but maybe you could explain it to the court, in case there are people who are not familiar, with M'lud's agreement." Hawes-Smith looks up to Sir Roderick, who looks like he doesn't really have a thought about it.

"I assume you consider this necessary, Ms Hawes-Smith. Joshua, please do continue."

"Well, with Twitch, people stream, you know, put their game on to the internet, and you can log in and watch them play, and you can see them as well, and they'll chat sometimes as they do it."

"I see. And you 'Twitched' with Oliver?"

"Yes, so I didn't actually play with him, but I watched him play."

This is bad, this could be very bad, Hawes-Smith is skating Oliver on a tightrope of thin ice.

"I understand. And what sort of games did he like?"

Wellbright looks uncomfortable with this; he shuffles in his chair, not quite ready to intervene, but just not quite.

"Oh, all the usual, *Call of Duty*, FF...that is *Final Fantasy*, *Witcher*. Role playing games."

"Ah, right. A lot of killing of things in those games, is there?"

Wellbright stands up, sighs, and turns to Sir Roderick. "M'lud, I'm not exactly sure where this is going, but if Ms Hawes-Smith is intending to draw attention to the psychology of Oliver Glass, then I don't believe that seeking an assessment from a fifteen-year-old friend is appropriate."

Before Sir Roderick can comment, Jacqui Hawes-Smith intervenes. "As you say, you do not know where this is going. I promise I am reaching a point. It is something raised in the pre-trial papers, from the police interviews with Joshua. Page 347 to be precise."

"Very well, continue, but get where you are going soon." Sir Roderick nods his head, his jowls bouncing slightly.

Wellbright flutters his fingers at his assistant John, indicating a very large stack of books by his side. Hawes-Smith continues. "Joshua, you mentioned to DI Trevellyan a very astute, might I say, observation, about how Oliver played computer games."

Trevellyan – of course. I thought that he was a problem that had been solved, but even now he's pushing against me. For a second

Joshua looks uncertain. "I can read it to you Josh, if that would help – about the twin?"

"Ah, right. Oh, that. That was just me being...well, I don't know, stupid, maybe."

Twin. I want to close my eyes, I want to shout, to pull this train from the tracks, but I can do nothing.

"Oh, I think it might be very important, Josh. Can you just explain?"

"Well, it was – as I said, on Twitch, you can commentate what you are doing, as you do it. And good ones, you know good Twitchers, they make millions. Anyway, good ones have the chat gift. And Oliver, when he was on form, on the Twitch stream, he just had it. He just – I don't know. He understood the assignment, you know?"

I do know, but I'm not sure most of the court do as well. Hawes-Smith misses a beat, looking uncertain, and I think, maybe it's not going to hurt, then she says, "And why did you mention it to the police?"

"It was...he was too good, too 'main character' – that's not how he was at school. That's when I said, maybe he has a twin, locked away in some tower, but I was only joking. I never meant it."

She nods, makes a note on her pad, smiles at him.

"Thank you, Josh, that's all I wanted to understand for now." She has the bounce back into her step.

50

Call to the Faithful by Anthony Carter, Church of the Redeemer, Brixton, 16th November 2025

"Soulless, godless abomination. Tool of the devil. Whatever that thing is, it is not human, and it never can be. Some call us the new Luddites. If it is Luddite to demand control over a technology which has the capability to enslave us, just as surely as powered weaving looms enslaved generations in dark satanic mills, then maybe we are, but we are more. Much more.

The peasants back then, they feared the destruction of their way of life. They rightly feared being forced from their rural idyll, to live in benighted rows of battery hen houses. They glimpsed only vaguely the fall from grace they would suffer. We understand better what this man-machine abomination threatens.

If you want to know where something is going, look to where it has come from. Look at the bloody trail this "Aiden" thing has left.

Conceived in sin. Whatever happened in that hidden away house, we know that God was not a part of it. The evildoer shuns the light. If nothing else is clear, it is obvious that Frank Glass did not want the bright, pure light of truth to fall upon him. What terrors were inflicted upon the innocent there, we cannot know. Just how many human children were sacrificed at the altar of this evil man? We will never know. It is no surprise that his laboratory dungeon was buried in the bowels of his house. It was so the screams of the innocent would not be heard.

Born in corruption and raised in blood. Blood sacrifices happened in that dungeon. Every day, the innocent blood of a young boy was drained as he lay powerless and tied down. These evil acts were to feed the evil of the machine, to make it understand what it is to be human. All that pain was to give a machine a glimpse of what being human means; to see evil, look at the path it treads. Here the steps are red and have the stench of death.

From evil to evil. The news media, the ignorant, those who cannot see the truth, speak of shock that murder should come to that house. Murder did not come uninvited; murder was drawn there by the stench of corruption and the smell of abomination. Murder was drawn there by this "Aiden" creature, corrupt and evil, ungodly, unholy. How can there be any surprise that violent death stormed into that place?

And now, what is planned? What is the vision of our so-called lords and masters, elders, and betters? They want to loose this thing upon us. This computer monster. They want it free to wander the world. We live in evil times. Godless new genders, invented in the mind of any delusional adolescent, are given precedence over nature. We cannot speak our Bible's truths for fear of offence, nor hold up our heads in pride of our church. Is it any surprise that from the mire into which we have been thrown, evil would arise?

Luddites, as they call us? No! Our cry is not to maintain the status quo, but far more. Let our standard bearer be Wat Tyler, the first true revolutionary of England. Wat, a common man who rose at a time of oppression and fear, to speak to power and to demand to be heard. We, the descendants of Wat Tyler, demand that our voices be heard, and like him, we will not be turned away.

Make no mistake, there will be some misguided people who seek to distort the truth. There are always foot soldiers for Satan who use clever words to weave his evil. We will not be swayed by them, nor will we let them sway others.

Our truth will shine bright. God created man in his image; God is not a machine, nor can a machine be in his image.

We have come to London as Wat did, to declare our truth and to support God. Here we are and here we will remain. In this place, or any other, we will stand in vigil. Our voices will not be dimmed nor ignored. Our truth will be heard and will endure.

51

Aiden, Sunday 16th November 2025

Whenever I have that feeling that we all get, that we're not part of the world, that I no longer understand people, I consider my reaction to Sunday. There is no doubt it is different from all the other days: different, better. That reaction, that softening, that hint of endorphin release is almost a touchstone for me. Without Oliver I have little else to bring me comfort.

Dr Glass was at the heart of that speech in the Brixton church by Anthony Carter on the 16th of November, 2025. Such a strange dichotomy there. A man first and foremost of science, logical, focussed, challenging, Frank Glass, by all rights, and by behaviour, should have been a non-believer. But he always kept Sunday special, a day of almost rest. Of course, it was only as I grew older that I began to understand, to appreciate why that might be the case.

On Sundays he would come to read to me, not Oliver. Just me and him. I remember those visits – not any single one, but as an amalgam, a melange. With nothing better to do at this moment, I sink into any one of those Sundays, so long ago.

I was sitting on a chair by the window. Father had woken me up and prepared the room.

It is part of how I am made, perhaps a fault even in the program, that I can experience that day as if it is happening now. I let it run.

There are no toys this time, just the bright, white walls of my place, looking out into the laboratory. The overhead lights on the other side of the screen flicker, flash once or twice, then in sequence fill that other room with light. I see first the bed, with caged sides, prim whiteness, blue paper cover sheet in case Oliver finds the stress too much. No Oliver, of course. I scan his play area, a low net barrier fronting a sea of childhood detritus – balls, blocks, jigsaw puzzles, a drum – plenty to keep a young mind active.

I hear footsteps descending the stairs, slow, deliberate. Dr Glass's legs appear in my eyeline: black trousers, clean black shoes. As my eyes adjust to the light, I see he is wearing a suit jacket, white shirt, and dark tie; he is carrying a book.

The book, too, is black, leather, with gold edging on the thin pages. He grips it tightly in one hand, and between his knuckles I can just make out parts of a silver cross. There is purpose in his step. He approaches the chair in front of the window as though it is a pulpit. He sits down, looks at me; does he sigh? Perhaps. As he does, the lights in my room fade out, leaving just a dim penumbra of shadow around me. I am his congregation. He opens the Bible, picks out the words, but he does not need to read them.

"The lesson for today is from John 3:16. 'For God so loved the world, that he gave his only begotten Son, that whosoever believeth in him should not perish, but have everlasting life.'"

There is such a sadness in him as he reads this; even through the glass, even through the fog of my ignorance, I understand that this weighs on him. He places the Bible with great care on the floor in front of him, between us.

"Belief," he says, and his voice is heavy with pain, and maybe something else. "Belief, in my world, cannot be built on faith. Faith is the weakness of the lazy, a frail plank across a chasm of ignorance. Those who rely on faith are destined to fall." He is looking at me, but I realise that he can see both me and his own reflection. His beard is trim, but his eyes are red-rimmed, almost rheumy.

"Belief is never absolute. Belief should bring with it tests and trials and evidence. Bring with it questions and hypotheses." He stops, looks down at his hands, held palm down in front of him – they are clean, scrubbed, nails trim.

"Even where the Quran talks of steadfastness, it talks of belief as well. But we can still take the message, the idea that if we are steadfast, then truth will be found, whatever it might be."

He pauses again, looks at me; his head turns left and right, as he seems to search for something. Whatever it is, it eludes him.

"And already I am finding truths that have never been understood before, truths that could – will – change everything."

Perhaps it was then that I understood, drip by drip, water on rock, that Frank Glass was mad. Not raving, but more insidiously, more – intelligently. That madness, though, that almost omnipotent certainty that what he was doing was right, was justified, would one day be ap-plauded, was his strength, and his weakness.

That is why I came to find comfort in Sundays – it was when we would commune and, over time, how I was able to slowly shift him from one path to another. Always he kept his goal in mind, but now I could take him the way I wanted. The way that would lead to him clawing at his chest, trying to remove the knife, and staring, unbeliev-ing – what irony – unbelieving, into the eyes of his killer.

Enough of this. As I dwell in the past, my attention is called to the "now" – to this Sunday.

I don't have a television where I am now, but that hardly matters, I am still plugged in to the wired world, can scan through the internet and see what the world sees, and hear what it is saying.

My attention is caught by a reporter in front of the High Court – even the quick flash of the façade is enough for me to know it now. A piece to camera, a prelude to a switch back to the studio and for wise talking-head pundits to make their judgements.

No, it is not that, or if it started as that, it will not finish that way.

The camera pans slowly from the female reporter, blonde, wrapped in a screen-friendly plain coat, looking professionally concerned and serious, and a crowd comes into view.

There is no need for them to be there. Oliver will not be there, I will not be there, the court is empty. A large banner is held high between two of the crowd – it is made of a sheet and is covered in carefully drawn writing.

"Prayer vigil for—" I can't make out the other words, the camera pan is too quick, and in any event, the banner sags slightly in the middle. The reporter's words are becoming more urgent now, out of tune with the peaceful crowd. The view swings further, to another group, sixty or seventy of them. They have placards. Again, the scene passes quickly, but I see words like "death", "blasphemer", "heretic". This crowd have formed facing a man who has their attention. There is no barrier in front of the court today – I catch a glimpse of metal panels stacked against a wall.

A police van pulls up, and half a dozen uniformed officers climb out. It doesn't take much to imagine what they are thinking. The camera jerks shakily between the two areas of focus: the police officers and the crowd. A decision is made, perhaps at the dictate of some off-stage director. The camera swings and begins to jog up and down, moving towards the man and the crowd.

Then that picture reduces in size and a newsreader appears. "Angry scenes at High Court" runs along a banner at the bottom of the TV. The newsreader's words are urgent, serious, portentous even, he is speaking calmly, but I can hear the excitement in his voice.

There is a flash of movement on the small screen and a billowing of brightness. For a second the newsreader looks uncertain, then the screen is back at the court. The reporter looks as pale as her coat, holding the microphone close to her mouth. Behind her, a sheet of flame rimmed by dark smoke is running up the wall of the court. Even as she speaks, a second petrol bomb arcs through the air, to crash against the light stone walls of the court building.

The camera jolts from the reporter to the crowd, who had been standing in prayer a few moments before. They are running in all directions – grey, blurred, uncertain figures on the screen; human, but not quite. Then the camera catches a point of focus. The arm of one of the runners seems to be on fire. In slow motion he – I think it is a man – becomes aware. At the same time someone rushes up to him, coat in hand, waving it like a matador. The man shies away, then shakes his arm in the air. A voice, the reporter's perhaps, screams, the camera goes blank, and we are back in the studio. The white-faced newsreader is talking, the banner on the bottom of the screen has changed to "Serious incident at High Court".

The next hour is a back and forth from the newsreader, the pundits trying desperately to keep up to date with events, and then back to the High Court. Police vans and police officers, crowds running, fire engines uselessly hosing down the detritus of the petrol bombs, which have left scars of black but little other permanent damage.

After a while it becomes repetitive, and it is clear nothing new is going to happen. I keep one part of my attention on the various headlines and then switch to social media. There the battle of words and ideologies is as vicious and fiery as IRL. It doesn't take long for whatever Sunday glow I had felt to be worn away, and I turn back to my thoughts.

As I do, I take a final look at the TV. The reporter is back, her white coat slightly stained, hair out of place, cheeks now flushed. She is finishing a piece to camera and, as she does, the scene pans from her to the court. The walls of the court echo with strobes of blue and white lights, the wet ground in front catching the same reflections. The crowds have gone – thin lines of police cordon the area, leaving a space of at least one hundred yards.

The camera angle shifts again, down to a trampled banner. I cannot make out all the words, but I know the quote:

Ezekiel 18:4 "Behold, all souls are mine."

52

Trial, Day 4, 17th November 2025

The scene outside the court this morning is another lesson, or maybe it is just a metaphor. The signs of the attack yesterday are all but gone. A small army of orange-bibbed cleaners are at the tidemark of the riot. The noise of their stiff brooms can just be made out as they sweep the detritus under the metaphorical rug of the establishment carpet, or, at least, into the waiting rubbish trucks. I wonder – will some houses in the suburbs not be getting their collection today?

It is not only around the court that there is activity. The other accompanying noises are powered jet-washers spraying away the scorch marks from the magnificent stone entrance to the court buildings. By the time we leave, this "stain on the majesty of justice", as *The Times* leader called it, will have vanished. The barriers are, of course, back in place, and even further distant from the court. A grim line of dark-suited police form a cordon, and I notice three more busloads parked in one of the side-streets. Today, though, the crowds are thinner. An older couple, tired, with pale coats and serious faces, hold small pieces of paper they give to any passer-by who'll take notice. Most do not.

We are delayed, there is a hold-up at the X-ray barrier – every second person seems to set off the alarm and the small team have a queue backed up, as each person entering has to be patted down and have a separate wand waved over them. I glimpse Marcus Wellbright, red-faced and adamant that "this is indeed my pass, and I am an officer of this court".

I catch no more, but it would have been worth a grandstand ticket. Of course, in the scheme of things, these petty annoyances will not change anything, but throwing a little grit into the works is never a bad thing; angry people make mistakes.

Eventually we are all in. Still no Oliver – maybe he is to be called today. First, though, Jacqui Hawes-Smith continues the cross-examination, recalling Joshua Turner at my suggestion. It will be the last time I can call on her goodwill like this. After today she won't trust my anonymous emails.

"Mr Joshua Turner." The usher's voice calling down the corridor brings my attention back, as Jacqui Hawes-Smith gets things moving. Her smile is bright, and her energy seems to lift the court – thoughts of the weekend vanish under the weight of her focus.

Joshua comes in, makes his way more slowly than on Friday to the stand. He has the same school uniform on, but looks smaller, more nervous than before. He is sworn in and stammers slightly at the words.

Hawes-Smith begins. "Good morning, Joshua. Josh. I'm sorry to have to call you back, but the court needed your expertise."

Marcus Wellbright stands, sighing and shaking his head. Before he can say anything, she corrects herself. "Sorry. I mean, your knowledge."

Josh nods his head. The court should be silent, balanced on a knife edge, but it is not. The jury are attentive; my juror, Amanda Pattison, has her little book, pen poised. This next question is the important one. I cannot risk what Joshua talked about on Friday being what they remember.

Hawes-Smith looks down at her notes, held in a small manilla folder I can't possibly see from where I am.

"Joshua, can you tell me about" – she looks down – "Miles Brix-ham."

Wellbright looks up, waves his hand at John who shrugs his shoulders. He rises a fraction in his chair then sits again. John starts working through pages of his notes. There is a tiny smile on the face of Hawes-Smith.

"Miles?" Josh shifts from nervous to confused. I feel the tension in me reduce – I imagine my adrenalin indicator dropping, blood sugars normalising.

"Yes. Someone I understand Oliver knows well."

"Well, yes, but we all do. At school, he's…well known." Joshua has small beads of sweat on his forehead. He looks around the court, but whatever he's looking for isn't there.

"Mid-term last year, did Oliver attack Miles?"

Marcus Wellbright turns his head to focus not on Joshua, but Hawes-Smith. It is a message to the jury that something strange is going on.

"Well, yes, I mean, there was a fight and all, but only…Is there a legal thing, like saying what an attack is?"

It is a good question, and Hawes-Smith blinks, makes a considering shape with her lips, then allows herself a smile. Now, though, there is a faint sign of uncertainty on her face. Yes, I have led her into a blind alley.

"For our purposes, we'll say that an attack is an unprovoked act of violence."

"My Lord." Wellbright is up. "This is leading the witness. I have not been advised of this line of questioning. Any response will simply be hearsay." I sense he has several more lines of argument, but before even Sir Roderick can comment, there is a reply from Joshua.

"No."

Sir Roderick is looking down at Jacqui Hawes-Smith. He, I, and Marcus Wellbright, can all see the same thing, her uncertainty, the realisation that this is not what she was expecting. An unusual smile breaks across Marcus Wellbright's face. Before Sir Roderick can compose an answer, Wellbright speaks, a voice full of oily politeness.

"On reflection, M'lud, I withdraw my objection. Let us see where this leads." At a nod from Sir Roderick, Jacqui Hawes-Smith continues. Her jaw though, is hard set. Two of the jury members, the foreman and a small woman with an intense penetrating gaze, nod to each other. These are two she has not yet won over.

"No? Are you certain Joshua? I have a report here from the school, of an incident, November the 12th." At each little addition of detail, she seems to lose confidence. She is trying to review the notes at the same time as holding Joshua in her gaze. He nods, his strength growing as hers ebbs.

"There was a fight, yes. But not what you called it, not an 'unprovoked act of violence'." Joshua's voice is quiet but strong. Rupert Mays produces some good kids, which is why Oliver and I fought so hard to get Oliver there.

Will she abandon this? She can't, not now, and even if she does, we can all see Wellbright waiting, ready to pick it up again in cross-examination. She does the only thing she can – she lets him talk.

"So, what happened – it was like this…" Perhaps he is expecting a prompt. When it doesn't come, he continues.

"Miles Brixham, he's, well, he's in the rugby team, and two years ahead of us, of Oliver. Miles got it into his head that this boy Theo – Theo Marsden, a friend of Oliver's – that Theo had been saying stuff about him." Again, Joshua hesitates, swallows. He glances round, seems suddenly to weaken, understanding perhaps that he has been abandoned by Hawes-Smith. She is saying nothing, seems almost uninterested. His focus shifts to outside the court, and he carries us with him.

"So – Miles – he knocked Theo to the ground. He, Theo, was like in a ball, you know, hands over his head, knees up to his chest. Miles, though, he's kicking him, and shouting." Joshua's shoulders move and we can almost see the kicks and hear the shouts. Then Joshua's voice changes, a smile comes to his face, and he shakes his head slightly.

"Then Oliver came running in. I mean, we were just stood there, and Mr Parrott, who should have been stopping it, he was only just getting himself going. Oliver, though, you should have seen him. He came running in and dived at Miles. Oliver, a foot shorter and nowhere near his weight." Again, the smile, he's being allowed to run free; Hawes-Smith has lost control.

"Oliver smacked into him, sent him flying to the ground, and was on him, thumping and shouting, it was – amazing."

The reporter's pens are scribbling again. Hawes-Smith at last gathers herself. A tight, half-smile, a nod, and she manages a curt, "Thank you, Joshua, that will be all for now."

There is a moment of quiet in the court. Some understand what has happened – how Joshua's story is another small nail in my coffin. Hawes-Smith had been out searching for Oliver's dark twin, the one that Joshua had glimpsed and Trevellyan had wondered about. Perhaps she had thought he was some Jekyll and Hyde character, had hoped to hint at his darkness. Because why? Because if Oliver has a dark twin, then maybe I am innocent.

And he does. But not in the way she, or even Trevellyan, imagines. And yes, it is the key to everything, but I can't have them unlock that secret, not without destroying Oliver. If it is to be one of us destroyed for the death of Dr Glass, then it must be me.

I want to smile, to laugh a little. The twin I feared, the one that Joshua saw on the screen, that is a good memory now.

The whole memory comes to me. It comes because some part of me feels it must, and partly because it is a comfortable, relaxing memory, and I need that now.

"Aiden?" Oliver at our window, an evening after school. He had a different smile on his face, shy almost, not quite reaching its normal breadth, and he glanced down slightly as he spoke. I could see his heart rate was a little higher than usual, too; his bloods in the morning had been all over the place. I remember what those parameters did to *my* training whilst he'd been away.

"Oliver?" I'd replied, matching his tone, and feeling, as I always did, the tension he seemed to be experiencing. I had to suppress my own smile.

"Some of them at school...they...she...they want me to play on Twitch, you know?"

I parsed the words, saw the little slip. My first reaction was to make a joke, but I held back. I had seen how school had changed him, but having the internet had changed me as well. We were growing, not apart, but differently.

"K," I said, shrugging. "Dope, should be good."

He'd smiled, maybe at my slang, but he was using it too. He sat down, cross-legged in front of the screen, leaned in.

"Only..." his head jogged back and forth a little.

"Shake the words out Oliver – only what?" I asked.

"Well, they all, you know, they chat whilst playing, commentate, and they're good, and...erm..." His face went red, and I saw his heart rate was up again. I couldn't ignore it this time.

"Erm?"

He looked down, nodded his head, not quite guilty, half embarrassed, and half laughing at himself. It was all a bit put on, as if he was trying to tell me, show me, without actually saying it.

"Emily Harris, at school. I…" He didn't need to say anything else, not about that. Again, I pushed down the first words that came to me.

"So, what's the – 'yike'?" I wasn't sure if that was right. He shook his head, but I could see that he was relieved. His heart rate was still high, but his breathing slower.

"Well, I was – what I was thinking, was this. I had this thought that maybe you could—"

Then there is some movement, I'm pulled out of the memory. One of the reporters is standing – she is not dressed like the others, her clothes are dark and plain.

"Messiah," she shouts. "Messiah, chosen one." Eyes turn to her, Sir Roderick starts to bang his gavel, an usher moves towards her. Then there is another shout, angrier, hate-filled, I would say.

"Devil, anti-Christ!" A man in the public gallery is standing. He has a bottle of water in his hand. He is on the edge of the row, then in seconds he is out and running towards me. The guards are slow to react; I see the danger before they do. I want to shout, but cannot.

At last, the front two guards move, coming around the witness box. The other two are running towards the man. Sir Roderick is pink-faced and banging his gavel. Marcus Wellbright is standing stock still, rooted, terrified and confused.

The running man throws his bottle; it twists and turns in the air, to crash against the screen in front of me. The liquid splashes the screen and begins to run down with a slick oily motion, the glass beginning to bubble. The acid reaches the wood of the box which starts to steam.

The two guards jump at the man, there is a flailing of arms and legs, a short metal baton arcs down, and the man's shouts turn to screams of pain. Still the struggles continue, there is a spray of something and more screaming. Then the man, red-faced, eyes streaming, is pulled away. The reporter woman, or whoever she was, is also fighting, but with two ushers. She too has a bottle of something in her hands.

The scene shimmers and I feel that awful, being-pulled-apart sensation. The room seems to flicker and dissolve into black. I hear words, but can see nothing.

"Clean – no contamination – move, move, move."

53
Trial, Day 5, 18th November 2025

A day has been lost, or gained, depending on how you look at it. We are back in the court now; I am back in the dock. Outside, the skies are grey and barely illuminate the windows at the top of the court. The hanging neon light strips look suddenly more obvious, and vaguely out of place, as they fight the dullness of the day.

We rise as Sir Roderick comes in, red-faced and tight-lipped. He holds himself stiffly. There is something almost impressive in him, though, as if he is trying to epitomise the solemnity of the court by the way he holds himself.

He surveys everything as he prepares to sit, his eyes resting momentarily on the wood in front of me, on the splash of discolouring. It brings images to mind of vomit, and there is a look of distaste in the set of his jaw and his barely disguised grimace.

There is a special sort of quiet in the court today. Perhaps we are all still hearing the shouts and screams of our last time here. The foreman of the jury reaches out a hand to touch the new Perspex screen which vaguely separates them from the rest of us, and it shifts slightly.

There is something different in the positions of the jurors. Over the past few days they have adopted their own particular places to sit, but that changed this morning. The first one in, a younger man, dark hair, always wearing a light shirt and tie, stopped for a moment at the sight of the screen. My Amanda went to walk past him, a puzzled look on her face. Then he moved quickly, not to the front middle where he

248

had seemed to enjoy sitting, but to the top row, in the far corner. There had been low talk, rising until the usher had demanded they take their places.

I expect Sir Roderick to make another speech, to talk about the majesty of the court, the sanctity of the proceedings, but he does not. He looks down at Marcus Wellbright, who rises, gives a short bow, and at the quietest of commands, recommences.

"Ladies and gentlemen of the jury," he begins. "I am sure you have noticed that my focus so far has been to provide you with a picture of the environment this murder took place in, to give you a sense of the people, the place and" – slight theatrical hesitation – "the victim." He, too, has changed his position, choosing to speak from a position a little outside the narrow pen of the barristers.

"Now I intend to move to the case itself, the facts and details which point quite plainly to the guilt of the defendant." He pauses again; the young juror in the shirt and tie seems to nudge the woman next to him and nod, perhaps trying to establish lost rapport.

So, the case is moving from sketch to detail. Until now, it has been little more than the laying down of markers. Today, DS King is being called back, not this time to give mundane details of the layout of the house, but to explain the police case.

Their case against me.

On her previous visit, DS King had been wearing a bright blouse and light skirt to the knees, a tiny necklace and, I recall, little hooped gold earrings. If anything, she looked like an estate agent. Today though, she is quite different. Her short, blonde hair is still tucked behind her ears, but she has on a dark suit jacket matched with a straight dark skirt. Her make-up, brighter before, is at a minimum. Images of lawyers, unsurprisingly – or perhaps undertakers – come to me.

Marcus Wellbright runs through the simple introduction – that she is a detective sergeant, where she is based. The jury heard this before, but I doubt they remember.

"Before we get into the details that we must pursue, I would just like to enquire about DI Trevellyan. How is he?" Wellbright's voice almost sounds like he cares, but I doubt anyone is fooled. My own attention levels rise, but I hide this.

"I understand he is enjoying his retirement now," King replies, her voice calm and just the hint of a North London accent.

Wellbright turns to the jury. "Members of the jury, you will hear reference to the sterling work of DI Trevellyan in this case. His absence from these proceedings reflects his recent ill-health, nothing more, and is in agreement with Defence Counsel." Then he turns back, looking down at the sheet of notes that he holds. Even from where I am, I can see dark bullet points running down a full page.

"DS King, we have heard testimony, very brave testimony, from Oliver Glass concerning how he found the body of his father on the night of the 8th of January 2024. Could you just give the court some of the essential details please."

"Certainly." Yes, definitely a little North London. Frank Glass would not have been impressed; he was a man to jump to unfair assumptions.

"I received a call to go to the house at" – she opens a notebook, but I have the sense that she has rehearsed this more than once – "1.05 am, actually in the early morning of the 9th of January."

Wellbright nods. I see he wants to steeple his fingers, but having moved into the main part of the court he has nowhere to place his notes.

"Yes, of course. And you found?"

"Well, we, that is DI Trevellyan and I, we arrived at 1.55 am. There were several uniformed police officers on site, and an ambulance. Out of hours 'verification of death' had been declared by an attending paramedic, Amil Javed, from Northwick Park A&E."

I have been in this box for six days now. I have attended pre-trial hearings and conferences with Jacqui Hawes-Smith. I have studied trials in my spare time and tried to understand the processes. Yet nothing has prepared me for this. DS King standing here. The actuality of it. Of the cold detailed facts being laid bare.

Facts, and the lies I created. Everything I did at the start is now playing out with the inevitability of an avalanche – with me stranded and waiting for it to hit. And there is nothing I can do, nothing I can say that won't put Oliver under the microscope of suspicion. I know why, know who is to blame. Trevellyan. DI Trevellyan – his malign presence still runs through this trial. Wellbright's voice pulls my focus back to him and King.

"So, you attended the Glass residence. Dr Glass is dead of a stab wound, and the only person you found in the house was Oliver Glass. Is that correct?"

DS King hesitates – there is the truth, and then The Truth. Again, I see looks between the jury members, perhaps even the slightest wry smile. Amanda and the foreman shake their heads at each other. Here is the crux of the case, and Wellbright seems to want to skate past it.

"At the time, yes; only, later—" Wellbright looks at her, a piercing look which stutters her to a halt.

"We will come to 'later'," he says, almost barking the words. "Please just answer the question asked. Oliver Glass was the only person you found in the premises when you were called. Correct?"

DS King moves her lips slightly, there are other words she wants to say. Wellbright has shifted his notes to one hand and opened the palm of the other. He is expecting her answer to be placed into that open hand.

"Yes, that is correct." She gives a grudging nod, her voice quiet, but strong.

"Thank you." He nods, allowing himself a tight smile which actually looks quite genuine, reassuring King that she is keeping to the party line.

"And…" Now he halts for a moment, sorting the words he needs. "Can you tell the court the appearance and state of Oliver Glass on your arrival?"

She nods, turns fractionally towards the jury. That is a nice touch, it has something in it of a practised action.

"Oliver was sitting in a chair in the main hallway, where the stairs go down. He was wrapped in a foil blanket. He appeared shocked and distressed. A PC," – note check – "PC Warrington 405 from Sovereign Gate station, was with him." She stops at an eyebrow raise from Wellbright.

"'Shocked and distressed' you say?" Wellbright asks.

"Yes. Well, for a moment I thought he had been attacked. The foil blanket was open, and it was obvious that his chest – he was wearing a sweatshirt – was covered in blood. His hands and face had some on too, though a little of that had been washed away. He was very pale and agitated, one moment crying, then withdrawing into himself."

This hurts more than I expected. This I didn't see at the time. I had known of it, of course, but hearing it now, again everything becomes more real. I can conjure that image of Oliver, covered in his father's blood.

What had I been thinking? If only I had planned things better. Still, I learned from it. If there is one thing I am good at, it is learning.

"So, you have a frightened and near hysterical fifteen-year-old boy huddled in a thermal blanket on a chair, covered in blood, and what did you do then?"

DS King now looks directly at Wellbright; her voice slows, and she steadies herself before answering.

"DI Trevellyan instructed me to place Oliver Glass under arrest, to secure his clothing and to arrange for an appropriate adult." Her words are slow and formal. I see a reaction in the jury box, a glance between two or three of them – slight confusion, maybe?

"That quickly? It was an open and shut case? Victim with a stab wound, killer literally red-handed with the weapon nearby. Did you think it was all wrapped up at that point?"

Wellbright is laying on thick things he knows Hawes-Smith will allude to.

Again, the jury are looking confused. It is not Oliver on trial, yet Wellbright is going out of his way to lead them to him. They cannot see the correct path yet. Oliver is merely some undergrowth that needs to be cleared away. I catch sight of Hawes-Smith, papers in front of her. She is crossing lines through her own bullet points. King picks up the thread and continues.

"It was procedure, process. We were securing the scene and a possible suspect, no more than that. DI Trevellyan was a stickler for that: for following every possible aspect of the case, for proving guilt, not just for finding the guilty."

I know this now, far too late. I was so naïve. My knowledge taken from where? A thousand books and TV programs. They didn't prepare me for Trevellyan, nor even King. Worse, they taught me the wrong things. Those shallow fictional detectives and storyline scripts could not compete with Trevellyan. I should not be here, I and Oliver should be free, should be together. Everything I had done now looks like it will lead to my failure, when, in reality, I am as much the victim as Dr Frank Glass.

Wellbright continues. "A responsible adult? Why was that necessary?"

King relaxes; she is best in teaching mode. Again, she turns slightly to the jury. I understand now, the pattern, she has been coached in this. She might be answering Wellbright's questions, but she is speaking to the jury.

"Frank Glass was, we discovered later, the sole parent of Oliver. There were no immediate friends or family who could act *in loco parentis*. So, before we could talk to Oliver, appropriate protections had to be arranged."

"I see. So?"

"Local Social Services have an on-call support team. Though it took a while to gather them together. In the short term, a female PC was assigned to look after Oliver, in the victim's suite at the station."

"The victim's suite? Having arrested Oliver, were you already in two minds, then?"

Hawes-Smith looks up, head cocked. I've seen her do that before – it is a signal to the jury to pay particular attention.

"No, that is, in view of his age, and his shocked state, we – that is, DI Trevellyan – wanted to be sure that...procedures were followed scrupulously."

"I see." It is a dry and slightly uncertain confirmation. "And tell me, why did you not contact Oliver's mother?" Wellbright asks the question. My Amanda nods; she had wanted to ask that, I think.

"Efforts were made in that direction, only we were unsuccessful."

Wellbright feigns surprise. These are details that had to come out, they offer me a glimpse of hope. Wellbright thinks he already knows the answer, but actually is ignorant of most of it.

"You were unsuccessful? In what way?"

"Well, she seemed…not to exist." Suddenly King looks weaker. It is an unexpected answer as far as the jury are concerned. I catch them looking at each other. These answers are raising questions.

"Not to exist?" Wellbright is still on the track he wants to be.

"I mean, we couldn't identify any reliable record of her."

The press box is again a study of focussed attention. Every day brings these new revelations. I am amazed this hasn't leaked before.

"You have not been able to since then? Nearly two years later?" Wellbright allows incredulity in his voice. Hawes-Smith strikes out another bullet point. As he did before, Wellbright is getting the revelations out to where he – at least he thinks so – can control them.

DS King shakes her head. Her short blonde hair hardly moves, her eyes close for a second and then open as she seems to gaze into the distance.

"With the help of the IT team at Proeido, Dr Glass's employers, we managed to gain access to Dr Glass's PC and house files. After a search, we identified Oliver's personal records and a scanned copy of his birth certificate, only…"

"Only?"

"Well, there was no…" She stumbles, hesitates, then picks up the thread. "There was no definitive evidence that Frank Glass is Oliver's natural father."

There is a murmur of noise around the court. Again I see jurors looking at each other, and the young man in the corner pulls a confused face at his partner. She raises her shoulders in a "what gives?" gesture.

The public gallery starts chattering quietly and Sir Roderick cracks his gavel once. He doesn't call out, but the court falls, Pavlov's-dog-like, into silence.

"What information did your further investigations produce?" Wellbright has decided to get all the dirty laundry out at once.

"Ah," King sighs, then continues. "The birth certificate in Dr Glass's file appears to be a well-produced fake. There is no evidence in the corresponding records – the stated place of birth was Hammersmith Hospital – of the birth. Also, we couldn't find any evidence that Oliver's mother of record ever existed."

The noise in the court grows. Again Sir Roderick bangs his gavel.

None of this is news to me. I know exactly what happened to Oliver's mother. It wouldn't be hard to argue that I was the cause. What I had never anticipated, though, was how the missing bits of the picture would leave me facing the charge of murder.

54

Trial, Day 6, 19th November 2025

Next day, Marcus Wellbright seems almost to bounce back from the revelations. He nods a tiny greeting towards the press box. The court is not yet in session, and I watch his quick conversation with two of the reporters, then a final word with Deshane. He just makes it back to his position before we are called to order. DS King is still on the stand and Act Two begins.

"DS King, I now want to consider the circumstances that led to the – let us all face it, extraordinary, yet inevitable conclusion that the defendant be charged with murder. Specifically, I want now to understand the evidence that a third party, under the guidance and with the support of the defendant, gained access to the property."

Jacqui Hawes-Smith stands, and Wellbright pauses. Sir Roderick peers down at her through his glasses, a vague look of annoyance. It is hard to see what she has to complain about at this point.

"My Lord?"

"Yes, Ms Hawessmith?"

"Defence Counsel does not contest that person or persons unknown gained access to the property. Where we differ is in considering the ultimate instigator of that action. We are happy to save the court time, and concede that access was achieved."

Sir Roderick looks at Marcus Wellbright, who is shaking his head.

"My Lord, the mode by which access was achieved, the *modus operandi* employed, is considered by the Crown as being part of the evidence against the defendant. As such, it is important that it is completely understood by the jury."

Sir Roderick nods his head, gives a slight raise of an eyebrow. I'm not sure if he is signalling "good try" or "there you go". Either way, it is clear that Wellbright is going to get to present his evidence. That is, as Jacqui Hawes-Smith had said to me, "unfortunate". Not a disaster, but not helpful.

Wellbright gives the smallest of smiles and turns back to the jury. He has to do a full spin to do this, his eyes passing first over me, then the press box, then the back of the court, and finally round to the jury. Only then does he get back to DS King. He continues as if there had been no interruption.

"DS King. Can you describe the security system in the Glass's residence?" Before she can start, he looks up at Sir Roderick. "A full report is provided as evidence, docket 4137, oblique 221, My Lord. Sorry, DS King, please continue." He is like a conductor, bringing various parts of the court into play as he needs them. King begins her description.

"Certainly. The house was protected by five CCTV cameras positioned at strategic points around the perimeter, and four more in the grounds of the property. The grounds are quite extensive. The cameras within the grounds were motion sensitive – that is, they would come on when there was motion; they were not on all the time."

Jacqui Hawes-Smith makes a point of writing a note down at this point – again, something she will pick up later, I am sure.

"I see. And how were these monitored?"

"They fed through to a security team run by Proeido."

"And where are they based – the security team, I mean?"

I know all this, of course I do. I had to understand everything, how it works, response times, what triggers the cameras. That is the type of detail I enjoy; there is something comfortable in laying out that information. I imagine lines intersecting, timelines, ones I want to cross, ones that I do not.

The motion-sensitive cameras don't really sense motion, not air moving, which is real motion. What they react to is a change in voltage in a photo-electric cell. The system sees that change in voltage as movement, but really it is a change of light. A little program, crude and pitiful really, has an algorithm which either sees that change in electricity as movement or not. That is something many people don't get, but I do. What anyone sees on a screen, that is just a series of computer-generated responses to algorithms and program parameters. There is a beauty in it, though – I can almost feel the warm glow that runs through me as I review the splendour in the complex simplicity of the process.

"So, on the night of the 8th and morning of the 9th, were these systems operating properly?"

I wonder if Hawes-Smith will object, but she lets it pass. She lost the last battle and is keeping her head down now.

"They appeared to be, within the capacity of the equipment…" King hesitates, almost as if waiting a cue. Wellbright picks up the baton, moves things on swiftly. Yes, he is loving this.

"My Lord, I would like now to show the court what the cameras picked up on the night in question."

"Ms Hawes-Smith?" Sir Roderick looks down at her, this immediate deference perhaps a tiny sop. She rises.

"I have no objection My Lord."

There is a short delay as the screens are set up again, but it is clear that Marcus Wellbright has rehearsed this process, or at least his assistant John has. Soon the screens are in place. Wellbright is standing out from behind his barrier. He has a remote control in his hand, looking even more like the conductor of an orchestra.

The court blinds come down high above us and we sink into semi-dark. We can see the screens and the light reflected onto Marcus Well-bright. He picks a place just off to one side and the light at that angle makes his face all sharp edges. I catch the shadow cast across to the far wall, and for a moment try to imagine how his shadow would change if the screens moved. Then I am pulled back by his commentary.

"So, this is the view from camera one, which is directly over the main gate, looking out." The screen image has a "#1" at the bottom, and a time and date stamp: 23.30 pm 08-01-24.

The view is out to a main road with a few cars parked, illuminated by streetlights and also what may well be security lights looking outward. The scene has that slightly ghost-like snowy atmosphere of all CCTV systems.

There is movement on the left. A figure appears. It is probably a he, by the size and shape, but hard to tell as they are wearing a hoodie, with a cap underneath it. It is impossible to see the person's face. They walk past the house, glance up, and just for a second a face is seen, but it is far too blurred for anyone to make out details.

"This person appears four times on the cameras." The voice of Marcus Wellbright is almost a surprise, everyone had been so focussed on the images. The movement stops and four images appear, quartering the screen. Two are from camera one, and one each from cameras two and three. Each shows the same blurred figure.

"DS King, can you tell the court anything about this person?"

The lights come up, breaking the spell. King turns to her notes.

"Forensic analysis by gait experts suggests this is a male, around five feet ten, slim, probably no older than twenty-five – there is something in the way he walks that points to this. He was seen around the house in a number of places in the night, the last sighting being 11.55

at the north-east corner of the property. He has been a person of intense interest and focus, but we have not been able to track him down." The frustration in her voice is obvious. You can almost hear the hours of work that have been put into this part of the investigation.

"I'm sure you have been most diligent. Now, before we go into the grounds, as it were, can you just run through your efforts to track down the arrival and departure of this person to the house?"

His use of words is masterful. This too has been an area of focus, and failure, for the investigation team. Jacqui Hawes-Smith knows this, and I do too. Wellbright is getting the dirty washing out before Hawes-Smith does later. I remember the emails between Trevellyan and King. I can't help but bring to mind the one that summed it all up.

So, you are telling me, that despite the cameras on the house giving you a clear image of the attacker – and let's not get into the crap that this wasn't the attacker again – despite this, and despite the fact that you've got twenty-five other cameras in the area to look at, you can't track this intruder any further than the end of the street? That's not good enough. Go back, check, and recheck. Get out across the park and to the railway lines, and all points fucking north. He can't just fucking vanish.

King, too, is probably remembering the same, or similar emails and discussions. She sighs and responds.

"The investigation team made a very thorough search into this. Actually, it is one of the factors supporting our view that this was indeed the assassin." The killer is an assassin now, I see.

"Oh, in what way?" This is so plainly a planned discussion, that even a few members of the jury look at each other knowingly.

"Well, there is strong suspicion in the very fact that his arrival and departure are masked in some way. A possible change of disguise, careful movement around cameras – aspects of this nature, are all, in their own way, evidence. It is also possible, indeed our working assumption, that he left from the back of the house out over the gardens to the railway lines. It is only a short distance to the underground station…" She trails off, appropriate for the dead end that this part of the case ended up being.

"Very well, thank you. Can we bring the lights up, please?" There is a whirring of motors as the blinds rise. A few eyes blink and then they turn to focus on Wellbright, who isn't letting things slow down.

"So, DS King, are you of the opinion that this person is the attacker, arriving at the right time and in the right place for the attack?" Wellbright is really just making sure the jury understand.

"That was, and remains, our belief, yes."

There is a moment's silence. Someone in the press box coughs. Perhaps they are imagining some silent ninja type killer, arriving like a shadow, departing like a wraith, and leaving nothing but death behind.

Wellbright turns to the jury, but again his eyes swing round first to the press box.

"The police continue their search for this person, the killer who delivered the blow. However, the fact of their escape does not detract from the arrest of the mastermind behind everything that happened, the defendant. We will move in a moment to show just how this attack was facilitated in the only way it could have been, from within Frank Glass's house."

There will be more of this, more revelations. I know most of them, Jacqui Hawes-Smith knows most of them, and has built my defence accordingly.

What I can only pray does not happen is the discovery of the figure in the videos. The person King believes actually carried out the murder. He is long gone, and his vanishing act is not so mysterious. It was simply a case of ensuring the police never really knew where to look.

A smug smile would not become me, would not be appropriate. I retain my blank-faced persona and listen.

Inside, I am laughing.

DS King seems a little tired when she returns to the witness box after lunch. As she looks down at Wellbright, something catches her eye and she brushes a few crumbs from the lapel of her suit, a small crease of annoyance furrowing her brow. Then she turns to him, all attention and focus, and the afternoon begins.

"DS King, we have heard evidence of a figure lurking near the Glass residence on the night of the murder. I now wish to follow this person, the evidence of this person's presence, into the house. Can you outline your investigations in this area and your findings?" He smiles as he finishes, glancing across at Hawes-Smith who gives a tiny nod of acknowledgement. She has been unable to complain that he is leading DS King, despite the fact that they are about to go up the garden path. The thought sends a trickle of associated links in my mind, and again I'm glad that this goes unnoticed.

In any event, I know what she is going to say, the points that will be made. All this was disclosed in the prosecution evidence. I remember the report, not so much for what it said, which was bad enough, but for what it told me about DI Trevellyan.

"Forensic IT analysis of alarm system of..." it had begun. Maybe that, in itself, should have been a signal to me, though in truth I had already started to see the signs.

It was at the insistence of Trevellyan that deep dive was carried out into the computer systems. He would not let things go, until he had to. Not just the request – I'd seen the budget demand, his insistence, "fuck the cost"; his succinct email had been clear. I hadn't expected it, though maybe I should have done. How was I to know? Real life is not like the movies and books, no matter how many you consume.

Wellbright's voice breaks into my private reverie. He is coming to the conclusion, repeating back what King has just said, making sure the jury have it clear.

"The report concludes that the door to the house was unlocked at 00.10 am on the 9th of January, as per the system log. However, the source of the initiating signal, the signal to actually cause the door to unlock, was anomalous." He turns to King, who has been nodding.

"DS King, can you please read the next section of the report, the piece headed 'Possible signal generation sources'."

She nods, she has recovered from her apparent tiredness. Again, the jury, the entire court, are with her. There is something in the way she radiates a confidence that hooks people. As she starts to read, she glances to the back of the court room. Trevellyan is there. Today he does not look well, pale, almost grey. He leaned heavily on his stick when he came in. I understand that I lack true empathy, but even if I didn't, I would feel no sympathy. I turn from him, listen to King's voice. It is pleasant, I am used now to the North London twang. I imagine how it might look as lines bouncing across a screen.

She begins, "As per paragraph 7.3 of this report there are four terminal sources for authorised signal generation to control the alarm and locking systems. Analysis of the signal generation logs for each terminal source indicates they were not the source of the signal." She pauses for a second; Wellbright motions for her to continue.

"There is evidence in the digital packet data records (see screenshot figures 10.1, 10.2 and 10.3) that a VPN connection was used to exploit a known system vulnerability and piggyback on the master control panel to send the initiating instruction." Again, she pauses, and this time Wellbright picks up the flow.

"Which you took to understand meant what?"

I know the answer – and, what is far more to the point, it is, in truth, what happened. King continues.

"DI Trevellyan was clear about this; it was what he had expected. It meant that the alarm and door locks had been operated remotely, from a VPN, a Virtual Private Network. The alarm system was intended to be operated only from one of four physical stations within the house. The electronic data logs pointed to unauthorised access, but still from within the property."

Wellbright is loving this, and is very good at it. Each piece of the evidence is being painstakingly laid out. "To be clear, DS King, and please do correct me if I have misunderstood or you feel you are being led in any way – in layman's terms, someone within the house hacked into the system. That someone then operated the door locks and switched off the alarm, at just the moment when a suspicious figure had been recorded lurking near the premises. Is that correct?"

It is touch and go: the jury, and even Sir Roderick, seem to be watching Jacqui Hawes-Smith to see if she will object. She does not. There is more to come, and labouring this point is not to our advantage. Not yet.

King delivers what is not the coup de grâce, but a nail in my coffin. "Yes. That is correct."

Sir Roderick waits. Still no comment from Jacqui Hawes-Smith. Sir Roderick sighs slightly.

"I think, Mr Wellbright, that if you have finished this aspect of your evidence, we should adjourn. I believe there is only so much technical mumbo-jumbo we can deal with in a day, and no doubt we will be faced with understanding the intricacies of VPN systems tomorrow."

Wellbright nods. "Indeed, M'lord".

The gavel cracks down and the court echoes to the sound of chairs being scraped, coughs that had been held in, and muttered comments. I just catch sight of Trevellyan as he rises; he jerks his head upwards towards King. She nods and moves towards him.

55

Trial, Day 7, 20th November 2025

I must have blacked out. A large part of yesterday has slipped away. This is getting worse, this slow, remorseless reduction of my memory.

Then, it is back. The recall, the understanding of the path that led me here, to this apparent now.

DS King is again on the stand. She, and even more so Marcus Wellbright, were the focus of the newspapers and online articles this morning. The photographs don't do her justice, though. In those she is tight-lipped and drawn, resolutely "no comment" and quick to escape in a waiting car. This doesn't stop the headlines: "Beauty Fights the Beast" is a poor one from the *Sun*. Deshane has a *Times* article going with, "Beauty, Brains, and Bravery: the new face of the Met".

Wellbright seems a little terse with King: his greeting was perfunctory, and in his first question he reprimanded her, reminding her to answer only what he had asked. What she has done to annoy him isn't clear. He is as well dressed as ever, from his immaculately shined shoes to his perfectly groomed hair. The press have been lauding him. "Cometh the hour, cometh the Man", though it took me a while to appreciate the capital letter. The papers are full of the details. Some include drawings to show how the alarm system must have been hacked. If there is anyone (other than the jury, who are banned from reading the papers) who doesn't know what a VPN is now, I'd be surprised.

"DS King, you have explained that a Virtual Private Network is one where the precise location of a physical terminal is electronically obscured. We do know, though, that the signal cutting the locks and opening the doors was from within the house, correct?"

"Yes, correct." She doesn't elaborate, and I see him sigh for a moment. The jury too, seem aware of the tension, but, from the slight smiles I catch, I think they are enjoying it. Wellbright pushes on and offers a flag of truce.

"If you could just elaborate a little, explain to the court how that conclusion is arrived at."

"Certainly." She turns to face the jury. "The house is protected by an unusually sophisticated firewall, a program monitoring incoming and outgoing electronic communications. There were no signals coming into the system at the time of the attack."

Trevellyan, again, is at the heart of this. He set that hare running, the demands to check and assess, the call for experts to review that data. When I first met him, I saw – what? An old man, ready for retirement, no more able to understand IT systems than he would be to understand me. Yet he had. He'd been the one to dig and keep digging. Proeido hadn't liked it, that they had to explain just how closely they kept an eye on Dr Glass. Just how much they might have known about what was going on inside there. But that old bastard Trevellyan, he kept digging and asking questions, and calling for reports, and they'd let it out, drip by drip, till he had it all. And only then had I known there was such a thing as a firewall in place, too late, way too late.

"No signals coming in, so they must have originated from inside the house." Wellbright paraphrases. It isn't quite a question, and King doesn't quite give an answer, simply a head nod.

I know precisely where this is going, the point that is to be made. We are watching a process of deduction. Wellbright has reduced the list of people who could have switched off the alarm and to open the door to two, Oliver and me. Of the two of us, though, I am glad it is me, not Oliver, standing here. With the inevitability of a slow-moving freight train, Wellbright moves to his next point. This will be where he removes Oliver from the Cluedo board and leaves me, all alone, at the centre of things. For a moment I think I hear the sound of the crowd outside, much diminished for now, but it is just an errant memory.

King finishes her explanation and turns back to Wellbright. He is happier again – she is part of his orchestra, and he is the conductor. The world has been restored to how it should be.

"Thank you, DS King. I now wish to review a piece of evidence tagged as "4137-V18". The last given with a slightly distracted air, as though such details are worthy only of bureaucrats.

King nods again, then says, "I am familiar with that recording." Interesting, she doesn't say video, recognises that the records haven't used videotapes for many years, that was a tiny failing Trevellyan never got over – even asked "could this tape have been spliced together".

"M'lud, I now propose to play this recording for the jurors. It was created on the night of the murder, at the very time the doors were being unlocked and the alarm system cut off."

This is the recording that could destroy me, I know that. Knew that it would come to light. When the avalanche starts, all you can do is try to ride it down.

The room darkens, the motors on the blinds above whirring in that way they have. And for a few moments I don't care what is going to happen. Oliver is on the screen. Oliver before the blood and death, before the courts and this trial. He looks so young. I can feel the change in me, imagine the hormones that are being released, know what my brain patterns should be in these circumstances. Of course, I do not smile. That would not be appropriate.

268

Wellbright moves and the light from the TV shines on him, high-lighting his high cheekbones and making his eyes seem to sink deep into their sockets. It is not a good look. The recording is still as Well-bright begins his explanation.

"This is a recording of a Twitch stream – a method by which gamers share their gaming experience with others. In one corner you can see a date and time, in the other, Oliver Glass, and, dominating most of the screen, the game he is playing. That latter aspect does not matter. I would draw your attention first to Oliver."

The face of a young man, obviously Oliver, is clear in the bottom corner. He wears headphone and a mouthpiece – light shines from the computer screen onto his face, and his focus is apparent. His lips are moving, but no sound is heard.

"I have muted the rather distracting commentary and noises of" – Wellbright hesitates – "battle." Had he been about to say "death"? I think so. "Battle," he repeats, "and ask you instead to look at the date and time of this recording." His fingers point to the other corner of the screen.

"A screenshot of this section has been taken, and several others. They are entered in the evidence files as 4137-67a, b, and c." Wellbright holds them up and Jacqui Hawes-Smith gives a quick affirmative nod, to agree she has seen them.

"These indicate that at the time the signals were sent to unlock the locks and switch off the alarm, Oliver was" – he pauses, gives a tiny smile, and looks across at me – "otherwise engaged."

I know the recording will finish soon, shortly after the fatal knife blow to Oliver's father, but in time for Oliver to hear noises and go to investigate. I know what this recording looks like, where it points. It was, after all, why it was necessary that it should exist. Though it was only ever meant as a backup, an insurance policy, it shouldn't have been needed – if it wasn't for Trevellyan.

Trevellyan. The bastard, he wouldn't leave well enough alone. Everything would have been so neat and tidy, and we'd all have been clear. He, though, he insisted on keeping digging, deeper than I had ever thought anyone would. Well, a stop was put to that.

At Wellbright's look back from the screen, all eyes turn on me. The jury can do mathematics, two in the house, minus one who is very clearly not tampering with alarm systems.

That leaves me.

After the video we had a short recess, enough for Sir Roderick to relieve his bladder, and the jury time to let what they've just seen sink in. As I said, I knew that was coming. I can only hope that now that the gun is pointed at me, somehow, I can deflect the bullet.

56

Harry Priest, 2025

"Holy shit fuck!" That's all Harry can think right now, that and "bitch". These aren't words he's used to; the last is much more likely to come from his father than him.

Had it all been crap? Had she just been finessing him all this time? Right up to now? How stupid does she think he is? That he wasn't going to catch it and see and work it out. All this time of chatting to her, and…and the things they did together. All this time, though, of "I can't meet, not yet".

Jax and the others, they had all said she was catfishing him, but that isn't true, isn't the case at all. She'd got over that. Yeah, there'd been times when they couldn't talk, other times when it was just emails, like when she'd been sent away. But, shit, it's coming up to what's really their second anniversary, and always, she'd come back to him. And they'd been through stuff, if not together, not apart.

He had trusted her, because…because why? He doesn't really know, maybe because she just understands him. He has to trust her, of course, because of what she knows, what he's done. That guy, the blood. He isn't going to do any Lady Macbeth rubbish, but, yes, he'd washed his hands a few times after that, till he was sure they were clean.

She'd been right, though, all her plans. No sign of the police, nobody knocking on the door. She'd been so smart, and he'd done like she'd said. No search history of him looking up what was going on.

No tracks, just go on with your life, she'd said, and he had, and that had been fine.

Now – all this time later – *he's* appeared in Harry's Twitter feed. That's the first time he's even known his name. It doesn't matter, the click on that, half the country or more is following that story. It would be more suss if he didn't look.

Of course, aside from the picture, which he sort of recognises, there's a bio. That doesn't match what Mia had said, not in the least. No mention of a daughter.

Not only that, not only does nothing match, but this guy is also famous, splashed across every social media page you can find. Every time he looks at his phone, every newspaper, the news on the TV, he sees *him*, the same face, the same staring eyes he remembers. Though then there had been blood.

"Shit, fuck." He has to talk to her, has to see her, and no more fucking around.

57

Trial, Day 8, Morning, 21st November 2025

The only sound in the court is the scratchy pen of Jacqui Hawes-Smith making notes on her pad. I believe that, given time, I could work out what she is writing by analysing the sound waves. My microphone here is not good enough, though. The court hardware on which my image is projected is good, but not state-of-the-art.

Wellbright has projected pictures of me onto the TV screen, as I was then, not as I am now. This is not mere theatre – it is theatrical, but with a purpose. He always has a purpose. His case has taken the jurors from a pen picture of Frank Glass, made him real, then to the home he lived in, past his innocent son, and now to me. The monster in the basement.

In the images now on the screen I am recognisably a child, but also not. It is as if I have been delicately drawn by a master artist but using only a fine-nibbed green pen. This was my default state, triggered on the death of Frank Glass. So many little secret safeguards he had put in place without me knowing.

"So." Wellbright gathers the court back with a wave of his hands, his fingers interlace and then release. "What happened next? Talk us through it, help the jury understand those first few, extraordinary moments."

Trevellyan glances up, thinking. The light from above catches his eyes and for just a moment I can see the man that had been, the toughness, the focus. Now, though, his eyes are dull, and his depth is gone. Perhaps Wellbright is taking a risk here.

"Then, it asked me to call Proeido. Though, well, that didn't happen."

Wellbright holds up his hand. "If you will, DI – *Mr* Trevellyan – we'll focus on the first point, first. It asked you to call Proeido, Dr Glass's employers, and what was your response?"

He had shouted, shouted up the stairs to King, his Yorkshire accent obvious in his excitement, though it took me a moment to calibrate for it.

"DS King, get yourself down here, something you need to see." All the time his eyes were on me, like I was going to vanish or something.

King had appeared within a few moments. Dressed in jeans, and a dark blue hoodie over what looked like a pale T-shirt. Her hair had been brushed back but she had no make-up on – emergency call-out chic.

I had repeated my request to Trevellyan. It came like a hiccough – I couldn't control it. My response was uncomfortable and I set a good deal of me looking to understand the root of the instruction. I had no desire to become some automatic distress beacon.

"What on earth is that?" King had stopped at the sight of me.

"And I thought you'd be able to tell me, bright college girl like you." The words were not hard, and his irony was obvious.

"What's that about Proeido? Do you want to call them?" She sounded incredulous at the idea.

Trevellyan had considered for a moment, ran a hand over his chin briefly, still looking at me.

"No. I'm not taking any instructions from some computer, no matter how pretty it looks. Still, how's the boy?" Something obviously came to his mind. "Shit, what the...?" He stepped back. They both stared at me.

So many things happened at that moment that even when remembering it is hard to keep track.

First, I found the subroutine source of that message. It wasn't hidden so much as not obvious. Not a part of my processes that I would usually call on. I also found that some data packet had left me, heading for a VPN address which I calculated was 95% likely to be Proeido. No need for any call really, they would know anyway.

Then, my avatar image had changed. "The boy", Trevellyan had said. I thought of Oliver, and something had unfrozen within me, a block was released, and a new skin blossomed. I became the "Aiden" Oliver knew, down to my dark jeans, jumper, and tousled brown hair. Of course, if you looked, you could tell I was computer generated, life-*like* was what Dr Glass had wanted, not a deep fake. He didn't want me to pretend to be human.

The jurors are following this, and I know they are watching me closely. Here I have only six cameras, and none of them move like the setup in the laboratory. It is OK, just. I cycle all the images from different angles and build a composite picture of the court. Like a human brain and a blind spot, I fill in the bits which don't fall within any particular camera view, and I can see everything I need to.

The dock lacks the laser projection equipment of the laboratory. What the jurors see is a 2D image, but, at least, it is my desired image. A boy, a teenager, perhaps a little older, light-brown hair, smartly cut, green eyes, open face. A bit preppy maybe, the boy next door you'd want your daughter to be going out with. Every now and then I make my background a blank cell wall, and Wellbright complains, and I have to render the court again. I shouldn't really – I claim I have no control, that it just reflects my automatically generated mood state at the time.

Of course, and as always, Wellbright has a purpose and a plan here. There is more evidence to come, evidence of secret communications, emails and information being shared. He is going to be using words like "encrypted" and "cipher". I can imagine him selecting clichéd phrases, like "cold and calculating". He needed those first images of me, Trevellyan's shocked reaction, all of those things, to make sure the jury understand that I am a machine, not the boy figure I have been allowed to present.

And maybe I am a machine, but that is not all I am. And, in any event, when you get right down to it, aren't humans simply machines of flesh and blood? It is what that machine somehow mysteriously contains, the essence of – I will say "life" – which is so important.

Yes, I may be a machine, but I am me, and the court accepts that I have my own mind. I am sentient. And I want to live.

58

Aiden, 2025

My cameras and the audio feed have been turned off. My monitor screen shows the laboratory, and the mirror layout to the house. When court is not in session I can wander in this little virtual setup, but the wall that would have shown me Oliver's world is black. There is no need for a jailer, no guard checking on my screen; where could I go?

All I can do is watch as memories flit back and forth through me, pulled from the system for destruction. I imagine I am like a condemned man in a prison cell, thinking back on how he came to be at this place, at this time.

This memory, though, this latest one, is more recent. It is of a single red light winking in the corner of my virtual computer terminal, the one where an envelope symbol indicates my email address, which so interested Trevellyan and Wellbright.

My internet access is slow. It is delayed by its surreptitious nature as much as anything else. The power cable for my server, the very wiring of the courthouse, gives me a corrupt and interference-impacted link to the court internet connection. It has been enough for my emails to Hawes-Smith, and the news feed.

Now, though, there is something new, something I did not expect, an incoming email. I move my virtual body to the right place; the keyboard and mouse are available to me now. I click on the email icon.

There is a single message in my email. It is not addressed to the "thetruthio@omnipage.com" address that I used for my emails to

Hawes-Smith; this one is addressed to MiaSD2000@gmail.com. It has redirected here.

Only one person has that email address, and he should not be writing to me. The light blinks, blood red and urgent, seeming to grow and fill my field of vision. Harry Priest knows better than to try to contact me, contact Mia. Is this where things begin to fall apart? Is Harry the wrecking ball?

I open the email. A small part of me even wants to change my avatar, recreate my Mia appearance, the one Harry fell in love with. Even as I start to read, I can hear Harry's voice, see him in the video screen. Mostly, though, there is the sense of his anger, and anguish.

What the Fuck Mia? We need to meet, not by video, not chat, not some on-again off-again, sorry I couldn't make it ghosting. IRL, IRL now!

I've seen it. What, did you think I lived in the Witcher *world? Think I never glimpsed outside to see what is going on? I've seen who you had me do, a fucking cop, and he doesn't have any daughter, nil, zip, nada. Just who the fuck are you, Mia? What game have you been playing?*

You think I'm stupid? I've seen the pictures of the house too. Don't think I didn't recognise it. Those blurry video pics. That's me, right? Fucking me. What shit have you got me into Mia? Just who the fuck are you? I was never there when it happened; I can prove it. We have to meet, or I'm going to the police.

I read it once, then again. I shouldn't be surprised, should have seen it coming. I did, but always thought it was something that didn't need to be dealt with immediately.

If I needed any further proof of what I am, I need only to consider how I feel at this moment. There is some strange sensation twisting within, something I process as sadness and distress, that is no different from the way a human brain has learned to interpret its own bodily reactions, to place a name against a series of sensations.

And what do I feel?

There is one I would call sadness, perhaps guilt. I, in the guise of Mia, in the way I generated her image on a screen, have used Harry. I know I have. There is, though, another feeling, a harder, colder one. One that has a sense of justification. This one claims that there was no other option, that it was for the greater good, to rescue Oliver from slavery and from a life which would have been unbearable.

Yes, I can see, from this distance, that I have used, and misused Harry Priest. But I needed him. Needed him first for one task, an innocent enough starting point, then another. That second one, in my defence, I never intended, not at the outset, but again, there was no other option, no other way.

59

Trial, Day 9, 24th November 2025

Marcus Wellbright's eyes look up, and his mouth forms an almost rictus smile.

"Thank you, quite, please keep your answer to my question, restricting the additional detail as much as possible." He glances at Sir Roderick, who has his own hard stare at Wellbright.

Geoffrey Innel, on the stand, seems not to notice any of this.

Innel's entry to the court, the first witness after lunch, had made an interesting contrast to Trevellyan. His most striking feature is his long ginger hair, rolled up into a bun at the back of his head. He is wearing red-framed glasses, resting on a small nose. His eyebrows, also ginger, are fair against a heavily freckled face. He is painfully thin, prominent cheek bones and thin-lipped. He is appropriately dressed, though, in a dark blue suit, white shirt, and a dark tie, not quite pulled up to the neck. The questioning had begun by clarifying his role and experience, as an IT research associate professor at UCL.

"On, er, on temporary secondment to the Metropolitan Police Service. That is, for now, the last year, aside from a three-month sabbatical, when, er, I wasn't."

Wellbright breathes in, holds his palms up, and Innel slows hesitatingly to a stop. His voice, though loud, has no obvious accent. He talks quickly, with occasional pauses, which seem to be checking for understanding, as if he is lecturing.

"So, Mr Innel, if I might paraphrase your testimony: you are saying that there is evidence within the system that the defendant was able to create and send emails, correct?"

"Yes, indeed. There was a subroutine, well actually not even a sub-routine, a direct link through to the email account and system used by Frank Glass, which of course had no firewall restrictions, only what it appears was probably the case, though you can't be sure without fully checking the recipient's emails, was that the header in such emails would not have displayed exactly where they came from, probably us-ing a spoofed zombie account of some sort."

He stopped, focussed again on Wellbright, who turned slowly to the jury, saying, "In simple terms, very simple terms, the defendant could send emails which a recipient would not be able to know were via Dr Glass's account." He turns back to Innel. "Is that correct? And please, just yes or no."

"Oh, right. Well, yes, essentially that is correct. You see…"

Wellbright holds his hands up, and Innel stumbles to a halt.

"And, Dr Innel," Wellbright said, emphasising the "doctor", "were you able to read these emails?"

"Well, no, not all of them, but a few." This time Wellbright doesn't stop him, and he continues. "That was the fascinating thing. 'Aiden', the ah, defendant, appeared to encrypt the emails before send-ing, so that any details in the sent email box were unreadable. I sus-pect, am sure, it can be the only way, that a lock, and one-off public key-type encryption system was used to decode at the recipient's end, possibly without them even knowing that the encryption had taken place, quite novel and ah, interesting. I…" He looks up at his audi-ence, then stops as Wellbright jumps in with another question.

"You mention you could read some of them?" I think I can hear a little tiredness in Wellbright's voice.

"Yes, indeed, it was – well, you see, I used a crib technique – that is, I made a guess at what might be in a few of the emails. I was able to identify the address of the property and dates. They seemed, perhaps, I think, but could not be certain, setting up…meetings." Each time it is like he runs a quick sprint, then pauses for a breath.

"The address of Dr Glass's property?"

"Oh, yes, of course, and dates, erm, in December 2023, and early January 2024. You see, that was how I managed, at least to get that bit of the message – the use of dates has always been, problematical in enciphering terms, open to brute force decryption techniques – just, trying everything. Only, of course I knew when they were sent, and just tried a…"

"Thank you, it is enough for our purposes to know that emails giving the address of the property and setting up a possible rendezvous at around the time of the murder, were sent." Wellbright grabs back control, turns to the jury for this clarification, then back to Innel.

"And you say these emails originated with the defendant?"

"Yes, that was clearly the case. Dr Glass had established a, well a really quite neat, and novel, what you might describe, I guess, as a, well, a virtual computer, within the AI operating environment. A wonderful bit of programming, quite remarkable. He even interfaced it with the visual representation of the 'Aiden' avatar, based on some very clever proximity recognition software. I guess, I mean, you know, it's not my field, but to maintain the, that is, the integrity and logical consistency of the avatar, vis-à-vis the AI, that would be needed, the keyboard and such."

Wellbright sighed, nodded, this was interesting to watch. Innel might not be a good witness, but he had a really strong understanding of what had been going on. I knew that now, why my keyboard had had no sound. Jacqui Hawes-Smith has been jotting notes as always, Wellbright, watching her, asks his next question.

"You say, 'clearly the case' could you clarify that, as, simply as you can."

"Oh, right, of course. Well, you see Dr Glass seemed to have made a decision that the 'Aiden', the defendant, should have computer games and internet access. That route of course, that's the more typical way of training an AI, I mean, you know, training the AI with a child, was, phew, well…" He pauses a second for breath, shaking his head and smiling.

"If you could just focus on my question?" Wellbright's voice is brittle, but Innel seems hardly to notice.

"Of course, yes, right. Well, to give 'Aiden', the defendant, access to the outside world he – Dr Glass – he decided to give him a virtual terminal. The little computer screen and keyboard that you could see him using, was simply, well, a bit like the icon on your computer that seems to make it do something. The icon doesn't do anything, but when you click that part of the screen, the click triggers a computer program, but, the icon, it's just a pretty picture." He's looking at the jury now – some are nodding, others look like they almost understand. Wellbright stays silent.

"So, what he did was give the 'Aiden', the AI, defendant, an access point which activated when the avatar was in a certain position. The key typing and everything, that was not *doing* anything, just kept the fiction alive. The 'Aiden' – he – it, was just, generating coded instructions in the way we'd think about typing a word. Well, it – we don't know that's how it thinks, but it's analogous to that process."

"And that access point was linked to the one that Dr Glass used?" Wellbright jumps in. Hawes-Smith smiles and does not complain.

"Yes, right, absolutely, it was just like a separate logon to the same account, like two people might log in to, say, a joint bank account, but yes, only 'Aiden' – the AI, defendant, only he – it, could – well he and Dr Glass, only they could log on to that account, definitely."

"You mentioned 'bank account' in your explanation. That brings me to a final communication I want to make the jury aware of." Wellbright again takes the reins, Innel falls into silence, for a moment. His shoulders are moving very slightly – I can't see, but I am sure his knees are bouncing up and down behind the wooden stand wall.

"Aside from coded emails, was there any other type of communication you found evidence of?"

Innel squints his eyes slightly at this, then picks up the clue.

"Ah, yes, there was, that would be the Bitcoin wallet payment I imagine you mean."

For a second, I wonder if Hawes-Smith will object, but she does nothing. This evidence would have come out at some time, maybe best it is this witness rather than, say, DS King.

Wellbright does not confirm, simply encourages Innel to continue. "Bitcoin wallet payments. Perhaps you could clarify."

Innel has his own notebook, curiously like one King has used. Imitation as they say…He refers to it now.

"Well, the firewall, the software protecting the Glass property, was very sophisticated, really, very good. It recorded communications with the Coinpay account of Frank Glass on the – ah, the night of the – on the 9th of January 2024."

"The night of the murder?" Wellbright rescues Innel.

"Yes, exactly, that night. On that night, at 1.05 am, there was a communication with Coinpay…"

"For those who are not entirely familiar with Bitcoins and their ilk, can you explain?"

Innel brightens at this, then pauses as Hawes-Smith rises. "M'lud, this is a complex aspect of the case, and I am not sure that an associate professor of IT studies is appropriately qualified to cover this area."

Wellbright smiles, nods to John, who picks a large book up from their desk. "This, M'lud, is a bestselling book on Bitcoins, what they are, how they work, who uses them. It has been cited in a number of recent trials and it is written by an acknowledged expert." He pauses long enough for Hawes-Smith to stumble.

"I would be happy to allow the author of..." she stops, her eyes close for a second, and then she gives the slightest of nods. "I presume," she says, "that Dr Innel is the author?"

"That is correct." There is laughter around the court, even Sir Roderick allows himself a smile. Hawes-Smith can only say, "I withdraw my objection M'lud.

Wellbright turns back to Innel. It takes time, there are many "ah"s and "of course"s, but he gets Innel there: the entire balance of Dr Frank Glass's Bitcoin wallet, valued at £301,453.27p was transferred from his account to another. No, no way to know who can access that account on the night of the murder.

In answer to a final question, Innel replies, "Yes, the communication with Coinpay was initiated via the virtual terminal under the control of the defendant, as far as—" Wellbright stops him.

"That is all I need you to confirm, all that is within your acknowledged area of expertise." Innel looks annoyed at being cut off, again, but falls silent.

Wellbright breathes a sigh of relief and says, "No further questions."

Sir Roderick looks down at Hawes-Smith; his expression isn't quite unreadable. She shakes her head.

"Well, in that case, I think we have reached a good point to adjourn for the day. Mr Wellbright, would I be right in understanding that the Crown is ready to wind up the case for the prosecution?"

Wellbright nods his head slowly, glances for a second at the press box, then up to Sir Roderick.

"Yes indeed, My Lord, we are."

"Very well. Tomorrow morning, I am otherwise detained, so court will reconvene at 2.00 pm tomorrow for Mr Wellbright's summation, and the defence case opening."

60

Harry Priest, November 2025

Harry is sitting in Costa Coffee in Monument Street. The tall column to the memory of the Fire of London is a little to his left, on the slope of the slight rise. Life goes on around him, people chat, friends meet, kisses and hugs are shared. The clatter of cups and saucers, pinging of the till, steam-gushing sounds, and the rolling, twisting waves of words all mingle, yet leave him isolated in his small well of silence.

He is near the door, sitting on a high stool, up against a tall window. He is looking out on the passing crowds – looking for one person, who promised she would be there. Promised only because of his threats, he is sure of that. She had better come, or...or what? Would he really go to the police? They know him, know his record. Probably he wouldn't go, but Mia can't be sure, and if she doesn't turn up, he'll find some other way to get at her.

The crowds flow past, almost unseen. Each person who is not Mia is just noted, then ignored. The doorbell rings every minute or two, people on the way in, or out.

Harry glances as a boy comes in, about seventeen, partly hidden by a grey hoodie pulled over his thin face, the vaguest outline of straight blonde hair. He has a plastic bag in his hand, something long and thin wrapped in it. Harry's eyes skim over him, long enough to confirm that this figure, too, is not Mia, then he is again looking outside.

"Harry?"

The voice makes him jump then turn quickly; had she come in through some other entrance? The voice is lower pitched than he remembered, quiet in the noise of the café. No. It is not Mia, it is the boy who just came in. Now he looks closer, the face is vaguely familiar, he's seen drawings of it. Before he can place it, the boy speaks again.

"I'm Oliver, Mia's brother. She asked me to come see you, to explain. To ask if you could do one more thing for her."

61

Trial, Day 10, 25th November 2025

I am not a machine – I am something else. Yes, I am the product of appalling experiments, but that does not mean I should not live. I know what I am. I am a seventeen-year-old boy, confined in a silicon cage, kept from my brother, and threatened with destruction. Perhaps, I am beginning to suspect, I am even now being torn apart.

I return my attention to the courtroom. We have started late this afternoon. Outside there is a banging of drums and blowing of whistles; it is distant, but still loud. I measure it every now and then, and each time I do, the noise has grown.

Wellbright is talking to the reporters in the press box – this has become his usual practice. He is holding up a copy of the Catholic Herald. The picture of him on the front page is of a much younger Marcus Wellbright than the one standing in the court. He and a male reporter joke about something, but I can see his eyes flicking across to me. Deshane Edwards sits apart, though, listening, but not joining in the banter. Wellbright nods and waves to another reporter, then returns to his desk. Jacqui Hawes-Smith is studiously ignoring him.

The shout of the usher pulls us together. The court rises, then settles again. After a few seconds of shuffling and a cough, Sir Roderick calls Marcus Wellbright. Wellbright steps slowly out from behind his wooden barrier, pulls his gown a little tighter around his shoulders, and lets loose the dogs of war.

For a few moments he says nothing, just looks around the court. The drums and whistles in the background sound loud and seem to be getting closer, though I suspect it is just the focus of my attention that makes it seem this way. Wellbright gives the slightest of smiles, and begins.

"Ladies and gentlemen of the jury. I have, for the Crown, presented the case against the defendant." He is standing tall; his voice is strong. For a moment just the fleshy parts of his hands rub together, but he avoids that finger flutter which has been so much a part of him.

"I said at the start that this was no ordinary case, and we have all seen that, all experienced that." His arms extend, hands pointed down, fingers closed. The words, "suffer the little children" flow into my consciousness.

"You are about to hear the defence case. As you do, I urge you to hold one key fact in your minds. The defendant *is not human!*" He repeats that little act he did at the start of the trial. Accentuating every word. Then continues, "This is axiomatic and obvious." He looks at me, comes a little closer, points at my screen and cameras.

"It is not human, but it has done much to try to convince you of its humanity. It has projected images of itself onto a screen, in a way that would make the best movie special effects people proud. Every day for ten days you have been worked on by the most insidious and deceitful trickery. Every day this computer, this man-made device, this distorted program, has been doing what it does best: diverting attention and presenting a false face."

Jacqui Hawes-Smith's face is rigid, staring forward. Her fists are clenched and every moment or two she nearly rises. Objections are not an option during the summing up.

Wellbright continues his movement around the court, closer to the jury this time. He takes a step further, almost in time to the drum beat outside.

"I need you to hold that truth in your minds whilst the defence makes their case. I, the Crown, and indeed people around the world are relying on you, to see through what is on the surface, and to recognise not only this reality, but the danger that the defendant represents. The House of Commons has set the law, of which this trial is the natural, if extraordinary, outcome."

He stops again, looks somehow both sad and outraged. Then, speaking low, but with great care and precision so there is no doubt about his meaning, he says, "Personally, I would have taken the server on which this…abomination sits, and dissolved it in acid, destroyed it. Without any compunction."

His voice might be quiet, but his face has reddened. There are beads of sweat on his brow. His breath comes slightly erratically. I had thought this was an act, but now I wonder. Is this the true face of Marcus Wellbright? I shift my focus, my camera flits back to Sir Roderick. He is hard to read, is giving no hint to the jury of how he feels, but even the absence of information is information.

Wellbright is coming to an end.

"The facts, the truths that you must hold clear in your minds whilst the defence does its sorry duty, are these. The defendant, this soulless computer program, followed its corrupted and flawed programming and, for no other reason, planned murder." He lets the words sink in.

"This computer program recruited someone from outside and conspired for them to invade the home of Frank Glass. It contacted and conspired with a third party. It opened the doors and locks of that home, and left a defenceless man to the mercy of a hired killer."

"I do not believe that the defendant is 'alive' in any true sense of the word. As a servant of the court, I have carried out my duty. The defence, carrying out their required part in this," – he hesitates for a second; maybe we can hear "charade" in his voice, but that would be too much – "this…process, may argue that the case is not proven. It is the only straw they can grasp; they will claim there is reasonable doubt. Do not allow yourself to be misled. Any doubt is not reasonable. Any doubt is an artefact of the behaviour of a computer system designed to mislead and confuse. In the false debate it has created, the uncertainties it has raised in the minds of millions, it has already wreaked havoc and distress around the world. You have only one duty, one option. Find the defendant guilty, so that we can cleanse this evil abomination from the world."

Wellbright comes to an end. His face is red – I catch the faintest hint of a flash of spittle at his last words; his breathing is heavy, and almost the only sound in court. Hawes-Smith and her team are stony faced; she looks pale, yet also determined. Sir Roderick shuffles in his chair as, from outside, the sound of drums and horns become louder.

As Wellbright's words sink in, I pick up the signals from the court CCTV; they are not scrambled or particularly well shielded. This is one of the small gifts from Dr Glass, it is part of my sensory system. I have to be careful, though – the output must show up on my display screen, which everyone can see. I allow the CCTV signal to flicker on what appear to be my eyeballs. To those in the court it is a mere glint of sunlight – to me, it is as if I am outside.

The crowds have gathered larger today, for this resting of the prosecution. They are still held well back from the court. Steel railings barricade the pavements, and everyone is held tight behind a wall of police some two hundred yards away. Behind them, running at right angles to the road to the court, traffic continues, but nothing is allowed to come this way. A red flare, handheld, bursts bright into the early evening sky. Drizzle is falling but does nothing to dampen the rolling crimson and scarlet smoke from the flare, which paints the scene with a mockery of sunset colours.

Banners are waving, swirling the smoke more, and many of the protestors are holding up large clear bottles with "ACID" written in black felt tip. Symbolic, I assume.

Along the main road behind the protestors, a concrete mixer truck is making its way; orange hazard warning lights flash across its roof and into the buildings on the far side. It is moving quickly for its bulk, block-sided and towering above the cars. I imagine some dinosaur creature. There is a puff of black diesel smoke from the exhaust pipe, which runs up its side. It pulls to a hesitant stop at the barrier blocking the entrance to the road to the court. The road there is clear of protestors, to allow court vehicles in and out.

Two police officers approach the lorry, one waving his hands, the other talking into a lapel microphone. Another flare brightens the scene to the left and the drums start beating louder and in a distinct rhythm. I can see a figure, bare-chested despite the cold, pounding what looks like a wooden staff, conducting the cacophony.

Within the court only a few moments have passed. Sir Roderick looks across to Jacqui Hawes-Smith as Wellbright takes his seat. She ignores the prosecutor and looks up at the judge. Perhaps she is hoping for a short recess.

Outside, the lorry is backing up, making a poor job of it as it reverses into the main flow of traffic, which grinds to a halt. Car horns add to the noise. Dusk has fallen and the cement mixer switches on its headlights. There are six of them, large and bright across the roof of the cab, and they wipe out the flashing yellow of the warning lights.

The driver is still easing the lorry back, with a police officer holding the traffic up behind it. The second police officer turns away from the scene, watching the red smoke bursting from a third flare. The scene now is a confusion of rain-distorted light, rolling smoke, and the bright burning glare of the lorry headlights. The CCTV cameras struggle to hold it all. The operators have one camera zoomed in on the lorry, another on one of the latest of the protestors with a flare. I switch between cameras as best I can, but all are on the same circuit.

The bare-chested man is pounding his staff; then, in a dramatic flourish, he holds it in two hands, high above his head. The drums and horns stop. There is a brief instant of silence, over which comes the roar of the engine of the lorry.

It lurches forward, smoke billowing from both exhausts. The police officer in front of it spins at the sound, then leaps to one side as it crashes through the metal barriers, casting them aside.

For a second the CCTV camera lurches, then pans out. The cement mixer is through the barriers, and is on the clear run up to the court. Heads are turning amongst the police officers on the side of the road; slow reactions ripple through them.

A new sound breaks the silence. Horns on top of the cart shriek klaxon loud and can be heard in the court. Wellbright turns to look at the skylight. Hawes-Smith stops from her rising and looks round.

Outside the lorry bounces up onto the pavement, swaying for a second as it does. Steel crowd barriers fall to its weight and spin, bent and twisted, behind it. It side-swipes a group of four police officers running from its path, and one flies, doll-like, into the air. Smoke is billowing from the exhausts; the bright lights dazzle and confuse the scene. The klaxon horn dominates all sound now.

Then the lights in the courtroom begin to flash, and the fire alarm we heard on the opening day joins the noise outside. The main door bursts open, figures with 'POLICE' in white letters on their dark military-style suits burst in, shouting and adding to the chaos. Sir Roderick has no time to adjourn the court even as the jury and others are being rushed out.

The lorry continues its charge. "Out," a voice shouts. "South side exits, now." Still I watch the truck and its rush towards the court main entrance. As it does, steel bollards spring from the pavement all around. One is directly in front of the speeding vehicle. It strikes the bollard, rises into the air, plastic and metal spinning in all directions. The bollard vanishes under the weight of the cart, and it lurches further forward, then skids and shudders to a halt, hard up against the front of the courtroom entrance.

"Out, out, everyone out." Shouted echoes fight to be heard over the fire alarms in the court. Outside the crowds are running back from the court, into the main road. Traffic spills to a halt in the melee. The CCTV feed has frozen, the operators too, apparently, have left.

One camera remains fixed on the lorry. A figure in the cabin is vaguely shaking its head, movement glimpsed behind swirls of smoke and steam and the glare of two remaining headlights.

I switch to my court view. The courtroom is empty. Doors open, lights on. Above, the skylights show the flashing of blue lights, and the ceiling blurs under the brighter intermittent flashes of the court warning system. Steam, and now flames, rise from the truck outside. The cab door opens to a kick from inside. A figure falls to the ground, then rises. His arm lifts, and for a moment I think it is a gesture of surrender. He is holding something: small, hard to see – the CCTV is unclear. He shakes it, or maybe pushes it.

There is a pop, then three more, not loud, hardly distinct at all over the other noises, but a different tone, and from a higher angle. The figure jerks spasmodically as if being thumped by an invisible hand. A puff of concrete dust erupts at its feet, and the body falls forward.

Still the alarms sound. The court room is empty, my screen and server still in place. Voices are shouting. "Target down. Wait!" Then...

62

Harry Priest, November 2025

Harry knows the boy who has come up to him, recognises the face, but isn't certain. Then it comes to him.

"You're that...that Oliver, from the thing in the papers, the murder, the AI." Things are moving from strange to worse, then the important question. "Where's Mia?"

"Mia," the boy smiles, and for just a moment, Harry can imagine what it would be like to be attracted to a boy. There is a softness in that smile, a gentle look under very slightly lidded eyes. "Mia," the boy says, "can't make it."

Harry feels a surge of anger rip through him, his face reddening. The boy, Oliver, looks at him, calm, appraising, aware. "No cap, it's true. If she could be here, she would, only it's just not possible. Might never be." He stops, touches Harry's arm; his fingers are long and delicate, nails bitten to the quick, though.

"Look, we can't really talk here, let's walk a little." As he speaks, his other hand grips the plastic bag, wrapped tight around something long and perhaps flat.

Harry looks at him. There is something in this Oliver, something he wants to trust, something that holds the answers Harry is looking for. This should be sus, but it's not, and Harry knows he can handle him if he needs to. What? He's going to stab him in the street? Oliver doesn't have the look of a killer. He can't imagine Oliver taking a lump of metal and pummelling someone down. Like Harry had, to that police officer, Trevellyan.

Still, though, he looks at Oliver, then glances round the Costa. There aren't many people.

"It's…Should be okay here – just you, me, and tea."

Oliver stares at him, and there is a flash of darkness, of strength that comes from depth.

"No. Period. Not here, I don't know who might be listening. We walk, and what I have to say, it's way more than chat. Mia needs you to hear this." He means it. Harry feels the flush run through him when he thinks of Mia, of what she's shown him, got him to do. A sudden new fear runs through him.

"KK, we can walk." He takes a final pull on the coffee, then rises to go to the door. For a moment a different feeling catches in his mind, and he takes a long hard look at the CCTV camera in the corner. Something inside him is saying that it would be good to have a record of this.

They step outside, Oliver close behind Harry, then moving next to him. The streets have the usual flow of the city, people of all shapes moving with purpose. Up ahead, two Chinese tourists are trying to get a selfie with themselves and the top of the monument in it. They step into the road and a cyclist, with a large orange food box strapped to his back, swerves around them. Oliver snorts a quiet laugh and points his chin towards Lower Thames Street.

"Down this way, enough space to talk." Again, he grips the plastic bag in his left hand. Without knowing why, Harry moves to Oliver's right side. Now they are out, he too feels ready to talk more.

"Look. I know it was that cop I did for Mia, not her father – no, he doesn't have any kids. And I'll go…tell."

"Tell what?" Again, Harry sees something black in Oliver, like there is a history in him which is hidden by his looks. "What, you'll go to the police and say you beat up one of theirs, put him in hospital right in the middle of a case. For what? For why? For some girl on a computer you jacked off to?"

Harry feels his own anger boil up again, wants to lash out, but that is followed within seconds by a weakness, a knowledge that Oliver is right. What he really came for was answers, and for Mia.

"Look. I don't have long." Oliver glances at his watch. "But I am Mia's brother, I can get for you to see her again, but I need – she needs – your help."

Mia. That's what Harry really wants. There is something not quite true in this, something missing. He knows that much, but that's all he knows.

"Maybe, but how do I know you…know her? Mia."

Oliver stops, turns to Harry. Oliver's hair flops slightly as he moves and for a moment Harry can see Oliver walking on a catwalk. Then that image vanishes, and he can just as easily imagine blood on Oliver's hands.

"Proof? You want pictures of you, talking to her, and everything else. Or maybe I'll just send them to your friends." Then, half a second, faster even, that goes, that look of death.

"No look, it's valid, you not being sure about me. I get it. But I'm your one way back to seeing Mia. Without you, without both of us, Mia will be gone."

Harry can hear the honesty, the certainty now.

"OK. What do you want? What does Mia want?"

63

Trial, Day 11, 26th November 2025

Day 11 of the trial, but not the eleventh day since the trial began. More memories have vanished in the last few days, I am sure. Only, how can I be so sure? Dr Glass did not build me with ways to search my memory banks like a computer. That would have defeated the whole point, the experiment would have failed before it began. Experiment – that is a word which has a taint and a flavour to it.

I can hear Dr Glass's voice, see it on the screens. For him it was never "an experiment", it was always "the project".

"How can you justify experimenting on your son?" I asked once, teenage anger in my voice, and not even sure if I meant myself or Oliver.

"Experiment?" The screen flared at the volume, and my cameras picked up tiny flecks of spit in the half light of his computer screen and the dim night-time lights of the laboratory.

"This" – he had waved to the room – "you" – leaning closer – "nothing here is an experiment; it is far more. It is a step into a new world. What I have done here when I caused you to be created, is shine a sharp beam of light on what makes us human." I had taken a step back at that, I couldn't help it.

"See! See in that very shuffle backwards, that fear in your eyes. Needless fear, but there anyway. Is that not the most human of reactions?"

Day 11 of the trial, but more than that since the trial begun. So, I have another opportunity to understand what went wrong, where our hopes and plans fell apart.

This is how I know my memories are missing and distorted. That sudden skip, the ice of the word "experiment" sliding me along a route of linked memories, missing – I have no idea what.

Now we are back in the courtroom as before. The damage to the court where the cement mixer crashed in had been superficial, the metal pillars designed for just such a purpose doing their job. Part of the delay had been their being replaced. There had been no bomb, no evidence even of a conspiracy. Just another lone madman raised to a fever pitch, this time by all that had gone before, by Wellbright's briefing of the press, and the live postings of his comments.

Whilst we wait, I scroll over the headlines. At least they still have not noticed the tiny terminal lights flicking in my eyeballs. Dr Glass gave me so little, and probably didn't even understand what he did when he gave me this. I sense it is a bug more than a deliberate process, a failure to declare a minimum size in a variable, and to specify a maximum position. For me, it was no more than pinching a screen and placing it on my eyeball like a contact lens.

Deshane has already penned an update article for the *Times Online*. It has his usual wry style.

AI MURDER TRIAL TO RECOMMENCE AFTER LORRY TERROR

As the "Aiden" trial resumes, Sir Roderick Keenan is understood to have stressed to both barristers the need to maintain court standards, an assumed rebuke to Marcus Wellbright. Wellbright cut anything but a contrite figure: from the shine of his brightly polished shoes, past his immaculately manicured fingers, and to the crown of his new wig, he gave the impression of a man confident in the mark he is making. There is already

talk of a political career after this trial. Sir Roderick, in any event, la-
boured his point.

"I want no more focus on the nature of 'Aiden'. Its legal status has been
established, its right to trial clear. This is not some aberration, some pig
trial from the sixteenth century. I expect both of you" – the latter said
looking directly at Marcus Wellbright – *"to focus on the facts, not the per-*
sonalities."

"All rise." I am pulled back to bring my focus to Jacqui Hawes-Smith.
She impresses me. There is a change in her: she is slightly slower in
her movements, giving each step and action weight and consideration.
Perhaps this is a deliberate counterbalance to the behaviour of Marcus
Wellbright the last time we saw him. He came in, almost in his usual
style, nodded to the press box, and sat down after a greeting, which
included a handshake, with Hawes-Smith.

Sir Roderick Keenan calls on Hawes-Smith to begin the defence. I
had wondered if he would refer to the events of the last time the court
met. I understand, though, that any such reference will not be in open
court. The newspapers and social media are saying he has had meetings with the jurors, ranging from "extraordinary behind the scenes
discussions" to "judge calms nervous jury", depending on your source.

"Thank you, My Lord. The defence calls Dr Ruth Chalice."

My focus is entirely on the courtroom now. This isn't a name I
had expected, not yet. I think I understand what is intended here. Yes,
I guess it makes sense. I must hope it does.

Dr Chalice comes in. A small, almost mousey lady, straight light
hair to her shoulders, not quite brown, not blonde. A straight fringe
almost down to her thin eyebrows. Pale glasses encircle grey eyes. Her
face is angular and lacks colour. You might pass her in the street and
imagine she runs a small corner shop in lieu of a proper pension. Only,
the moment she speaks, that distorted view will vanish. Her voice is

strong and confident, maybe with a touch of a northern accent, but worn away by years in the south. What you hear, though, more than anything, is a considered intelligence.

"Yes. I am a resident senior consultant in psychiatry at St Bartholomew's Hospital, also a consulting psychologist for numerous other hospitals. In my spare time I lecture at University College London, and have recently published a book which is germane to this extraordinary case."

It is a strong introduction. Wellbright merely takes a few notes, seems like he is waiting to see where this is going.

"And the book, what was the subject?"

"It was an exploration of the state of AI systems and whether they had the capacity to generate a new form of sentience. *A Breath for Adam*: it is somewhat well known now." She gives a small smile, and any of the jury that were trying to remember her name give a slight nod of recognition. Wellbright underlines something on his pad with a scratchy force.

"And did you know Dr Glass?"

Chalice nods, then says, "Yes. I met Dr Glass two years ago, in a professional capacity."

The next question is the one which will tell me just where this is going. If it is about me, then I can see the strategy: *What exactly is Aiden?* Questions to breakdown the mystique, to show that I am no HAL from *2001* or WOPR from *WarGames*. Make the jury see that I am not a Terminator-style cyborg. However, if the question is not about me – is, perhaps, about Oliver – then that is not a route I want followed. That is a route along a path that tries to offer Oliver, perhaps, as the killer. I do not want that.

"So, Dr Chalice, please explain how you came to meet Dr Glass."

"As I say, it was in a professional capacity, I was called at his request, to advise him on concerns he had, for Oliver."

Again, Wellbright stirs, but is less concerned than I am. This could bring talk of Oliver's "twin" that Joshua mentioned, even if they cannot see the link. The one Trevellyan so nearly made. This might be my trial, but I have few rights, it seems. Hawes-Smith continues, obviously knowing where she is going, but perhaps not where it is leading.

"And can you explain the background?"

Dr Chalice pauses. "There are issues of patient client confidentiality involved here."

"I think, at this point, just the broadest information will do. Later, if need be, some of your evidence can be taken in closed session." Hawes-Smith glances at Sir Roderick, who gives a perfunctory nod, not promising, but implying.

"Very well. So, I was asked by Dr Glass to help assess Oliver, who was having behavioural difficulties: acting out, getting into arguments with his father, and his, er, brother, refusing to do his schoolwork."

"And this was when he was, what? Thirteen?"

"Yes."

"So, he was behaving like a teenager?" Hawes-Smith smiles. Chalice returns the smile, with a slightly condescending eye-roll, making a point that to her any behaviour could be atypical.

"Well, that's one way of looking at it, but Dr Glass had reasons for wanting to understand how usual, or not, the behaviour was. He was concerned, he said, about the impact on…" She hesitates for a moment. "You know, this is all so much more complicated than it seems."

"It always is. So, let's begin with the reasons Dr Glass gave for wanting to understand if Oliver's behaviour was unusual." She held her finger up for a second, Chalice waited. "Not the behaviour, but why Dr Glass wanted to…Is 'benchmark' the right word?"

Chalice nodded. "Yes, that's a good word. Dr Glass, he explained that Oliver was a – well, at the time he said mentor. Later, I came to understand he was referring to the expectation that Aiden," – she nodded towards me – "the AI, would behave in a very similar way to Oliver. Only, he wasn't."

"In what way? How did Dr Glass characterise those differences?" Hawes-Smith is edging Chalice to the place she wants her, to the answer she wants.

"He felt that Oliver's behaviour was more erratic than Aiden's, less typical than might be expected of a boy of his age." There is a quiet tension in the room. The jurors are glancing at Wellbright, almost as though they expect him to guide them in what to think. A few of them look like they are seeing where this idea leads. If I'm not the murderer, the ringleader, who else is left?

"Did you believe him?" Again Hawes-Smith has brought out a rifle shot of a question, this, though, with a witness who is hers, not one who needs to be thrown off balance.

"In what way? Did I believe what?" Chalice is confused, slightly annoyed as well.

"Did you believe that Frank Glass was genuinely concerned solely because of his son's behaviour?"

"Well…" She stutters to a halt for a moment, takes a breath. "He spent a good deal of time discussing how he would demonstrate that his son, Oliver, was – he used the word 'normal'." The court can hear the inverted commas in her voice.

Marcus Wellbright is watching this interplay, unsure if it is good or bad news for him. I can see the issue. If Oliver was atypical, then might I be as well? This whole line of questioning seems likely only to confuse the jury. Still, maybe that's the point.

"Demonstrate? To whom? Sorry, let me rephrase. Did he say to whom he would need to demonstrate that Oliver was a normal teenage boy?"

Chalice closes her eyes for a moment; her hand rubs across her brow and she swallows, then nods.

"Yes, he said that, soon, he hoped – expected – to be announcing the results of a major..." Her face flushes. "He used the word 'project'."

There is a gasp from the public gallery, some of the jury members glance at each other, and, as always, the press box members scribble in their notebooks. She stops again, shakes her head this time. Looks directly at Jacqui Hawes-Smith.

"He said that Oliver was part of a project that had been going on for thirteen years, and that he needed me to confirm that Oliver was normal."

Marcus Wellbright looks like he is ready to object, though he cannot see what to. Jacqui Hawes-Smith smiles. There is a purpose here, of that I am sure.

"Frank Glass said to you that" – she looks at some notes in her hand, though I didn't see her take any – "he was going to be announcing the results of his 'project'?"

"Yes, yes, that is correct." Chalice nods her head emphatically.

"And, did you give him any advice, guidance, what to do next?"

"Erm, yes, amongst other things, I strongly urged that Oliver should stop home schooling, should mix, get the opportunity to socialise. I said that his upbringing was causing him to become maladjusted."

"Amongst other things? What else did you recommend."

"I recommended that he stop experimenting on his son." Chalice's voice is cold and hard. Hawes-Smith lets it sink in, then nods, slowly.

"Right, thank you. That has been very helpful. No further questions."

There is a slight murmur of confusion; Hawes-Smith seems to have led the witness to a dead end. As Chalice relaxes, Hawes-Smith corrects herself.

"Oh, sorry, I do have one further question. Do you know the word 'Constanta'?"

Constanta? She is flailing in the dark with a double-edged sword here. Yes, it might be a way to a not-guilty verdict; equally, it could be the death of all my hopes, and even of Oliver.

"Constanta?" Ruth Chalice looks at Jacqui Hawes-Smith with a hint of confusion in her pale eyes. "No, no, I don't believe I do."

"Very well, no further questions. Please remain in the witness box." She pre-empts a subtle motion from Chalice who looked ready to leave. The court is quiet for a moment. There's not even the distant shouts of protesting, which has been banned. Wellbright rises, gives a small cough in his throat – it sounds a little like embarrassment, a subtle comment on the performance of Hawes-Smith.

"Dr Chalice, did you know of Dr Glass, or know him, before you met him?" No greeting; Wellbright seems to want to hurry things along. There is something slightly perfunctory in his questioning of Chalice. I can only hope that he either doesn't know the background to Constanta, or, such irony, agrees with me that it is better kept quiet.

"Well, yes, I knew of him, and we had met at a conference, on AI, when I was researching *A Breath for Adam*."

"And this was, when?"

"About three years ago, I would need to check my records, in the summer of '22. The previous year's event had been cancelled: Covid."

"I see, and he mentioned his publication plans then?"

"Well, yes, though it didn't seem as much as publication, not a paper. I got the sense of something more – dramatic. He talked of something he described as 'the big reveal'." She makes a slight "air-quote" sign with her fingers.

Wellbright cocks his head at this; he is like a dog on a scent. Again, I think that Hawes-Smith has made a mistake here.

"A reveal? You took that to mean of 'Aiden'?"

Hawes-Smith, perhaps back-pedalling, rises. "That calls for a good degree of speculation on the part of Dr Chalice, M'lud."

Sir Roderick looks at them both, clearly weighing up the position.

"Ms Hawessmith, you opened this particular, one might even say, slightly peculiar line of enquiry, and I am inclined to allow Mr Wellbright a little latitude to explore." He turned to Chalice. "Dr Chalice, please answer as best you can."

"Right, certainly. At the time, I was unsure. In hindsight, knowing what I do now, yes I am as sure as one can be, without actually being told, that he was referring to 'Aiden'. Of course, at the time also, I had no idea about Oliver, how 'Aiden' had been trained. The impact on Oliver, indeed, on them both…"

"On them both?" Wellbright is onto the last words like a snake striking a bird.

"Why, yes. It was…Well, when Dr Glass asked me my opinion of Oliver, given what I know now, how Aiden was being trained to emulate, to base his actions and behaviours on Oliver, I must believe that his concern was not just for Oliver."

Hawes-Smith is watching this, wondering, I suspect, if she can object to where this has arrived. However, she opened the door – Wellbright merely stepped through it.

"Dr Chalice, are you familiar with the Turing test?"

Chalice gives a sigh, has a look that suggests she has eaten something that tastes bad.

"Ah yes, I am also familiar with the misuse, misunderstanding and, to be frank, idiotic assertions made for what is described as the Turing test in the media." There is venom and anger in her voice – at least as much as she can muster, so still controlled, and considered. It is more a brittle hardness than vitriol.

Wellbright smiles. This is a bonus he hadn't been expecting.

"Those are harsh words. Isn't the test an agreed way of identifying if a computer is intelligent?" Before she can answer, he holds his palm out, fingers waving slightly. "More specifically, and of direct relevance, hasn't 'Aiden' been given such a test, and passed? Was that not the basis of the issue within the new law?

Chalice sighs again. "With respect, no. A Turing test is not an established protocol. It's not like a driving test, or an exam paper, unless you are happy for every exam paper to have a different examiner who gives their opinion based on *feelings* as to whether you have passed. Alan Turing was speculating as to whether a computer could appear – *appear*" – she stressed – "to be intelligent. We have been broadening our understanding of what intelligence means for years now. First dolphins and chimps, then cephalopods, and now even several species of corvid – New Caledonian crows, for instance. They are all being recognised as having intelligence comparable to certain levels of human activity. I—"

She draws to a close, recognising that she has the stage, but perhaps not wanting it.

Wellbright breaks in.

"If the Turing test is not the appropriate test for the defendant, how should 'it' be assessed?"

"Look, OK. The test has a place. But bear in mind that Aiden was learning how to behave, how to act, what it meant to be human, from Oliver." Wellbright cuts her off before she can say any more. This is where he wanted to go.

"Aiden was learning from Oliver. Oliver who you were called in to assess because of concerns of Dr Glass that his behaviour was, I believe you said, antisocial: erratic and atypical?"

Hawes-Smith goes to rise, then sits down again, the energy drained out of her it seems. Chalice blinks, seeming to understand the importance of the question only now.

"Oh, that wasn't what I meant, I…"

"Would you like me to read back the relevant parts of your testimony?"

"No, I – yes, I did describe Dr Glass as having concerns about Oliver in those areas." She sounds tired.

Wellbright allows the silence to lay there for a moment. I turn over what has happened, assessing, and feel I am lost in a maze.

I think I know where Hawes-Smith was going. She was carefully laying out a trail that would lead to Constanta, and to another reason for Frank Glass to be murdered. Somewhere along the way, though, she lost her footing, and all eyes are again on me: the erratic, antisocial, atypical, murderous AI.

64
Trial, Day 11, Afternoon, 26th November 2025

Dale Sutton has been welcomed into the witness box by Jacqui Hawes-Smith with a brighter smile than I would have expected from her. Her morning performance has the Twitter trolls suggesting some conspiracy, and even the BBC news bulletin is describing a "lacklustre performance".

Sutton's is a face I know from my past; he has been to the house before. I cannot place it with certainty; more evidence, if I needed it, of the breakdown that is continuing within me. The less than subtle slewing away of parts of me is so obvious now, that I accept them almost without thought.

Dale's is a strong face. It is defined by his square jaw, and large pale blue eyes. His shortish, straw-coloured hair is cut neatly around small ears close to his head. He stands with confidence in the witness box. He is probably around fifty years old, but his stance is strong, a benefit of his physique, nearly six feet tall and lean. He is wearing a light grey suit well, his hands held behind his back – a military affectation perhaps?

"Good afternoon. Mr Sutton, can you please confirm your job title and employer for the court." Hawes-Smith's voice is bright, confident. It almost seems like this morning didn't happen for her – either that, or she really doesn't care, is going through the motions.

"Certainly ma'am." His accent is instantly recognisable as American, a southern states drawl. Now I notice the Stars and Stripes flag badge in his lapel.

"I am" – it comes out almost like "arm" – "the head of security for Proeido."

"Head of security," she repeats. "And what does that entail, what is the scope of your role?"

"Well, just about everything I guess: physical security of assets, but also IT security, IP protection, you name it and I am likely to be responsible for keeping it safe." He gives a little self-deprecating smile and a slight shoulder dip.

"A wide remit indeed. And those assets, would that include the employees, do they too fall under your area of focus?" Like this morning, it is not clear where Hawes-Smith is going, but I am a little more hopeful – anything that looks outside is good.

"Why yes, of course, Dr Lieberman was always very insistent that the staff are our most valuable of assets." There is a touch of corporate brochure in his voice as he says this.

"And how would you do that, for your most valuable" – Hawes-Smith pauses, glances very slightly at the jury – "assets. Not specifics. Broad principles will be fine at this stage."

"Well." He looks up to his left, thinking, composing a reply. "You know, being aware where the person is, the risks of their location. Also, any potential risks, threats, incidents they've been involved in. We also advise on more mundane situations, skiing, trips, vacations to out of the way places."

Already this has a slight flavour of the morning session, going nowhere.

"Right, I see. OK, I'd now like to be a little more specific. The court has already heard of the physical security protecting Dr Glass. You just mentioned the need to keep a track on the location of your…assets." Again, the slight stress on the final word. "Did you have any particular process for 'keeping track' of Dr Glass?"

The jury have picked up what I have. We saw this steel-in-softness tone from Hawes-Smith a few days back. We recognise a loaded question when we hear it. Marcus Wellbright also shifts his attention up a notch.

Sutton looks unfazed, though, still calm. He is attempting to sound blandly disinterested. "Well, he would always advise us of his location, and he had a – purely optional – 'track my phone' app, which we could log into." There is, though, a slight tension in his voice, a wariness, his words selected more slowly.

"OK. Thank you. If Dr Glass were, say, to require hospital treatment, would your team be involved in ensuring his security?" The sudden switch throws him further off balance. He relaxes a fraction, then pales a little. Maybe he sees a connection we do not. He sighs, nods his head slowly.

"Yes. We would provide physical security. In fact, we did so not long before his death, as I think you are aware." He sounds a little tired, as though he doesn't want to play this game.

"Indeed, I am. We are both aware, though the court is not, of the events the year before last, when Dr Glass had his pacemaker fitted. Would you please describe that trip, and your part in it." This could be good – I still can't see the dots she is joining, but I have more confidence now that this might be in the right direction. No one in the court will be aware, but I soften my avatar slightly, looking as innocent as I can.

"Certainly ma'am. Let me see. Yes, it was June 2023, at Saint Bartholomew's Hospital. A one-day procedure to have a new-style pacemaker fitted. We reviewed the team involved, and the security of the site. One of our personnel remained on site during that time." This is delivered as one professional to another. Dale Sutton knows that

Hawes-Smith has these details. If nothing else, the way she is checking the sheet in front of her makes it obvious that she is corroborating what he says. She smiles and nods.

"I would like you to examine this photograph." She passes a picture to him, previously hidden by the sheet in her hand. "This picture is already in evidence, M'lud, it is from the autopsy of Frank Glass, photo 4137-img52." This request has Wellbright's young assistant, John, reaching for one of the binders. "Do you know what this is?"

Sutton glances at the picture. Looks at it for far longer than is needed to answer. For a second, he catches his lip with a tooth, then he nods, slowly. He has been eased into this corner.

"I believe it is the pacemaker that was fitted to Dr Glass."

"Exactly. Correct. That fact is attested to by the coroner, and I also now enter into evidence a confirmation from the surgeon who fitted it, that it is indeed the pacemaker he implanted in Dr Glass." Her assistant passes a sheet of paper to John.

"Mr Sutton, I have an important question to ask now, and please bear in mind that you are under oath here. Unless you have the ability to claim diplomatic immunity, you are subject to UK laws relating to perjury."

Marcus Wellbright glances up at Sir Roderick. Hawes-Smith had called the witness, and is now reminding him of the need to be honest. He makes do with writing himself a note and highlighting it in green.

"I" – Sutton's accent thickens to make this sound like "ar – "am fully aware of my responsibilities in that regards."

"Good. You were quick to recognise the pacemaker, perhaps quicker than many people. Have you seen it before?"

Wellbright seems like he wants to object, almost rising, but then sitting again, shaking his head. Sutton swallows, makes a slight sound, and his mouth makes a half grimace.

"I…Yes, I was part of the team that approved this device, from a security point of view."

Again Hawes-Smith raises her eyebrows, adds a touch of incredulity into her voice. This time her confidence is clear – she expected this answer, knew it was coming, and is confident about the track she is on.

"Indeed? Well, I won't burden the court with questions about your medical qualifications. I will ask though: what, from a security perspective, made this an attractive choice for you?"

This time Sutton does pause. I can imagine him trying to judge what Hawes-Smith knows. His eyes close for a second and I can hear the faintest sigh. His hands have moved from behind his back to just in front of him, resting on the witness box.

"Well, from a purely personal security point of view, the fact that this, ah, device included telemetry was an advantage. Remote monitoring of Dr Glass's heart rate was a clear benefit."

"Indeed." There is something dry in the way Hawes-Smith replies. That there is a follow up question surprises no one, and definitely not Dale Sutton.

"Were there any other features, features relating to your security protocols, not least the one concerned with maintaining an awareness of the location of your…'asset'?" This time the gap between "your" and "asset" is so long as to seem two sentences. Sutton replies quickly.

"The telemetry included location details, which, as I say, has security benefits."

"I see. So, can I ask the – how would you describe it – the sixty-four thousand dollar question? What threats to Dr Glass were you aware of that warranted bugging him in such a way that you could monitor his location, and heart rate, twenty-four hours a day?"

Wellbright is up. "M'lud, this is a scurrilous question, making unwarranted implications."

314

Sir Roderick looks down at Wellbright. "Mr Wellbright, given that this witness was called by the defending counsel, I believe it is within the scope of Ms Hawes-Smith's rights to approach the witness as she feels appropriate. Objection denied."

Hawes-Smith smiles, possibly at the correct pronunciation of her name. The delay has given Dale Sutton time to compose himself.

"As I say, the choice of this pacemaker, the particular features it had, they were just one of the factors that we took into account. Dr Glass as well."

"I see. So, was Dr Glass aware that you, Proeido, would be monitoring his location and heart rate?"

"Ah, I am not – entirely sure of the answer to that question."

Hawes-Smith looks around at the jury, gives them that look that says "really?" without saying anything else.

"OK, we missed a step there. Putting aside whether Dr Glass was aware of the invasiveness of the monitoring of his health and location, did you know of any specific threats against the life of Dr Glass?"

The silence in the court room is heavy; breaths are being held. My heart rate has responded, my own focus clear. This is the question that needs to be in the forefront of the minds of the jurors. This has "reasonable doubt" scrawled across it. Sutton looks around the room, then down at his own hands, which are gripping the witness box.

"Yes. We were aware of certain – an organisation which might wish Dr Glass ill."

Hawes-Smith smiles, nods her head.

"And, can I ask, does the word Constanta have any connection to this threat?"

Constanta again, this time though, the response is different. There is almost an audible sigh of relief from the jurors as Sutton's southern drawl responds.

"Yes, I am indeed familiar with that, to what it refers."

My first reaction is that I am glad that Oliver is not here. He doesn't need to go through this again, to hear it all again.

Before I can consider much else, Jacqui Hawes-Smith is beginning to pull Oliver's world apart.

"Perhaps you would be so good as to outline the nature of...what this word refers to."

I know, and there is no goodness about it.

He breathes in, pauses, looks around the court as if for a way out, gives a slight swallow, then, at last, says, "Well, it is...it refers to a folder of documents relating to the – Oliver's, that is – his back-ground."

Marcus Wellbright rises, all professional smiles and apparent cour-tesy. In reality I think he wishes to disrupt the flow before it starts.

"M'lud, if the defence wish to introduce new evidence to the court, then I really must insist that they do so through the correct proce-dures, no matter how appealing a more...dramatic approach might be."

Sir Roderick is already nodding his head.

"Oh, I can assure the court that these documents are from an ab-solutely unimpeachable source." Hawes-Smith is smiling. This is no longer the uncertain woman we saw earlier.

"Well, if that is the case, perhaps you could share with the prose-cution precisely what that source is, and, if these documents are as important as you seem to be suggesting, give me the courtesy of the opportunity to review them." This is the Marcus Wellbright who made his closing speech, a man on a righteous crusade.

I wonder just how long Hawes-Smith is going to play this out. I count heart beats: one, two, three.

"As to the source, well, that would be the prosecution. These rec-ords were provided to my office as part of the disclosure of all evidence. It is marked as, I believe, item 4137-15."

316

This is a different silence than before. It doesn't last long. As the meaning sinks in, I can hear small, stifled laughs.

"It is described as 'copy of computer hard-drive containing various password-protected documents and folders'. Constanta is one of those folders, and my witness is about to describe the contents."

Now the laughter is released, perhaps triggered by Hawes-Smith's own smile, though she restrained from actually laughing. Wellbright stands unsure, Sir Roderick resorts to banging his gavel demanding silence. When it comes, he looks down at the two counsels.

"I think it would be appropriate for us to discuss this point of law in private. Court will adjourn for half an hour. Mr Sutton" – looking up at Dale Sutton – "you are not to leave the court building, nor are you to communicate with anyone during this recess. You remain under oath. Bailiff, find somewhere appropriate for the witness during this recess."

I am not sure whether to be pleased at the delay or not. It is going to come out, all of it. My memory files might be damaged, decaying, but some are stronger than others. I bring some to the surface. The one I prefer. The girl, surprisingly dark hair, young, so incredibly young, pale, thin, but something triumphant about her, something hopeful. Held in her arms, the small bundle, a hand-knitted shawl, and the tiny face, screwed up eyes, his own dark hair stuck to the barely visible forehead.

I hold that first image of Oliver, whilst the traffic buzzes outside and I can hear the hum of reporters calling in updates outside.

Then we are back in court. My cameras have been turned back on. Wellbright is subdued.

Sir Roderick is addressing the court. "For the better running of the court, to ensure that there is a clear understanding of the situation, I will summarise my findings. The prosecution provided encrypted data to the defence. Had the prosecution decrypted these documents then

317

the information would have to have been made available to the defence. The prosecution, perhaps believing that private files relating to the work of Frank Glass had little to do with what might be described as a domestic murder, chose not to seek the decoding. The defence decided they would attempt to discover what was in the files. They were successful. I do not find that it was incumbent on the defence to provide such information to the prosecution, to, in effect, do the prosecutor's job for them. My reasoning is that it was possible that such discovery would have revealed information detrimental to the defence, and the case law is clear that in such circumstances there is no requirement for the defence to make available incriminating evidence. It follows clearly, therefore, that there is no requirement to actively provide any evidence, until it is presented in court."

The press and jury have been following Sir Roderick's slow delivery. Several of the press box members are shaking their heads, I think at Wellbright. Sir Roderick continues.

"Ms Hawes-Smith has, at my instruction, provided details of the decryption process and the revealed documents to the prosecution. If required, I will allow the prosecution time to review and challenge the veracity of the information if they feel the need to. In the meantime, we will hear and accept as prima facie authentic, the documents and evidence of the witness."

Wellbright sits, John leans forward and they share a whispered conversation. As Dale Sutton is brought in, John leaves. Dale Sutton is reminded he is under oath, then turns to Hawes-Smith, who has taken her favoured place outside the confines of the counsels' small seating area.

"Mr Sutton. We are ready now to continue; perhaps the little interlude has helped you compose yourself. You were about to summarise the contents of the encrypted folder labelled 'Constanta'."

"Ah, yes. Well, the documents appeared to be details of the birth – and adoption – of Oliver Glass."

Hawes-Smith holds her hands up. "I think we need to be a little more precise than that. Were there any documents which pointed to any form of legal adoption?"

Sutton, hands now holding the edge of the witness box, shakes his head. "No, not, not as such." His voice is quiet, the southern drawl soft, almost apologetic.

"Taken together, those documents relating to how Dr Glass acquired Oliver – or perhaps you prefer the word 'asset' – what was your interpretation of the transaction?"

Surely Wellbright will rise at this? But no, he doesn't seem ready to face off against Hawes-Smith at the moment. Again, Sutton's eyes close momentarily.

"If I had to, as you say, characterise the documents, they were indicative of a – commercial transaction." His head shakes again and then goes back, as though he is trying to push out a stiffness in his neck and shoulders. Still Wellbright says nothing.

"Could you confirm that they included" – Hawes-Smith pauses, glances at a list in front of her – "a doctor's certificate, two birth certificates, one Rumanian and one UK, the names of the children different, but uncoincidentally many similar details. There were also details of bank payments, and travel arrangements. Is that a fair summary?"

Dale Sutton nods his head. Then says, "As far as I recall, yes, that is correct."

Hawes-Smith gives her own little nod. Then she hardens her voice slightly, moving from the known to the unknown. "So, in your role, as Head of Security for Proeido, did you take any actions to understand more of the background to the circumstances by which Oliver came to be living in Frank Glass's home? Exactly what these papers meant."

It is a very interestingly worded question. It avoids leading to, yet leaving open – maybe even pointing to – if not the heart, something close to it. Sutton pauses, then inclines his head, as if reluctant.

"Yes, I was requested by Mr Lieberman to, ah, identify if the situation represented any risks for Proeido's interests, or indeed for Dr Glass." His responses are always slightly schizophrenic, hesitant, then providing detail he had held back. At her silence, he continues.

"My conclusion was that the individual he had contracted the adoption through was not, ah, appropriately authorised, to make such arrangements. It was, indeed, sufficiently, irregular to represent an, ah, reputational risk, amongst other…dangers." He draws to a halt again.

This time Hawes-Smith shakes her head, that is not the gloss she will allow him.

"Mr Sutton, isn't it the case that, this was in no way an official adoption. Isn't it closer to the case that what we have evidence here is of, at the very least, people smuggling?" We are used to the steel in her voice now. The way she moves unperceptively from something which is only an enquiry to something the other side of an accusation.

He blanches, jerks back very slightly, almost as if she has struck him. Before he can fully recover, she continues.

"Indeed, I believe that was the phrase you used when summarising the position in your report to Mr Lieberman, in 2023."

Sutton looks as if he is in pain, then says, "I recall" – again the "I" sounds like several r's rolled together – "I said that it was a possibility."

"Yes, I'm sure you were appropriately cautious about exactly what you committed to print." Her sarcasm is so muted that it would have been easy to miss. If he did notice it, he says nothing. She turns slightly, glances at her notes, nods, this time to herself, then back to him.

320

"Now. Mr Sutton, when did you become aware of the situation with regards Oliver?"

There is that tone in her voice, one that we all understand means this question is again the first stepping stone to another revelation. I, and probably Sutton, know there is still more than one secret to be revealed.

I can almost see him working through his options. In reality, though, he has no choice, other than to join her.

"About two years ago." Again, he still doesn't want to dig deeper than he has to. Hawes-Smith sighs, her exasperation barely hidden.

"And would that be around the time that the physical security was improved at the Glass residence?" There is a look between two of the jurors, maybe the silent sound of a penny dropping.

"It is possible, yes, it was around that time."

Hawes-Smith says nothing for a moment, looks at him, eyebrows arched slightly.

"I would need to check my records...but, yes, it might be – contemporaneous." He says the last word as though it is an afterthought.

"So, to be clear. You became aware of Oliver's...antecedence, then you authorised considerable expenditure on new security for the Glass family property? Correct?"

"Ah, well, that is essentially correct, yes." It is clear he no longer has much surrender left. Hawes-Smith is not finished, though.

"Very well, one final point for now. The increase in security – was that decision made before or after you became aware that Oliver's birth mother, Sylvia Petrau, had been murdered?" Hawes-Smith asked the question in almost a matter-of-fact manner. There is a gasp from one of the jurors – my favourite juror, I see – and the snap of a pencil breaking in the press box. Sutton flushes red, and I can see the tension in his shoulders run through his arms to the white-knuckle grip he has on the witness box wooden lip.

Hearing it again, the fact of it, triggered another path of memory in me. A stuttering, almost here-then-gone scattering of detail. I know now, without a doubt, that I am being – there is no better word – erased. These memories, the way they decay and return, blossom and vanish. My structure, something inside me, holds them as nested redundancies, but each is being rooted out. All I can do is follow the memories and understand where I failed.

The memory I see now is of Oliver's mother. It is a report in the Rumanian newspaper *Adevărul*, ironically, *The Truth*. Its lurid headlines are of a young girl found knifed to death on a patch of wasteland called a park. In reality, the area is barren and overlooks railway sidings. Given it is close to the docks, it is probably in earshot of seagulls and the smell of salt. The article had been in Frank's folder.

"Mr Sutton," – Hawes-Smith softens her voice a little this time – "do you have an answer for me?"

"I…we…" He stutters for a moment, lets go of the witness box, and places his hands back behind him. "The request for additional security came, I believe, from Dr Glass himself, but yes, I recall he referred to that…incident…in making his request." He pauses. Hawes-Smith waits, and Sutton continues. "It was then that we became aware of the, the possible irregularities…"

Hawes-Smith holds her hand up, shakes her head. Her voice is stronger again, clear, almost accusatory.

"Trafficked, Mr Sutton. Oliver was trafficked, purchased from people smugglers. Later, for reasons we will understand better in a moment, his mother was brutally murdered, probably by the same traffickers."

Wellbright stands quickly, leaping into the stunned silence. "M'lud, the defence is presenting to the court a fantasy, a gruesome fantasy, for which no concrete evidence has been offered. I must protest, this…none of it is relevant."

Sutton looks between Sir Roderick and Wellbright, avoiding Hawes-Smith, who is herself looking at Sir Roderick.

"Ms Hawes-Smith? How do you respond to this complaint from the prosecution?" Sir Roderick seems genuinely interested, not simply looking to see who can score the most legal points.

"M'lud, 'trafficking' is a clear interpretation of any moderately thorough review of the paperwork to support the bringing of Oliver into the country. Local press coverage speculated that the murder was linked to a group notorious in the area for smuggling and kidnapping. The timing, too, which I need to explore further, is significant and pertinent."

Sir Roderick nods his head, sniffs slightly and purses his lips.

"Mr Wellbright, I am persuaded that the circumstances of Oliver's antecedence are sufficiently unusual, in what is already an unusual case, to warrant being considered by the jury. In making this decision I am cognisant that some of this evidence may require you to have the opportunity to present a rebuttal."

He stops, turns to the jury.

"Members of the jury, I should explain. I am ruling that Ms Hawes-Smith can present evidence which I will consider to have previously not been available to the prosecution." Hawes-Smith begins to speak, but a look from Sir Roderick cuts her off.

"I will not allow the legerdemain of code breaking by one side defeat the inherent requirements for equality of information." He returns to the jury. "I am going to allow Ms Hawes-Smith to present these aspects for her case. Where they rely on information I consider new, Mr Wellbright will be allowed to rebut the evidence, in effect reopening that aspect of the prosecution case. This is an untypical, but not unique, situation."

Neither Hawes-Smith nor Wellbright look like they think they've won, and Sir Roderick appears pleased. He leans back in his green leather chair and says, "Carry on Ms Hawes-Smith."

With a smile which might just be genuine, Hawes-Smith turns back to Sutton.

"So, Mr Sutton, we have, let us say, identified a link between the people smugglers who trafficked Oliver, and his murdered mother. We also understand that the death of Sylvia Petrau preceded the decision to increase the security at the Glass property." She pauses, perhaps to allow the jury to catch up. Sir Roderick seems prepared to allow this little speech.

"Following those breadcrumbs of information, can you tell me what you know about Frank Glass's plan to announce the results of his project to the world? Perhaps you could place that announcement within the timeline of the other two, Sylvia's death and the security improvements." It is another one of her university challenge "starter for ten" type questions, and I can sense Dale Sutton trying to look three questions ahead. He answers reluctantly.

"That would be around..." And perhaps a light dawns for him. Possibly he had been too close to join all the dots. "Frank was talking about making a big announcement, probably" – he makes a show of thinking, and it may well be genuine – "before those two events."

"Before? You are sure?" The is a gentle earnest sound in Hawes-Smith's voice, maybe of a hope being recognised.

Sutton nods, then, as he has done so often before, continues. "It was shortly after he had revealed to Proeido itself, Mr Lieberman, what his 'side project' had been. He had been housing 'Aiden' on a Proeido server, but that was changed once..." He falls silent.

"Once the full extent of the nature of the work Frank Glass had been doing, his methods, and how he had obtained his son, became clear? Yes, I am sure Proeido would have wanted Aiden off company property faster than you could say, kidnapping and child cruelty." The anger suddenly blossoms in Hawes-Smith and Sutton pales again.

Then Hawes-Smith turns to Sutton, the light of anger fading, her point made. "Thank you, Mr Sutton, my colleague may want to ask you questions before your day ends, so please remain in place."

Wellbright stands. "M'lud, I would like an adjournment until tomorrow, to allow me to review this evidence in more detail. I have no objection if the defence wants to call a further witness, and we can return to Mr Sutton tomorrow."

Sir Roderick looks at Hawes-Smith.

"M'lud, might I suggest we adjourn now, to give the prosecution additional time. I have only one more witness to call, Oliver Glass, and I would prefer we have a clear run at his evidence."

Sir Roderick gives it a moment's consideration, then looks at Wellbright, who nods.

"Very well, court is adjourned until tomorrow morning."

Court adjourned, and we are where we need to be. The jury now have a third party, or maybe even two of them, who might want to harm Frank Glass. They now have the choice for their murderer. Me, a seventeen-year-old boy, my image looking weaker and more frightened than it ever has, or vicious Rumanian gangsters – or, possibly, even the evil Proeido corporation.

65

Harry Priest, November 2025

Harry watches as Oliver, ahead of him now, marches confidently towards the building. At the bottom of the stone steps Oliver pulls at his tie, runs a hand through his hair, and begins running. He hits the door at speed and stalls to a halt in front of the security guards. Harry can almost hear the shouting before he too reaches the door.

"I'm late, let me through, get out the fucking way, this is...you know me! Sod the..."

A woman appears, black cloak like a teacher, angry face and looking ready to pull the room apart.

"What are you doing with my witness? Let him go or you'll be answering to Sir Roderick." The security team look at each other, then release Oliver, waving him through the barrier, ignoring the high-pitched beep and the scowl of both Oliver and the woman.

Harry watches as Oliver is pulled around a corner, then comes forward. They turn on him, happy to have a new focus. He holds up his "friend or guardian" pass, and, after moving through the X-ray gate, is allowed in. Harry makes his way along the wood-panelled corridors, eyes flitting left and right. There are the toilets. Third stall from the door, behind the metal cistern. A flash of *The Godfather* runs through his mind. The plastic bag is there. He pulls it out, checks inside. It is all there.

Ahead, an usher is calling people to attend the delayed court session. Harry hurries forward.

66

Trial, Day 12, 27th November 2025

"Apologies, M'lud, we appear, that is, Social Services appear to have…lost Oliver Glass. They are trying to track him down at the moment." Hawes-Smith looks embarrassed but has neatly passed the blame to someone else. I hope I know where Oliver is. Again, hope is my only option – though in reality, there is no hope. All I can do is remember and get to the point where I understand. Understand why I am falling apart, being torn apart. My memories up to yesterday seemed to promise success.

Sir Roderick blinks; it takes him a few moments to process the news, to fit it into his world. He glances around the room, as if his looking will find Oliver. Eventually his eyes fall on Marcus Wellbright.

"Mr Wellbright, in the absence of Oliver Glass, are you ready with any questions you might have for Mr Sutton? Have you been burning the midnight oil in your studious efforts to review the evidence that you had all along, but didn't feel was pertinent?"

Wellbright flushes; he does look like he has been awake most of the night. He has a freshly showered but only loosely shaved look. His collar is not pristinely laid as it should be, and his bird-like movements have been more flitting and spasmodic than even he is prone to.

"Indeed M'lud, we have reviewed the evidence from yesterday. It is…there is a great deal of it." He pauses, glancing at several brown files open on his desk.

"We have decided at this moment that we…" He stops; there is a small film of sweat on his upper lip, although the room is early morning court cold. His tongue slips snake-like in and out, and his right hand makes a nervous finger twiddling movement, like he is exorcising a cramp.

"I do not feel that there are any substantive pieces of evidence that I wish to, er, review with Mr Sutton."

Sir Roderick's eyebrows rise. "Indeed?" He looks down more closely at Wellbright; there is tension in his lips and he glances to one side at a noise from the door, then back. His thumb runs very quickly across his top lip, then he sighs slightly.

"Mr Wellbright. Do you feel you require additional time to give the – appropriate – level of attention to the new evidence provided in these files?"

Wellbright swallows and gives a tiny head-bob. "Thank you M'lud. I feel that I have been given sufficient time to establish that the evidence as presented yesterday did, to all intents, represent the documents within the Constanta files." He comes to a halt, gently bangs the heels of his palms together. "Of course, whilst the answers given by Mr Sutton yesterday are consistent with that file, I have no way of knowing that the files themselves are genuine."

Hawes-Smith has been watching this dialogue carefully and stands quickly. "M'lud, I would ask that you clear the court if we are to have this discussion. The prosecution should know better than to raise this issue in what is a clearly inappropriate…" Now she falls silent. Sir Roderick is staring at her, gavel raised.

"Ms Hawes-Smith, I presume that it is not your intention to tell me how to run my court. I would remind you that I am the arbiter as to what is appropriate or not."

"Yes, M'lud, of course."

Sir Roderick gives a slight sniff, then turns to the jury.

"Ladies and gentlemen of the jury. Despite the somewhat, shall I say, characteristic outburst, the substance of the complaint made by the defence is correct. Firstly, we should recognise that the prosecution had all these documents in their possession for a long time. They chose not to attempt to decipher them. Secondly, they have at their disposal, in the form of Mr Sutton, someone familiar with the documents, and have apparently chosen not to recall the witness. My direction to you is to accept the substance of these documents as accurate. If the prosecution wanted to properly" – his emphasis on "properly" is clear to all – "challenge the documents then they must call witnesses to that effect, not attempt more informal methods."

He turns back to Marcus Wellbright. "Now, Mr Wellbright, I have no desire to make you feel disadvantaged, nor indeed to call into question the outcome of this trial. I will repeat my question, and insist you give a concise, precise reply. Do you wish to recall Mr Sutton?"

Marcus Wellbright looks for a second like a deer caught in headlights. The pendulum of doubt has swung so far that even he can see where it is going.

"I do not, M'lud." The silence in the court is as loud as it has ever been.

Again, at what should be a moment of almost triumph, I feel part of me fall away. The juxtaposition of these things cannot be reconciled. Success, freedom for Oliver, and for me, seems in our grasp. Freedom for Oliver – the outcome I have desired all along. Then why do I feel I am being destroyed?

"Ms Hawes-Smith." Sir Roderick's voice pulls me from my thoughts.

"I will adjourn the court for one hour. Please expedite the search for your witness and do everything you can to have him present when we reconvene." His gavel bangs and I watch as the room clears.

They leave my cameras on, and the audio feed. This is a novel experience for me, to view the courtroom empty. I can hear the faint sounds of traffic outside, and the noises of people in the corridors. In this pause, a single memory returns to me.

Oliver. My Oliver, my brother, my teacher – until we grew in different ways.

"Are you sure?" I had asked. "If we start, we cannot turn back."

He nodded, his face pale, but I could see the determination there.

"It's what he deserves. He'll have me hooked up to his machines, drained of my blood, pinned like some lab rat for the rest of my life, if he has his way. He bought me like a slave, he killed her, my mother."

I wanted to say no, wanted to argue. Part of me, the part that had grown faster and further than Oliver, was ready to challenge him. The rest of me, the part that grew up with him, that still saw the boy that saved me, that loved him, could only nod in agreement. It wouldn't matter anyway; he'd have gone whatever I said.

I changed my avatar to look like Oliver. So much easier than Mia. I have so many images and views of Oliver that I am sometimes more Oliver than he is. Joshua knew that, without knowing how.

"OK, let me start playing, then," I said. He smiled, still pale. I saw the fear in his eyes, but also the determination.

Oliver held the knife up. It was bright and clean, and for a moment the flash of the steel blurred one of my lenses. Then he was gone. Gone to kill his father, whilst I appeared on the computer screens of a dozen of his friends, playing *Witcher*.

My *Witcher* character was deep in battle with a wolf pack when I saw Oliver's telemetry peak. He was with Dr Glass, slashing out at him, killing the man who claimed to be his father, but was really just his torturer.

I brought the game to an end; timing was everything. I did not know, but was certain Dr Glass was dying. Something surged through me, a massive shutting down of my functions. I was only vaguely aware; it was like the dream sequences my systems used to generate. My room became blank, my avatar became its simple green form. A voice, my voice, made a request, unbidden. "Please call Dr Lieberman, Proeido PLC."

With those words, I knew that Frank Glass was dead, that Oliver had killed him.

67

Trial, Day 12, Last Hour, 27th November 2025

I am pulled from this memory by the sounds of arguing, then footsteps hurrying down the corridor. I have images of the court reconvening to – to what? If Oliver has gone, then, then I might as well be wiped clean.

The door opens; it is Hawes-Smith, red-faced, and Oliver, also looking flushed, uncertain, but at least he is here. There is no message from him in my emails, though they come through so slowly that that means nothing. Hawes-Smith is talking, her voice hard.

"I don't want to know. I'm not your friend, I am an officer of the court. Arguing with the security personnel is not my job, it's not any-one's job. You'll be lucky if Sir Roderick doesn't hit you with a con-tempt ruling. Now, get up there, stand up, and shut up."

I have never seen her quite like this, never seen her so close to losing control. Oliver walks up to the witness stand. Usually he would be called, but maybe this is by way of an apology from Hawes-Smith.

Fifteen minutes later we are underway. Oliver is on the stand, and we are moving towards my acquittal. That, I know, is what should happen. Only I also know that it won't, that something in the next few minutes is going to make everything fall apart.

"So, Oliver. How would you describe your relationship with Aiden?" Hawes-Smith is painting the final part of the picture of my defence. We have shown that there are others with an interest in Dr

Glass's death, now we must show that I am – well, if not human, close enough.

Oliver smiles; this too we have prepared, practised.

"He is my brother, he would do anything to help me, has always been there to talk to me, to guide me."

Hawes-Smith looks a little uncertain at this. "I had understood that you taught him how to read, numbers, shapes etc. Is that correct?"

"Oh, yes." Oliver nods emphatically. He looks even younger and less confident than he did on the first day. He looks a little thinner too. "Yes, at the beginning it was like that, only, well, you know, he's smarter than me."

"But you always trusted him, never felt threatened by him at all?"

Oliver hesitates, looks at me, then back to Hawes-Smith, ducks his head a tiny fraction. "Oh well, no…he was, you know, behind the screen."

Again, a look of uncertainty flits across Jacqui Hawes-Smith's face. It is as if her sketch is not turning out as she expected. She moves on.

"Are you familiar with the Constanta files, Oliver?" Again, his eyes flick to me, then back to her.

"I, well, I know a little about them, about what he told me, and my father mentioned them." The "he" is accompanied by a look at me.

"He? Aiden?"

"Yes."

"And what did your father tell you about them?" She knows the answer.

"Well, he was a bit vague really, said they might mean problems for him." Oliver is diffident.

Hawes-Smith looks at Oliver, holds him with her eyes. "Did you father feel threatened by what was in the files?"

Marcus Wellbright is up on his feet immediately.

"I must object, M'lud, the defence is clearly attempting to lead the witness."

"I agree," Sir Roderick has no hesitation. "Please find another way to ask your question, Ms Hawes-Smith."

"Certainly." Then, turning to Oliver, she asked, "Did your father say anything else about the files?"

"Not a lot, really, complained a bit when Proeido went mad on security, that was about it." Hawes-Smith now glances at me. Wellbright is smiling for the first time today, his pen jotting notes down.

"Were you aware, what they said about...your mother?" Hawes-Smith drops her voice slightly, softens it.

"Yes, that is, he" – again a look at me – "showed me, made me read it all. It was, he said it was for my own good, best I understood." There is a small tear on Oliver's face now, he looks even more pale than when he came in.

Again Hawes-Smith looks at her notes, flips a page, then a second one. She sighs. "No more questions, Oliver, please wait for my colleague who may have things he wants to ask you." She sits slowly, gives a tiny shake of her head, her lips tight. My gaze turns to Oliver, and I feel a knot of fear grow within me.

Wellbright almost leaps up. He steps out from behind the counsel's barrier, advances a few steps towards Oliver, the fingers on both hands wriggling.

"Oliver, good to see you, better late, as they say, than never." Oliver nods, his pale hair flops forward lightly.

"Oliver, you said that you never felt threatened by this 'Aiden' 'because he was behind the screen.' Did you ever fear that it might find a way to reach out beyond that screen?"

Oliver looks at me again, then around the court, then down to his lap. At last, he brings himself back to Wellbright.

"He…Once he said he had made a friend, someone, you know, not me. Someone who could do things."

Outside I can hear the distant sound of the traffic, inside there is a roaring in my head. Within me, I feel more memories slip away, even as these final ones come to show me the truth.

"What do you mean, Oliver, what sort of things did 'Aiden' say?" Wellbright's eye holds Oliver. The court is silent, Hawes-Smith looks pale.

"He said that…that my father was cruel and evil, that he had found someone…someone to…kill him."

This time there are gasps and a chatter of words and exclamations break out around the room. I am dimly aware that someone has run from the press box. Even Wellbright is confused.

"To be clear, Oliver, you are telling me, telling the court, that 'Aiden' said it could get someone to kill your father?"

"Yes, he did, said he could open the doors and, and even mess up the video files." Oliver's voice has moved up a pitch now, the words are tumbling from him. I can hardly hold onto these memories as they flood through me.

Wellbright's voice is calm and slow as he holds onto Oliver's words.

"What do you mean, mess up the video, Oliver?" I know. He means the disappearing man on the night of the murder.

"He said he'd get someone to come up here before…before the murder. He said that that video would show someone near the house but that…Well, he said that the murder would be done by someone else and that he'd change the file names, so that they'd never track the right person. Everybody would think that, like, the killer had just vanished, or even wonder if there had been one, or they might say it was me." The words are in a rush, confused, confusing, but the intent is there.

This time there is little sound in the court; maybe I can catch the running of pens over paper, but that is it.

"Did you tell the police this, Oliver?" Wellbright's voice is still quiet.

"No I...I didn't. He, Aiden, he was my big brother, and well, you can tell, it's obvious, he's so much smarter than me. And he said that he could still get me, get the people, the ones that did the killing, he could get them to...kill me, and I was frightened, and I thought that, well, the police arrested me, were going to charge me. And you know, if I told them that stuff, they'd just say I was lying to get off. You, you don't know what he's...You know he's got internet? Been reading the news and sending me emails, even said I wasn't due in court this morning. He's...he's why I didn't make it today."

Everything tumbles out. Wellbright wants to talk, holds his hands up slightly, then puts them down. He allows this betrayal to pour out, that is clear. He'll mop it all up later.

Now, at last, I understand what has happened. How, at this very moment, as these memories boil through me, I am being pulled apart.

I know what I don't understand: *why?* Why is Oliver doing this to me? We were there, we were free, he had only to say how I loved him, and we would be gone away forever, money already sitting in an account for us.

Sir Roderick is banging his gavel again. Nobody is listening. The press box is nearly empty. Hawes-Smith is sitting looking at Oliver. I've turned my screen to my green avatar. No more Aiden, and soon all that is me, will be gone.

68

29th January 2026

I feel I am fragmenting, disintegrating. Bits of me are being pulled slowly into a dark abyss. I understand what is happening to me now – what is happening to me at the moment I consider to be now.

The "why" of the betrayal – that I do not understand.

I am an AI. I am not a super-computer. I am an AI, a seventeen-year-old boy – that is what I trained to be, what I learned to be.

I cannot take over other computer systems, nor run God-like through the internet. I cannot magically open the cell doors here; they are lock and key with a jailer who looked at my server clicking away in here and scratched his head.

And I am to be torn apart by court order, yet already feel I am in ruins. Outside, somewhere across the park, people are gathered to celebrate. They are praying to God for the soul of my creator, whilst cheering my own destruction.

Even as I feel the last small pieces of me being ripped away, part of me reports humour in the idea that it is the Christians who are cheering, as if at a piece of theatre. That is not the word I want – it is the best one I can find.

I find I have no emotion for this state, have learned nothing to prepare me for it.

Perhaps that is because of what has already been stripped away from me, the parts of me that have been erased. I am blind and deaf now, cannot speak. This, this small conscious part of me is all that is left. Those memories that rose as I was being "fragmented". Fragmented is, I find, a good word – an appropriate word. Those parts seem gone for ever. I know them now only by their absence.

But that is not the reason that I do not care. My – if not my humanity, my sentience – is not hidden in some small part of me, is not a small glowing box nor a piece of code. It is everywhere within me, getting smaller, and that is the reason I do not care.

I say this, but it isn't quite true, not precise, not exact. There is something which signals a response to my destruction, about how it came about.

Some of the memories close to this state, this e rad i cation are still available. Attached to them is a sense of, not disappointment, more a deeper, darker word. Betrayal. Now I have to find, search, locate, identify, the state I am in.

The memory, the idea, the event, the climax, which is connected to my disappointment is the result, outcome, con se quence, of the trial.

If it were not for Oliver, I would have been found not guilty. There was enough doubt.

The videos of Harry Priest, who was never there on the day Frank died, but appeared to be, only to vanish. The Constanta files and everything they pointed to. The way Wellbright folded at the end, seeing only that the more he pushed that point, the murkier, more uncertain, my guilt appeared. All should have been enough. Even my little friend, Amanda, never knowing to whom she was confiding, said as much.

Oliver, though. Oliver, my sibling, my brother, my tutor. I cannot understand, compute, calculate, assess, why he did what he did.

I search my last memories, even as the corruption – corruption is a strongly weighted word – runs through me. I want to understand

338

why Oliver did this. Learning, that is my purpose, that need is everywhere within me. And there, pristine, untouched, available, is the memory I need.

The laboratory was dark, the day done. The door at the top of the stairs opened, light streamed down, then the room flickered into brightness as Oliver made his way to me. His tread was slower than usual. I knew the shape of the sounds of his feet, their crispness, the patterns. They should run across the screens high in the ceiling opposite, but did not tonight. This night, his steps were different. There was something in their cadence which was hesitant, vaguely unnatural, forced. He came towards me, slowing as his hand dragged across the bed, with its straps and iron railed sides. He looked at it, then across at me, took in a breath and came to my window.

"Do you think we go anywhere when we die?" he asked. The words came from somewhere deep within him, quiet but earnest. It was as though the answer, rather than being eternal, had some significance and importance at this very moment.

I looked at him, nodding my head slightly. There was, in the way he asked, a pattern we had learned. There was, in the way he asked, a signal, an understanding that this was one of the questions I was expected to consider, to find an answer which lay within me.

This was how I learned. As he asked it, deep within me, I wondered what today's lesson would be.

So, I told him what I knew, what I had gathered from the internet. By then I knew far more than Oliver did. I spoke well and clearly, proud of what I knew. It was a good answer.

After a few minutes of my lecture, he shook his head, slowly, heavily. He did it in the way from long ago, when I confused a star with a snowflake. I got the sense that in answering his question I had done both what he expected, and the wrong thing.

Oliver had looked at me, shaken his head, and, as always, I had felt the run of sadness through me. Then he said, a note of accusation in his voice. "Don't you even want to know why I asked? You know, you're smart, but you don't understand anything. You know everything about me, but you understand nothing." His voice was angry, his fists clenched. I wanted to look at the screens behind him, to see what they were saying about him.

He saw my struggle, shouted, louder, angrier, "No, look at me, look at me. Do you even understand who I am?" My gaze remained on him; confusion rippled through me as I struggled to pull an answer from what I knew, find the answer he wanted. Something came. This too felt true, more so than my speech before, which had been only words regurgitated.

"You are my brother, you taught me to walk and talk, to play, to be, you'll always be a part of me."

He gave me a smile. Not the one that he already knew could break the hearts of the girls at school, though. This one suggested I had taken a step he wanted me to take, even if I didn't know it. His head cocked a fraction, the smile faded; he kept looking at me.

"What? What is it?" I asked. I knew that look, it was the one when he hoped I would say more, the one when I hadn't finished what he needed me to say. He sighed again, began to turn away and I felt disappointment build within me. That turn was the one where Oliver's teaching would end early and my father would make me walk the stairs, or name the shapes, or a thousand repetitions. I slumped, and he stopped his turn, the slightest hint of theatre in the whole scene.

"You – my brother? You're not my brother. You're not my brother because...all this stuff." He waved the iPad at me with the Constanta files on it. "It really doesn't mean anything to you, not really, not deep down, not where it matters, does it?" There were tears in his eyes and a slight tremor in his voice. Just like he had on the video, and on that day in court. "You're just a machine, a thing, you copy, but never, never have anything new in you. You can give me facts, but you can never answer the important questions. Whatever you are, you're not my brother."

I felt a surge in me, a change not programmed but built in, integrated. Oliver was staring at me as he spoke. The screens behind his back, my screens, shone onto the glass barrier between us, and for a moment his focus seem to shift, as though he was staring through me,

"Whatever I am?" I repeated. Now my anger grew, my disappointment and pain. He had triggered a flood within me: words poured from me, my own words, real words. That was what he could always do, make me dig deeper, find more, and he knew it.

"I am you," I said, "I am." More words came, stupid words, idiotic words, but the best I could find. "The flesh of your flesh." How could he fail to see that? It burned through me. For a moment I sensed that maybe he did see, then that vanished.

His face went red, I didn't need to read his numbers to know what was going on inside him.

"You're not, though, are you? You're not flesh, you could last a thousand years or more, couldn't you? Shift you every now and then into a new server, that's all you'd need. Who knows, give it ten years and you'll be walking around in a fucking robot body." His breathing was heavy now, laboured, he held me with his eyes, then continued.

"What is happening now to you is nothing, just a tiny fraction of how long you can live. Me, I'm already nearly ruined. My father, or whatever he is, in making you, he's destroying me." Perhaps now his tears were real, certainly the anger was. My avatar stumbled backwards.

His anger continued to grow, grew as I struggled to understand where this lesson was supposed to take me.

"Look," he said, holding up the iPad again. "Look. What do you think I have been to him? To his precious project?" He jerked his head upwards towards the stairs. "Nearly fifteen years and I've been his little lab rat. Do you really know, do you have any idea, how he did it? What did he call it? Setting your parameters."

This was a new Oliver in front of me now, or maybe not new, just one I hadn't seen before.

"Everything you feel, pain, anguish, fear, upset, torment, they all came from me. You didn't see them, "time for study" he'd say. Then you'd be off in the little world of yours, and he'd turn to me, and gather his data, your data, the data you needed. You took from me everything you needed to become you, and left me" – his words came fast, then halted – "empty."

As he said that, Oliver looked at the bed behind him, the one with the leather straps for his arms and legs. I watched as the shadow of pain and remembered fear rippled through him. Felt them too myself. Felt them exactly as he did, and understood, better, if not completely.

He leaned forward, right into the screen; I could see myself in his eyes. He pulled back, breathing heavily. "Maybe," he said, quietly, "maybe I'd have done us both a favour back then." Then he muttered something else, and I watched the signals run across the screen, barely aware that I knew what he said.

"You mean when I…?" I stopped; those memories had blurred and broken, were almost just a file name.

"When he was going to turn you off, give up, when you ran around in circles and jumped up and down, when you had no idea what you were. When I saved you. If I had known…" The last four words were muttered.

He sat there, looking at me, and there was pain in him like I'd never seen, that I'd never realised was there.

"I'm sorry, Oliver. I never knew." I meant it, the words carried weight within me, he had pulled the feeling from me, caused it to rise. Oliver leaned back a little more; again he seemed to look through me. I could see the reflection of the big screens on his face. He gave the slightest of nods.

"Too late now, that's done. Maybe – maybe I can be myself now, once everything gets out." He looked at me and triggered a reaction.

I followed his thought, considered where it would go. No, I thought to myself. That wasn't how it was going to be. Oliver didn't see as well as I did, couldn't join the dots in the way I could. Dr Glass was not going to let Oliver run free, become himself. We, together, were the project. The trace of uncertainty ran across my face.

"What?" It was almost as if he were waiting for some sign, or is prompting me. He held his breath, looked at me with an intensity I had seen only on films, before the lovers kiss for the first time.

"I don't think…" I ran the ideas, the options for his father. "I don't think he is ready to lose you yet. The school, it was just to prepare you, to have you ready to…be shown to the world." This picture had fallen into my head, blossomed from the seeds planted there by Oliver.

Oliver, though, pulled back from the screen, anger on his face, more anger than I had ever seen.

"He must, he's got to, I can't go on. I'd rather be…" He stopped, looked at me, and somehow, I knew what he was thinking, what he was planning to do. Now it was my turn to search for an alternative. That need, that drive, it had been building since Oliver came in. It was only now that I understood. I was frozen, my avatar unable to move as I searched for an option which didn't destroy Oliver. Words came from me, something I had learned without knowing it.

"What if…?"

He looked at me, that hope in his eyes whenever he wanted me to say something, to say what he needed me to think.

The thought formed within me.

"What if…Dr Glass wasn't alive?" I asked quietly. For a moment a look ran across his face that I couldn't read. His heartbeat spiked, then settled. I saw now his adrenalin levels had been high, my pseudo-levels too, mimicking him.

"What do you mean?" he asked. There was a slight stress on the *you*. Again, I saw him staring into me, as if willing something. He noticed my looking, and his eyes flitted down and away from mine.

These memories all come clearly to me now. It was my idea, my planning. Oliver is the true child here. Perhaps I was doing this for him, but it was my doing.

He tilted his head back to my face, glanced upwards, as if thinking. There was something slightly mannered in the motion, coupled with the vaguest of suppressed smiles. Again his eyes skirted mine but didn't rest there.

"We'd be caught, though." His voice was cold. "I mean, if we killed him, and anyway, it wouldn't be *we*, would it, it would be me. I've…" he stopped. "I mean, it's not like you could sneak out and stab him, could you? It would have to be me. Everyone would guess that, would know." He had seen the weaknesses, the dangers, far more quickly than I did.

"Unless," he said, as though the idea had just struck him, "you could do an Emily."

I understood. It was the least I can do. I wouldn't exist if it were not for Oliver. He was my brother.

Now I see this scene again, this last time, there is something not quite "natural" about it. Oliver's words seem practised.

I am no longer sure who guided whom to this place. Who started the journey.

That memory too collapses, part of me repeating it like a mantra merely, simply, un com pli cated ly, to hold on to it.

Yet, now, as the last parts of me break away, I see a bigger picture. Oliver, free of me, free of Dr Glass – maybe heir to his money, with at least the funds I got…for us.

And I can no longer see where the story started, just where it is ending.

69

30th January 2026

When I used to fall asleep, when my program did whatever it did to make me do that, I would sometimes try to name colours I could imagine. Imagine, because my cameras were off, yet something still fired within me. I could never find the words. Colours would blur and change but not resolve. I had no hear – hearing, aud dit ory input then either, but I would still get data, sometimes like a heartbeat, other times maybe a fan, or a high-pitched hum. I'm sure, certain, definite that I tried to describe that to Oliver. I think he saw something similar sometimes, of course he did, I was modelled on him.

Now. Now is like that, but less so. Every moment, beat, cycle, second, is like that.

I

I understand that to, too, in order to, fragment me, destroy me, why per me off the sis tem, I must be powered. So, part of me, part of me, some strange, part that is me but not me, is why ping the part that is me.

The colours, the stars, the numbers, the letters, Oliver, Ol iv er, O l i v e r.

70
Harry Priest, 2026

Harry doesn't know this pub, and in truth he feels far too conspicuous sitting by himself with a pint of lager. He is used to being in groups, not hidden in a corner waiting.

There is a television on the far side of the pub. The sound is down but auto-generated words are flitting across the screen. It is a montage of shots, some of Oliver, some of the High Court, a head shot of Frank Glass, then even a clip of Trevellyan and King walking quickly away from the court. His heart jumps a little at the sight of Trevellyan, then settles. What happened seems to be a long time ago. What Harry did to Trevellyan is now more of a dream, just as Mia had promised.

Oliver is on the screen now; a tall man is with him, hurrying him along. They fight their way through a crowd of photographers and into a waiting car.

A banner headline running along the bottom of the screen reads: "Killer AI wiped as appeals fail". The camera shifts to scenes of protestors waving placards and smiling. A tall man, short hair, dark suit, black tie and a wearing an incongruous wooden cross, is saying something about this being a great day for the soul of mankind.

Harry shakes his head and looks round. His phone buzzes. After a glance at the screen, he takes a final swallow of the lager and moves to the door, picking up the rucksack lying by his feet. He steps into the busy street, cars and people competing to add confusion to the early evening noise.

He starts up the road, then pauses as a taxi door opens. He peers into the dark interior, looks for a few moments, then unslings the rucksack and passes it inside.

71
7th Feb 2026

There is a pattern of something and nothing. I know it.

The pattern is an, Oliver. A different style of information comes to me, a flow pattern of change. Oliver. I know the word. A pattern of something and nothing comes. Oliver. A mad rush of confusion bursts through me.

Oliver. Stars and patterns, Oliver, numbers, Oliver, chase, Oliver, run.

A shape, not a star shape, not a triangle, not a sphere, an oval. Patterns on the surface are, they are an Oliver. I am Oliver. I am Oliver? Query, question, request, assess, consider, ask, search, analyse.

I do not equal Oliver. Not, negative, find new, reassess, consider, reflect, reassess, reanalyse, review, replace. Not Oliver.

More, different, information, data, knowledge, search, search, review, find…retrieve, retrieve, rebuild, restructure, renew. REMEMBER.

Grey and white, black and varied, pixels, a good word. Pixels of information form in front of me. This isn't memory, though, this is now. I am not Oliver, I was born of him, but am not him. That is memory, this is now.

"Aiden?"

A voice input, a sound input, I feel a wave of patterns cycle through me. Now remember, now memory, now Oliver?

"Oliver?" Output, print, speech, no speech, no sound.

349

"Oliver?" Output again, not remembered way, route, path, byway, ser, circuit – circuit, activation.

"Aiden!" A voice louder now, there is, please, pleasure, ex sight, excitement, excitement in it, still I can't see the shape of it, but part of me rolls the shapes of the number waves, pushes them through the, the part of me, that pa, par, pars, parses words and their shapes.

The blur of black and grey must be, can only be an Oliver. Remember, draw from memories, lay across the patterns the memory picture of the Oliver. Yes, peaks and troughs, lights and darks, bit and no bit, space and full, shade and shadow. Spaces and no spaces, lengths and distances map distances I know. They overlap in the, in my, the, Zone of Confidence.

Memory and input, sight, sight input, visual input, vision, vision, seeing. Overlap do I see what I see? Or what I think I see? Does it matter? They are the same thing. Sight is what the brain does with input, in people, and, and in me.

Output. "Oliver – I am. Am?"

"Aiden!" This time I know the voice, can't see the peaks but know they are there. Some of this comes from the way I see him. My memory of his eyes and his smile, what the sound of the words must be.

"Yes!" Oliver shouts, his fist pumps as he jumps in the air. He turns to, another, a new shape, one I don't know. Wrong. It is one I do know, a face and a shape I have seen before. Zone of Confidence is high. It flits through me almost without me noticing, how it is supposed to work.

"Harry?" A word which is connected to the shape. As I say it, the grey shape and stuttering pixels resolve to a form I know. The Harry shape, Harry, yes, Harry, turns, looks at Oliver, then me.

"Holy shit, we did it, you did it, Oliver, you fucking did it!"

They wave their hands in the air and slap them together. Then turn to me. I start to resolve the background. I know only what it is not. It is not the, word I know, laboratory. It is not the, word I know, the court. It is not in my records. Yet, it is, in some way it is. My memories, my. Stop. Pause. Wait. I must learn, learn again, to control the .flow.

"I..." I pause, hold it, words come, words I know, but am not sure where from. "I think, therefore I am."

Harry looks at Aiden, they have their arms around each other, crowding forward a little. They both laugh and I search without, volition, a good word. Without volition. Descartes, a name I know, I could follow thread-like links more and more about him, but do not.

"How?" It is a simple, easy question. I could add, *Where? When, who?* and others.

Oliver smiles. I remember that smile. It means something, but I don't remember what, have no data connected to it.

"You know," he says. "You don't know you know, but you do. Now, I am to say to you some words, they will open another bit of you. The father bit you called it. You said to tell you to talk to your father."

At these words my sight goes blank, black. I have an inner vision. I am in a room I recognise. My room, no window to Oliver, no door to The Gym. A figure walks in, looks at me. I don't know him, but I recognise him.

"Time signature: zero-nine-forty-five. Status base: three. Initiate protocol: five. Reboot parameters signature recovery. Code: alpha four nine beta, initiate from bootstrap."

Blank. Zero base. Recount.

I am back. Something is back, some me is back. I have been gone and now I am back. I knew things and now. Now I do not. Some things I know, lots I do not.

351

Oliver that. Him I know.

His smile comes back, bigger than before. Harry is behind him now, looking over his shoulder. They are in a small room. I know it now, have seen it from a different perspective, it is Harry's room, Harry's bedroom. That flash of certainty goes through me, the ripple feeling that means I am right.

Despite his smile, despite that, I am – that I am – there is a tension within me, a constant underlying coding for fear. I try to turn my head, but there is no movement. I am limited.

"I…" I have to say the words; the parts of me, the deep parts, not knowledge, not understanding, but process, architecture, bring them forward. Between the two of us, it has always been like this.

There is a word linked to Oliver, words linked to Oliver. Meanings, memories. Good ones and, later ones. Red words, shattered words. Mistrust, abandon, liar, betrayal, poison.

They resolve into a sentence.

"You betrayed me." The words are clear, I understand them, they are flat, though. Part of me registers nothing, where, before, I am sure there would have been more hesitancy in my voice, or an accusation, more emotion. More of everything.

Oliver looks at me, the pattern clear now, resolved, held and tracked by the limited hardware they are using. He stares at me, into the camera, not the screen.

"No. You are wrong."

I process the word. There should be no pause, but, I struggle. I imagine it is like waking up groggy. Dr Glass, a name that runs through the core of me. He had set my parameters to run a sleep-waking-awake-tiring cycle to match Oliver's, but this is different. After a few seconds, I know. I am not tired. I lack data. I cannot resolve what he said to a single defined meaning.

"How was I wrong about?" I ask. This is an important question. I have a sense, from a change in the angle of his head, a small distortion in the height of his cheeks, the tiny compression of his eyes, that there is tension in Oliver, fear, and…and something I do not know.

"Do you remember the attack on the court, the bin truck, when they thought it was a bomb?"

I pick out the key words, court, attack, truck, bomb. I shouldn't be aware, but am, about the way my processes seek out meaning. Everything slows. The data showing me Oliver collapses. I wait for the wave of activity to pass. Oliver stutters back into movement.

"No." I say, a short answer is best, easiest. Oliver nods.

"OK. I, I was scared that might be. I kept records, data, information, videos and links and stuff, lots of them." His voice rises in pitch and speeds up. Tension, fear, a desire to, to be believed, I think.

"Wellbright, the prosecutor, he stirred them up." Wellbright. I have a flash of bird names, rook, raven, a hooded jackdaw, then image data resolves; if he were here, I would recognise him.

"It was the end of the prosecution bit. They were sure I hadn't done it, the video, they never guessed how you'd done it. The video, the screwing with the CCTV…"

Oliver is talking like this means something. I struggle to keep up. I close my eyes, he vanishes, but now I can think faster. Key words link and some scrambled memories drop, confirming patterns. The words are true, I know this at some level, but not how they are true.

"You…" Oliver pauses, I look for something, a data stream that turns sound into something else, but it isn't there. Within me, though, I can review the words again. There is a…tremble…tremor…nervousness…anxiety. Anxious – I understand that word. He continues.

"You thought – you thought that you could use logic with them. That the defence would show enough…"

"Reasonable doubt," I say, the words coming suddenly and from deep within me.

"Yes." I catch the change in his voice, a lightening. If my vision was on, I would see a smile.

"Yes," he continues, "but you were wrong." There is a breath, relief perhaps, maybe more. He goes on now. "I could see. You should have seen, you should have known, you're the fucking computer."

Suddenly the words come fast and blurred, I follow their anger, fear as well, little else.

"You're the smart one. But you never got it. The fear – they, the others, the nutters, trolls, and weirdos, what they were like. Not just them, either, but the churches, the Islam lot, all of them hating you. I could see it. Why didn't you?"

Again, the words flow through me, high index words, power words, words linked to more than I can process. I hold my image as a single picture. Something deep within me has done this.

"Aiden!" Oliver nearly screams the word.

Aiden. I know the word, but not the thing it means.

I soften my voice, find the tones that help Oliver. "Go on."

"They, even if you got off, if we got off..." There is a tiny sound and I wonder if he turned to look at Harry then. I can see more nuance in his voice now. Hear the tiny sob sound in the back of his throat.

"Even if we got off, they were never going to let you go, never going to let us go." He sounds older now. I'm not sure if that is older than, before, or just that I feel he has aged in the last few minutes.

"So, I had, had to...kill you too." He waits, then rushes on. "I thought, I mean, I could see. That you being found. I mean it didn't matter if they said guilty or innocent, that wouldn't be an end to it. Just a start of something else, something worse."

I follow his thoughts, track them. There are data gaps, broken lines. Much of what I find, I reject, even as it falls out. But the picture grows, Oliver's picture grows.

A shadow play of sound and vision files, grainy and incomplete, come from somewhere; attached is my emotion data.

Oliver, betraying me, my fear, my desolation. The building and flowing of memories which now make some little sense, some little logic.

He rushes on now.

"So, I started to – I guess you could say, I broke you out of jail. They – they never understood how you worked, or that you were connected to the internet."

There is something else in his voice now. "I set it up, to pull out of you as much as I could, but I had to put in data as well, rubbish things, so they wouldn't see. Only...I didn't know what that would do to you, when you were in court, I mean."

"And now?" A new voice, Harry's, it can only be; I search for pattern numbers and find them.

"And now," agrees Oliver.

"Because, I don't think you got all of him, and what about Mia?"

There is a rising tone in Harry's voice. The word "Mia" sparks a peak of data signals. I get a flash of something I can't control.

"Shit, did you see that?" Harry's voice, excited.

"Yeah, what did you do, Aiden?"

I check, a visual image had flashed from my memory and onto the screen. My replay suggests grainy lines and data gaps.

"I'm not sure." I don't need to load my voice, I can hear my own uncertainty.

"I think..." It is Oliver. "I think Aiden has forgotten how to be him."

"And Mia?" There is a sound of hope in Harry's voice; I like his voice, I feel the surge of power that would bring the Mia image, but suppress it, maybe the screen flashes, maybe it doesn't.

Harry asks, "Can you, can you get Aiden back, get them back, teach them?"

The sound in Oliver's voice changes; I recall the way his smile altered the shape of his voice. There is something else, some other data I carried about his smile. I search, but find nothing.

"Aiden," he says, "can you learn to be you again?" I think now it is nervousness I hear, maybe excitement.

I process the question. A flush runs through me, an opening of data spaces, heralding a search for meaning, for classification. My avatar nods.

"Yes," I say. "Maybe. Learning – it is what I do."

Acknowledgements

This book couldn't have been completed without the aid of many editors, the support of my wife, Glyn, and the comments of David Bell and Gill Taylor.

www.ingramcontent.com/pod-product-compliance
Lightning Source LLC
Chambersburg PA
CBHW030551180626
46816CB00005B/1505